Follow me on Twitter - @

Facebook - @

And please check out Amazon

for my latest releases.

THE LANNWEDHENEK
AND THE BATTLE
OF CADIZ

Joshua Barraclough

Dear reader.

As a local lad myself, I walk past the riverside most saturdays whilst walking my dog, Benji.

Please feel free to "check out" my book, but kindly return it to its place or else donate it to another community library. Finally, please sign your name on the cover.

J. Barraclough

*With thanks to Lucy, who always believes in me,
regardless of how much I sometimes struggle. And
to Karen, my mum, for hours of tireless editing.*

CONTENTS

CHAPTER ONE

Four bells. Four bells on the morning watch. Four bells. That made it six in the morning on land time. Commander Henry Smythe had promised his first mate, no, his first Lieutenant, that he would relieve him at six bells. The boat, no ship, was bobbing slightly on the water, as he lay back in his cot. Six bells. Another hour. He had another hour of peace, should he so wish it. But what was peace aboard this ship? Lying awake, alone in his cot, tight and squashed up. No, he might as well just relieve his Lieutenant.

He stood, and at five foot eleven, he was taller than the average man. His face, worn through years at sea looked as tired as he felt. He steadied himself, for the wash of a wave had hit the ship hard and began to dress. He rinsed his face, thought about a shave, then decided better of it. His five a clock shadow complimented his dark thick hair. His steward, read his younger cousin, had laid out his clothes the night before, but had forgotten his socks, forcing him to rummage through his chest. This was nothing new, Will often forgot something or other.

Stepping out on deck in the fresh morning air, Smythe looked around him. Fishermen come militia, that is all this was, and he was no better. Having worked the American coastline as a boy, he was the most experienced seaman aboard. That is why he had been given command of this little Sloop. They had harboured the night around the bay of Perranporth, and sails had been loosed in accordance with

his orders, around the start of the morning watch.

"Mornin' Commander," acknowledged Coxswain Jones. He was a sailor, one of the few which had been given to *The Lannwedhenek* by the Navy, assumably to ensure that the venture did not entirely fail. "We are slower than yesterday, down to six knots, it's cruising speed."

Coxswain Jones had been in the Navy for the majority of his life. Coming from Cardiff Bay, seafaring was in his blood, or his water, depending on the day. The cool breeze hit their faces as they stared out into the fog ridden sea. His curly ginger hair was thinning on top, but he was making up for it with a wispy beard he insisted on growing. He was shorter than Smythe, but not by much, making him around average height.

The fog of the morning was customary on the North Cornish coast, even now in early summer. "It's the fourteenth," Smythe forced himself to remember the date every day in the morning and reminded himself of the date every night whilst writing up his reports.

Every day the fog would burn off during the morning, leaving a clear day to sight any shipping coming into the Bristol Channel. Sometimes it would be larger vessels coming in to restock, having been at sea for months, others were little gigs and cogs passing round Lands' End and using Bristol or Cardiff, rather than that of Falmouth or Plymouth.

They were sailing ten points north of west, into a westerly breeze, slowing their progress. The wind was biting, and Commander Smythe looked over to the Cornish coast.

"We should turn fifteen points south, I want to veer more towards the coastline and ensure nothing is untoward in the bay."

They were twelve miles east of St. Ives, with a full mainsail, a topsail, and a foremast at half sheet. The two masted Sloop kitted out with ten six-pound guns on the deck below was a sight to behold to the fishermen of this county. To the men of the Admiralty, it was a tiny speck within the Imperial machine.

"Sir, turning into the wind will simply slow us, it would do better to keep on course and turn south when the time is right."

"For speed, yes," acknowledged Smythe, who felt he was growing into his Commander role more by the day, "But for visibility, Mister Jones, I want a slower approach. I want to ensure the fishermen of St. Ives know that they have one of His Majesty's ships looking out for their interests."

Coxswain Jones had to admit it was a valid point. They were here on "the Barbary Watch", a completely pointless venture. The number of Barbary raids since the bombardment of Tripoli some thirty years previous had seen a rapid decline. And on the northern coast of Cornwall, there had always been less issues.

The ripe fields of Munster were more accessible, as were the southern Cornish coastal towns like Penzance, Saint Michaels Mount

and other such small coves. Like the Viking raids of old, the Muslim Berbers of North Africa cared not whether you were a clergyman, layman or atheist. They just wanted slaves.

Six bells. A whole hour had passed since Smythe had woken in his cot. The morning watch was coming to an end and the forenoon watch was starting.

"Lieutenant!" shouted Smythe over the general din of the ship.

"SILENCE DOWN THERE!" bellowed Jones, "The Commander should not have to shout to be heard, you dogs."

"Erm, yes, quite," Smythe looked uncomfortable at the sudden use of his rank to quash the noise. "Lieutenant," he said quietly now that he had his attention, "the morning watch is over, I trust you have nothing to report."

The tone was that of a Parish council meeting between the two men. Lieutenant Treen stood tall at six foot, two inches tall, in his evidently second-hand uniform which was slightly too small and with a stuttering manner.

"Nnnoo. Sir," stated Treen "Nothing at all sssiiir,". He was a young man, he had not had much seafaring experience, but he did have one quality which helped him secure this position. His grandfather had owned the ship.

"Then I relieve you of the watch.", said Smythe gently.

Smythe was around fifteen years the young man's senior, and always tried to be kind to him. "Go below and get something warm in you."

"Aye Aye Sir.", and with a nod and a salute the young man went below. There may have even been a hint of a smile from him. "Looks like I'm not the only one growing into the role," thought Smythe.

"Begin' your pardon Sir, but you should have informed him,"

"Coxswain?"

"You altered course. You're the Commander of this ship, but you still should have informed the officer of the watch."

Smythe sighed. Jones was of course correct. He should have informed the officer of the watch about the change in course.

"Well, it's too late now," he murmured to himself more than Jones.

"All the same, write up the report, keeps everything official. It's nothing really, but if it becomes something, it would do well to be in writin'"

"Yes, yes, as soon as my watch is over."

The Forenoon watch was working away, as were the ships hands. The decks needed swabbing, and ideally so the noon sun could dry them, and the sails needed shortening, so that they would not dry out too much in the sun. Lieutenant Treen had returned to the top deck and asked if he could observe the Commanders' actions.

"Of course, young man," smiled Smythe, impressed with the young man's energy.

"Pace has slowed Sir, as I advised." came over Jones's voice. "'Course shortening the sail added to it,"

"Pace are we setting?" Smythe was not in the mood for a lecture

about his speed. He simply wanted to know the speed itself.

"Around four knots, we'll be in view of the bay within the hour Sir."

"We'll be in the view of the bay already."

"Sir?"

"St Ives is an inlet bay with a watch on the Western outcrop. It's raised on the cliffside, between fifty and a hundred feet above sea level depending on tide and whether they are high or just on The Head. We are sailing five points south of west, but St Ives bay is approximately on a south west course."

"Agreed," nodded Jones.

"Meaning that we have been travelling at approximately four knots for around an hour and a half, meaning we have travelled approximately seven miles."

"Again, agreed,"

"Well, we are then, with an unobstructed view less than nine miles away from the bay, considering our course and that of a straight line. Our topmast is approximately forty-five feet above the horizon. The only thing stopping them would be the mist." Smythe smiled to himself knowing he had won the argument. Even Jones

smiled as if to show the approval of a Commander he had clearly had doubts about. Treen looked on in pure amazement.

"Make a turn into the bay, they will have fish from the night catch, and we could always do with fresh water, being so close to home we never keep much on board."

They turned due south, pushing steadily now towards the bay.

"Shorten the sail some more," shouted Jones, "Best not to come in too quick Sir, people don't like it,"

"Agreed, I assume I can leave the command of the ship in your hand Coxswain?"

"You may Sir,"

"In that case, I will go ashore and speak to the Mayor."

St. Ives is a large double bay town with a headland in the middle and eastern and western bays respectively. It lies about halfway down the northern Cornish coast and the main industry of the town, was and still is fishing. The church in the town is set on the hill, and is dedicated to the Irish St. La or Ives, to which the town is named after. It was built in the fourteen century, and it is the cornerstone of the community. The quayside is at the western end of the western bay. It is not large enough for a Sloop or Brig to come directly up to it, especially when the tide is out, and it relies on smaller luggers to supply these larger vessels.

Mayor John Hawkins was sitting in his office. It was his first year as Mayor of St. Ives and he was determined to stamp his own authority on the office. The Mayoral office was elegantly furnished with furniture from over the last forty years or so.

"Sloop spotted coming into port Sir," his clerk said to him from outside the room.

"Ours?"

"Yes Sir, flying a naval ensign at any rate."

"Fire a saluting shot then, no doubt if it's coming into the bay, they will want a word."

A seven-gun salute was issued to the ship as it entered and anchored in the bay, as was required by the grade of the ship. John walked down to the stone harbour which a small rowing boat had started to pull toward. Aboard was a Commander by the looks of him. His ship was too small for him to be considered a full Naval Captain at any rate.

"Mayor John Hawkins, Mayor of St. Ives, and you are?" he asked with a rudeness that was hardly concealed.

"Commander Henry Smythe, of his Majesty's Ship the *Lannwedhenek*, at your service."

Both men shook hands and looked at each other with apprehension. It was Hawkins who spoke next.

"Well Commander, as I'm sure you can see, we have no need for your protection here, so you can…"

"I was rather hoping to resupply and provision my ship, Sir," Smythe interjected before the Mayor could finish his sentence and dismiss him.

"And what do I get out of this?"

"A promissory note from the Navy, I'm afraid I do not have any guineas on me,"

"A promissory note!", it took nearly everything Hawkins had not to laugh at the man standing on his harbour, "Look good Sir," he again barely concealed his rudeness, "this isn't Greenwich or Portsmouth or even Bristol. By the time I got the money from that note, I would no longer be Mayor of St Ives.

I cannot accept. No, if you want to deal with the provisioners here you will do it without my assistance, now, be quick about it too."

And with that the interview was seemingly over. Smythe rubbed his head. The water was simple enough to refill, even if it would take time without the help of the aid of the Parishioners, but his food problem was rather more difficult.

"I am a day out of Bristol Sir," he shouted back, as Hawkins was walking away, "I would appreciate one day of provisions on a note Sir."

Hawkins stopped. It could be useful to have a naval Commander in his debt. And he sounded rather desperate.

"Say I were to accept your offer. You are to sail to Bristol immediately, restock and show the receipt. I expect my town to be paid in full by the end of the week." This was not a negotiation and Henry knew it. He was stuck between a rock and a hard place. There was probably enough food onboard ship to get them to Bristol easily.

But how would the Admiralty react to his acceptance of terms from this Mayor. He was Commander now, but that could easily change, and he knew it.

"Done," he said eventually, and Hawkins smiled. "See," he said, now more smoothly and soothingly, "You can always find a friend here in St. Ives. Richardson, see to it that the Sloop has *one* day of food aboard it."

The loading took time, with around eighty souls aboard the ship. Smythe had thought about buying himself some chickens, but that was out of the question. He would not show Hawkins that he had any gold on him whatsoever.

The re-vettling of the ship took around five hours, and the Dogwatch had started when Smythe eventually returned to ship.

"Plot a course for Bristol if you please, Mister Jones. Whichever course you deem fastest would be preferable,"

"Aye, aye Sir."

"Sir?"

"Yes Treen?"

"There's a small ship out to sea Sir, and it has been anchored all day."

"What do you mean all day?"

"I mean I've been watching her, and she's been sitting there, out of range, almost waiting to come into the harbour."

"Well, we haven't stopped her."

"No, but maybe our presence has.", said Jones.

Smythe stopped to think. A ship out to sea probably meant one thing. Smugglers. It was not in his remit directly, but he was charged with protecting the Northern Coast and surely this counted right?

"Smugglers?" he voiced to the group.

"See I thought that at first too," said Jones. "But then why draw attention to yourself. Only reason a Sloops in harbour here is to restock, could have easily of ran us, they had the wind."

"Not if your port of entry is St. Ives."

The ship was around five miles ten points west of north of them, with a light easterly breeze.

"Make a course as if leaving the bay fifteen points east of north," he said slowly, the plan still formulating in his mind.

"Call the hands, quietly, dose the fires. We should make about five knots when we are moving. Depending on when they set off, we swing a hard port tack and intercept them before they enter the bay."

"What if the bay fires on us, Sir?" Treen looked positively petrified at the idea of hotshot ripping through the vessel he was aboard.

"They won't," said Jones, calmly coming to the same realisation as his Commander. "They know we are a Ship of his Majesty's Service. They would not risk sinking her and having to deal with the might of the British Navy and her legal system. If they sank us, at the very least, the cost of the ship would be on the town. No one is that stupid, not for a bit of sugar and cotton."

Ship's Captain Jenkins was rather pleased with himself. He had managed all day to avoid capture and avoid detection from the English Sloop-of-War which was situated in St Ives Bay. It was late afternoon, and the ship was now moving away from the Bay, clearly it had done its re provisioning, in an easterly direction towards Bristol.

"Better get movin' Capt'in", said his first mate.

"Why?" questioned Jenkins, scornfully "They haven't looked like moving all day and they finally up and move. There's no rush whatsoever. Loosen the sails slowly, I do not want to arouse too much suspicion. Let's see what you can do about some lunch.", they had killed the fires upon observing the Sloop entering the Bay in case of action.

"At this point Sir, its dinner."

The Sloop seemed to slowly move away, trudging towards an easterly direction when the mist completely burned away from the Bay of St Ives. The main sail was loose and the top sails started to

ring down but the little Pinque began to move in a southerly direction.

"I'm going below," said the Captain "If you need me for anything just shout but it better be bloody worth it."

"Aye aye Sir," said his first mate.

Jenkins went below deck his eyes adjusting quickly to the changing light. He could feel the ship underneath start to pull slowly away and he could hear the groaning of the oak on the swing of the rigging as the ship moved.

They were six weeks out of the Bahamas, with sugar and cotton from the plantations. Smuggling was simply part of the way the world works.

You could either smuggle your contraband past the guards and the check points of His Majesty's Navy or you could pay the exorbitant taxes which His Majesty requested. No puny little Sloop-of-War was going to cut his profit margins.

"Sir," came a voice from outside his cabin.

"What is it?" he shouted back, rather frustrated having ordered them not to disturb him.

"They've taken a new tact Sir,"

"What you mean that taken a new tact?"

"They're already straight for us Sir."

"Shit," thought Jenkins simply. Six weeks crossing the Atlantic, a couple of days passing by the Scilly Isles and making sure they were

not spotted and now in the last home stretch some poxy little Sloop was going to ruin the whole goddamn operation.

"Roll out the guns, let's get ready to fight them" said Jenkins simply.

"Sir it's a Sloop-of-War we don't stand a chance,"

"We're not going to fight them we're going to push them off until we can get into the Bay. Then the contraband will be already on shore and my contact will make sure that it was legal. We just have to get to the Bay."

Back aboard the *Lannwedhenek*, Smythe smiled to himself. His guns were loaded on both sides, as well as one-pounder swivel guns which sat on the top deck.

"Their ships are rolling out their guns, Sir," came voice from portside bow.

"Yes, I can see that thank you," he replied calmly "We need to fire soon. We need to make it obvious to the Bay that we have spotted an enemy or at least unrecognised ship."

"Sir?"

"The shore needs to know that we know that they shouldn't be here. I also want the shore batteries to be at alert that we are a known ship of His Majesty's Navy and we are coming under fire. Therefore, harbouring the said ship which is fighting against us is completely unacceptable in terms of war. They will be harbouring officially a vessel which had attacked His Majesty's Navy. This would

not stand."

His speech which had been aimed merely at his Petty Officer Coxswain Jones and his Lieutenant Treen had also been heard by other members of the crew. They seemed to not realise that they were at war. Indeed, this had gone from merely watching waiting and looking for vessels with which to engage, to a battle situation like none of them had ever expected.

"You will shorten the sails to ensure they are a smaller target come the battle. And now gentlemen we are nearly in range. To your

positions! Gunner!" he roared to get the attention of the man below.

"Aye Sir?"

"You may draw the guns as you please, Mister Gunner."

"Aye aye, Sir"

The six pounders had been primed and loaded and were ready to go. But first, the popguns on the deck, which fired one pound shot, would be within range sooner.

This was crucial, as an early shot or early salvo could make all the difference.

"Lieutenant you may fire all top guns as you desire."

"Aye aye, Sir," was the response that was given.

Smythe took a deep breath. The last time he was in combat had been in a fishing vessel just off the coast of Newfoundland this was something entirely different. This was actually going to be a battle.

His first main battle as a Commander. The first battle he had ever been in his life. He took another deep breath.

The ships are closing in on each other now, it would not be a simple surrender as he had hoped but a full scale battle. Could you call it a battle however with that being merely a Sloop and a Pinque? No, this was more skirmish than anything, but just because it was a skirmish did not make it any less deadly. His pulse was quickening as the ships came in range.

"Fire!" shouted the Lieutenant as loud as he could, and two popguns fired. Smoke filled the air and a thud of metal against wood rung out.

Aboard the Pinque the first shots were felt. Jenkins heard a man scream as the single-pound ball struck his shoulder on the ricochet off the decking. It shattered in seconds causing the man to cry out in pain. Mercifully, a second ball hit him in the stomach, again off the ricochet, but this one was more of a glancing ricochet and he bled out on the floor of the deck.

"Return fire damn it!" Jenkin shouted out as loud as he could to his small crew, and the six pounders that were on deck fired towards the Sloop. Two large sprays of water, one to portside, and the other starboard, showed that his guns were not aimed correctly.

"Reload and realign you lazy buggers!" he yelled, as more one-pound balls smashed into his deck, this time injuring no one but causing wood and splinters to fly up in all directions. Turning slightly onto the starboard side, allowing his four six-pound starboard side guns to fire, they fired in unison, causing the whole ship to slide exposing her starboard side vulnerably. Had there been a better gunner aboard the Sloop, they would have been in real trouble. But the gunner did not seem to have taken his advantage and the boat rocked back into the water without any major issue.

The reply came almost instantly after this, however. The six six-pounders the Sloop was carrying, along with the two pop-guns on the deck seem to fire almost instantly and simultaneously. Jenkins dare not look. He could hear the screams of his men, as the deck had clearly been raked across with cannonballs. Again, another example of the inexperience of the gunnery crews that were against him that aimed too high, but fortunately for them, had hit the main deck. Wood splinters and what sounded like part of the mast creaking underneath its own weight, the mask must have been hit by one of the cannonball's almost plum.

"Sir, we are in real trouble," shouted his first mate.

Smythe was witnessing the destruction his crew was causing with a smile. His volley of guns although high, had still hit the enemy target, and with the creaking and evident billowing of the sails he could see even from this vantage point he knew his opponent was not long for this world.

"Gunner I'm going to make an about turn, see that your guns are lined and ready,"

"Aye aye Sir," was the simple response. He fully understood the implications of this order. They were going to be pointing towards St Ives they were going to break this ship. It was already struggling and becoming crippled shot after shot, and they were then going to sail her into the Bay under a flag of surrender. They would have a prize.

"Lieutenant continue firing with those pop guns for the entirety of the time I don't want to give them a moments peace!"

"Aye aye Sir," the young Lieutenant seemed to be growing into his role and the battle seemed to be helping him do this.

The Pinque erupted in flames as the guns fired at the Sloop. The screams below were evidence of the lethality of the cannonballs, but

that would be the last major shot they would receive judging by his calculations.

Smythe had deduced about the enemy, that they would possibly have time to reload once. That was assuming that they had an experienced gun crew, none of them had died in the previous volleys from his Sloop. The Pinque's guns were all on the main deck and as the main deck had been raked by cannon fire, it was highly unlikely that any of the crews were still full. Yes, they could replenish from the starboard side but in the confusion and the unfamiliar crews the reloading will take longer and likely not be in time.

The popguns fired once more and again screams could be heard coming from the enemy ship. "A couple more down," thought Smythe, "might be couple more seconds on that reloading time" It was a curious thought to have, but every time an enemy went down, it increased the likelihood of your own survival, but that was what was going through his mind. They were about turned now and couple more seconds and the guns would be in line. Then came a sound which he had dreaded. He had miscalculated. The sound of guns roaring from the enemy ship. He could hear screams coming from

below and some screams coming from above he looked around and could see man dead on his deck he had to hold back the vomit the smell of their burning flesh from cannon balls rip through them.

"Fire!" came a shout from below and the guns ripped through the chorus of smoke and screams. The enemy must surrender now surely. To come under such heavy fire from a larger enemy was too much. The deck of the Pinque now covered in the blood of its gunners and sailors, and the mast creaking more by the second, as the weight of the sails it bore caused more damaged to the already splintering wood.

Jenkins knew his time was done. At least a quarter of his crew were dead or maimed. His ship was a wreck. If he could use the tide to

push his little ship into harbour, perhaps he could play the victim.

But there was little to no chance of that working either. Everyone in

St. Ives knew it was a Naval ship that they had encountered.

"Throw up a white flag, we're done," he said over the din and noise of the ship. No one heard him the battle was too deafening and all-encompassing for his men to pay attention to such a trivial order. He ran to his first mate blood trailing down his face as the popguns again from the sloop ripped through more of his men. He reached his first mate grabbing him by the arm and shouting in his face.

"Throw up a white flag damn it." His first mate merely nodded in acknowledgement and ran towards the bow of the ship. They would

pull down their previous flag and throw up a white rag.

Smythe saw the white flag being slowly pulled up the rear of their
ship.

"Cease fire!" he shouted, but the ill-disciplined crew did not react quickly enough and another salvo of gunfire, both from the six pounders and from the muskets as they were in range, brought death and destruction down on the little Pinque.

"I said cease fire," he again shouted this time with less energy in his voice. He was tired and he was weary. This time the crew did respond, and as they ceased firing, they started to cheer. They knew that they had won this little skirmish with an unknown enemy.

"Hook her on Commander," came the voice of Jones.

"Beg your pardon?"

"You need to go aboard and accept the surrender Sir," he stated, as if this were obvious to everyone.

"Yes, yes of course," he replied, as if he had already been planning to do it. "See to it Mister Jones."

"Aye, Aye Sir."

The grappling hooks were thrown, and as was custom on a surrendered ship, the sailors did nothing to hamper this. Once the two ships were connected, Mister Jones returned.

"All's ready for you Commander."

The gangway was not the largest, but it would suffice. He wobbled
across with as much dignity as he could muster under the circumstances.

"Commander Henry Smythe of his Majesty's Sloop, the *Lannwedhenek*."

"Captain Jenkins of the merchant ship, the *Greyhound*, and I demand…"

"You demand nothing." Smythe cut across him before this inevitably well-rehearsed speech could be made. "Everyone knows that there are hundreds of ships known as the *Greyhound* for this exact purpose. You are smugglers, it is simple."

"How dare you Sir!" exclaimed Jenkins with all the fake anger he could muster, "We are an honest merchant vessel, out of St Kitts and Nevis, and are returning to St. Ives after twenty weeks at sea."

"I wasn't aware St. Ives had a merchant vessel," said Smythe calmly.

"Well, as you're not a man from around these parts."

"I'm from Padstow."

Jenkins looked deep into the eyes of the Commander who had boarded his ship. If he were indeed from Padstow, he might as well stop lying now. Padstow was only twenty or so miles up shore, and he would indeed know that St. Ives did not have a merchant fleet as he had claimed.

"So, let's start again and maybe you will avoid the rope!"

"The rope?"

"You fired at one of his Majesty's Ships and you fly no national colours. Therefore, I assume you are a pirate."

It was a very big leap. Even Jones who was stood at the side of Smythe knew it was an empty bluff really. "I shall sail your vessel into

St. Ives and I shall present you to the local magistrate."

Jenkins paused. He knew he had contraband with clearly faked details on each crate from Nassau as everything from the free-ports of the Bahamas did.

"I accept your offer Sir," he replied simply.

"What?" Smythe had not been aware he had made him an offer.

"To go into St. Ives and be presented to the magistrate. It will of course all be settled then easily enough."

Smythe was furious with himself. He had overplayed his hand and he knew it. At the worst, his opponent would be tried for smuggling and no doubt pay the fine. It was unclear as to whether Jenkins was even his real name, and it would be up to the locals to prove this was not a first-time offence. And what if he did have enough credentials to pull this off. Smythe was not being fooled, but this Jenkins was a smooth talker.

"You will tow us in I presume?" continued Jenkins calmly. "As you can see my ship is in no shape to be sailing anywhere thanks to your treatment. I will be billing you of course," he added.

So, the towing ropes were attached and the *Lannwedhenek* pulled the *Greyhound* into St. Ives bay. They had returned less than a couple hours after leaving.

CHAPTER TWO

Jenkins had been taken aboard the *Lannwedhenek*. He knew that this was not going to end well for him. His smuggling career was over, that was for certain. His ship was a wreck, half his crew were dead or maimed, and his cargo had been taken. And that was the least of his worries. Smuggling was a capital crime. Not to mention he had fired on a Navy ship and killed sailors of the Navy. No, he was in real trouble and he knew it. The fact he was in irons confirmed this. He was in danger for his life.

And what if he managed to get out of this? What then? He owed people money, that was for certain. How was he supposed to repay them? And how would they react when they found him, penniless and broke? Pity? Or punishment. He was dammed by the courts or dammed by those who had employed him. The rope or the bullet? Or a knife in the back, he was not sure how they would do it in all honesty.

John Hawkins was on the docks watching the Sloop pull in the Pinque. He knew the ship; it was a regular round these parts. Bugger the Navy for insisting a ship be stationed along this coast. There had not been a Barbary attack in years along the northern coast and here it was that stupid little Sloop, and it was ruining everything.

Smythe, along with Jones, a group of sailors and Jenkins still in irons, boarded the jolly-boat which would take them into dock. "See to it that the reports are ready for me once we return Mr. Treen."

"Aye Aye Sir," replied the young Lieutenant. His respect for his Commander had increased during the skirmish, he had shown poise under fire, and that was invaluable aboard a Sloop, or indeed any ship. Even Jones, who to begin with had been very sceptical of his Commander, was coming around to him, with the way he had acted during the skirmish against the *Greyhound* and the accuracy of his calculations aboard the ship that morning.

"Commander!" he exclaimed as Smythe walked onto the gangway. "Please explain to me what the hell I've just witnessed! You have destroyed the only merchant vessel this town has, and what's more you have killed lots of young men of this parish, it cannot, it will not stand."

"You have no merchant vessel registered on the logs my Lord Hawkins," replied Smythe coolly. It was evidently going to be a battle of who blinked first. "Now, to the charges."

"Charges?" said Hawkins a combination of outrage and confusion in his voice.

"Yes, charges. I am merely informing you as a formality your Mayorship. I intend to draw up charges of smuggling and piracy upon this gentleman. His crew will be offered employment in my ship, but he is clearly the ringleader of this whole operation and therefore must be brought to justice."

"I will not hear of such a trial!"

"It matters not what you will hear of Mayor," Smythe replied continuing with his tone.

"Officers arrest this man!" shouted Hawkins, clearly losing his cool over the situation.

"On what charges?" Smythe almost burst out with laughter, having just issued some empty threats himself, he knew one when he heard it.

"Destruction of private property, false accusations of an honourable man."

"How do you know he is an honourable man?"

Silence. Jenkins, who had been silent throughout this exchange now stared at Hawkins with a look somewhere along the lines of you idiot. Smythe continued to look without worry as he continued in his speech.

"So, the Mayor of St. Ives is actively working against the government of the day to aide and abet a smuggler."

"I told you men to arrest him!" an out-of-control Hawkins bellowed.

"Enough," roared Smythe, clearly, his patience had waned thin. "Let us make this simple. You cannot arrest me. I am a Commander in His Majesty's Navy, and you don't have the authority. I will arrest your friend, no," he saw a quick look between the two men to have surmised what was going on, "Cousins perhaps? Anyway, I will be arresting him on piracy charges, before you interrupt, there is nothing you can do. I will take him to Bristol, where he will be

escorted to London for the piracy trials. This is an Admiralty matter and nothing for the civilian courts or officials to, or more importantly can, do. Most likely, as he fired on a naval ship, found guilty and will be hung from traitor's gate as a warning to others who fire upon his Majesty's ships."

The mood on the dock had dropped. Hawkins had gone from a confident Mayor making demands and threats to a snivelling wreck. Jenkins was kneeling, motionless and looking at the Commander.

"What do you want?" he asked simply. There was no fear in his voice, a man who was steady under fire and stress.

"I beg your pardon Sir?" questioned Smythe, trying to keep his face as neutral as possible.

"Come off it," exclaimed Jenkins, a small smile coming over his face, "We both know you made a big speech to give us an offer. No one is that pretentious that does not work in Parliament. So, what do you want?"

Smythe smiled. "Your ship is out of contention, its de-masted and not going to sea anytime soon," summarised Smythe. "No, what I need is twofold. Firstly, my ship needs recrewing and refitting. We took some damage during the battle, both with men and materials. My carpenter is currently assessing the damage, and I intend to take any wood I need from your vessel first. Also, as I have said, crew. Any of your men can join my ship. As, will you."

"Me?" said Jenkins confused at the request.

"You have experience in a ship, you're cool under fire and you're bold and decisive. Yes, I would like you aboard my ship."

"And your second demand?" asked Hawkins curtly. He had some idea of the cost of his to his town.

"The debt the Navy has incurred whilst here is clear. The town, or you, will pay for these provisions we have acquired during our time in the bay."

"I cannot simply…"

"Use the money from the goods that I will let you keep. All I want is any cannons to return me to a full complement aboard the *Lannwedhenek*. The rest of the goods are yours to do as you wish with."

Jenkins was still in irons and kneeling, but he was not a fool. He knew a good deal when he saw one. "Done," he said, not waiting for Hawkins to interject or ruin this.

"But the money, the town," exclaimed Hawkins, spluttering his words.

"You fancy doing a hangman's jig, cos I don't!" yelled Jenkins, furious at this interjection from his friend. "The deal is fair. You get your goods, I don't die!"

It was evident from the strain in his voice that he understood the potential implications of the actions against him. Piracy was a bit of a stretch, everyone knew that. But this was not going to go away

anytime soon. His life was in the balance, and he had been offered a

way out.

"Then shake," said Smythe, returning to his controlled, slow voice. He outstretched his hand to Hawkins first, who begrudgingly took it, his eyes filled with frustration and his grip slightly tighter than was welcome.

"Un-shackle him," said Smythe simply, and the handcuffs were released from around his wrists. And he again offered his hand. "I've put my faith in you, what's your real name?"

"It is actually Jenkins," he said, and quickly remembering he was no longer in command of his own ship, but subordinate to someone else, "Sir."

The two men stared at each other for a moment, trying to work out each other's intentions.

For Smythe it was simple. He needed men, and he wanted his ship repairing. For Jenkins, it was less clear. Did he want freedom? Money? Or simply did he not want to die. All of these things were perfectly possible.

"Carpenter is ready with his report Sir, when you are," came the voice of Jones.

"Excellent," replied Smythe calmly, "If you would join me Mister Jenkins, I would appreciate your opinion on the matter."

The two men walked from the dock and sat in the dingy which would ferry them back to the *Lannwedhenek*.

"I have yet to take a report from my surgeon either," said Smythe to

Jenkins, "How about you? How are your crew faring?"

"No idea," replied Jenkins simply, "Your men had me separated from them once we had surrendered. I would like to take stock of them and explain the situation."

Smythe looked at his new crew member. "I think that we should address them together. I would like it if all your men joined us, but if some feel it would not be acceptable, I am sure we can find an alternative arrangement for them. One that does not involve the noose," he added, as an afterthought. He did not wish to seem too callous.

"I'm sure most will sign up," said Jenkins, "They just want payment and food. They are not fussy about who provides it."

The honesty of the man made Smythe smile. In his short time in the Navy, he was used to maybes and vague promises down the line. Here was a man who unashamedly knew what he wanted and was willing to get it whatever the cost.

The little boat slipped up to the side of the Pinque, careful not to be caught in the wash too much. The boat was drawn in by the men aboard and the salutes were signalled as was customary of a Commander.

"At ease," he said. The skirmish in the bay seemed to have given him the confidence he had been previously lacking. "Bring up the men from below."

The confused look on the face of his mariners made Smythe smile.

Not an hour or so ago, the man standing next to him had been in irons and was being carried off into the town. Now he was stood aside him, like an old friend holding his position as a deputy.

The men, battered and beaten, slowly walked onto deck, eyes straining in the sunlight. The sight of their former Captain confused the men, just as confused as were the mariners of the *Lannwedhenek* had moments before.

"Gentlemen," Jenkins said, with a voice not that dissimilar to someone addressing a church choir. "We fought, and we were beaten. This gentleman, Commander Smythe, respects the effort you went to in the defence of our ship and he has an offer for you, Commander,"

As Jenkins spoke the word "Commander" he stepped back, as if introducing some great Lord and then trailing off into the shadows.

"Thank you, Captain Jenkins. And may I formally welcome you aboard the *Lannwedhenek*," he turned to the men assembled in front of him.

They were a rag, tag bunch of all ages. Some barely out of their teens, some well into middle age. There were different races too. Blacks, and Mulattos as well as Whites and what looked like men from the Far East.

"You men fought valiantly. You shot your guns against the odds and held firm until it was evident that you would not survive. I respect that."

He paused, staring at the dead strewn across the deck. "I must apologise," he added, the words becoming stuck in his throat. "The final volley from the popguns and muskets, I should have ordered the ceasefire sooner, you had already struck your colours, and we could have saved more lives."

Jenkins looked at the Commander with interest and bemusement. In the thick of a naval battle, the fact that one order was not heard was not anything to be ashamed of. And yet, Smythe seemed to carry this burden with him, as if every ounce of blood on the deck was his personal responsibility.

"Your ship is to be scrapped," Smythe continued callously. "As part of our terms of surrender, I am to use any timber from this ship I see necessary to repair mine. After that, and the mast being damaged, I'd wager the town will strip the rest of it for their fishing fleets."

"He guesses right," thought Jenkins. The fisheries were not enamoured with the idea originally to be part of a smuggling team. Now, with a perfect excuse to break it down and be rid of it forever, he was sure that the ship he had sailed halfway around the world on would be scrap by the end of week.

"So, you gentlemen will be unemployed. Not a nice place to be in." again Smythe paused, looking at these men. "However, you are all experienced seamen. And that is something my crew is distinctly

lacking. I would like you all to come work on my gundecks."

There was a general murmur amongst the men, a combination of nods and scowls in equal measure. "You know that my crews are

inexperienced. And I lost men too in the fight, that goes without saying. I want you to help train them to be the best crew on the peninsula. You will all get paid as of today and…"

"What about this prize?" asked a voice from the back of the group.

"There is no prize," interjected Jenkins, "The *Greyhound* doesn't exist, or at least, not according to the Navy."

"What's our pay for the last three months then."

"Gone." Said Jenkins simply. His was too.

"I've got an 'effin' family to feed you robbing, thieving…"

"Silence!" shouted Smythe. "You engaged in criminal activity, and you have been caught. I have no intention of prosecuting anyone, but if you cannot abide by the terms given, then you're on your own. No pay, no job."

The prosecution was an empty bluff. With the *Greyhound* being stripped of everything of value, and most of the crew eagerly ready to join the ship with guaranteed pay.

"The Blacks and Mulattos?"

"Are all freemen." replied Jenkins, "I do not have slaves aboard my ship. No man is a slave."

"Well said," smiled Smythe and the two men understood each other. Had Jenkins said they were slaves, then Smythe would have

freed them. The few men in the back who were affected by this conversation stepped forward at this.

"We will join you," one said, with a heavy French Creole accent, "but

we need certain assurances,"

"Assurances?" Smythe did not understand what assurances he could give.

"None of them have their papers," said Jenkins simply. "Not exactly easy to acquire. They acted as my slaves whenever we were somewhere which it might be an issue, but they are all free men."

"Then we shall have a clerk in town address that," said Smythe. "Anyone else wish to join?"

The men stepped forward one at a time to shake the hand of their new Commander.

Some came, obviously willing to join and receive the benefits of going from poacher to gamekeeper. Others, seemed more re-luctant, seemingly thinking they simply needed a job.

"Do you have any powderboys aboard?"

"A couple below deck, they know not to come up during the fighting."

"Then I shall take them too if their guardians are willing."

"I am their guardian," said Jenkins uncomfortably, looking at his feet at these words.

"Ex-slaves?"

"Strictly speaking, still slaves." A look of extreme discomfort came
over his face. "They speak very little English and I didn't want them
ending up lost or harmed. They haven't left the ship since I purchased them."

"Well, we can sort that, I need powder boys and some midshipmen, are any suitable?"

"A couple, Abraham and Gabriel. I picked boys with more English sounding names."

"Why?" it seemed such an unnecessary thing to have done given the circumstances.

"So that when they are free, no one will know they were once slaves," said Jenkins simply. "They have begun their studies under my first mate, and those two can read and write in English. I know it isn't much but…"

"It's a start," nodded Smythe in understanding and acknowledgement. It took a lot of guts for Jenkins to admit he had slaves onboard after making such a fuss about his freedmen sailors previously, but his reasoning did make sense.

"How many Jones?"

"Fifteen Sir, and the six boys. Makes twen'y one in total."

"Then we need to speak to our surgeon."

"That will be difficult Sir,"

It took a moment for this to sink in.

"Dead?"

"Not yet. But I wouldn't hold out much hope."

"If I may Sir," interjected Jenkins trying to show both his usefulness and deference to his new Commander, "Yin!". One of the men who had signed up walked towards the three men talking. "This is Yin, he
has no formal training, but he sorted us out throughout our voyage."

"We need an acting surgeon if nothing else Sir. And then he could become the surgeon's mate, should he prove useful." Jones murmured in Smythe's ear.

Smythe shrugged his shoulders, "What have I got to lose? Welcome aboard Yin." Yin bowed his head politely in acknowledgement. "Go aboard the *Lannwedhenek* and make your primary assessment of my crew if you please."

"Si, Si Senor!"

This took Smythe and Jones by surprise, but Jenkins merely smiled and shook his head. "He first worked with the Dego's," he said simply, "He understands English, but sometimes struggles to vocalise it. So, he responds to orders in Spanish, not like it hurts anyone." Jones looked horrified. But Smythe simply shrugged his shoulders. What difference did it make, so long as he followed orders?

"Carpenter Sir," announced Jones, and the boat returned from taking Yin to the *Lannwedhenek*.

"Report?"

"The foremast has a few nicks out of it, but nothing major. One of the topsails is damaged, not sure how that happened, but that's the sailing master's issue. We've been holed a few times, but nothing which can't be fixed in the bay. Where are we getting the wood?"

"You're standing on it," replied Smythe simply.

"Oh, in that case I will start getting measurements. Couple of the gun-

holes need repairing too but we can do that on the move if needs be."

"Good," replied Smythe, "how long?"

"About an hour to ensure the sizes, once I have the wood about another couple. We could be out of here in the morning easily."

"See if you can have it done before low tide, that is..."

"Three bells on the middle watch" interjected Jones. He knew his Commander was about to say half past one in the morning and did not want him to embarrass himself in front of Jenkins.

"Not a timekeeper?" asked Jenkins with a smile, and Jones scowled at him.

"Aye, Aye Sir," nodded the carpenter, ignoring the new man.

"Gunnery mate Sir," said Jones, as the conveyor belt of mates and men came to report to the Commander.

"Sir, we lost three cannons during the engagement, along with thirteen gunnery crew members."

"The crew has been replaced; see to it they are integrated into current groups. If there are any men who would prefer to be transferred to the sailors or mariners offer that too until you have

filled up with the new recruits. See to it that three of these six pounders are moved over. And any other weapons you think you would find useful."

"Aye, Aye Sir."

The *Greyhound* was a hubbub of noise still. With the old crew removing their personal belongings, the men from the *Lannwedhenek* moving the equipment back to their ship and men from the dock removing the cargo from below. Jenkins looked upon his ship with grief. He knew that the whole thing was about to be gutted of anything valuable.

"Time to return to the *Lannwedhenek*," announce Smythe. "I will give you fifteen minutes to get any personal belongs Jenkins. Then we must be off."

In the distance, the first dogwatch bell sounded four bells. It was early evening and Jenkins was hungry. He had not eaten since before breakfast. He went below deck into his cabin and started packing. It would not take him long. His chest had been packed since yesterday. Yesterday when he thought he would be home free and paying off his debts. He grabbed the wine, he might as well drink it down now, or else take it as a peace offering to his new bunkmates. He was a common sailor again, after commanding his own ship for the past two years, he was not sure how he felt about that. He grabbed the last of the cheese they had picked up in

Boston, ate it quickly, which was a mistake as it was starting to turn, and walked back above deck.

The sun was still high in the sky, it was another couple of hours before the sun would set at this time of year. The light was, as always, dazingly having been below.

"Right Mister Jenkins, you're Coxswain's mate. We didn't have one,
and Jones has agreed to have you work with him."

"You mean he doesn't trust me, so wants to keep an eye on me?"

"Something like that. You'll bunk with the other Mates, there will be a spare couple of bunks down there, and good luck."

The carpenter, with a few men, was back aboard the *Greyhound* with saws and hatchets. It seemed his measurements had been made. Smythe led Jones and Jenkins to the jolly boat. The crew began to pull off, with Jones at the tiller. The *Lannwedhenek* had sailed away slightly to give themselves room.

"A peace offering," said Jenkins to his Captain, and he handed him one of the two bottles of wine he had taken from his cabin. "It has been at sea for about three years, and I have no idea how good it is. But you have made me a petty officer. It wasn't just the rope and be done with it. I am thankful Sir."

Smythe was taken aback. He had not expected a present from his opposing Captain when he went into the skirmish, that was for certain. But today had been an odd day for many reasons, why not add to the confusion.

"You are most welcome; however, you can keep the wine. I don't drink heavily, and the bottle would be far too rich for my taste."

"He's a Quaker," came Jones's voice from the rear.

"A member of the Society of Friends, thank you Mister Jones."

"Oh, I didn't realise," said Jenkins awkwardly and then shook himself. There was nothing to have realised, and it was not a disease or
anything.

The pumps were being worked by the men to keep the water out of the holed *Lannwedhenek*. Jenkins smiled at his work. His ship had caused this. A few well aimed shots had seriously hampered the *Lannwedhenek*'s ability to keep afloat. But the holes were being filled as they spoke, and Jenkins could see the water flushing out of the pumps was less with each flurry.

Moreover, the ship was clearly becoming more balanced. A mere inconvenience rather than larger victory. Jenkins inwardly sighed. He would have never won that fight.

"Welcome aboard the *Lannwedhenek* Mister Jenkins, Mister Jones will show you to your bunk. Mister Yin!" he shouted over the general din of a ship on dogwatch but without food. "in my cabin if you please, I would like that report."

Yin stood still and to attention as his Commander read the report, he had handed him.

Talle – 34
Lesionado, pero se recuperara – 12
Muerto o no volvera – 18

"This report Yin," began Smythe, trying not to lose his cool with his new recruit.

"Top line; ok. Second line; will recover. Third line; not recovering."

"Right, ok." At least it made more sense now, "Details?"

"No detail yet, Senor," replied Yin, "Will be in follow up report. Will take a long time."

"Why?"

"You no read Spanish. My English is slow."

This was an issue.

"Do any of your old crew speak Spanish and write English?"

"Abraham, Senor."

"The boy?" said Smythe recalling the name. "Steward, call for the boy Abraham, tell him he isn't in trouble, but to come here at once. Send for Mister Jenkins too."

It took a little while for Jenkins and Abraham to reach the Commanders quarters. It was becoming increasingly busy with now four people in this small office space. Jenkins and Abraham looked confused as they had both been summoned without warning.

"Abraham," started Smythe. "It's a lot to ask, but could you translate Yin's report into English for the wounded and in-jured?"

It would not be a pleasant job, especially for a boy, but it would keep him from having to do any manual labour. Abraham looked at Jenkins for his opinion.

"It's up to you lad," replied Jenkins simply, not wanting to in-fluence his young ward one way or the other. Abraham looked back at Smythe and simply nodded.

"Very good, in that case Yin, find somewhere quiet if possible and

dictate to young Abraham what it is you wish to explain about each wounded and killed man."

"Si si Senor," came the reply, and Yin beckoned young Abraham to follow. With an uneven bow Abraham departed.

"I appreciate what you are doing Commander," said Jenkins after the other two had left. "But kindly, would you stop?"

"I beg your pardon?"

"You are trying to include me in any orders and dealings with my crew and the boys. But it is your ship. And they are your men now. The sooner everyone realises that and conforms the better."

"I'm sorry, I did not mean to offend."

"Nor have you, Sir," replied Jenkins "Just remember, it is your ship."

Jenkins bowed and dismissed himself. Smythe was frustrated with himself. He had indeed tried to interject Jenkins into his decision making, giving his orders another level of legitimacy. But he had no need to give these bits of charity to Jenkins, nor re-legitimise his orders. He was the Commander and that was all that was needed.

He sat back in his chair, he was exhausted and could feel his eyes drooping more by the moment.

There was a knock at the door of the cabin, bringing back from the twilight between awake and asleep with a start. He shook himself before he spoke.

"Enter,"

It was the carpenter, smiling rather pleased with himself.

"Ships ready to sail away Sir, whenever you are."

"Very good, I will be on deck shortly. Please have Treen, Jones and Jenkins ready on deck."

"Aye, Aye Sir."

The night was drawing in, but the tide was still going out of the bay. This was exactly what Smythe had hoped for. The tide would help pull the ship out into the Atlantic coastline, allowing them to sail down the Bristol Channel and into home port. There they would re-provision once again, amend the crew lists at the Admiralty, and then back out on duty.

The papers ensuring the men would be free had been supplied by the clerks, along with guardianship papers for the *Lannwedhenek* for the boys. Although in effect a form of slavery, it ensured they received pay, and food and had basic rights. It was better than nothing, he thought.

Stepping out on the deck, the sun was just about set. The cool night air had set in and the men worked away on the ship as was to be

expected. Many of the men were below, playing dice or cards. Smythe did not approve of such actions, but he knew that it kept his men occupied on the longer nights. Lord above only knows what they gambled on. Food probably, or drink. But that was irrelevant now.

"Mister Jones," he said, as the Coxswain approached him, "And Mister Jenkins, thank you kindly. I would appreciate your opinion on the matter of returning to Bristol. Unless you have an issue with the

plan, sail directly north, letting the tide take us out, then sail west up the channel."

"Seems like a good plan to me," said Jenkins. Jones, who seemed to want to argue with Jenkins more than Smythe, simply nodded and shrugged.

"Then set the course Mister Jones. Mister Treen, the ship is yours. Mister Jenkins, thank you for your input. Send for Mister Yin. I will be in my cabin when he is ready."

The lamps had been lit throughout the ship. The deck was lit with a low-level light and it meant that the eyes did not take as long to adjust to the light change of dropping below deck. The light in his cabin had been lit by his steward, and his crab dinner had been set out. He ate alone as he often did, in silence, re-reading his bible.

"Sir, Mister Yin is here,"

"Send him in,"

Yin walked in and bowed as he always did as his sign of respect.

"The report, Sir."

Smythe looked down at the report. It was flawlessly written by the young man Abraham; Jenkins was right he would make a decent midshipman. It read as follows.

Injured men and their return.

1. *J. Bodilly – injury to eye. May need removing. Return possible but delayed.*
2. *C. Cargeeg – bullet wound. Left shoulder. Graze. Will return shortly.*
3. *T. Carlyon – Splinter from ships wood. Will return shortly.*
4. *A. Carthew – lost finger, index right hand. Will return shortly assuming no infection.*
5. *D. Carthew – Broken foot, two weeks light duties.*
6. *H. Davey – large wood piece in leg. Will need surgery. Return possible but delayed.*
7. *F. Dyer – also missing a finger. Ring, left hand. Will return shortly assuming no infection.*
8. *G Gilbard – swelling of the hand, suspected broken. Light duties required.*
9. *H. Pascoe – lost right hand. Has been bandaged up. Will need further medical attention. Could return but may not wish to.*
10. *P. Penhaligon – broken arm, hit by flying object. Once reset will be fine.*
11. *B. Trevethan – lost lower leg. Surgery required. Insisted*

he would remain in the ships company. Something about a wife not having a cripple in the house.

<u>*Dead or incapacitated.*</u>
There are now 19 men who are injured or incapacitated. I know Commander I said 18 originally but J. Toms has taken a turn for the worst. He has lost a lot of blood and unfortunately will most likely
now not make it through the night. I am sorry for misleading you.

Smythe read and reread the report to ensure he understood it. Yin stood in silence as he read, stood to attention, an anxious look on his face.

"The report is excellent," commented Smythe, trying to relax Yin, "My compliments to young Abraham for writing it so eloquently."

"Thank you, Sir."

At least he has stopped calling him Senor. "You look uncomfortable Yin, what's the matter?"

"I. I," the words seemed to be failing Yin as he hung his head in shame, "I mislead you, Sir."

"How so?"

"I originally said eighteen who would not be able to return. It is now

nineteen. I should have seen Toms' injuries for what they were."

"You cannot be held responsible for other men's injuries," replied Smythe kindly, then remembering that actually, Yin may be responsible for the crew's injuries. "In any case, you have told me as soon as you were aware. I am not angry in any way Yin. I am grateful. You may go to your charges. Steward?"

"Sir," came a voice from outside the cabin.

"Send for Mister Treen if you please, tell him to leave the ship in command of Mister Jones." As the conversation ended, Yin made his bow and left the cabin without delay.

Smythe sat at his little desk in his cabin in thought. It had been a long day. They were moving out of the bay, as far as he could tell, the slow-moving tide aiding their movement.

There was a gentle breeze from the land pushing them away too, it would not be long before they were heading up the Bristol Channel as planned. And then what. He had half a new crew, the other half looked battered and beaten. How on earth would he explain this to the Admiralty?

Treen knocked at the door as was his custom, and Smythe smiled at him to put him at ease.

"Mister Treen, thank you for joining me,"

"Anytime Sir," he replied. It was an odd custom that Commanders on ships thanked their subordinates for following orders. It had to be done. The newly confirmed Articles of War, which needed to be

read out to the new recruits at the earliest convenience, put down the punishment for failing to follow orders. Death by firing squad or the rope, depending on your rank.

"Today's action was," Smythe paused to find the word which would correctly identify his thoughts on the matter.

"Unexpected, Sir?" came Treen's interjection, trying to assist his Commander.

"Yes, let's go with that," replied Smythe, "unexpected. We have lost nineteen men and have had to patch up the ship as best as possible. And moreover, we no longer have surgeon, which will make more

difficult."

"Agreed Sir," came the stock response from Treen.

"I feel the best response is that we sunk the *Greyhound* further out than the bay. And although we managed to salvage some of the materials from the ship, she was otherwise damaged beyond repair. Furthermore, we pressed her remaining crew into joining."

"I see no other option Sir."

There was truly little else that could be done. And the *Greyhound* would indeed be stripped down by the fishing fleet in St. Ives, then lost to the ages. It would be as if the ship were at the bottom of the Atlantic.

"Then I shall write my report to say as much. I will write it before I

turn in for the night. Thank you Treen. I shall relieve you at the usual time, what speed are we making?"

"Around 5 knots Sir."

"Well, the first bell of the middle watch just sounded. Six bells of the morning watch means we should have travelled about half the distance to Lundy Island. Gives us plenty of time to get into Bristol, and read the new recruits in."

"Aye aye Sir."

"Well, goodnight Treen, I assume your watch will be peaceful."

"Aye aye Sir."

Treen turned and left the small cabin. The report, although could wait, should not, and it would take all the energy he had left to write, read, and edit his report as best he could. He listed the injured and the dead, that would need dealing with tomorrow also. If any men held on till Bristol, they could be dropped there at the naval hospital. Otherwise, it would simply be to Davy Jones with a stitch through his nose.

Smythe remembered the first time he had seen that custom done

by a ship's crew. He had been fishing off the coast of New England in the Americas, and an old mariner's time had simply come. The harsh waters, not to mention the cold weather, caused him to simply die.

"Stitch him up, last one through the nose, if you can't do that boy, ask one of the other lads to do that last stitch."

Smythe had not struggled with any of the bunk stitches. Nor did he struggle putting the lead weight in the bottom of the hammock to weigh it down. He got to the old mans weathered face. And he held

the needle.

"You know why we do that stitch?" asked a voice from one of the other fishermen.

"No," replied a young Smythe.

"Make sure they are dead," replied the fisherman. "If he's dead, and his heart has stopped, the blood may trickle, or it may not even move, but it won't flow. If he's alive, blood will keep pumping out. It might sound grim. But if he bleeds heavy, he ain't dead, and we don't wanna send him to the deep with that."

So, it was a kindness which caused the final stitch through the nose, rather than disgusting habit. Smythe had never from that day had a problem with drawing that final stitch. But not everyone was so comfortable with it.

He found it funny that fishermen, who gutted fish and were often covered in blood, and mariners and sailors, or ever gunners, who now shot balls of lead at each other in the hope of killing and maiming their enemies often struggled with this final act.

The night-time drew in on him as the bell struck six. He had four

hours sleep from this point. It was common that this was his regular

amount of sleep aboard his vessel. It was also common that he did not get a great night's sleep, despite the privacy which being Commander gave him.

Five bells on the morning watch sounded. Will had shaken him awake from the twilight zone which he had been in and had laid out his clothes. He had laid out his best uniform for him.

"What's the occasion?"

"Funerals Henry,"

It was a sign of the familial bond and the dourness of the day that Will had used Smythe's Christian name. It was not something which often happened.

Smythe stepped out into the morning air and walked towards his Lieutenant. "Before you issue your report on the ship, I would be extremely grateful of your opinion on something if you please, Mister Treen, you also Mister Jones if you would be so kind."

Jones and Treen walked cautiously towards their Commander. "We

have new crew, who have not been told the articles of war. They need to be read in. However, there is the matter of funerals. I wish to perform those first. It will show our new crew members that we have compassion aboard this ship and allow our men to grieve their fallen comrades."

"Agreed," said Jones simply. And Treen looked from the old Coxswain and his Commander and shrugged.

"Then see to it all hands-on deck, Treen, you may go below should you wish and sleep. Jones, the ship is yours. We should be about

eight leagues from Lundy Island, so we have plenty of time."

"About seven and a half, we picked up a bit of speed in the morning breeze."

"Then I bid you the ship," he said quietly before turning away from the small conversation, "All hands-on deck, bring up the bunks!"

It was like spilled liquid, how fluidly the men moved, the skirmish seemingly focusing their minds.

The bunks were brought up onto deck, and even the new crew members seemed to understand the need and wished to help their

new comrades to lay to rest their previously fallen foes.

"Attention!" shouted Smythe, and the men, stood around their fallen comrades in perfect silence. "I would before we commend these bodies to the deep, like to thank the new crew members for their assistance with this. I know there will be some animosity, I know there will be pain and grief. Some of you have lost family or lifelong friends. But we are here now, together. That is what should be remembered."

The silence aboard the ship continued as the memory of the dead

was observed. Then Smythe spoke again.

"Unto Almighty God we commend the souls of our brothers departed, and we commit these bodies to the deep; in sure and certain hope of the Resurrection unto eternal life, through our Lord Jesus Christ; at whose coming in glorious majesty to judge the world, the sea shall give up her dead; and the corruptible bodies of those who sleep in him shall be changed, and made like unto his

glorious body; according to the mighty working whereby he is able to subdue all things unto himself. Amen."

"Amen," came the chorus of men who surrounded the bodies. "Now, for the names of the commended," and he went on to name each of the men in turn. There was a stony silence throughout the proceedings as he continued through, naming each, their previous profession as known, and their hometown, Perranporth, Padstow, Porthcothan to name a few. There were men in the group with tears in their eyes as friends and relatives of theirs were given their final stitch and lowered down into the black waters below.

"Coxswain Jones, you have an announcement I believe?"

"The auction will be on the last Dogwatch for the men's belongings. All monies are to go to families of the deceased. Relatives of the deceased have until then to claim said belongings before sold."

"Thank you, Mister Jones. Well gentlemen, back to your postings."

The *Lannwedhenek* after being as quiet as the graves they were commending the bodies to, became a hive of energy.

The hands were, after all said and done, seamen at heart, even if not usually one on such large vessels. The sails had to be loosed as the wind picked up taking them into the Bristol Channel faster. They

were approaching eight knots now and approaching Lundy Island. Three bells rung out on the afternoon watch.

"We'll have to slow down Sir, before we reach Bristol."

"Agreed, we are not going in at night, if we shorten sail, we can steady down to five knots, that will make it around sixteen hours to Bristol. That will put us in around half seven in the morning."

"Perfect, the nights catch will be in, and we can breakfast whilst we wait."

"Mister Jenkins, would you be so kind as to assemble your old crew?"

"Sir, I've politely asked you,"

"They need swearing in Mister Jenkins and it would be quicker if you were to arrange them all to meet me on deck. Furthermore, you speak several languages or at least the basics of them, it would be useful to have your assistance on such matters if the need
arises."

"Oh, of course Sir," said Jenkins slightly taken aback. This was not a request as he had been receiving. It was a direct order. The crew of
the *Greyhound* were assembled on the deck, stood at ease, looking towards their new Commander.

"Some of you may have served in the Navy before. Others of you, this may be your first time. In any case there are certain rules which you must follow in order to be successful and prosperous." Smythe was trying his best to give an aurora of confidence and command. He was not sure he was achieving this, however.

"In due course we will go over all the rules you must obey. But a few simple rules to start you off. One; do not steal. It results in a
gauntlet and I will not spare any man from it." The gauntlet was a commonly used punishment in the Navy, whereby the offending party had to walk, a sword pressed against his stomach and back to dictate his pace, between rows of his shipmates where they were hit on the back with any weapon they could get their hands on. It drew blood.

"Secondly, if any man endangers this ship, strikes a superior officer, or ignores a direct order from a superior officer, there is only one punishment. Death."

Although many men merely shrugged, some looked on with absolute horror. However, after looking around at their fellow

sailors, they realised that this was a formality, and not different to any other Naval ship. After a small amount of shuffling,
the men gave a grumble of consent.

"Thank you, gentlemen, in that case, if there is no complaints,
to your stations."

And so, the *Lannwedhenek* sailed on without incidence all the
way to Bristol docks.

CHAPTER THREE

The docks at Bristol were growing steadily as the trans-Atlantic trade was increasing. It would not be long surely before Bristol took over as the main port in all of England. The *Lannwedhenek* was anchored at the mouth of the Avon, waiting for the pilot to lead them into the main dock. The Avon ran through the city and is its lifeblood.

"Won't be long now Sir, just had a word with the pilots' team, they have a couple of luggers they need to get in first with sugar, then us."

The *Lannwedhenek* was just languishing in the wash, as the cook made breakfast for everyone. The hands seemed to be incredibly happy during this time.

"They don't have to work," said Jones cynically to Smythe.

"Nothing to do in port."

"We letting them off Sir?"

This had been on Smythe's mind all the previous evening. If he allowed his men off, they would blow off some steam, and undoubtably, some money. But Bristol is a large town. And men could easily go missing in those streets of vice and sin.

But they would only be ashore for a day at most. Smythe had some business to attend to at the Admiralty house. And the ship needed refitting. The powder needs refilling. And more cannon balls, both six and one pounders needed to be procured. The water barrels

were the most important of goods to be added. This would take time and idle hands in port would cause trouble aboard. No, it was better to lose some men in the taverns and brothels that stood by the quayside than have fights and anguish aboard.

"Treen!" he called, and his Lieutenant came over to his side.

"You will be in command of the ship whilst I am away. I have business with the Admiralty and Mister Jones will be procuring the supplies we need. Mister Jones, we will be allowing the men ashore, however, offer a double rum ration this evening to any man who stays aboard to help with the loading of the cargo." He hoped that it would be enough to keep enough men aboard that they would be able to sail away again this evening should the weather and tides permit it.

"Mister Jones, a word if you please." Jones turned to his Commander, a look of confusion on his face. "Take our new shipmate along with you. You're right, I want you to keep an eye on him. I'm not a hundred percent sure about his motives, but I wouldn't mind a close watch on him."

"Aye aye Sir."

The dock's pilot came aboard to lead the *Lannwedhenek* through the turbulent waters of the dock. The River Avon led into the city of Bristol, and the cut in canals and quaysides which followed.

"Mister Jones see to it the ship's supplies are sorted. I will be at the Admiralty's offices should you need me."

"Aye aye Sir."

Unlike that of Greenwich or Portsmouth, as Bristol was a commercial dock, it was deemed currently, an unnecessary luxury for the Admiralty to have their own building here. However, the rooms within the Custom house which the Admiralty rented were beautifully furnished, in the fashion of the Restoration. The oak panelling, laced with gold leaf, gave the impression that one was aboard a great Ship-of-the-Line.

Admiral Ashore Sir John Molesworth was in the office doing his usual paperwork. He often had little to do, but that was more than fine with him. As Vice Admiral of the North Cornwall coast, he had few ships in his jurisdiction, and often spent his days filling in paperwork and idling away. He shared the office with his Devon counterpart George Courtenay, who spent most of his days dealing with the Bristol affairs, as the positions overlapped in jurisdiction.

"You got any ships in today John?" asked George, in a rather bored drawl.

"Just the one I think, the *Lannwedhenek*. They were due in for supplies yesterday, but no doubt they will have spotted a fishing boat and mistook it for pirates."

"That's the fisherman's Sloop, isn't it?"

"It is, yeah, they mean well by god, but they just ain't sailors."

Lists. Molesworth was sure that the Navy ran on lists. Forget the ships and the men, the powder, the shot and anything else, lists. Lists of men. Lists of ships. Lists of stock, and supplies. Lists of healthy. Lists of sick. Lists of Captains, Commanders and Commodores. Lists, lists, lists. It was never ending.

A knock at their collective office as Molesworth's secretary stood at the door. "Commander Smythe of the Sloop *Lannwedhenek* is here to see you Sir."

"Send him in, send him in."

"Commander Smythe, of the Sloop *Lannwedhenek*, Sir" said Smythe as he presented himself to his superior officer.

"Very good Smythe, report."

"Engaged a smuggler in St. Ives. The *Greyhound*."

Molesworth looked up from his paperwork. He had expected a mere request for funds to restock his ship, not report an engagement. Even Courtenay, who had not even bothered to acknowledge the Commander upon his arrival, looked up now, intrigued to the goings on. Of course, it was *a Greyhound* they encountered. There was a joke at the customs houses that even Derby had a sailing vessel named the *Greyhound* officially registered.

"Well, report then man!" came an excited Molesworth. Even as Admiral ashore he was entitled to some of the prize money acquired by the engagement.

"She sunk Sir," said Smythe and Molesworth's face dropped. Of course, it had. No major prizes were earned along the north Cornish coast, why would this engagement be any different.

"Well, what's the damage." The disappointment in his voice

was audible.

"The ship has been repaired Sir. We knew we couldn't salvage her, but we could take some of her wood to patch our damage."

"Guns?"

"Also replaced by the *Greyhound*,"

"Cargo?"

"It was sugar, Sir, but it was ruined as we had holed her."

"Men?"

"All pressed into service Sir, they have replaced the men we lost in the skirmish." He felt it would be overselling it slightly if he used the term battle. "I have the updated lists of my ships company Sir and would be obliged if you would update the lists here in Bristol."

"My secretary will see it to, anything else?"

"My Coxswain is currently restocking the ship; you will be receiving a bill from the suppliers."

"Basic rations don't forget; I am not paying for any extravagancies."

"No Sir, of course not Sir."

"Anything else?"

"I require a new surgeon. We have a surgeon's mate from the pressed men, but no such luck with a full surgeon."

"There are no free surgeons currently on the lists," said Molesworth simply. "I will advertise in the local gazette, but you will have to sail for now without I'm afraid. Not like you are going far."

Smythe nodded. He had expected as much. Aboard one of the sloops on Barbary Watch he was unlikely to be a priority. Nor would the pay be large enough to entice a surgeon from another ship over. No, it would be a young doctor wanting to see the world who might foolishly sign up. And if they were lucky, they would see as far as the Scilly Isles.

"Very good Sir. Unless you have any new orders for me?"

"No, you can go Smythe. When are you due back?"

"Couple of weeks Sir,"

"Then I shall see you then, but probably be the last time for a while, I will be at Parliament after that."

Of course, the recent election had returned Molesworth as a Member of Parliament. Courtenay smiled to himself. Molesworth had told everyone and anyone he was due back at Parliament later this year, whether it was relevant or not.

Smythe nodded, turned and made his leave.

"He's a menace that one," said Molesworth after he had left.

"You mean he didn't capture the ship,"

"Few tonnes of sugar and a small trading vessel. I would have been about two hundred guineas richer damn it."

Courtenay shook his head. Forget the fact that England had one less

smuggler and enemy, Sir John Molesworth was slightly worse off.

"What do you mean, there's no rum?"

"We have no rum in stores."

"How the hell can you have no damn rum in stores?"

"Well, we don't."

This conversation had been going on for about twenty minutes.

"There is a ship due in from Kingston, when that arrives you will have your rum, until then, you'll have to wait."

Today had been a frustrating day for Jones. Acquiring the ships biscuits had taken far too long, the salt beef seemed to be taking forever to be loaded and now this.

"Mister Jenkins, my compliments to Commander Smythe. Inform him we will not be leaving tonight as desired and he will need to acquire a letter of stay from the dockmaster."

"Aye aye Sir."

Jones was furious with the situation. The longer they were at port, the more trouble the crew would get into, the more likely they were to fight with the locals. Most importantly, the longer they were in port, the more likely they were to desert.

There were around twenty-five thousand people who lived in and around Bristol. That did not include the multitude of sailing vessels currently docked, ships just arriving from the Indies and the Caribbean, ships due to set off shortly to the slave coasts of Africa,

and finally little ships aiming for the continent, to the ports of Bordeaux or Bilbao. There were at least fifteen taverns, inns and brothels on the streets of St. Thomas and Thomas Lane alone, and the money that many of the men had hoarded during their time at sea would be spent probably in the one night they were here.

Plus, there was the Commander's broken promise about rum ration. They would receive it later without question, but the damage to his reputation would be done. The men would not care that there had been supply issues on shore. They would only care that they had been promised double rum to stay aboard, and they would be receiving none whatsoever.

"Do you have any beer?"

Jenkins was stood a couple of steps back of this initial conversation talking away to the other labourers on the quayside.

"Beer?"

"Yeah, you know, made from barley, made in a brewery, often brown in colour, beer."

"I know what beer is."

"Well, we have men aboard who want drink. And you have no rum yet. So, what can we buy off you?"

The Quay-master stood silent for a moment, looking at the new man. He had worked with Jones, on and off, for the better part of a decade. In all that time, Jones had never permitted one of his subordinates to join in the negotiations, and yet, here was a new

man who was as presumptive as they came. Jones stood there too, looking at Jenkins, but he turned to the Quay-master and said, "Well?"

"Well, what?"

"What have you got that could see us through till the rum arrives."

"You can't be serious?"

"I need drink for the men aboard. What have you got?"

The Quay-master looked stunned at this statement. Had Jones gone completely mad? "Gimme the lists!" he shouted at a boy who was walking past him at the time. "Lemmie see here, right," his Bristolian accent coming out more now that he was busy in thought.

"I've got six bottles of wine spare and a firkin of ale, nothing more."

Jenkins looked at Jones. Seventy-two pints of beer and six bottles of wine. The wine would go to the petty officer's mess for them to enjoy. The beer would go to the lads working away for the to divide out however they saw fit. It was not a double rum ration, but it was something at least.

"Alright we'll take it," said Jones at last, "And mind I'm the first bugger you tell when that ship from Kingston arrives won't ya?"

"Aye, you old git, I will do." The two men shook hands as the orders were confirmed.

"It'll take all day to shift this lot," grumbled Jenkins to himself.

"Good, keep you out of mischief," Jones replied.

CHAPTER FOUR

The *Lannwedhenek* sailed back out of Bristol the following day once the rum had arrived from Kingston. Life aboard ship did not alter much for the next four months. They would return to Bristol to be re supplied, the only difference currently being that their bills currently went to George Courtenay as, he had reminded Smythe yet again before leaving, Sir John Molesworth would be at Parliament. Drills were introduced to the gunnery crews at the behest of Jenkins, and he was in charge of leading these weekly drills.

"Barrel out at half a mile on the starboard side. Mister Gunner fire as they bear."

The first shot was extremely short, causing a spray of water in the air.

"Up your trajectory damn it, it's well short!" roared Jenkins at the crew.

The second shot was fired too early. This time the spray was off to the right of the barrel, not far off in line for distance, but off for accuracy.

"Patience lads, patience," came again Jenkins who was spotting up on deck. The third cannon was closer still, this slightly to the left.

"Off by a few feet!" came the excited voice of Jenkins, "now let's finish it!"

The fourth shot was closer still. The fifth shot hit, causing a splintering of wood to match the spray of water.

"Shot by god!" yelled Jenkins, "An extra ration of rum to that gunnery crew!"

"Great, drunk gunners, what could go wrong?" Jones remarked.

On the port side, Treen was giving the newly minted midship-men's their trigonometry lesson. Today it is simple open sea calculations.

"If we are travelling on a course of thirty points south of west at seven knots for three hours, and change your course, moving twenty points further south and slow to five knots, how far away from your origin are you? You have thirty minutes boys." Treen walked over to his Commander who was watching over the lesson and the training.

"Everything going well Mister Treen?"

"Everything is fine, thank you Sir."

Snow began to fall gently in the November air. It was early winter now, and the cold wind was blowing in from the north. The cold air was being felt by all aboard the *Lannwedhenek*. The shortcomings of the thin uniforms of the Royal Navy were literally being felt by every man aboard.

"Jones, the course we are on, take us slightly further out to sea, see if we can shift away from this snow."

"Aye aye Sir, turning a point or two north of west. That should do the trick."

The snow was falling quicker now as they began to move out to sea.

The winter waters splashing high on the bows of ship, and the wind was becoming more erratic as time continued.

"We should turn into a bay Sir!" shouted Jones over the din of the wind and snow, "Find a more sheltered place."

"Not yet Mister Jones, we continue at sea, Mister Treen!"

"Sir?"

"Get the Midshipman below, let's get the deck clear of men unless needed above,"

"Aye, aye Sir,"

"And continue with the lesson, a bit of snow shouldn't stop their studies."

The snow and wind began to become blinding in the north Atlantic. Smythe stood to his usual attention on the deck, staring into space. He began to pace, up and down along the deck, giving his pleasantries to the men who had to remain above board. "We need to invest in some winter clothing," he thought.

"Commander?" came Jenkins voice from aloft.

"Jenkins,"

"There's a square sail off to portside."

"What do you think?"

"I think I can see oars Sir,"

Oars. And a single square sail. The only thing that sounded like was a slave galley. The British Navy did not employ slave galleys. Some of the Scandinavian countries and the Prussians did, but it would be

the wrong side of Britain. The only country that would be using slave galley to the south would be those of the Barbary States. But surely the Barbary nations would not be so bold or so brazen in this weather.

"Are you sure Mister Jenkins?"

"Certain Sir,"

They had been on Barbary Watch now for eight months, since around February. Besides their encounter with the *Greyhound* and some stops on trading vessels heading north into Bristol, they had merely been on a pleasure cruise up and down the Cornish and Devon coastlines. But now, could they finally be employed in the business they had been intended.

"Mister Jenkins, a course if you please?"

"They are going toward the coast, not on a direct course, if I had to hazard a guess based on where we are, I'd say they were heading towards Port Isaac or Padstow."

Padstow. Home. It might not be home for all this crew anymore, but it was home for at least half the crew. Their wives were there, and their children. There was no debate on the action to follow.

"Mister Jones chase down that Galley! All hands, chase down that bloody ship."

The deck was a flutter with excitement and movement. The crew, which had been drilled more and more through the weeks, mainly due to the cold weather and keeping them busy, now were all a

rush. Those who had been on deck had heard their Commander's conversation and there was no doubt. The galley would not reach the coast.

"Jenkins! Stay aloft man, keep me posted on that ship!"

"Aye aye Sir!" came the emphatic response. All men aboard knew the cost of failure on this venture.

"Gun crews be ready, you men, get aloft and loose all sail. Let's get a move on you slackers!"

The panic aboard for many of the men was thick enough to cut with a knife. The movement of the crew had however become like a well-oiled machine. Treen was ordering men to do their duties quicker, the young boys were moving the powder quickly, preparing for the battle ahead.

"Mister Jones, how are we doing?"

"Gaining but slowly Sir,"

"How far?"

"Couldn't see the ship when Jenkins first pointed it out, but now its faint in the distance. I think he's right Sir."

"Then let's close that distance Mister Jones if you can, instruct me when you think we are about a mile and half away."

Smythe was reminded of the song his mother used to sing him relating to these pirates of North Africa.

Gonna sing you all a song,
about a ship that haunts my dreams,
Blow high, blow low,
And so sail we.
A song to curdle up your blood,
And makes the banshees scream,
Sailing down the coast of high
Barbary!

The song was playing through his mind as they chased down the Galley.

"Mister Jenkins, any colours flying from that ship?" As much as he was sure it was a Barbary pirates ship, he had to be sure it was not a Prussian vessel. Or Danish. Or Russian. He didn't want to start a war for a trading vessel which had got lost in a storm."

"Nothing Sir, they aren't showing anything. The oars are working hard Sir, I think they may have spotted us."

That would, in some respects, make it more difficult, but on the other hand easier. They would not wish to go into port and be caught by the naval vessel chasing after them, they would continue to keep sailing at arm's length where possible away from the Sloop. They also would keep their rowers at full pace as long as they could. The galley had to get itself over the horizon, away from the eyeline of the Sloop, then it could continue with their ghastly intentions. Failure to do so would be dire for the galley.

Algamir Al Daye stood on the deck of his galley, the *Niazmehr*. The snow was beginning to fall around him. He had not known snow since he was a child and that had been on the Hoggar Mountains close to his homeland of Algiers. He was older now, in his forties and was ready for one last voyage. He had cut his teeth on the waters for years now, from his youth, capturing slaves from Iberia, Gascony, Brittany and the British Isles. Interestingly, he had never raided Provence, himself feeling that there was too much water with French and Spanish ships to intercept them on their return voyage. He had spent his life enriching his masters back home in north Africa. But now he was his own master.

Having fought and assisted the bid for independent rule of the Regency of Algiers, he had been rewarded for his efforts with this slaving Galley. He had ransacked the Catalonian, Valencian and Murcian coastlines for people to sell, riches to be had. But the fairer, lighter skin of the north was a far richer prize.

He stood and watched over the North Cornish coast debating where to land his ship. He could land in any of these bays or harbours. It would be like child's play. And once done he would have all the captives he would need to become a rich man. All his crew would become rich men too and they would follow him to the paradise which would await them back home.

"It's cold Sayidi," spoke one of his subordinates, rubbing his shoulders as if to exacerbate the point.

"It is indeed my boy, but to riches we go!" he was a giddy child again, waiting for the presents that Eid brought.

The snow and wind were coming thicker and stronger now, his vision was becoming impaired. His vision was not the best on clear days on the North African coast, let alone in a snowstorm in the north Atlantic.

"We should venture further out Sayidi," said the young man again, "Away from the landmass and this dreaded weather."

"They didn't have to be Cornish men," Algamir thought to himself. "They could be Welshmen or Irish. Or, at a push Bretons on the return south." There was no point risking his crew, and his ship, when he could get just as good a deal in other markets. "Give the slaves a rest," Algamir ordered, "full sail, directly west, let's get away from this heathen land." The snow slowed as they ventured westwards. They slowed down to around two knots, but it did not matter. No fishing ships would be leaving their ports today. The captures would be slower, and he might not get paid as much. But if he did not flog his rowers he could use them again later, and more importantly, none of them would die on route.

"Sayidi!" yelled a man from the bow with panic in his voice.

"What is it?" he yelled back. What in the name of Allah was his problem that required that much of an issue?

"A ship Sayidi!"

"Yes, the ocean is full of them." One little fishing boat was not going
to change his plan.

"No Sayidi, it's a proper ship!"

Algamir turned back to the man at the tiller. "What the fuck do you mean a proper ship?"

"A naval ship Sayidi, a Sloop I think they call it."

Algamir took out his glass and turned to the bow of his ship. He cursed the tillerman in his mind. If this turned out to be a large fishing boat, he would put him down with the rowers. He reached the bow of the ship and looked through his glass.

It was a Sloop alright, like ones they had brought during the battle of Tripoli. They would have about sixty men aboard that vessel. Three times his active crew. And if they were boarded, he could not rely on the rowing slaves below.

"Row master! Get them bastards moving!" They could not out-fight them. But they might outpace them.

Aboard the *Lannwedhenek* Smythe could see the galley moving away from them westward.

"How far till they are over your view Mister Jenkins?"

"About six miles Sir. At best they are a knot faster. We have about six more hours Sir!"

Six hours would take them into the darkness. The galley would surely kill all their lights and try to evade capture in the darkness. But they were in foreign waters. They would not dare go toward

land and risk running aground or worse, hitting some concealed rock.

And their rowers would tire. They were rowing flat out now, but they could not continue at that pace for the entire time. Perhaps they would flog them till night and let them rest during the evening. If only the wind would pick up.

Their single square sheet had nothing on the fore, main and top masts of the sloop. In square feet the galley could call upon around a hundred and twenty, perhaps up to a hundred and forty. The *Lannwedhenek* would have around thirteen hundred square feet, a clear advantage in a larger wind.

"Mister Treen!" shouted Smythe over the general din. "Mister Treen stand the men down. We will not catch them with the hour, that is for certain and as such, there is little to no point having more men above deck than necessary."

"Aye aye Sir."

"Until I state otherwise, normal watches are to resume, as is dinner," There was a smile from the crew members around who heard the words dinner. "But no rum, I want clear heads when we do engage." The same faces which had been smiling moments before turned to grimaces.

"Aye aye Sir," came the stock response.

"Mister Jenkins!"

"Sir?"

"I'm sending someone up to relieve you,"

"There's no need Sir!"

"It's slowing?"

"No Sir, but I'm fine Sir,"

"That being said, I will send someone up with some warmer clothing for you."

"That would be welcome Sir!"

The wintery weather would bring down the darkness of the night sooner than expected and having a man aloft in this weather at night could be dangerous to his health. Smythe would not put his men in danger wherever possible. He wanted to catch that galley this afternoon. The wind turned a point or two westwards, giving the sheets even more power.

The *Lannwedhenek* was travelling at seven knots now, with the Galley moving what appeared to be slightly slower. On their current course, they would be moving further out to sea, running slightly away from the south westerly curving coastline.

"Mister Jones, do we have a time to catch them?"

"I think we are about half a knot faster Sir! A few hours at least,"

It was a sign of how the crews' professionalism had improved that the bells were now rung on the dot regardless of what was going on around them.

During this time, when the ship was readying for action, it fell to the Midshipmen to ring the times, and they did so with the usual levels
of excellence the Royal Navy expected.

The bell chimed out seconds after, four bells on the forenoon watch. Ten in the morning. They had about six more hours of light at the most.

They were half a knot faster, with the ship visible from the main deck. The horizon in this tossing sea would be a few miles, and the sheet at full furl made the galley visible for about six or seven miles. But from the tiller, slightly raised, the galley would be in view for over ten miles at least. With half a knot, although they would remain in view, they would not catch them before nightfall.

"Mister Jenkins. We can see the ship from here. Come down Sir and get yourself warm."

"Aye, aye Sir," there was an unquestionable hint of relief in his voice.

Smythe's frustration with the situation was evident. He was doing his duty, he was chasing down this galley. But it would remain out of reach till the morning.

"They won't keep it up Sir," came Jones voice from the tiller behind him.

"What?" snapped Smythe, his mind busy with the calculations of the chase.

"Their rowers Sir! They are flogging them to the bone, they'll slow, mark my words."

He was right. Their pace was only being kept by the slaves rowing

away. And although they were unlikely to become overheated, a common issue they had in the Mediterranean, the tides and the high waves of the Atlantic would surely slow and tire the crews. If they were half a knot faster now, in an hour it would surely be a knot, and then two, then perhaps four! They would catch them in about three hours by that rate, just as darkness was falling.

Algamir stood on the bow of his ship, looking through his glass at the Sloop chasing down on them. In his mind he was working it through. They would not keep the pace they were at now, and the sloop was chasing them down.

"We've slowed Sayidi," the young man had clearly been made to tell his superior rather than any of the other more experienced seamen.

"I can see that." He did not need his subordinates telling him what he already knew.

"No, the rowers Sayidi, their row rate has slowed."

"By how much?"

"Couple of rows per minute, but it will probably drop us by a knot." Dropping a knot was not the end of the world, it would still be hours before they were caught. But a tiring rowing crew was a problem. Their pace would only slow, dropping them down to a couple of knots at most. They would be caught within one hour at that point, with a fatigued crew and outnumbered and only stern

chasing guns.

"Turn us around," said Algamir.

"Sayidi?!"

"I said turn us around. I'd rather fight them head on than running away. It'll happen either way, might as well make it on our own terms. Allah will protect us."

Smythe was below in his cot. He was trying to get some rest before the pursuit which would climax later. By his calculations, his ship would catch the galley in around three hours. The ship's bell rang six. It had been at an hour since he was last on deck. Will rushed into his cabin, he looked flustered.

"Sir, they've turned around!"

"They've what?"

"They've turned around."

Smythe was stunned for only a moment before coming back to his senses. They were electing to fight rather than run. Not a completely irrational move considering the inevitability of them being caught in the current circumstances. With this tactic, they could try to cripple the Sloop with a couple of shots from the bow mounted cannons which galleys often used.

"Tell Mister Treen I will be up on deck in the next five minutes.

And thanks, Will."

Smythe put his overcoat on and his hat. He looked at the chart in

his cabin. They would be almost directly north of Tewynblustri. He noted that in case of danger. They could retreat to that harbour should the skirmish not end as planned and regroup in the winter weather. It was essential that they at least cripple the Galley, to prevent her from entering the civilian bays quickly. Most bays had at least some defences, and a slow-moving galley would allow a local militia force to be arranged. He looked up from the chart, steadied himself and marched out onto his deck. The Galley had indeed turned around, and was now rowing, albeit slowly, toward them.

"Mister Jones, how long before we engage?"

"About an hour Sir,"

"Then let's get the men prepared, I want that vessel sunk!"

"Or captured," said Treen from his side.

"Either way it needs to be removed from these waters."

The *Lannwedhenek* was a bustle of movement. From preparing previously, to being stood down and again now being told to prepare again must be draining, but the professionalism was now shining through.

"Only thing I don't get is why the hell did they turn?" asked Treen.

"Improves their odds," replied Smythe, "if they turn and fight a lucky shot, who knows, but running would lead only to their eventual capture anyway, might as well go out in a blaze of glory."

"If they aren't careful, it will be a blaze," remarked Jones.

"Then we must make sure we give them a wide berth should that occur Mister Jones. The last thing we need is a fireship hitting our vessel."

The time ticked away slowly as the two ships began to engage together.

"We are about two miles apart Sir," came the voice of Jones.

"Then to your stations gentlemen. And may God bless us all."

"Our bow guns are ready Sayidi," came the young man who again must have been told he had to tell the Captain any news.

"Then fire at them!" Algamir's voice rung out.

The crew did not need telling twice, as the guns from the bow fired off towards the Sloop engaging them. Both shots were off target however, the left bow chaser firing short by about hundred yards and the right one was wide of the target, and clearly had not been aligned enough. The rocking of the ship in the high waves off the Cornish coastline was disorientating compared the relative calm waters of the western Mediterranean and his crew had not accounted for this.

"Alter your aim!" he yelled. "The waves aren't going anywhere, so you need to adjust you morons." Algamir was frustrated with not only his men but himself. He gave the shrill order to fire and his men merely reacted to their Captain's wishes. He should have been more explicit; he should have told them to wait and not to be over

eager. Instead, they had lost one of their few shots which would not be answered by the enemy.

The bow chasers took around three minutes to reload safely and effectively. They were travelling at around two knots. The Sloop was travelling in the opposite direction around six knots. They would therefore converge, as they were two miles apart in around fifteen minutes.

That meant he had at most four shots before they received a broadside of however many cannons the Sloop had aboard. His crew of twenty men would not last long. And his slaves below might have even less time depending on their aim.

"Steady as you go men, set an aim and fire true!" Accurate shots would be needed if they were to survive this. The galley's bow cannons fired again, the smoke slowly passing back towards the stern.

Splash! The water sprayed from the second salvo sent from the galley's bow guns. Both shots missed, but they were closer than their previous attempt.

"Mister Jones, if you please put us on an angle to give them a broadside in the next few moments. Mister Treen, you may shoot the swivel guns on the deck as you see fit, aim for the main deck if you please, that's where their men are, and I would rather they stop firing back at us."

"Aye, aye Sir!" came the response from the two men, both having waited for a second to ensure the orders were complete. The *Lannwedhenek* moved on the turn of the wheel from Jones, they were about three quarters of a mile apart, at the extent of the range which Jenkins had been doing his gunnery practices from.

"FIRE!" came the order from Treen, and the lighter guns on the deck fired out, smoke and the acrid taste of gunpowder lingering in the air. The one-pound balls flying towards the galley, hitting their deck. The wood and splinters flew from the deck of the galley, only viewed through the glass of Smythe. He could not see if any men that had been hurt, or carried off, and the bow chasers being reloaded by their crews.

"Same again Mister Treen as soon as you are ready, the aim was fine, bit more luck needed!" came over the din from Smythe. He knew that enough shots would have their toll on the galley with the small crew. The deck bellow roared with flames and smoke as the first broadside came from the five cannons on the starboard side. Smythe stood, his glass fixed on the galley about half a mile away now. She fired her guns too and the mixture of roaring from his guns, the whistling of metal from the balls overhead showed his opponents this time had fired over them. They must have fired just as they hit a wave, causing the balls from the light galley to travel harmlessly overhead. The balls from his cannons made contact with the galleys main deck, causing more wood to fly in all directions.

Smythe was still singing the song his mother had sung him in his head.

When we fired off a broadside

The balls went right on through.

He could thankfully say that those balls did not simply pass through.

"Their oars Sir! On their port side by God!" called Jones from the wheel behind him, and Smythe retained his glass upon the portside of the galley. One of their balls must have gotten below onto their slave deck, ripping through the men pulling the galley on their port side as several oars were pulling at a much-reduced rate. This gave Smythe an idea.

"Mister Treen! Mister Treen," it took a couple of shouts of his name in the din of battle to get his Lieutenants attention, "Mister Treen aim for their oars."

"Come again Sir?" It was such an odd order that Treen was sure he must have misheard his Commander.

"Their oars man!" shouted Smythe, as if this had been obvious from the beginning. "Without them they will be sitting ducks and we will turn them into matchsticks by God!" Smythe inwardly cursed himself for using God in such a fashion as that, but the expression seemed to resonate with Treen.

"Aiming for the oars, Sir!" came the response finally from Treen,

"You there, realign them, aim just of the portside."

"Sir, the chances of hitting an oar at this range is..."

"Small, I know Mister Jones," Smythe curtly responded, "but a single damaged oar will either slow them down or else pull them offline."

This was of course true. A galley could move at approximately two to three knots and had ten oars on each side. The removal of a single oar would slow the pace of the ship by around a fifth to a third of a knot. Removing two oars would slow her by around half a knot. This was not just beating her down for the sake of it. Should the unthinkable happen, and the *Lannwedhenek* be defeated in this battle, Smythe was doing his upmost duty to ensure that the Galley was crippled to the point she could not complete her mission.

"Turn her about Mister Jones, let's have the portside guns having some fun!"

Smythe was treating this skirmish as nothing more than a training exercise. The enemy were heavily outnumbered and outgunned. But all the same, he wanted to pound this ship into submission. This was the first Barbary ship to trouble these waters in over four years, he wanted to make sure that they understood that England was not for the taking. The clouds of smoke from the one-pounders on deck obstructed his view of the Galley as Jones made a hard turn to starboard in order to use the portside guns.

The Captain was a skeleton,
The first mate was a ghoul.

He hoped that, like the rest of the song, this line was also part of the fable.

"Sayidi, we can't row!" came the voice from below.

Algamir had enough problems to deal with and now this.

"What do you mean we can't bloody row?"

"They've shot away four oars on the starboard side Sayidi!"

That was either pure bloody luck or an excellent shot. In either case it was a disaster for his ship.

"We should kill the slaves," came a voice from below. This was common practice. Each slave was worth around seventy to hundred guineas in England. The around two hundred men they had bellow would be worth around twenty thousand pounds.

"No, Allah would not approve,"

"But their value?"

"They are lives; all be it forfeit. That is final!"

His ship was lame, his men were frustrated, and he would probably be executed. This was not going well.

"Fire the guns!" he roared, and the formidability of his character seemed to have steadied his crew. The bow chasers again

fired, and this time the wood and splintering of their nemesis flew away from
the Sloop. It was the first accurate shot they had hit all day and might just be their last. The Sloop was turning to give yet another broadside, this time from her portside guns. It ripped through his crew, as a mix of blood and screams were emitted from both the main deck and below.

"Run up a rag!" he shouted over the din. It was hopeless. He was down to at most fifteen men, and it would not take long for that to decrease again. He would probably be hung, but his men may avoid such a fate. It was unkind to endanger the lives of his men anymore. A couple of one-pounders hit the deck again causing splinters to fly, but thankfully nobody seemed to have been hurt. His guns fired again, the smoke choking him as he had not expected it. He turned in panic to see if the white flag was flying yet, but thankfully it was not. It would have been another crime to add to the list had he fired under a flag of truce.

Smythe stood on his deck, looking through his glass at the galley in front of him. He knew it could not take much more punishment, and he was reluctant to cause more damage and death than necessary. That being said, he could not and would not relent until they surrendered. If he did, he would be putting his own men at risk, and if it were a choice between some Barbary Pirates or his own men, he knew which he would take.

"Sir, a white flag!"
It was the news he had been waiting for. The galley would not have
been able to take much more punishment and now at least there would be something to sell back to the Admiralty.

"Time to board her." Smythe was in his best overcoat and hat and would board the galley with all the pomp and pomposity the Navy could muster in such circumstances.

The little boat rowed across as the *Lannwedhenek* positioned itself to tow her prize. The damage on the galley was evident even from afar. The portside deck had been damaged thoroughly with both balls of one pound and six pounds. There was blood covered wood in places, bits of bones and screams from dying men below. The crew had lined up to give a guard of honour, with who he assumed was the Captain stood at the end of the guard, sword out and ready to surrender.

"Commander Smythe, of his Majesty's Ship, the *Lannwedhenek*."

"Algamir Al Daye of the Galley *Niazmehr*, out of the port Algiers. It has been a pleasure to fight with you in these waters Sir."

It surprised Smythe the quality of the English spoken by the Captain of the galley. His surprise however, quickly faded. "I am to hand over my ship now?" It would appear that Algamir had learned a single statement just in case it was needed.

"Erm, yes, you will hand over your ship, your men will be bound for now." He placed his hands together to show the idea of arrest. This caused a stir amongst the assembled crew, clearly the idea of being

in chains was not in their interests.

"We are not slaves Sir!" protested Algamir. Perhaps his English was not as poor as he was letting on.

"No, you are prisoners," replied Smythe, his usual calm demeanour shining through. "We will be taking you to Bristol under lock and key. I intend to bind you until you are in my brig. From there your hands will be released."

Smythe was cool in his orders, giving them without question or hesitation. Algamir simply shrugged, knowing that this was common practice in these parts.

For him, free men were not chained, that was for the slaves and criminals. Here, it was anyone who was not doing what the government thought they should. His crew were less receptive, however. A couple of scuffles broke out as the Englishmen tried to bind and arrest the crew.

"Perhaps they would prefer to be down there with the rowers?" suggested Smythe to Algamir. The look of horror on Algamir's face made it evident he understood what the Englishman had said. He frantically shouted something in Arabic. His men looked furious with both their treatment and their Captain but accepted their fate.

The crew were ferried back to the *Lannwedhenek* in small groups. Smythe had given instructions to Treen to escort the men cordially to the brig below, and he knew that he would carry out these instructions to the letter. The Captain however would not be placed

in the brig as was customary. Although he knew full well that they had intended to capture people in order to force them into slavery, they had yet to achieve it, and therefore, they were merely an enemy ship in English waters, and as such, the crew, and the Captain must be treated as prisoners of war.

"Do I have your word as a gentleman you will not attempt to escape?" asked Smythe.

"You do," came the almost customary response from Algamir. This would allow the Captain to remain above deck, be able to walk freely and, so long as he did not affect the running of the ship, basically be a free man, until they reached Bristol at least. "Make a tow rope for the galley." ordered Smythe to the men around him. "And let's go below, speak to the men under-neath."

Down in the depths of the galley were the rowing slaves. It was a fate usually worse than death, but normally, should a man survive long enough, he was granted freedom. Sometimes it would be a set period required in a galley, as punishment for a crime or another. The great irony, was that men who were enslaved to row these ships, took their masters to places where they in turn enslaved yet more people.

It stunk. Sweat, faeces and urine. With two hundred men chained together down here, it was hardly surprising. There were white faces, olive faces and black faces staring up at him. Their legs and hands chained to the benches where they were to row. Smythe

could also smell and sense the presence of blood, a product he was sure of his own making.

"Does anyone speak English?" he asked hopefully. That would make this exchange between them easier if it were the case.

"Yes!" came a relieved voice from halfway down the rowers. There were other men too who nodded, some with vigour, some who may understand the basics, but might not be of much use.

"Then if you men would be so kind as to translate. My name is Commander Smythe, of his Majesty's Sloop the *Lannwedhenek*." He paused for the men who spoke English to translate this message to the men surrounding him. "We are going to unchain you. This vessel is now property of his Majesty. We do not have slave galleys in use in England."

"Are we free?" asked a voice with a Basque accent.

"That is not for me to decide," said Smythe. There was a war brewing in Europe, and undoubtedly England would be pulled in to aid her allies. Not all men on this ship would be free. But they were currently not a threat.

"We are around three days out of Bristol as we are towing you. We are not going to man this ship; we are pulling you. So long as you do not try to free this ship from its tow, you will be able to walk around and be free above board however you wish."

It was fair terms to men who could have been left chained. Some men looked unhappy about the lack of full freedom. Other men seemed to understand the freedom they had been given was the best that the man in front of them could offer.

"Do you have a surgeon on board?" asked Smythe to the chained men, and they looked at him with a look of derision. Smythe smiled to himself for his naivety. Even if there had been a surgeon aboard the *Niazmehr* the slaves would not have been able to have his expertise. They would be simply left to die, and other man would be found to take his place. Life was cheap like that.

"Once my surgeon has completed his rounds of my ship, I shall have him sent aboard should you wish," said Smythe matter-of-factly. And with a nod, he bade the galley men farewell.

Back aboard the *Lannwedhenek* acting Surgeon Yin was busying around with Midshipman Abraham. Until the last shot had hit, the *Lannwedhenek* had gotten away with no casualties whatsoever. However, the final shot had hit through a gun hole, causing a six-pounder cannon to fly along with their gun crew.

"A broken arm," Yin said simply to the gunner, "It will need resetting, but you should be fine in a month or so, now." He turned to the next man who was clearly in lots more pain. "Now, now, now, now, now. Your leg is broken." He said simply.

"I fucking know that you fucking…"

"Now, now, let us not say something you'll regret. Especially as I will need to remove that leg I fear."

"Remove it?"

Yin appeared not to be listening to him and was examining the leg intently. It was a very bad break; the lower leg had completely shattered as the cannon had been thrown into it. "It will need to be removed to ensure infection doesn't take hold. I would advise you make a quick will just in case. It's going to be a nasty business. Master Abraham, please inform Mister Treen that I will need an operating table to be ready if he would be so kind."

It was the matter-of-fact way in which Yin, to which English was a third language, which unnerved some men, but his professionalism under fire and the closeted racism which he underwent almost daily seemed to steel him to it. He was used to it by now, and this was by no means the worst ship for it. With so many blacks, mulattos and gods know what else now, the racism aimed at the man from the "Far East" as they put it was minimal.

"Ah, Mister Treen Sir, I was just saying to young Abraham I needed an operating table."

"Can it not be bandaged until Bristol?"

"I am afraid not Sir, infection would set in and it may be more than his leg he loses. Everyone else will heal in time, but that leg needs to come off."

"Very well Mister Yin, then I will sort you out a table. The Commander should be back soon, and he would no doubt appreciate your report." Yin gave his customary bow, rather than a salute, which always made Treen feel uneasy, as if he were some kind of Prince or King.

"Abraham?" Yin turned to the young Midshipman who assisted him during his rounds often. As surgeon, he often had the Midshipman assist him with duties, especially after any action.

"Sir?"

"You have been writing the report for me, haven't you?" Yin asked.

"Of course, Sir."

"Good boy. Perhaps you would like to assist me in the task at hand?"

"Of course, Sir!"

"Excellent! Now, you Sir," he said turning back to the gunner with the broken leg, "will be in a lot of pain now and a lot more when I am done, but it's the only way you'll live." He looked at the saw in the tools of the previous *Lannwedhenek* surgeon he used. That would be put to good use now.

CHAPTER FIVE

Sir John Molesworth was sitting in the Custom house, and he was in a foul mood. His mood had been poor since Parliament had been dissolved. And it was highly unlikely his mood would improve until he was back in the halls of Westminster. If he were to return.

"Relax John," said George with a smile on his face. He had enjoyed teasing his friend since his return earlier in the month.

"You understand that I have to win the election. Again!"

"Yes, that's how Parliament works. Come on, cheer up old friend, you'll be fine. You represent a rotten borough anyway."

Their little office was warm thanks to the large fire in the grate, being constantly stoked and added to by the off cuttings from the dockyards. The snow was continuing to fall softly outside and November was drawing to a close. Soon it would be the festive season, a reason for joy and merriment. Perhaps this would bring John back to the land of the living. The morning had not been a particularly productive one for either of them, John because of his poor mood, and George because he was thoroughly enjoying watching his friend in such a poor mood.

"Will this infernal snow not end!" demanded John to no one in particular. He was becoming more and more irritable as the day's past. George smiled to himself.

There was a knock at the door and the office clerk came in. He stood to attention in front of John, who completely ignored him and

continued with his paperwork. Eventually, George spoke.

"Vice Admiral Molesworth, will you kindly acknowledge the gentleman in front of you, I am sure he has a thousand things to be doing and standing in front of you waiting for you to stop being so rude to someone merely doing their job is not on that list."

John looked up at the young man standing in front of him. "Well, what is it?"

"Commander Smythe to see you Sir. He says its urgent."

"Urgent, is it?"

"Something about a prize Sir,"

This made George look up with interest. As Smythe's admiral, Molesworth would receive around a third of whatever the captured prize was. That would most assuredly help fund another run at Parliament.

"A prize?" John looked up with a smile on his face. George could not help but laugh. John had been in a mood like thunder for the past two weeks, and one single event had caused his mood to lift like a child on Christmas morning. "Send him in then!"

Smythe walked in with whom Molesworth assumed was his Lieutenant. Both men stood in front of his desk, stood at attention, and saluted.

"Commander Smythe, introducing to you first Lieutenant Treen of the ship *Lannwedhenek*." Treen gave a small bow to Molesworth who in turn nodded his approval.

"Report Mister Smythe if you please."

"Three days ago, we encountered a ship just north of Padstow bay. We persisted to follow her as we felt that she had no business being in these waters. She engaged with us causing damage to our ship and forcing the amputation of a leg of one of my gunners. We then went on to capture the Slave Galley *Niazmehr* from the Port of Algiers as she realised that the overwhelming force that came with our ship would clearly overpower her."

"Slave galley?" Molesworth's eyes nearly doubled in size. Slave galley meant slaves. And that of course meant even more money from the prize.

"There is an issue however Sir."

"Of course, there was a problem" thought Molesworth.

"Let's hear it then." His face had dropped significantly.

"The slaves are a mixture of men. Some are English, some

Dutch, Frenchmen, Spaniards. You get the idea."

"You mean to tell me that the majority of them are freemen and not slaves?"

"Yes Sir."

"George?"

"Yes John." George was certain he knew what was about to happen here.

"Please convene a court to decide upon the extent to which these men may be free."

"I had an idea Sir?" interjected Smythe. Molesworth raised his eyebrows with frustration. Smythe took this as a tacit agreement that he would at least listen. "Any man who can be pressed is a free man?"

This was not the worse idea in the world. It would speed up the process. Furthermore, many men who would have been freemen might sign up just to speed up his own ordeal. Molesworth nodded. Smythe continued.

"As for the ship, it is mainly unhindered. The rigging will need refitting but otherwise."

"The ship will take time to sell."

"Sell?" Normally prizes were refitted to match the needs of England and her Empire.

"The Galley is not a ship employed in his Majesty's Navy. It will have to be sold, most likely to Sweden, or Denmark or whichever side we are currently on in that Northern war."

The Northern war was an ongoing war between the Countries of Denmark-Norway and Russia on one side, and the great Swedish Kingdom on the other. England, or Britain as it was becoming, had a simple policy when it came to this war. As long as they are fighting each other, they are not fighting us.

"What was the Galley doing here?"

"Her Captain claims to have been blown off course from a storm in the Bay of Biscay, intent on trading with Britany coastline in Brest
and other such ports."

All four men in the room smiled at this. It was the usual story to come out of any ship captured in English waters. We were blown off course, obviously we were not doing anything that would harm England, however could you think such a thing. The usual rubbish.

"So, no proof of wrongdoing other than we don't get on nicely with other children. I don't care who fired first, because I know they did, or that's what the report will say to the Admiralty at any rate." He added, and Smythe believed him.

John Molesworth knew that the *Lannwedhenek* had done her duty either way, there was no point worrying about technicalities now.

"So, a Galley with no slaves or criminals. Worth about six hundred pounds. We will probably sell her on the cheap for four hundred. The ship gets a third of that of which you get a whole half, giving you fifty pounds. Then the young Lieutenant here gets his share of around twenty pounds. Then your petty officers will get twenty to split between them and the Midshipman. Meaning the remaining forty or so men aboard will get around ten shillings for their work. Not a bad payday."

It was not a bad pay day at all. However, ten shillings was hardly the pay of kings, it would get them a warm bed for a night with a lady or two. That was of course on top of their normal pay, which was an added bonus. It would clear some debts for some, be extra pay for wives and mothers for others.

"I have new orders for you at any rate Smythe."

"Order's Sir?"

"Yes, those things we all have to follow if we wish to remain in employment and with breath in our bodies." Replied Molesworth sarcastically.

"You are to report your ship, and crew to Portsmouth. The *Lannwedhenek* has officially been absorbed into the Navy proper. You are no longer acting on some crusade on the north Cornish coast looking for ghosts."

"Respectfully Sir," Treen began to interject, but a swift nudge from his Commander silenced him. The sentiment was not missed by Molesworth, however.

"Yes, I see that ghosts they are no more, but orders are orders. I shall send my report to the Admiralty that you were thrilled to engage in new duties and that your prize money should be paid forward to Portsmouth."

It was very final. Either Smythe nodded and walked away. Or he could argue. Be court martialled for refusing to follow orders. And his ship would still be sent to Portsmouth without him and with a new Commander at the helm.

"Of course, Sir," said Smythe resigned. This was the way of the Navy. You followed orders. At least they had stopped the Barbary ship before it hurt anyone. That was a success.

"Portsmouth?" exclaimed one of the sailors aboard the *Lannwedhenek*. There was a general grumble by the men when they had learned that they would not be going home for Christmas, but sailing around Lands' End, all the way down into Spithead. "Orders are orders!" barked Jones, although he himself was not too thrilled by the outcome. "Now get to your bloody stations before I make this deck bloody!" The stout ginger man's face was going a similar colour to his hair, and many of the men simply shrugged their shoulders. Many might not have signed up for this work, but it paid well enough, they knew a bonus payment was coming from the prize at some point, and it was employment, which was never guaranteed in this world. The old crew of the *Greyhound* seemed especially unfazed, but the fishermen from Port Isaac, Padstow and the like seemed to think this was more than they had signed up for.

"To your stations lads!" shouted an exuberant Smythe upon returning to the deck. It was evident from his manner he knew the issues aboard and was merely trying to make the most of a bad situation. "You there, sailor, unfurl that sail, let's get ourselves out of Bristol if you so please gentlemen!" Jones had to smile at the use of the "You there, sailor." Smythe was becoming notoriously bad with names, often getting even his petty officers names mixed up.

The sails were unfurled, the tiller set, and the course plotted.

All that was left was a smooth sail around the coastline of England.

The snow which had plagued the coastline in the previous week had

passed and in the late cool November air, the *Lannwedhenek* gently pulled out of the Bristol channel.

"We are hoping for around eight knots with the wind we are carrying Sir," said Treen.

"Yes, but upon turning round Lands End, the wind will be working against us. I expect our speed will drop to four or three knots at the most." It would take them around twenty hours assuming they kept the eight knots pace they had set so far just to reach Lands' End. However, once they had rounded the peninsular, assuming they kept a good pace of four knots, it would take them around two further days to reach Portsmouth. If it slowed down to three or less, it would be at least three and a half days.

Keeping discipline on this ship would be the first major test of Smythe's command, from a non-military point of view. Prior to this, all the men in his command had always been happy enough, feeling they were protecting their homes and families. Now they were merely a cog in the immeasurable machine that was the English Navy.

Eight bells of the After-noon watch sounded out as Treen and Smythe stood on the deck of their ship. "We should hit Lands' End by noon tomorrow if the pace you wish to set is kept to.," said Smythe to his subordinate. It was not a criticism if they did not manage it. But Smythe often struggled with small talk with Treen. "I would appreciate it if you were to dine with me tonight Treen. I will

invite Jones as well; would you like to add anyone to make up a foursome?"

"How about Yin? He doesn't have many friends aboard, and we can ask him about his medical knowledge. I know we haven't managed to get a surgeon yet, but Portsmouth is bound to be more fruitful place to find help." It was a good suggestion and would allow Smythe to talk to his two main petty officers on board.

"Yes, that sounds good," he said after a long pause. Treen seemed to visibly relax that his suggestion had not been rejected out of hand. "I shall see you at the half point of the Dogwatch, I will arrange for Jenkins to man the tiller and arrange for the food to be ready, etc. The ship is yours Mister Treen, but I will have you relieved halfway through the first Dogwatch to enable you to get yourself ready." With a nod, both men parted ways, Treen to take command of the ship, and Smythe to make the arrangements.

Firstly, there was the cook to be informed that he wanted the ham he had bought in Bristol, to be prepared. Will had to be told as well to ensure that the table would be set and prepared. He had to negotiate with the other petty officers to ensure the ship would be running smoothly during the time in which the two warrant officers would be indisposed. It cost him an extra ration of rum for each petty officer not in attendance. He could have ordered them, but he found it was better to keep the men onside, and for an extra bit of rum, it was simple.

Secondly, he had to prepare himself. He did not gamble, so cards were out of the question. He would open a bottle of wine for his guests to share, but how much wine, and how many bottles was the correct amount. His own modesty would have normally limited him to a single bottle with friends, but these were sailors not Churchmen. But they knew of his beliefs, would they expect more? They had accepted the invitation after all. But it had been a request of a Commander so of course they had accepted the invitation, to not do so would be both rude and poor judgement, allowing another young man to discuss the world around him.

He had bought three bottles in Bristol, and he had no idea if the wine was any good. But he would offer it to his guests. And then there was the thoughts of Yin who he had invited. Did Yin eat pork? He knew some religions banned the eating of pork, but was Yin a follower of one? It was dangerous waters which he had to navigate through, trying to keep a modicum of decorum about himself and his station.

The dogwatch bell rang five times as Smythe stood by his cabin entrance ready to meet his guests. Treen was first to arrive, wearing his best uniform to mark the occasion. His hair he had combed, a rarity as he usually was not so formal, and the buckles on his shoes had been polished to the best of his abilities. He smiled politely as Smythe welcomed him into his cabin, the table having been already set, and asked him to take his seat.

The silence in the room thankfully did not last long as Jones arrived not two minutes later. Jones had worn a shirt, which was highly unlike him and a thick woollen jumper in a dark Navy blue. He was cheerful and seemed to be cheerful about something.

"The wind's turned a few points Sir!" he said excitedly.

"I thought we'd slowed," said Treen from his seat. "How is that good?"

"Because it will keep our speed higher around the southern side when we turn East. We should improve our time into Portsmouth. We'll be there before the end of the month." The mood in the cabin had lifted as the three men pondered what they would do in Portsmouth, a day or two earlier than expected.

Yin knocked at the cabins door and the three men smiled to him. He bowed as always and was wearing what appeared to be a silk robe of multiple colours of blues and yellows. "Sorry for my lateness Commander," he said as he continued to stand by the door.

"It's perfectly ok Yin, please, sit down, have a drink,"

"Thank you, Commander."

The four men sat together, ate food and drank the bottle of wine, all served by young Will. The conversation started with Jones discussing his history in the Navy, where he had served, what waters he had been in. Jones and Smythe discussed at length the North Atlantic coastline of the Americas, where

Smythe had worked in the fisheries and Jones had worked ensuring the shipping lanes
stayed open from Privateers aboard a ship of the line. He had
sailed most recently on the *HMS St. Andrew* and had seen
action against the French at the battles of Barfleur and La
Hougue.

Treen sat in silence and listened to his Commander and the
Coxswain of the ship reminisce about their previous adventures. A second bottle of wine was opened, and Treen told
them of his youth, how he had always dreamed of being in
the Navy. The *Lannwedhenek* had been his grandfather's ship,
an Indianman travelling back and forward transporting spices
from the Indies. Finally, attention turned to Yin.

"So how did you come into the medical profession Yin?" asked
Jones, his face red thanks to the wine and ham.

Yin did not answer right away. Smythe was not sure if it were
because he did not wish to answer, or because he was trying to
formulate the answer in a foreign tongue.

"My mother was a," he paused, evidently trying to figure out
the words, "I guess the word we would use is healer in my
village. She taught me to set bones, fix dislocations that sort
of thing." Yin was clearly enjoying the memories of his child-
hood, Smythe was imagining rolling hills and little boats on
the river. "Then when the trade ships sailed into my village, I
thought, well, why not? A Spanish ship was looking for a surgeon's mate, I reset a man's broken arm in front of the Captain
of the frigate *El Santiago*, he offered me money, I did not care
which nation they were from. I
had a chance to leave my little village. And I took it."

Smythe and the others around the table listened to Yin's story.
Yin spoke slowly, trying to use the English he had to convey his
story. "We travelled through the Philippines, then south round
the Cape. We stopped in Cuba for a while. And then over to
trading in Nassau. I was offered a place in the *Greyhound*, better
pay, well it was meant to be." A wry smile came over the faces
of all the men, including Yin. He had received no pay from his

adventures on the *Greyhound*, but to Yin, life seemed to be a great adventure. He regaled more of the time on the *Greyhound* and *El Santiago* and it seemed he had gone from one adventure to another.

The lamps were burning gently as the night drew later. All four men were sitting in their chairs, slowly falling asleep in the rocking of the ship. It was four bells on the first watch, and the men bade each other goodbye. Smythe smiled to himself on the completion of a successful evening with his Lieutenant and a couple of his petty officers. He felt he had gotten to know Yin much better. That would serve well for the voyage ahead, wherever King William sent them.

CHAPTER SIX

Portsmouth is a town just off the south coast of England, in and around the area of the Isle of Wight. It is itself an island, situated on Portsea Island. Due to its advantageous location, it is a sheltered bay as the Isle of Wight protects it from the wind, it is an ideal base for a Navy to sit and wait. The expansion of the dockyards, built by the Stuart monarch Charles II in 1663, and the expansion of the fortifications, an ongoing project shared by those in the Admiralty and those in Whitehall, make it probably the most fortified and prosperous naval port in Europe.

The *Lannwedhenek* sailed gently into Spithead to await piloting into the bay. The travel around the south coast had been an uneventful one, with the wind picking up slightly allowing them a smooth passage straight along the channel. Over the water, the French coastline was looming ominous as ever, the great enemy which plagued this nation.

A small gig approached them from Portsmouth, carrying the ensign of the British Navy.

"Must be the smallest ship in service," joked Jenkins to Jones and even the old man smiled at the sarcastic comment. The gig continued to approach as Smythe, Treen and the petty officers stood on deck awaiting the boat.

"Jones?" said Smythe out of the side of his mouth.

"Sir?" he replied, unsure about what Smythe wanted.

"Is there anyone aboard that gig I should recognise or know?"

Jones had a quick look at the gig. Judging by the uniform, the man in charge was a Lieutenant, and a young one at that. He might have a father or an uncle who was higher up in the service, but that was inconsequential so long as Smythe was his usual polite self.

"No Sir, not that I can see."

It could destroy a Commander's career, and all his subordinates within the crew, if he snubbed a superior officer. Thankfully, it was a Lieutenant aboard, and judging by his opening remarks news of the *Lannwedhenek*'s exploits must have reached Portsmouth prior to their arrival.

"So, this is the ship which took the slaver off Port Isaac?" he asked cheerfully. He was a youngish man, in his late twenties, early thirties, with a boyish smile and thick blonde hair. He was evidently looking to see if the Commander was on deck, and as he saw him his demeanour changed almost immediately.

"Ah, Commander Smythe I presume? I am First Lieutenant Richards of the Admiral's Flagship *HMS Royal Sovereign*." He gave a small bow as part of his introduction, followed by a salute.

"Lieutenant Richards, welcome aboard, may I present my First Lieutenant Treen, and my Coxswain Mister Jones." The gentlemen shook hands as was customary and then all stood back. It was Richards who spoke first.

"I have been requested to invite you aboard the Admirals ship *HMS*

Royal Sovereign, for a meeting with Sir Rooke at the earliest convenience to you."

At the earliest convenience was the polite way of saying that you are coming back in the gig with me to meet him.

"Of course," nodded Smythe in understanding. "Just allow me to fetch my hat and I will be on my way. Mister Treen, the ship is yours whilst I am gone,"

"What if the pilot comes whilst you're away Sir?"

"The Admiral, I am sure, can send your Commander back on a gig into Portsmouth Harbour," smiled Richards kindly. "We will be giving way in around five minutes Sir, please be as prompt as you can, the Admiral is not used to being kept waiting."

It was evident from his smile, despite his politeness and pleasantries he would not be kept waiting for Smythe. Will had been listening to the conversation as the Commander's Steward and had already gone below. Smythe's hat, overcoat and sword were already set out in his cabin and upon arrival Will quickly set about putting his coat on.

"A real Admiral," said Will to Smythe, whilst brushing down his coat.

"I've met Molesworth loads of times."

"Yeah, but he was a politician. Closest he's been to the water is a leisurely row on the Tamar. Sir Rooke is a real hero! He's been in battles, fought his way through. This is huge Henry!" Will seemed to be hero worshiping their new admiral. It was true that Sir Rooke

was a veteran of nearly thirty years. And he was not just there for the victories, but the defeats too. He had come through steady under fire and his reputation came from that.

"He's just a man Will," replied Smythe, although he had to admit he was nervous. "How do I look?"

"Like a Commander should," replied Will, as they walked out of the small cabin.

On deck Treen had begun to give orders under the eye of Richards. Richards was evidently a keen young officer, diligent in his duties, but also clearly more experienced than Treen. It was clear to Smythe that Richards was judging not only the orders being given, but the manner in which they were being issued. As Smythe came on deck, Richards stood to attention and saluted his superior officer. "Are you ready Sir?"

"Yes I am."

"Then let us not delay," Richards nodded to the portside of the *Lannwedhenek* and both men took the lift down into the gig. "Have you ever met an Admiral?" asked Richards.

The words of Will were ringing in Smythe's ears as he answered. "Only an ashore Rear Admiral," he replied as tactfully as he could. Richards smiled.

"You remove your hat as you are told to enter. You stand to

attention and present yourself, despite the fact you have been asked to come aboard. Don't be overly surprised if the Admiral ignores you for a moment, it's his nature to finish the sentence he is on prior to speaking if he is doing paperwork. You will remain to attention until told otherwise. Don't forget he has come under fire by Frogs, Dego's and Dutchmen alike. So, your little exploits against the galley will not impress him. Don't try to oversell it, he will not like that."

The gig was heaving away slowly towards the *HMS Royal Sovereign*. Richards was smiling calmly in the cool November air. "How long have you been with the *Royal Sovereign*?" asked Smythe, trying to keep the conversation going.

"Since she was commissioned," replied Richards. "I was slated to be one of her Lieutenants before she was built."

They approached the portside of the *HMS Royal Sovereign*, and the first thing Smythe felt was one of awe.

The hundred-gun first-rate ship of the line had a combination of guns throughout her five decks. Larger thirty-two pounders on the gun deck, all the way down to six pounders on the quarterdeck, she was a sight to behold.

"Largest vessel you've ever been aboard?" asked Richards politely, looking at the awe inspired face of Smythe next to him. "This way Commander, if you would be so kind."

A ship with an Admiral aboard came with its own differences to most ships. There was the Admiral, who oversaw the whole fleet,
and a Flagship Captain who ran the day-to-day activities of the ship in question. It meant that each would have his own Steward, would both have cabins, and both have guests and fellow officers in their quarters for dinner and discussions.

Sir George Rooke was in his cabin awaiting the newest arrival of his fleet. It was a large cabin, larger than average at least, with the windows taking up the entire stern. Beneath the windows, there was a cushioned bench also running the length, and built into the ship. Off the main cabin was Rooke's berth, with a small wardrobed area and his cot. It was nothing like his bed at home, small, cramped and at best passably comfortable, but having spent most of his adult life at sea, he had grown accustomed to discomfort, and now he was an Admiral, he at least, had his own space.

He was sitting reading a letter, a personal one, from his wife, who was expecting, and had spent the last hour or so re-reading the letter from the Admiralty, issuing him with his orders. He was a portly man, with small, warm eyes, and a deep gruff voice. He was in his large armchair of red leather, with a glass of port, wondering if he were to be at sea for the birth of his son. It was highly likely. A knock at the door brought him back from where his mind had been wandering.

"Enter!" he said loudly.

First Lieutenant Richards walked in first, with a tall, thin man in a shabby Commander's uniform. They both stood to attention in

front of him, and after a small nudge from Richards the man seemed to realise his faux pas. Smythe removed his hat, tucked it under his left arm and spoke.

"Commander Henry Smythe, Sir. Of the Sloop *Lannwedhenek*. I was instructed to come aboard Sir." Rooke looked at the Commander with interest. He was a seaman, that was for certain, the weather-beaten face and rough hands were evident of that. But was he a Commander? That was a different matter.

"Commander Smythe," he said softly, "Man who took both the *Greyhound* and the galley *Niazmehr* and has very little to show for it."

"I did my duty Sir; it was not about gain."

Rooke looked deeply at the man in front of him for a few moments. "Good," he said finally. "Kind of man I want in my fleet. Now to business. I won't keep you long, I know you have things to do. But a have a couple of things that need sorting immediately. Your guns, they are?"

"Six pounders Sir."

"Six pounders as your only guns?" Rooke exclaimed.

"We were a trading vessel before we became Royal Navy."

"Gun ports?"

"Nine on each side Sir."

That was more like it, thought Rooke. "Then whilst you are in Portsmouth, you will be refitted."

"Refitted Sir?"

"Yes, not having some small poxy guns on a ship, when there are guns sitting on the dock. Get them to refit you with some twelve pounders at least. You can have a couple of the six pounders for the deck if you are so attached to them. One-pounders on the deck I presume?"

"Indeed Sir."

"Secondly, how's your German?"

"German, Sir?"

What on earth did German have to do with this? Were Prussia entering the Northern war which England had been assisting with? Was that their destination. He would need warmer clothing for the Baltic in winter.

"Yeah, German, you know "Sprekenzie Dotitch" and all that." Richards had to suppress a smile. "Well, you do better then, boy!"

"You asked the wrong question really Sir," replied Richards. "You asked do you speak German, when you wanted to know if his German was good. You should have said "Wie ist dein Deutsch?". That would have been preferable in this situation." At the quizzical look from Smythe, "I went to grammar school in Hannover," he said simply.

"So Smythe, how is it?" asked Rooke again bringing the conversation back.

"I don't speak German Sir."

"No, me neither," said Rooke, not at all concerned. "Richards, grab him that book off the shelf, the one on the left, no not that one, the red one." Richards pulled the book from the shelf and handed it to Smythe. "It's a book about teaching yourself German Smythe, dammed if I have time to read it but I have young Richards here to translate. You any good at languages

Smythe?"

Smythe remembered back to his rudimentary schooling. Knowing he would be a sailor and fisherman; he had focused on mathematics. As a member of the Society of Friends, he had studied some of the German teachings of Luther, but he had no grasp of German, or any other language for that matter. "No Sir," he replied, "Little French from fishing days off Newfoundland. Otherwise, nothing at all."

"Any men aboard who are a dab hand?"

"Yin!" thought Smythe. "One comes to mind, Sir."

"Well offer him the book too once you've given it the once over," he said, and Smythe nodded. "Thirdly, and most importantly." He looked extremely grave at this final statement, "I would be honoured, if you do not have plans, that you join me and the other senior officers for Christmas Dinner in Portsmouth." He broke into a large smile after this statement.

Smythe was taken aback, "Oh, of course," he said, still trying to compute what had been said, "Sir." He added as an afterthought.

"Good!" roared a cheerful Rooke, clearly wanting to have all his Captains and Commanders on hand for such an occasion. "In that case, refit your ship. Any men who do not wish to remain can only leave once you have replaced them. Otherwise, unless I have any other pressing issues, I will see you Christmas day, I will send you the details."

"Yes, Sir. Thank you, Sir." And he gave a small bow as he left the cabin.

"He likes you," said Richards simply as soon as they were out of earshot.

"How can you tell?" asked Smythe.

"Perhaps not like," Richards corrected himself slightly, "But he doesn't resent having you in his service. You're a life-long seaman. When he first found out he was getting a Barbary watchman, I think he was worried, now, he sees you can handle a ship at least. He will take that."

"I thought he," Smythe paused.

"He was unsure of you," said Richards kindly. "Right," his mood again changed into a professional manner, "I have a thousand things to do Commander so if it is alright with you Sir, I will remain here on the *Sovereign* rather than escort you back to the *Lannwedhenek*?" The use of the word "Sir" reminded Smythe that he was actually Richards superior officer. He tried to return to a profession and superior manner.

"Erm, yes of course, carry on."

"Thank you, Sir." Said Richards. "I shall send for the gig to return you. And don't forget your book."

The next month passed without incidence on the *Lannwedhenek*. Payment for the prize of *Niazmehr* had arrived aboard and about ten men decided it was their time. They could return to Cornwall with an extra months wages, set themselves up, put a deposit on a shop front and become sellers on land. The new guns had been fitted on the gun deck, and for the main deck they had retained four six-pounders on rollers. This caused a problem with crews. They needed four men per gun, with now twenty-two guns in total, meant an increase in the crew to around a hundred men plus officers and petty officers. They could get away with sailing with three men per gun, decreasing the need for the stores and other such provisions, but this would leave them short should the ship come under fire and lose gunners. This in turn would reduce the firepower of the ship, making her a potential paper tiger.

They needed however around a hundred pounds of biscuit per day, not to mention salt beef, rum, water, and anything else the ship needed. Restocking whilst in Spithead, they had been moved out as they did not need the dockyard itself, was simple enough, daily in fact. But the longer they were in Spithead, the more comfortable the crew were becoming, and this was a worrying sign. They had had to recruit landsmen, a phenomenon that Smythe had never encountered before. Even his original crew had been made up of mainly fishermen. Not large ship sailors by any stretch, but men whose lives had been spent at sea.

Now however, the crew were sloppy and undisciplined. Even the two Midshipmen aboard seemed mature sailors compared to the new landsmen they had recruited. They needed moulding into shape. And here they were, sitting in Spithead and unable to train, develop or improve these men. They would integrate the new landsmen within already established crews, meaning breaking up friendship groups, which in itself was causing friction with his proper crew.

Christmas day had arrived, and Smythe was wearing his best uniform. He had agreed to do a couple of extra watches the day before, as all officers and petty officers were expected to do a watch on Christmas, but he had wanted to be free. The ship, as he was leaving, was under the watch of Midshipman Gabriel, being guided by the petty officer in charge of the guns. He was also nominally in charge of the seven or eight mariners they had now been allocated as part of the Naval ships. That put the total number of souls aboard the *Lannwedhenek* to around a hundred-and-twenty.

"Your boat is ready, Sir," said Gabriel, himself wearing his best uniform for the occasion of Christmas.

"Thank you, Midshipman Gabriel, I leave the ship in your capable

hands." It was in his care, but anchored in Spithead, it was not exactly a risk.

The dinner was being held in the Admiralty in Portsmouth. It was inside the home of the Captain Henry Greenhill, the resident Commissioner of Portsmouth dock, but he was, like Molesworth, not a naval man. The dinner itself was being hosted by Sir George however, and Greenhill was merely the conduit through which it was being done. It was a late luncheon which Sir George had arranged, for three-o-clock, with the Captains and Commanders of his fleet arriving from two.

Smythe arrived and was introduced to Captain Greenhill, to whom technically he was subordinate to in the Captains List, but in effect this evening was his supposed equal. This was of course fanciful today; the fact he was in his house, which was fully paid for by the Admiralty was evidence of the difference in their stations. Greenhill was a kindly man, with a small nose and long flowing hair which was in the restoration fashion. Smythe was shown to his seat by a servant, who had obviously come with Greenhill from the West Indies and was pleased to see Richards sat next to him.

"Ah Smythe, good to see you. Merry Christmas!" The formalities usually shown by Richards appeared to have disappeared in the festivities of the day.

"And to you Richards," replied Smythe.

"I have the upmost excellent task of telling you who everyone is,"

he said with a smile. Clearly Rooke had known that Smythe would probably not recognise his fellow Captains from Adam and had therefore seen it prudent to sit someone next to him who could politely whisper in his ear who everyone was. They were sat in the middle, evidently as far away from the two heads of the table as possible, which Smythe wished was to allow him to get to know more people, but, in reality, knew that it was because of how unimportant he was in relation to other Captains attending.

The table was set for twenty people or so, and Rooke and Greenhill would evidently be at the ends. "Will Mrs Rooke be joining us this evening?" asked Smythe to Richards.

"No, she is still in London, they are expecting a child, and it was thought best not to move her," replied Richards. "Ah now," he interjected, "The man who's just walked in is John Jennings, prominent anti-Jacobite, commanded the *Experiment* stopping troops getting to Ireland back in '90. Currently Captain of the *Kent,* seventy guns." Jennings wore a large black wig, shook hands excitedly with Rooke and Greenhill and took his seat toward the end of one of the tables. "They have worked together in the past," said Richards, "Rooke helped in the stopping of Jacobean troops too during that war. Now, that's Thomas

Hardy. Used to be Captain of the *Pendennis*, not sure what he's doing now, don't know that much about him I'm afraid, but still, useful."

The Captains filed in one by one, shaking hands with Rooke and

Greenhill. It was interesting to see reactions as they were introduced to both men. All the Captains seemed thrilled to be speaking to the lifelong naval man in Rooke and seemed to tolerate the merchant come politician Greenhill.

Dinner started promptly at three, with a goose, ham, beef and pork joint laid out across the table. The wine was poured, Smythe took a glass for politeness, and drank to the health of feast. The clanking of plates, knives and forks chinked away, and the topic was, as it had been recently about the recent Article of Succession, which had gone through Parliament this year. Greenhill sat and listened, having taken part in the debate himself in Parliament.

"What do we know of these Hanoverians?" asked one man.

"John Baker, Captain of the Monmouth," whispered Richards out of the side of his mouth.

"They are good and proper Christians," said Greenhill, finally weighing into the argument. By that, it was obvious that what he meant by "Good and proper Christians" meant Protestant. After the toasts to the King, the Navy, everyone drank to the health of Rooke and Greenhill as the hosts, the noise simmered down. Rooke stood up, evidently to give a speech. His face was already rather ruddy with all the wine and food, and he swayed a little as he stood.

"Gentlemen, it is wonderful to have you all here with me, at this Christmas feast.". His accent, of that from the Garden of England, although mild, was more pronounced due to the drink. There was a clinking of spoons on the side of the toasting glasses at this statement. Rooke raised his hand for quiet, which was granted, and continued, "But now gentlemen it is to business. When we all first met, I asked every one of you if you could speak any German." Smythe squirmed slightly in his seat. He had started to read the book he had been given by Rooke, but he had not really looked at it since the middle of December.

"As you know, we are at war with both Spain and France."

The previous year, the King of Spain, Charles II, had died child-less. This had caused a crisis in the Hapsburg house. Though the house had controlled the two great Empires of Europe, The Holy Roman Empire in the East and the Spanish Empire in the West, the house had been separated for some time into two distinct areas of influence. This had worked excellently, until Charles died childless. Now there were two claims to the throne of the vast Spanish empire. Firstly, by the heredi-tary forebears of the Spanish Monarchy, House of Hapsburg in Vienna. And secondly, through marriage and diplomacy, the House of Bourbon, the Kings of France. England, who's eter-nal enemy was the French, feared a united French and Spanish Monarchy, so supported the Hapsburg position.

"Our ally, Austria," there was a look of understanding now as to the question of German initially, "has asked us to drop off a few dignitaries in Spain to further the call of the rightful King of Spain, Charles." A chorus of "here, here!" came out across the room. "This matches with England and Holland's desire to have a port in and around the Mediterranean to call our own. So, the Admiralty has come up with a joint plan. I must admit I am excited and apprehensive about the idea, but if it pleases our allies, and helps us gain a foothold in the region, it's a win, win all round," more clinking of spoons on the glasses fol-lowed. "Now, for the German element. Everyone here will have a dignitary aboard their ship. I expect you to give them every courtesy that they would expect from one of my Captains. Fur-thermore," he added, clearly giving all the bad news at once, after all the wine had been drunk, in an effort to stop any objec-tions being raised during the dinner. "We will be hosting some Lobsters,"

The mood changed immediately. "Lobsters?" whispered Smythe to Richards, as the general hubbub of the Captains who had now broken into private conversations with the people around them.

"The army," smiled Richards, "It's the red coats."

It was funny that the idea of having a German Prince or Duke aboard their vessels, a dignitary they would inevitably have to share their berths with, their cabins, and their private stores with caused a lot less commotion compared to the idea of the Army being placed on the vessels of the Royal Navy.

"I know, I know," voiced Rooke trying to regain control of the situation at the table. "It will take time to organise this, as I am sure you will expect. Furthermore, the location of the rendezvous is yet undecided."

"Why don't we know where we are sailing?" Jennings spoke up curtly.

"His Highness the Emperor Leopold, Holy Roman Emperor, King of Hungary, Croatia, and Bohemia, goodness," he broke off, "I severely hope he shortens that title if I am going to have to say it every time we refer to him, is making contact with some dignitaries in Spain to have them come and listen to the Hapsburg's claims. We also don't know when we are sailing either."

The gentlemen were now discussing the ins and outs of the mission. Sailing to an unknown location, with an army on board at an unknown time of year was not exactly the ideal of professionalism the Navy was becoming used to.

"There are concerns I have with the operation; of that I have no doubt," said Rooke as neutrally as he could. it was evident from his tone however, that he felt that the planned expedition might not be as fruitful as those in the corridors of power believed. "However, we shall be ever vigilant in our endeavours against the Bourbon tyrants." "Here, Here," rang out the chorus of Captains. "Finally, gentlemen, before I invite you all for a brandy and a smoke, I wish to let you know that in the new year I intend to discuss your role in the operation as we find out more details." There was a general murmur of consent and understanding from the Captains around the table. "Now gentlemen, to the parlour."

"I think," said Smythe softly to Richards, "This is where I will make my leave,"

"Make your leave?" Richards looked astonished, "You know that brandy and cigars is where all the real decisions are made right?"

"I feel I have had enough to drink, and I don't smoke," said Smythe simply. Richards looked on with interest at Smythe.

"You really aren't a normal officer, are you?" he said with a smile. "Right, ok, but make sure you say your goodbyes to Rooke first, he would see it as extremely rude if you dined and then ran."

Trying to get to Rooke however, as a junior Commander surrounded by these more senior Captains around him was proving rather difficult. These career naval officers were clearly trying to get closer to their Admiral, whether trying to curry favour or trying to get an idea of what the plan was going forward. It took Smythe a good half an hour, as slowly his fellow Captains went into the smoking room.

"Thank you for a lovely evening Sir," he said sheepishly to Rooke, looking like that of a naughty schoolboy.

"Leaving already Smythe?" Rooke asked, looking rather disappointed.

"I know my limits Sir, and I am there. The wine was lovely, as was the food. But my faith demands control and self-discipline, and I fear the brandy would force me beyond that."

"Bloody bishop" thought Rooke cynically. But then he stopped and paused. He had a Commander of a vessel under his command, who took both his health and his duty seriously, and that should not be discouraged.

"Very well," said Rooke as cheerfully as he could muster, "Well, have a lovely Christmas evening Smythe, and don't work too hard. I shall see you aboard the *Royal Sovereign* in the new year. Merry Christmas!"

CHAPTER SEVEN

It was early March before Smythe was summoned to the *Royal Sovereign.* In this time, his ship had barely moved. His crew had once again changed, as men were taken from it to stock ships which were now on patrols up and down the English Channel ensuring the shipping lanes to and from London were accessible.

He was not foolish enough, however, to give over his crew who had followed him from Cornwall wherever possible. He would simply be told that this ship needed ten men from his ship and send the men they had most recently recruited. There was a double motive for this. Firstly, and somewhat selfishly, it would ensure when it finally came time for the *Lannwedhenek* to set sail she would have a crew which could handle her appropriately. Secondly, it ensured that landsmen who had no previous experience at sea were becoming better and better, something England needed. As many people as proficient as possible. Finally, when men went into larger vessels their impact was less felt. In the *Lannwedhenek's* case, a crew made up of around forty percent landsmen would have a clear impact. Whereas should they be aboard larger vessels, the impact of forty men would be less so. The *Royal Sovereign* for example, had a crew of around seven-hundred men, then forty men spread across this vessel would have little to no impact.

He, Treen and his Petty Officers often ventured into town. To complete all the tasks required of the ship would be impossible for Smythe to do, but also it was good for the common sailors to see that Petty Officers were given both additional responsibilities, and extra freedoms compared to them. There was the inevitable need to recruit more men, which was almost a weekly task at the moment due to the draftees being taken to ships which were in the Channel. There were the usual jobs to be done, filling in paperwork, changing the crew lists, provisions, changing the gunpowder. And a nice drink in the *Dolphin*.

It was once again Richards who came aboard from the gig. His face was not his usual boyish self. His uniform was immaculate as always. The only time Smythe had seen him this smart was during the Christmas dinner. "Commander Smythe, you are to report at once to the Admiralty. The plans have changed."

This was never a good sign. Jones stopped doing what he was doing, as did Treen. Smythe coughed to remind his crew to return to work. "I shall get my hat and coat. Thank you, Lieutenant Richards."

Will had been so preoccupied with the brief conversation, that he had not even thought about going down below to see to his Commander. It took Smythe a couple of minutes to sort out his equipment and come back above board. Richards was still stood, ready to move as soon as Smythe was ready to do so. "Mister Treen, the ship is yours."

"Be ready to call all hands upon Commander Smythe's return," said Richards curtly. It was so unlike Richards to behave in such a way; it confused the majority of the crew who had gotten to know the young likeable Lieutenant whilst they were stationed in Spithead.

It was a long row back into Portsea town, and the mood in the gig made it feel even longer than usual.

"Why are we not heading to the *Sovereign?*" asked Smythe, trying to create some conversation along the way to pass the time.

"Orders came from Greenwich, all Captains and Commanders to be told the new orders together. Only the Admiral has been given the orders in advance, and that was only this morning."

"Do you know the orders?"

"Officially? No, I have no idea Sir," a little smirk came across his face, making him look more like his usual boyish self.

"So, yes then," smiled Smythe to the Lieutenant.

"God above I shouldn't be smiling, not in the circumstances, no Commander," he said, slightly more forcefully than perhaps he should have done to a superior officer, "You will have to wait till you're with the Admiral. Not long now however."

The dockyards in Portsea were unseasonably quiet. It was like the entire town had gone to sleep last night and not woken up. The Admiralty officers were silent too, only Captains of the Navy were there.

"Admiral Rooke?" said Richards, and Rooke looked up from his desk, "Commander Smythe is here. I think that's the last of the Captains and Commanders, Sir."

"Very good, thank you Richards. Gentlemen, please take a seat." The Captains around the room understood this was out of the ordinary and followed the orders without a sound. "Gentlemen, this morning, the tenth of March, I have our new orders. We are to attack the port of Cadiz this summer, in order to land dignitaries from the Holy Roman Empire." There was a general murmur amongst the Captains of the fleet that this seemed at the very least a sensible suggestion of a location. "Before I convey any more information about this, there is another message. I will not be here after this meeting, nor will Greenhill. We are due at Parliament. It is my unfortunate job gentlemen to tell you, that His Majesty William, Prince of Orange and King of England, Scotland and Ireland, passed away on Wednesday at Kensington Palace. Her Majesty, the late Queen Mary's beloved sister, Queen Anne, will be addressing Parliament tomorrow. I need not tell you gentlemen, that our position may change in the future weeks and months ahead, and moreover, we may have less to do with our allies in Holland, but by the Grace of God we will still fight against those Bourbon oppressors." The usual cheer of nervous energy came from his Captains. "A toast!" he called out, as the glasses of sherry were handed out to all the Captains and Commanders, "The King is dead, long live the Queen!"

"Long live the Queen," returned the chorus of assembled Captains and Commanders gratefully. William had not been very well liked in recent years throughout his Kingdoms. An outsider, he was King through marriage, his wife Mary had been the true heir, and now, the country had returned to an Englishwoman again.

"Now, return to your ships. It is now," he checked his pocket watch, "Twenty minutes past eleven. At four o'clock this afternoon, the bells will ring throughout the dockyard, and you gentlemen will fire a salute. If you have them, it will be a full twenty-one guns. For those that don't, a single broadside will of course suffice." The gigs and jolly boats were once again waiting in the docks. Some flags were already at half mast, Smythe now noticed on his way out of the Admiralty. Many in his crew would be slightly saddened, William of course had ended the reign of the tyrant James II. However, in recent years as in Parliament, William had become everything that was wrong with Monarchy. Perhaps a change would be good at any rate.

The little gig hove to against the *Lannwedhenek* and Commander Smythe went aboard. "Assemble all hands!" he barked as he retook command of his ship. Jones and others looked confused at the sharpness of their Commander's voice but followed orders regardless. It took only a few minutes for the crew to assemble as Smythe paced upon his deck. He could already see, or at least he thought he could, a lowering of the flags to half-mast upon the ships in the dockyard, he would be one of the last ships to do it.

"Men, at ease," said Smythe. He sounded tired and weary. "This morning I was issued with our orders. We will be sailing to Spain to capture the port of Cadiz." There was a general contentment at this news. For some members of the crew, they had been at Spithead now around four months, the warm waters of the Mediterranean sounded a much nicer prospect than another winter sat in the icy waters of the Channel. "However, there was another piece of news to add to the orders. Gentlemen, it my duty to inform you, that a couple of days ago, the King, William III, passed away in his sleep. Her Majesty Queen Anne will address Parliament today. I know some of you have served his Majesty," Jones had assisted during the transporting of troops prior to the Battle of the Boyne for example, "and this may be a disheartening time to for you all. An extra rum ration will be issued today at eight bells on the afternoon watch. We, along with the rest of the fleet will be issuing a broadside salute and toasting the memory of His Majesty. Coxswain, see to it that the Naval Ensign is dropped to half-mast. Other than that, I have little else to tell you men, the orders are now being finalised with the new men in the Admiralty, and I am yet to receive details. Back to your stations."

It was a cool March morning, and the men, or those who could, were glad to get back below into the ship. Charges needed to be moved, guns needed boring out to ensure a clean shot, uniforms needed cleaning and pressing where possible, and shoes needed shinning. The pomp which would follow due to the death of his Majesty was incredible. And the uncertainty. Anne obviously would continue the war, that was for certain, but how would Holland react? The closeness between England and Holland had been there due to the personal relationship between William and Mary. Now, there was no clear link between the two nations. Moreover, Anne was childless. That would cause problems in the future too. Would the Catholic Stuarts try to return again? The Succession had officially been settled, with the House of Hanover taking over after Anne's death, but was a declaration by Parliament enough? And should the Stuarts manage to force a return what then? Would that change the war, as a Catholic King would allow for an easier peace with the Bourbon's in France and Spain. This was all for men in Whitehall to decide. Smythe would sail his ship wherever he was ordered.

At seven bells, the hands were called once again to get into position. It was a sombre mood that the *Lannwedhenek* found itself in. Despite William's recent fall in popularity, the other option was a Catholic who may try to reverse the reformation, as had happened in France and other countries, and this would and could not be allowed.

Smythe, as always as a lay preacher amongst the Society of Friends, gave a speech about death.

"Though his Majesty has died, he has moved on to the House of our Lord, and is reunited with his Beloved Wife, Her Majesty the Queen

Mary, now and forever. Amen,"

"Amen," came back the response from the crew. The broadside salute from the gundecks of the assembled fleet rang out at precisely eight bells. "Gentlemen, to the King!" shouted Smythe over the din. "To the King!" replied the crew, as they all took a swig of the extra rum ration Smythe had allocated. Perhaps, it was the allocation of rum, but the men seemed genuinely moved. If they could keep that passion once they were in battle, they would be a fighting force to be reckoned with.

With the change in Monarchy, and other issues such as legitimacy and change at the Admiralty, the plans for the invasion of Cadiz were effectively placed on hold. The *Lannwedhenek* had been allowed out to enable some of its more inexperienced seamen time at sea. This, Rooke thought would be essential for the long-term health and productivity of the fleet. It was late June when the *Lannwedhenek* returned from its latest venture out into the Channel. These trips were only around a weeklong, and the *Lannwedhenek* spent its time escorting the merchant vessels through towards Greenwich as far as Dover. They saw the occasional French merchant or fishing ship, but most of them were within range of any shore defences, and therefore not worth the danger it may cause to the *Lannwedhenek* in the pursuit of such small prey.

Breakfast was being served, and the men were busying themselves as they came into the relative safety of Spithead. The Admiral's flagship was in dock, and Smythe was finishing his report in the early morning sunshine on deck. It was not his typical way of writing reports, indeed he usual did this in the relative calm of his cabin, but as nothing of importance had happened during their last trip, they had not even seen a single French merchant vessel, it would be a simple one, which if a crew member read over his shoulder, it would not matter in the slightest.

"Gig coming Portside Sir!" came a voice from up aloft. "Looks like Lieutenant Richards Sir."

Lieutenant Richards should probably relabel himself as Rooke's personal messenger, as this was the majority of the tasks he was undertaking these days. He was his usual cheerful self however in the morning air, a large boyish smile which the *Lannwedhenek* crew had come to know. He was always a kindly man, and whether that was his persona when visiting other ships, or his true nature did not matter to the sailors who interacted with him. Smythe had come to like the young Lieutenant, and the two had struck up, if not a friendship, then at least a cordial professional relationship.

"Lieutenant Richards, won't you join me for a quick bit of breakfast?" offered Smythe, as he always did, and as always Richards would politely refuse stating they had duties to do.

"That sounds lovely, thank you Sir, you will need to pull up three

seats however Sir."

Smythe had gone back to finishing his report for Rooke, so it had taken him a moment to realise that firstly, Richards had said yes, and that secondly, he was telling him to pull up an extra chair. "Is the Admiral coming?" Smythe asked like a naughty schoolboy worried about his homework being late.

"No but may have the pleasure of introducing you to Lord Hempleman, of the Landgraviate of Hesse-Kassel." He then turned and indicated the man stood behind him who, politely held out his hand for the Commander to shake it. He was young, in his early twenties and it was obvious this would be the young dignitary he would have the pleasure of transporting to Cadiz when the time came. "Dies ist Kommandant Henry Smythe, von seiner Majestät Schaluppe *Lannwedhenek*," and the Lord bowed his head politely at Smythe. "I think I got that right," said Richards to Smythe. "It's been a lot of introductions today. I'm also not sure if they understand the difference between Commander and Captain, but it's irrelevant really. No, my task is to introduce you to each other. And breakfast sounds like a fantastic idea." He again turned to the young Lord, "Der Kommandant hat uns Frühstück angeboten, um uns kennenzulernen."

"Vielen Dank, Vielen Dank!" replied the young Lord, clearly appreciating the care the Commander was taking of his interests. The table was changed from the outside office to breakfast in minutes. Two extra chairs were found from the Petty Officers' berths.

"Wait a moment, can someone send for Yin? He's been practicing his German, this would be a good test for him." It would be the second time that Smythe had dined with Yin, the first occasion had been pleasant enough, he had no reason to think this occasion would not be equally splendid. The table was set, and thankfully, they had bought some mackerel from a local fisherman, which would provide a better meal that the salt beef and biscuit the crew were on.

"Why is the Lord interested in supporting the Hapsburg claims?" asked Smythe with interest. Richards, probably less blunt and with more diplomatic tact, asked Hempleman in German and the young Lord replied to him. "He says that his territory is rather west of Vienna, and rather closer to Paris. If Bourbon influence came in, his autonomy would be reduced. He enjoys his freedom." So, it was a position of both self-interest and politics rather than fidelity to his Emperor which caused this man to be here. Richards smiled to himself. He knew that the pragmatic and honest to a fault Smythe would like the answer which had no frills. The mackerel were cooked well, with a little butter and some early seasonal greens that Smythe must have hidden away and Lord Hempleman seemed to be genuinely appreciative of the food. He again spoke to Richards in German, Richards, paused, possibly trying to think

how to phrase
whatever he had been asked as politely as possible.

"He would like to know where he will be sleeping during the voyage down to Cadiz." Richards said, as politely as he could. Smythe had not even thought of this, he had been concerned with getting his crew seaworthy.

"Tell the Lord, that regretfully I have not considered the matter," replied Smythe. Richards again paused.

"If I may Sir," Richards said, pointedly, "It is customary for you to give your cabin to guests and dignitaries and for you to bunk with the Lieutenants. Does Smythe have a spare bunk in his quarters?" By quarters, on the sloop, he meant a curtain between him and the petty officers and midshipmen.

"I am honestly not sure; I assume there would be room."

"In that case my advice is you offer your cabin. It would be seen as good manners. It also means that if you end up with some Lobsters on board, it means you have already been moved. Short of you housing a general, you wouldn't have to move yourself or Lieutenant again." The logic made sense, and Treen was a pleasant enough fellow.

"Yes, yes," said Smythe finally, as he realised he had not actually acknowledged Richards suggestion. "Tell him I will give him my cabin, it is both the biggest and the most private on board. There is also a Stewards berth down there, which means if he has a servant, there will be a place for him."

This again was conveyed, rather more slowly this time by Richards, who seemed to be making the offer sound as good as it could be. A Sloops Commanders' cabin was not the largest, it was big enough to have a table in as well as a bed, but it would be comfortable enough hopefully.

"Danke, Danke," said Hempleman, this time with noticeably less enthusiasm than he had shown for breakfast. He was starting to look a little queasy.

"This is his first-time aboard ships," explained Richards, "Perhaps some buttery fish wasn't in his best interests," he said supressing his usual smile whenever he found something inappropriate funny. He spoke to Hempleman about something, and he nodded in acknowledgement. "I just offered him a look at his berth, hope you don't mind? And then we will get out of your hair, I know you have things to do."

Smythe escorted them to his own cabin, which he knew he would have to vacate for at least a month during the time in which he was hosting the Lord. He knew that England needed this alliance if they were to prosper in this war. Hempleman spoke softly to Richards, who looked on and smiled. He nodded supportively, and Hempleman, who looked sceptically back at him, simply continued to stare. Richards said something again in German, and Hempleman nodded appreciatively.

"If you would be so kind Commander, as to give us a full tour of your ship, I feel that would make the Lord feel more at home here." Smythe nodded, and they walked through the gun decks, down into the stores, across to the Lieutenants and Petty Officers' berths and back on deck. Whatever the conversation between Richards and Hempleman had seemed to cheer him up. The two men were even laughing as they began to leave the ship. "The report can be sent this evening if there is nothing major to report, Sir?" asked Richards as he was leaving the *Lannwedhenek*.

"No Lieutenant, there is not."

"Then I bid you farewell," he dropped his voice down to a whisper, "Well done Henry, sorry you have got this little Lordling, none of the other Commanders wanted him. He will be a pain in the arse, but at least you don't have to speak to him."

Smythe smiled and shook Richards hand.

"Hempleman thought you were lying." Yin said from behind him after the gig had heaved away.

"What?" said Smythe, the lack of formality in Yin's tone was not uncommon.

"When you showed him your cabin. He thought you were lying about it being the largest cabin. That's why Richards suggested a tour. It was to show him that even if it was small, it was still the best you could offer him." That explained why Hempleman's mood lifted as they continued around the ship. It was not because he was impressed. But because he realised that the man in front of him was being honest with him. He had earned some respect there he was sure.

"Hang on," said Smythe after a few moments of contemplation about what Yin had said to him.

"Yes, Sir," smiled Yin, anticipating his Commanders next statement.

"They only spoke in German," Smythe said.

"Yes, Sir." Replied Yin, still smiling knowingly at his Commander. "Not fluently Sir," added Yin, not wishing to oversell his abilities in the matter, "but that book you gave me without reading yourself was rather insightful. Perhaps, if you have free time, you should try it, Sir." He added the "Sir" with a smile, which Yin, perhaps because of his clear use to both the ship and Smythe, he often got away with slightly more than any other seaman aboard.

Smythe nodded to his surgeon, coughed, rather louder than probably necessary and paused. "Are you finished with the book Mister Yin?"

"Not quite, Sir," answered Yin, "I thought it would be more prudent for me to finish the book first for when Lord Hempleman comes aboard properly in the near future and, if the need is, be your translator, Sir." It was the little statements like "if the need is," which reminded Smythe that English was not Yin's first language. Although now, due to the amount he used it, English had overtaken Spanish as Yin's second language. He no longer made reports in Spanish, and he was needing the literacy assistance of Abraham less and less. That being said, Abraham did often assist with any minor surgeries, as despite being in Spithead, at the literal home of the Royal Navy, they still had been unable to get a registered surgeon aboard.

"Yes, Mister Yin, that seems prudent, thank you for your assistance in this."

"Ever your servant, Sir," and this time, as Yin bowed it was clear he meant it. The weather was holding fair and it was turning into a lovely summers' day.

"Mister Smythe," he said to Will, who was earwigging into his conversations. "If you would be so kind as to bring up the table for me to work on again, and a glass of lemonade, it would be most appreciated."

CHAPTER EIGHT

June turned into July as preparations continued to begin the voyage south. Rooke was pacing in his cabin, frustrated with the lack of movement being shown by the Admiralty and the Army combined. Both sides had been frustrating in their lack of vision in his eyes, with the Navy not considering supply ships with either fresh supplies or enough to make a prolonged siege possible. Or the Army's clear lack of desire to send enough troops to be able to hold Cadiz for any period of time. The Government seemed to not realise, that as much as this may be a diplomatic mission that the Austrians wanted, the English and Dutch had a larger, and more pressing matter. A port in which they would be able to restock and refit their vessels in and around the Mediterranean. Without this, England's Navy, despite being formidable throughout the Atlantic, would be potentially stuck, without supplies in the Mediterranean should Spain successfully attack the port of Trieste.

There was a knock at his cabin door, a requirement for any common sailor to do, besides the steward of a Captain, or in this case, an Admiral. "Yes?" asked the usual gruff voice of Rooke.

"Sir," it was Richards' voice from outside the room. "The Army is here."

"Brilliant," thought Rooke, just as he was trying to assemble his stores and sail around forty ships of varying sizes through the Channel, past Brest, which would be massive risk in its own right,

sailing straight across the Bay of Biscay, not interact with any of the Spanish Ships coming out of Ferrol and A Coruña, sailing down past Portugal, which at any moment may declare in alliance with the Bourbon's extending empire, and into Cadiz, but now, the good men from the Army had decided to grace them with their presence finally.

"Bring him in!" growled Rooke, not wanting to be too rude to the man he would be entertaining.

"Sir George Rooke," Richards said in his finest and most regal voice that Rooke knew Richards only used for such occasions as introducing dignitaries, "I have the pleasure to introduce, the Duke of Ormonde, James FitzJames Butler."

The Duke walked into the Admirals Cabin. He was a tall thin man, with watery brown eyes and a pronounced jaw. He walked with the arrogance and pomposity of his breeding.

"I think this is where I shall take my leave gentlemen, if that is alright Sir Rooke," Rooke nodded to his young Lieutenant. He himself was not looking forward to this discussion, putting another unfortunate human being through such an order would be completely unfair.

"Odd young thing isn't he," remarked the Duke, "Duke of Ormonde, at your service Sir," he held out his hand for Rooke to take. They had of course met, through both being members of Parliament, but as was typical, anyone that Butler thought was below him, he
clearly did not spend the time to remember.

"Sir George Rooke. Recently promoted to Admiral of the Mediterranean fleet."

"Yes, I heard we were to leave some boats in the Med." He continued to try to keep his voice above that of Rooke's in what he considered the correct way to speak, but his Irish roots were unable to be completely hidden.

Rooke had to hold his tongue as best he could. "Some boats" was the only way the Army which Butler led would leave England. But to argue with the Commander of the Army before the expedition had even set off would be ill advised. A subtle correction was the more tactful way of dealing with this.

"Our *ships* are due to leave soon Lieutenant-General." He said as politely as he could. "However, I still need to know approximately how many men we are taking with us." It was a simple enough question, or so Rooke thought. Ormonde however looked on almost helpless at the notion.

"I have no idea as of yet Sir," he replied simply. This was not very helpful.

"It's a matter of food, and water my Duke."

"Well, bit of an odd way to ask me to lunch Admiral, but very well, thank you."

Rooke was taken aback. In his mind there had been no doubt to the

intentions of his words. He had clearly in his mind meant supplies for the troops, mariners and sailors under his command. How Ormonde had construed this to mean his own stomach was beyond him. "Erm, yes, I shall call my steward." The table was laid for a late breakfast of ham and eggs, with a little rum on the side. It was easy to keep the stores, even his personal ones, fully stocked here in Portsmouth. That would not be as simple once they left Portsmouth, that was for certain. During breakfast they talked about the ongoing war, the state of affairs in Parliament, and the ongoing issue of English succession.

"You know Anne wants the Union with Scotland making permanent," said Ormonde, his voice barely concealing his displeasure at the idea.

"Is that so?" asked Rooke. He had not attended Parliament since the Queens speech, and he did not know when he would have the opportunity to do so again with the current military situation in hand.

"Yes," replied Ormonde with a rather bored drawl of the situation. "Seems to think it would create a form of stability. When have the Scots ever been known for their stability?" he chuckled to himself. Rooke had to supress a smile. Considering that Ireland had been the hotbed of sedition during the War of the Two Kings, and that he himself had fought in the war, he could hardly consider his homeland stable, let alone criticize any other realm.

"The eggs are slightly overdone for my liking," said Ormonde, his air of arrogance evident even at this minor point.

"I am sorry that is your thoughts," replied Rooke. He was beginning to dislike Ormonde more by the moment. "Now, to business, I know about the majority of the details, however I am unsure about a couple of things."

"Oh, how so?" replied Ormonde, trying not to smile at what he saw as the buffoonery of this Naval officer.

"Well, who am I to be escorting down to Cadiz?"

"Well, myself of course," replied Ormonde. Seemingly this had not been something which had been discussed between the Admiralty and the Army. Made sense. Nothing was ever discussed properly. "Who did you think you would be transporting."

"I was under the impression I would be transporting someone of Germanic heritage."

"Ah," smiled Ormonde politely, "No, you were to be, but instead you will be collecting him from Cape Saint Vincent on the way."

"Cape Saint Vincent? As in Portugal?" This would be rather a way into the voyage. It would take them between three and four weeks to get down to Cape Saint Vincent, this would put them heavily into August. They would not have long to secure Cadiz during this campaigning season, and now he had to pick up extra people on route too.

"Yes, as in Portugal. King Peter II has signed a treaty with the Bourbon's. His Royal Highness Prince George Louis of Hessen-Darmstadt is currently in Lisbon trying to show Peter that his best chance of survival, and prosperity, is not with the Bourbons', even if just in assistance to them, but aligned with us in the Grand Alliance." As grandiose as it sounded, the Grand Alliance was the major alliance between the three main powers within it. The Holy Roman Empire, which was quickly becoming simply the Austrian Hapsburgs Empire, the newly resurrected United Provinces of the Netherlands or Holland and England, Ireland and Scotland, or what was becoming known as Britain. There were other minor Kingdoms, Principalities, Dukedoms, and other such minor nobles within it, but they were merely pawns and rooks, in this ever-changing game of European chess.

"Then I must insist that you speed your plans along General. My ships will not stock themselves and I am sure you have plenty of tasks to be completing." It was a courteous dismissal of the General, but not impolite enough that Ormonde could take offence.

"What?" said the General, with a look of absent mindedness evident on his face, "Yes, yes I guess so. Well, to your good health Admiral, let us try to sail away on time!"

The General put on his overcoat, a rather redundant item of clothing in the July weather, made a small, polite bow and left the cabin.

"Landsmen," thought Rooke to himself, although he was careful not

to say it out loud in case anyone around would still hear him. For the good of the service, hell for the good of the country he must look like he was keeping up polite appearances with the Duke.

There was another knock at his cabin door, which brought Rooke back from his continued thoughts about the misgivings of this whole venture. "Come in,"

Richards walked in through the door, a polite smile on his face, "Sir, the Captain would like a word about supply if you would be so kind."

"Yes, yes, give me a moment," he grumbled in response. "Don't you do any work around here Richards?" he added in a rather gruff tone.

"Me, Sir? No, Sir, I am merely a messenger boy I am sure of it," Richards replied, and Rooke smiled. He had been unfair to the young officer, who decided to reply in kind. He was a sharp wit that Richards, who could go far in the Navy.

Salt beef. Salt beef, salt beef and more salt beef. Smythe had asked for his ship to be restocked, and he had been given tonnes of salt beef. The crew were busying themselves trying to put it all below deck, getting out of the direct heat of this glorious July morning.

"You know what this means Sir?" asked Jones, excitedly.

"I presume it means we are soon to be setting sail Mister Jones," replied Smythe. The amount of Salt beef that had been produced

would be enough to feed the ship for around three months. He knew, of course, they would be also transporting soldiers from the army, but still. This much salt beef coming aboard today could only mean that they were preparing to sail.

"Mister Treen, new standing orders, no man is to leave ship without a very good reason, do you understand me?" It was a warning of dire consequences. They were due to set sail any day now. The stores coming aboard were clear of that. The last thing he needed was his crew, who were starting to come together nicely, going absent without leave. He would not be able to merely replace them, they had trained and drilled their men hard. And so what if the deserters were caught. They would be tried and hung or flogged most likely for sure, but that would not help the *Lannwedhenek*, she would be halfway to the Bay of Biscay by then.

The stores kept coming that morning as ships biscuits arrived soon afterwards. Again, the amount of biscuit was not for a few runs up and down the Channel. They were going on a longer voyage. A gig could be spotted bobbing along in the water, with the ever-cheerful Richards at the tiller. "Sir!" came the voice Richards from the gig. "Sir, if you please, Sir Rooke wishes to issue you with up-to-date orders."

This was hardly shocking. Smythe had not failed to, indeed no Commander would, the at least two months' worth of stores which were being added onto his ship. Therefore, it stood to reason that

new orders would be being issued soon. Apparently however, sooner rather than later.

"Yes, Mister Richards, I shall get my coat and hat." Smythe felt like he should have his coat and hat permanently attached to the side of his ship rather than in his cabin. Will, who had seen the gig evidently before Smythe himself had, was already moving with haste with both items. "Sooner you know what's what the better Henry," he said, forgetting that they were above deck and not in his private cabin, "Sir," he added as quickly as he could. A few sailors who had been with them for over a year now aboard the *Lannwedhenek* smiled. It was not uncustomary for this to happen between the cousins.

Smythe got into the gig with his usual unease at being aboard the small rowing boat. A fishing trawler, absolutely fine. A Sloop-of-War, or even a Ship-of-the-Line, not an issue at all. But these little gigs made him feel incredibly uneasy. It was a short row across to the *Royal Sovereign* leaving very little time for small talk. Smythe usually quizzed Richards, in a nice way, trying to pry out of him if he had any ideas as to the orders in question. However, today this seemed like a mere formality. There were sailing. And soon. There was no other explanation as to the filling of the *Lannwedhenek* to the brim otherwise.

Rooke was in his cabin, maps and charts spread wide across his desks. He had his plotting compasses all set to different widths,

clearly he was trying to anticipate the best course of action throughout this voyage. The knock at the cabin had been what he was expecting. "Enter,".

Smythe walked in, hat neatly tucked under his arm and stood to attention at the side of the Admiral who was still looking over his charts with intent. "Commander Smythe of the Sloop-of-War *Lannwedhenek*, Sir."

"At ease," murmured Rooke, still pondering over the papers. "Now, Smythe, how goes the restocking of your vessel."

"It goes well Sir," he replied, and then thinking to add more detail, "The Salt beef is all on board, we are working it down into the hull and the biscuits were arriving just as I left Sir."

"And the water?"

"Hadn't arrived as I left Sir,"

"Hmm," said Rooke, "Richards!" he roared.

"Yes, Sir?" he said from beyond the room.

"Get down to Portsea and see what the fuck is going on!" Any time wasted on supplies would be potentially deadly to all concerned. Moreover, if the suppliers thought they could be slow on refilling the *Lannwedhenek*, they may try to repeat the feat when restocking the larger vessels of the fleet. An extra twenty minutes allowed for the *Lannwedhenek* would be potentially a whole day for the rest of fleet.

"Aye, aye Sir!" shouted Richards, and Smythe could hear the footsteps of the young Lieutenant fade away into the distance.

"Try to get that sorted for you Smythe," said Rooke in a kindly fashion. He clearly was frustrated with the lack of movement on the plans, and any delays from what he saw specifically from seamen would not be tolerated. He knew the shame of the last attack on Cadiz back in 1625. It had been a disaster from start to finish, and Rooke was adamant this would not happen to his invasion. "To orders, you know of the overall plan,"

"Indeed Sir, sail to Spain, capture the port of Cadiz. Work from there." That was the limit of the plan as Smythe knew it.

"Pretty much, but there are some problems potentially getting down there."

"Sir?"

"We have to pass a couple of rather large Bourbon ports on the way at Brest and A Coruna. A large convoy of ships will hardly be missed."

"How large are we talking about Sir?" asked Smythe out of interest of the size of the fleet he was to be a part of.

"Around fourteen thousand men give or take," replied the Admiral, "All of which I have the pleasure of being overall responsible for. I would rather they not all get killed going round the end of France."

Smythe agreed it would be an unmitigated disaster should the Navy be sunk just off Brest. It would give the Bourbon's an un-

impeded shot, directly aimed at England. "So, we are going to send a ship
ahead to keep an eye on Brest, making sure that the French don't move any time soon."

Smythe was not a fool. He knew that "a ship" meant the *Lannwedhenek*. "When do we set sail Sir?". Rooke smiled. He liked Smythe. He was not a lifelong naval man, but he was a seaman, and he had an astute understanding of how the world worked. "As soon as is practical," replied Rooke, "Ideally as soon as the water is aboard, however, I know you are hosting a dignitary from the Holy Roman Empire, so you may wish to improve your own personal stores."

Smythe thought for a second. The only thing he knew about German food was sauerkraut, and all he knew about that was it was some form of fermented cabbage. Other than that, he would try to get food that would keep, pickled onions, salt cod and other such foods which would allow him to have some variation in the normal food provided for the crew.

"I think we should be good to sail in the morning Sir," said Smythe, "Providing Lord Hempleman is ready."

"I shall instruct the Lord's effects to be loaded aboard this afternoon," replied Rooke simply. This would be useful. Assuming that everything went to plan the *Lannwedhenek* would be at sea tomorrow. This was the best place for a Commander to be, alone at sea, in command of his own destiny.

"Your orders, which will be confirmed in writing," said Rooke, in a professional manner which Smythe had not seen since his first visit to the *Royal Sovereign*, "Is that tomorrow, at the earliest possible time, probably around three in the afternoon when the tide is highest, you will take fifty soldiers and Lord Hempleman, of the Landgraviate of Hesse-Kassel, to here." He pointed at a point on the map, outside the port of Brest, "and keep watch for movements of the French Navy there." It was a simple enough order, effectively anchor around twenty miles of the Brest coastline and watch. "You are not to engage under any circumstances," said Rooke, "That includes to support any merchant vessels of ours or capture any prizes until you have signalled to the fleet and have a response. Today is the fifth of July. I expect the fleet will arrive between the fifteenth and the twentieth."

Ten days. Ten days just off the French coast trying not to look too ambiguous and signalling to an oncoming fleet which could be several days away. It would take around three days travelling at five knots to arrive at the rendezvous point, leaving him alone for potentially eleven days.

"What should I do if the French do come out in force Sir?" asked Smythe politely.

"Run like hell boy!" said Rooke, and there was no inclination of humour in his voice. "You are a support ship, you are a lookout ship, but by God you are not a fully fledged fighting ship. They would turn

you to matchsticks or worse capture you. No, you will have it in writing also that you are to withdraw should you see an attack upon you. Anything bigger than a sixth rate, I think. You might be able to handle a sixth rate if it were crewed by Frogs."

"Very good Sir,"

"Turning of the tide. Tomorrow afternoon. Be ready Commander."

There were stores to sort. Gunnery teams to sort. Watches to be finalised. Midshipmen and Petty Officers to be confirmed in charge of watches and teams. Food to be sorted. Water butts to be sealed and put below. And a multitude of other tasks and jobs that ships which were about to leave port had to undergo. Everything was being done under the watchful and experienced eye of Jones, with Jenkins stood beside him ticking off each crate or bucket as came in.

"Seems to be taking forever," commented Jenkins. "We could fill the *Greyhound* in half the time."

"You were trying to smuggle things," said Jones cynically, "Doing illegal things tend to make you move faster." Both men, who originally of course had not always seen eye to eye, smiled. The water was being loaded on now, enough water for at least a month and half.

"Those stores won't last forever," commented Jenkins, who knew a prolonged engagement would not be possible with what they had on board.

"We are going out ahead of the fleet," said Jones, "heard Smythe saying it to Treen as he came back aboard."

"Fucking great," Jenkins remarked. "We are bait."

"More like a lookout," smiled Jones.

"I only know one thing about fishing," said Jenkins.

"What's that?" asked Jones.

"It never ends well for the bait, no matter what."

Jones smiled at his younger colleagues' analogy of their predicament. "We are a look out," he said, "The fleet needs to know it isn't sail into a trap, that's all. Now, to the fresh foods." The limes and oranges were being loaded on board now. It was customary to load up on fruits on long voyages, it reduced the chance of illness setting in. The stores were almost full now, but they would not be sailing until the following afternoon.

"Ahoy there!" shouted an unfamiliar voice from the gig coming upon the portside bow.

Both men turned to see the young German Lord they would be escorting as part of the Hapsburg delegation coming along. He was wearing what looked like a Naval uniform, which was fine, apart from Jones knew that Hessen was a landlocked territory.

"Ahoy there!" shouted back Jenkins, a clear amusement in his voice, which Jones hoped the German Lord would not detect. Behind the Lord's gig was a small barge with items such as a wardrobe and dresser.

"Stupid Kraut doesn't think he's gonna fit all tha' in Smythe's cabin,

does he?" said Jenkins quietly to Jones out of the side of his mouth. It became evident however, that yes, Lord Hempleman did think he could fit all of the furniture and books inside the cabin. He also did not seem to appreciate that Jones and Jenkins felt that the ships stores were more important than his own possessions. It was causing such a commotion on deck, that the Lords Valet drew his pistol. Jones and Jenkins drew their weapons in response, but thankfully, Lieutenant Treen was on hand to defuse the situation.

"Gentlemen, what seems to be the problem here?"

Lord Hempleman started shouting in German, which Treen had absolutely no idea what he had been saying. Thankfully, his Valet spoke some English. "Zeese fools are refusing to load Lord Hempleman's effects." It was clear that the Lord was angry, and his Valet would do everything to please his master. Jones and Jenkins seemed to be equally frustrated, and they were not even at sea yet.

"Where is the Commander?" asked Treen trying to cool the high tempers on deck. Jones looked visibly tired, and Jenkins was hardly better than him. The sun was beating down on both of them, and unlike their comrades they had been on deck all day, organising the stores and instructing men where to take things. This had equally meant that neither of them had probably had a drink of water since this morning also. Fatigue and dehydration were causing their tempers to fray.

"He's ashore Sir, filling his personal stores, at the behest of Admiral

Rooke," said Jones, clearly frustrated with this order from on high. It had left a ship to be restocked without its principal officer aboard. Treen, however could not be too disheartened by this information. Due to the visit of the Lord, Treen was sharing his small berth with both the Commander and his steward. This would probably mean that he got invited to dinner more often, get to spend time with the Commander, and hopefully build some good will with this young German aristocrat.

"Yes, of course," he had known that because Treen had of course been handed the ship by Smythe, and he was yet to relinquish it. "Mister Yin perhaps?"

"Also, ashore Sir, restocking out medical supplies. He felt having a fully stocked medical room was probably for the best on a long voyage."

"Damn him!" thought Treen. Yin was the only person aboard who had a good grasp of German. "Then we must accommodate our guests as best we can gentlemen," said Treen calmly. "You will bring on his Lordships possessions post haste, and I will assign four men and a Midshipman to assist you. Midshipman Abraham!" roared Treen over the din.

"Sir?" squeaked the young man from across the sloop.

"Bring your team over here, you are to assist his Lordship, Lord Hempleman of the Landgraviate of Hesse-Kassel." Abraham gave a small bow to his Lord. It was evident from the way Lord Hempleman

looked at Abraham that he did not agree with the ship's choice of Midshipman. Jenkins' scowl became more pronounced. But no words were spoken, perhaps Lord Hempleman did not think it was a good idea to argue about something just after it had simmered down, or perhaps he knew he did not have the English to create such an argument in a polite manner, but he simply nodded. "Excellent!" said Treen, trying to use the energy of his voice to overcome the anger being felt. "Now, Jones, bring over enough that these men can carry at once, then move back to the stores until they have returned. How does that sound Mister?" he indicated to the Valet who was yet to give his name.

"Wagner," bowed the Valet at this, "Seems acceptable." And he tried to explain the outcome to his Lord. Lord Hempleman still looked angry at the entire situation,

"Erkennen sie nicht, dass ich ein Herr bin?" said the Lord in a rather unflattering tone which was used to evidently show his displeasure to both his valet and the men assembled. "His Lordship has asked if you understand his position?"

"His position?" asked Treen as politely as he could.

"Yes, his Lordship vishes to know if you understood he was a Lord."

"Yes, the point had been made to me. We are doing the best we can Sir." replied Treen. He gave a small bow whilst trying to keep his face neutral. Did this German fool realise that he had a ship to try and run? The German Lord continued to look down his nose at the

young officer, and with barely concealed contempt at the Midshipman.

"Im Großbritannien haben sie schwarze Jungs, die um Männer herum bestellen," he said to his valet and both men chuckled to themselves. His Lords luggage was loaded next as Treen had requested. This took rather longer than Jones would have liked, as many of the items were rather bulky and instead of simply loading whatever was nearest, his Lordship insisted on specific things being loaded next.

"Nein, das hier!" he shouted back at the Coxswain. Jones sighed. The most efficient way of dealing with this, probably was to baby this young Lord, but that would create resentment amongst the men who were working hard to restock their ship. Treen, whilst on his rounds came back around to see the frustrated Coxswain.

"Will we be ready to sail by tomorrow Mister Jones?" he asked, possibly too loud, and as he approached, "Look, I know he's an arse,"

"And racist, you should see the way he looks at young Abraham."

"I know, but there's nothing we can do about that, look, just get his stuff aboard, and he can bugger off to his cabin all voyage."

He then turned back to the assembled crew, "Another quarter ration of rum to you all if it's away before the Dogwatch! That might get them to move faster Jones," he left with a smile.

"Amazin' what officers can get away with aye?" said Jenkins, smiling

to himself and moving a sack of potatoes down below.

CHAPTER NINE

Seven bells rang out on the afternoon watch of the *Lannwed-henek* as it pulled away from Spithead. There was a gentle Easterly wind, pushing them down the Channel towards their destination.

"Making six knots Sir," said Jones to Smythe. He knew that Smythe could probably have made the calculation himself, in fact he was certain of it. The men had now been together for over a year, since the *Lannwedhenek* had been commissioned into service in the early spring of 1701. Jones had been thinking about retirement, having served as a Coxswains mate on much larger vessels than this, and a quiet life in Abertawe, selling his stories for grog. But one last task England had asked of him, and he had obliged, thinking he would be kept close to home. How foolish he was to think he would remain on the North Cornish Coast.

"Shorten the sails, if you please Mister Jones, I do not wish to arrive at our destination too soon if that is all the same with you."

"Don't wanna get caught Sir?"

"Don't wish to be seen Mister Jones. No point being the lookout if you are the one who gives the Frogs the heads up."

Sitting outside of Brest, keeping lookout on the French's Atlantic fleet was an essential task that was required for the success of this mission. But arrive too early, and the *Lannwedhenek* may inadvertently tip the French off to the goings on of the Navy.

The sails were shortened, slowing the ship down to four knots. The

sudden jerk as the wind re-tacked the sails caused some of the less able seamen to slide on the ships deck. The deck was overly crowded at any rate with the extra fifty soldiers aboard. There was a Major, and a Lieutenant couple of Sergeants, which all needed "adequate" bunks. So, the Lieutenants Berth, which usually simply occupied Treen, now had five people in. This also affected the required formalities of the ship. This morning Smythe had been dressing in a hurry when the young army Lieutenant came into grab something. Smythe had been about to reprimand the young officer for failing to knock upon entering a superior officer's quarters, before realising of course that it was also his room currently and therefore there had been no need to knock.

There had been vomit too. Some of the soldiers were seasick, but this was a serious issue for any military. If it were merely seasickness, it would most likely pass, or at least not affect any other seaman. If it were something else however, this could rip through the crew turning it into a quarantine vessel, a fate no Commander could allow to happen wherever possible.

Therefore, before they had even stepped aboard whilst still on the gigs, and in some cases whilst vomiting, Smythe and Yin had assessed each soldier. Well, more Yin, Smythe was there for the legal authority to carry out any orders or suggestions issued by the acting Surgeon. The Major had made to protest but was powerless to stop such suggestions.

Despite being of equal rank in their respective services, a Major was the equal of a man who Commanded or Captained his own ship, so long as they were at sea and on the *Lannwedhenek*, it would be Smythe who had the final say. In practice, this rarely caused issues, a Major could always state "on the record" he disagreed with the decision and at any subsequent court marshals would be acquitted. But it rarely came to that. In the case of the soldiers in Spithead turned away, the Major merely shrugged, evidently feeling that if the shoe were on the other foot, and a sailor came into his camp with fever, he would not allow him to mix with the other soldiers either.

"Mister Yin," said Smythe politely, and Yin in his usual deference turned and smiled. "Be so kind as to speak to Lord

Hempleman's valet. Ask him, if he would be kind enough to allow me to host the Lord, the Major, and yourself in the Commander's berth tonight."

"Me Sir?"

"I need a translator," said Smythe, possibly too quickly, and Yin smiled. He was not there due to his position on the ship, he was there because he spoke German.

"I will ask Sir," he said, smiling, "Shall I ask the valet if he would be so kind as to help Will prepare everything?"

"Yes, that would be preferable. He can advise Will on how the Lord likes his food." It was around two and a half days to Brest. That meant three dinners before they anchored. If tonight he ate with

the Lord and the Army Commander, tomorrow he could dine with Treen and a couple of his Petty Officers, he would also invite that young Lieutenant out of politeness, then the third night he would be inevitably busy issuing orders to worry about food.

"Mister Treen, Mister Jones," His two subordinated smiled, knowing that some instructions they could probably guess themselves were about to be issued. Smythe was a good, kindly Commander, but he liked to micromanage, choosing to leave nothing to chance. "Will you come below with me and look at the charts. We have things to discuss."

In the Lieutenants berth, the young army Lieutenant was lazing on his bunk, reading *Ways to discipline in a siege.* As the Commander walked in, he jumped to his feet and gave a salute. Evidently the look that Smythe had given him this morning before he remembered they were sharing this space had stuck with him.

"At ease Lieutenant Potter. If you wish to learn some seacraft pay attention, if not, stay reading your book."

Probably out of a combination of boredom, curiosity, and the fact his book would be there once they had finished, Potter walked over to the charts, laid out over the desks. The plotting compass was set, as best as Jones could see to around four knots, and there were two courses plotted.

"As you two know, we are going to be lookouts in Brest. Sailing straight there will leave us in the wind, without support for around

eleven days potentially. Rooke has given me *some* leeway with this. So long as we are there with plenty of time to spare, he doesn't care." He picked up the pencil which was on top of the chart. "Route A – around three days at four knots, will get us there on the tenth. The rest of the fleet is due around the twentieth, wind permitting."

This was the most direct route, sailing down the centre of the Channel, giving as much visibility as possible. Treen nodded, but Jones was almost certain that this was not the route that Smythe intended to take.

"Or there is route B."

"Route B?" asked Jones. He could see it hugged the English coastline much closer.

"Route B. We have been instructed not to interact with any French fishing vessel under any circumstances. However, we can interact with any English fishing ships so long as they are within the area of English bays."

"We shall sail into St. Austell Bay. There is a small fishing village called West Porthmear, which has a small fishing fleet. It will take us a couple of days to get there and restock. Fresh food is preferable whenever it is available. And we have been stuck in Spithead now for months, let's get some Cornish air in us before the journey onward!" There was a practical aspect to his desire to go to West Porthmear, but undoubtedly a personal one too. "We can

refill the water barrels we have begun to empty, get some fresh fish for the crew that night, save them having salt beef for an evening, and work from there. The bay is also sheltered, which will assist our army friends," a quick nod to Potter showed he was trying to think of him too, "and we'd be staying closer to England to avoid detection."

"What are we saying to the locals?" Treen asked.

"We are sailing around to Glasgow to pick up some iron to make into cannon balls from the Scottish mines," said Smythe. "We will keep his Lordship and the Army below deck or at least out of uniform; save a few men who would look like Marines to the untrained eye, and we won't let any locals aboard."

It was a testament to the secrecy trying to be upheld by the Admiralty, that Smythe in his written orders had specifically been told not to allow a soul aboard the *Lannwedhenek* until the rendezvous had been established. So, if they were to get any fresh produce, it would have to be done carefully. And ensuring that there was not an abundance of men on the deck when in view of the shoreline.

"What about the Major?" asked Jones.

"He can be above deck, should anyone ask, he is the quality assurance for the cannon balls."

It was a fair ruse. He could be a member of the artillery, unless anyone knew any different it would not matter.

"I think route B," said Jones finally. "Keeps us closer to home should something serious go wrong and allows fresh food. Always a morale booster on longer voyages Sir."

Treen did not show a preference in either case.

"Speaking as a non-sailor," spoke Potter, causing the three seamen to all look up from the chart, "Anytime we are sheltered from the weather would be preferable." He had looked a touch green since they embarked and the three experience seamen smiled.

"Yes, of course," smiled Treen, "Well, I have no objects to the plan Sir, so route B it is I guess."

"Excellent," said Smythe, glad his subordinates were at least on side even if not in full agreement, "In that case gentlemen, I wish to extend an invitation for you both, and the other Petty Officers, to dine with me on the deck tomorrow evening, assuming a fair weather. You too Mister Potter." This caused the men to smile. That meant whatever fresh food could be acquired in West Porthmear would be theirs first.

"Who's gonna be looking after the ship?" asked Treen.

"Mister Yin," said Smythe. "We will most likely be at anchor in the bay and it isn't like we are going anywhere, so no harm can come of it. He's dining with me tonight," he added, as Jones was inevitably about to ask why Yin had not been invited in the first place. Jones closed his mouth, stopping the protest before it begun. "We have the pleasure of dining with the Lord Hempleman, and the actual

pleasure of dining with your Major, Potter,". All four men smiled at this. In the around twenty-four hours since he had been on the *Lannwedhenek*, the honorary Lieutenant in the landlocked German state of Hessen had insisted on telling seamen of over ten years in some cases how to properly do their jobs. Needless to say, it had not gone down well. Some of the men resented the tone, even in German, in which he spoke to them. Others resented the fact that he clearly had no idea what he was doing. He had upset many of the men for the way he had treated the young Midshipman Abraham, who clearly he felt above, not only because of his status in society, but also because of his skin colour. Finally, some simply did not like the fact he was a Lord. That may not have been his fault, but he did not have to act so high and mighty.

The bell rung out eight bells on the afternoon watch. Dinner for the Commander would come at four bells. This would be an interesting dinner as no doubt the Lord would have some helpful advice for his running of the ship too. He had one of the gunners shine his shoes for him for an extra bit of rum, had Will press his best shirt and presented himself at the Lords cabin at four bells sharp. The Lord, in his kindness as a host, had produced some wine for the occasion, and Smythe was pleasantly surprised to see that the Major had already beaten him in being the first one there. The two men were speaking in German, evidently the Major's schooling had included that.

"Gentlemen, thank you for accepting this dinner invitation from me," he said with a polite bow.

"My pleasure Commander," replied the Major. "I know I haven't been aboard long, Smith isn't it?"

"Smythe," he corrected the major, who was around his age, with grey, thinning hair, clean shaven and about average height.

"Connolly," he replied. Smythe's reputation for forgetting names had preceded him, and he thought he would politely remind him. The three gentlemen talked politely, with the Major translating where possible for both men, and Lord Hempleman seemed to be enjoying his time with the two men of war, both several years his senior, his valet and Will trying their best not to get in the others way as they finished the preparations.

Yin joined shortly afterwards, once again wearing the silken robe he seemed to only wear on special occasions. Smythe introduced him as both his surgeon and his translator for the evening. The Lords eyes were unreadable, but undoubtably this may have made him uncomfortable.

"Gentlemen, if you vud be seated," said Wagner, and the first course of potato soup was served. Potatoes had been one of the things which there had been plenty of in Portsmouth and using it in a soup with some onions made for a very delightful starter.

The conversation turned to the homes of the gentlemen in turn. Yin told his story, which both Hempleman and Connolly seemed very
interested in. When he said he had been aboard a Spanish ship, Connolly's knuckles turned white, but his account seemed to convey that Yin simply wanted out of his little town and to see the world. He had started recounting his tale in both English and German, until Connolly stopped him midway through. "Mister Smythe, I assume you have heard this story before?"

"That I have Sir," perhaps it was the fact he was Yin's Commander, or the fact his eyes had glazed over during the recounting, he was unsure what gave it away.

"Then in the interests of time, Mister Yin if you would be so kind just to recount your story in German, I am capable of understanding I am sure." This did indeed speed up the telling of the tale, and it was not long before the attention turned Connolly.

"Well, as you all know I'm Irish. My family went over around forty years ago during the plantations, so we are protestant thankfully." Wagner shifted uncomfortably. Austria was of course Catholic, whereas the other two members of the Grand Alliance were both Protestant nations. Although Hesse-Kassel was officially Catholic, its place within the Holy Roman Empire required it to be, the larger population there were converting to a branch of Protestantism, whether Lutheran or Calvinist remained to be seen. This obviously caused friction on occasion throughout the Holy Roman Empire, and the Church as a whole, as towns and villages, isolated from the watchful eyes of the Holy See, began to fall away from the *One True Faith*. What caused larger geopolitical problems, however, was the rhetoric given out by the Houses of Westminster. However, the world made strange bedfellows, and this alliance was not about religion. It was about stopping the Bourbons' owning everything from Coruna to Calais.

"We live on a farm, where locals come and work the land for us. We grow a variety of crops, mainly for domestic consumption. Both me, my brother and father are all in the Army, and the wages supplement the farms meagre income." Smythe smiled. He knew that the Crown were giving the members of the Protestant Plantations a stipend for living in Ireland, in an attempt to change the faith of those Catholic Irish.

"My father and I fought at the Battle of the Boyne alongside the late King William III. Obviously, this somewhat increased our favour with his highness. I had been a Lieutenant at the time and was bumped through the ranks quickly. Then with this declaration of war, I've been promoted again to Major." Smythe smiled. Promoted quickly during war, laid off and retired after. Should this be a quick war, there would be lots of land promised out to ex-service men of high enough rank to need paying off. But he had seen action, which would be useful should they come under fire. Most of the troops he had under him were very green, and a Major above them would at least be a steel rod for their nerves to rest on.

As the dinner of lamb and vegetables was served, it was Lord Hempleman's turn to tell his tale. Smythe was having to wait for Yin to recount events of Hempleman's life. From what Yin had gathered, Hempleman's father had been a Knight of Hessen, and during a dynastic struggle, had pinned his colours to the mast of the eventual Landgrave. As a reward, the Landgrave had raised his son, this Hempleman to the position of Lord Hempleman I of Hesse. Along with this, he was given honorary positions. Whilst on deck he had been aggressive, combative and sullen. But below deck, in this private room with three other men, he was charming and pleasant. The wine was being drunk a little too quickly by both Connolly and Hempleman, whereas Yin barely ever drank, and Smythe of course kept to himself.

Eventually, it came round to Smythe. He talked again about his time at sea which Yin had heard before. However, when he first started talking about Padstow, this was something Yin had not heard. "I grew up in the fishing village of Padstow,"

"Is it a large village?" asked Hempleman or words to that effect through Yin's translation.

"No, not at all," replied Smythe, "it's a faithful village, lots of chapels and a lovely church. You either preach, fish or drink. That's Padstow."

"And family?"

"Will and his parents." Smythe indicated to his cousin, "Otherwise, no, I was married." He stopped there. It looked as if Hempleman,

with his lack of life experience was about to blurt out "What happened to her?" but thankfully Wenger had read the room well enough to interject and save his master the embarrassment of such an outburst.

"More wine gentlemen?" he asked, quickly breaking through the momentary silence, and walked over pouring wine into the dinner party's glasses.

Smythe quickly placed his hand over his wine, "No more for me thank you," It was testament to the knowledge which his crew had of him and the esteem in which he was held by them that neither Yin nor Will batted an eyelid at this outcome. Connolly and Hempleman however looked confused.

"But Sir, you have only had a couple of glasses,"

"And that is my limit." Smythe replied. "I'm a member of The Society of Friends, and don't drink heavily, smoke or gamble. So, I fear Wagner will have to fill in as a fourth if you wish to play those cards I can see behind you."

Connolly had the good sense to translate this to Lord Hempleman, who merely smiled. Religious zealotry was commonplace in this world, and the fact that Smythe merely practiced his beliefs and did not force them down others' throats, made him a man who could at least be both worked with and reasoned with. Smythe bade the threesome goodbye as the cards were brought out, put his overcoat on and went to relieve Treen on deck. The summer air was nice on

his skin after being in the relative stuffiness of his own cabin. It was odd to think he would not be using that room for at least the next few weeks, probably longer. He knew he would come to miss his personal space, his privacy aboard ship. He had never had to endure this in all his time on the *Lannwedhenek*, and it was an unwelcome new experience.

"Winds slowed Sir," said Jones from behind him, "We are down to three and a half knots."

"I assume we will still make Saint Austell's Bay by tomorrow?"

"Aye Sir, even at this pace Sir,"

"No worries then. Good evening to you Jones, go get some rest man."

"Aye aye Sir."

As Jones walked away Smythe noticed more grey hairs in that wispy, balding head. "He'll die on the deck that man!" thought Smythe.

The *Lannwedhenek* was making fair time along the southern

coast of England. Nothing really of interest happened that day. The ship was tense, Smythe could feel it, but that was due to a combination of lots of none working men aboard, the army had been told it was not allowed to interfere or assist in the running of the ship, and the knowledge that action was if not imminent then at least highly likely. For the former problem, this would eventually subside. The
crew and their guests would become accustomed to their now more cramped conditions, and the crew would learn to work around the soldiers, who mainly played dice and cards and sat around rather bored. It was, however, the Commanders wash day.

The Commander, and any sailor who wished to be indulged also, could be washed by the pump using salt water. This meant standing naked or in their underclothes, and using some soap, to clean yourself. It caused a stir often for any new members of the crew, and currently, that meant nearly sixty people, when you took into account the army troops, newish crew members and of course the Lord Hempleman. Smythe washed his face and spat out the salt water. It was cold. But it was highly refreshing.

"Coming into the bay, Sir!" shouted Jenkins from aloft. Despite not needing to, Jenkins often volunteered to go aloft, and Smythe wondered whether the man actually enjoyed being over the ship, having a birds eye view of her.

Smythe towelled off and ran through the deck, still half naked, to check the progress of his ship. It had indeed come into Saint Austell's bay, with the small fishing villages dotting around the waters edge.

"Send a gig to West Porthmear, see if the catch is in. Tell them any excess at that they have we will buy off them, and if possible, load it into the gig."

The orders were clear enough, and Midshipman Gabriel took them
along with the oarsmen which followed. Lord Hempleman, though not a seaman could clearly tell that they were anchored

in a sheltered bay due to the ships change in fluctuations came up on deck.

"My Lord," began Smythe, unsure how to phrase this delicately enough that he would not be offended, but stern enough that he would undoubtably follow the orders, "My Lord, I request that whilst we are in this bay you do not wear your uniform."

It was an odd request on the face of it, and as Wagner translated this, both he and Lord Hempleman's face were contorted in a strange confusion rather than annoyance. "And why is that?" eventually came back the response.

"I have orders to ensure that nobody knows you or the Army are aboard," Smythe said slowly, allowing Wagner to translate, "and a foreign uniform would be somewhat of a giveaway Sir."

Hempleman seemed displeased at this request, however Wagner must have thought it was a reasonable enough request, as he continued to speak to his master in a mild manner. Hempleman was frustrated, his eyes gave that away, but he relented, Wagner clearly making the point that although Smythe had used the word "request" he was certainly not just asking.

West Porthmear's fishing fleet was that of around nine boats. Six had made catches that morning, but one had already gone into Saint Austell. Another one was needed to feed the village itself.

That left four fishing boats more than happy to sell their pilchards to men in naval uniforms who guaranteed to pay. They managed to acquire some butter too, so fried pilchards would be on the menu this evening. They had managed to get hold of some of last years cyder too, although it had fermented well.

Jones had managed to get the portside gun crew to put on a jig, with men playing the fiddles and dancing. Songs were being sung, songs which were fun, songs which made the Midshipmen blush. Simple songs such as *hearts of* oak. Another such song started with the lines of;

When I was just a little lad, or so me mammy told me,
That if I didn't kiss the girls, me lips would go all mouldy!

It was a sight to behold. Both Connolly and Hempleman, despite having dined with the Commander the previous evening, had joined them too, and in the warm summer air and with the cyder flowing, the night was shaping up to be a good one.

There were a few sore heads the next morning aboard the *Lannwedhenek*, especially those of Potter and Connolly. They were clearly still not used to the sea moving the ship as they slept, and with a stomach full of cyder and fish, Smythe knew at least one of them part way through the night had lost a large amount this.

The ships bell rang out to mark the fore-noon watch. There was a

loud groan from one of the officers' bunks, which caused Smythe to smile. This is why he did not drink to excess. He was feeling rather smug with himself, and then he gathered himself. Pride was a sin after all. They pulled out of the bay in the around two, another couple of days out of Brest.

"Keep our speed constant Mister Jones if you'd be so kind, it would be better for our guests and the ship as a whole."

"We could get there slightly faster Sir, if you wished?"

"No, Mister Jones, I don't want us anchored just outside a French port for longer than needed thank you."

A ship sailing past was not in itself suspicious. A ship stationary in the water outside of Brest, however, would indicate something more interesting to the French fleet. Even if a ship of his Most Catholic Majesty Louis XIV were not to harbour out to have a look at this small British vessel just off the horizon, trading and fishing vessels which also used Brest would be able to report daily on the goings on of the *Lannwedhenek*.

"Aye aye Sir," came Jones' response. Knowing that the speed had to remain constant put more pressure on the old Coxswain, but he was more than up to the task. "Get a man aloft with the wind gauge!" he shouted out, and a couple of men clambered up the rigging to be in position. The wind gauge would inform Jones how much sail to set. The *Lannwedhenek* could easily go much faster than its current speed, around three to four times faster in fact, but

Jones agreed with his Commander, that a slow and steady pace would suit best. It gave an air of calmness to the ship, and those aboard, both normal crew who knew they need not rush too much in their duties and therefore be more consistent and diligent with them.

They passed The Lizard at around midnight of the tenth of July, having not left Saint Austell bay until mid-afternoon with the tide, and the constant three knots was being safely kept by Jones.

"Take us a wide route round if you please Mister Jones, make it look like we are following the trade routes."

"Aye aye Sir," replied Jones. It was to appear, for as long as possible, that the *Lannwedhenek* was simply going on a normal run without incidence. Anyone who got close enough might notice the men sleeping on deck, but during the summer months this was not altogether uncommon, as the heat below deck became unbearable.

It was the morning of the eleventh of July when they were finally out of sight of any English land, the Sicily isles being the last thing to be observed. "Only half a day until Brest Sir," said Treen.

"Yes," said Smythe, seemingly rather distracted. "Mister Treen, would you be so kind as to come below to the charts with me, Mister Jones, your opinion would be appreciated too."

Although they were used to being consulted, they were unsure what the Commander could possibly want now. They had completed their voyage and arrived in good time at the rendezvous. The chart this time was a different chart, a more detailed map of the port of Brest and the surrounding waters.

"Admiral says he's due in at a minimum of four days. Sitting outside the largest naval port this side of the French nation is bound to attract attention. I would like your opinion on this idea. We sail in a figure of eight. First south, round and back up to this point here," he pointed on the map their approximate location, "then north, again around, and back to our position here."

"I thought the Admiral said to stay put?" asked Treen, not wanting to show any open opposition to his Commanders plan, but remind him of his duties.

"I worry that at most Sir, for a couple of days of sailing we will be away from our post as requested," said Jones, also clearly apprehensive about the suggested plan from his Commander.

"A spotted stationary ship is clearly doing something," said Smythe, clearly feeling that his idea was not being considered by his subordinates, "But a ship following the trade routes south and north is unlikely to do so."

"I think it will still look suspicious, Sir," said Jones, who clearly had not been won over by this reasoning. Smythe stood in the Lieutenants berth and sighed.

"Very well," he said, "then we stay put. Mister Treen and Mister Jones, I have a new task for you then."

"What's that?" asked Treen, looking rather uncomfortable at the

fact he had so recently disagreed with his Commander that the task would be very unpleasant. Jones was not however worried, that was not Smythe's style and he knew it.

"You have the pleasure of keeping the crew occupied until the fleet arrives," said Smythe with a smile.

Jones inwardly groaned. Maybe it would be an unpleasant task after all.

CHAPTER TEN

Rooke was tired. There was no other word for it. He was tired in every way. He wanted his ships filling with the required stores. He wanted the army to come up with an actual plan. Currently it seemed that sail to Cadiz and see what happened, was the extent of Ormonde's plan.

He was looking over the charts for what felt like the thousandth time. He was equally frustrated with the Navy, who seemed to think that this escapade would be highly fruitful, despite all the conflicting interests. The dignitaries for example, felt that only the smallest military intervention should be used to subdue the locals. Whereas Rooke understood that either a full military expedition was needed, or else the whole plan would fail. The higher ups in the Admiralty however, had decided to slam right into the middle, not sending enough troops to allow for victory, but equally sending enough that it would inevitably be Rooke's fault should the venture fail.

Then, there was the problems with passing Brest. The entire Atlantic fleet of the French was probably stationed there, with hundreds of guns to pass by, and a sheltered port for the enemy to retreat to should it not go well for them. The French could afford to lose some ships in that fight, delaying the English and the people she escorted would be enough. But delay was not an option for the Grand Alliance. The Bourbon's were already consolidating their

power in Spain, and a Papal assent to the confirmation of Philip, was making this an ever more difficult prospect.

A knock at his cabin door brought back Rooke from his considerations of the Geo-politic of Europe. "Enter," he said, as calmly as ever. His steward entered the room, with his dinner and what looked like dispatches. It was not uncommon, even though he had no need to, for Rooke's steward to knock prior to entering. "Mutton Sir," he said calmly, "and your new orders Sir."

Rooke sat at his desk and smiled at the dinner his steward had prepared for him. He knew it would be a long time before he received a side of mutton whilst out at sea. The mint gravy which it had been cooked in smelt divine. "What are the orders?" he asked whilst tucking his napkin into his shirt.

"No idea Sir, they are your orders," replied the Steward. Rooke looked suspiciously at his young steward. Yes officially no one was to open orders except the person it was addressed to, but that rarely happened. More often than not, by the time it arrived at the officer due to read them, it had been read by at least three or four subordinates. Some out of curiosity, some out of boredom, some out of a need to know where they were heading, from a logistical point of view. Did they need that overcoat that their wives or mothers had packed them, or could that be pawned for something more useful? Some may look through the eyes of espionage, but this was few and far between. Spies, where they did exist, were

pencil pushers and desk men rather than serving soldiers. It was easier for those men to get information back to their masters than whilst stationed on a ship in the middle of the ocean.

"Well, lets 'av' 'em then," said Rooke, and the dispatches were opened.

To: Admiral Rooke, Mediterranean fleet, Portsmouth, HMS Royal Sovereign

New orders issued Tenth of July by Thomas Herbert, 8th Earl of Pembroke, First Lord of the Admiralty, Greenwich.

Good afternoon George, I hope these orders find you in good health. You are to venture from Portsmouth at the next available time that the tides allow, head round the coast of Spain, and meet with

Prince George of Hesse at Cape Saint Vincent. He is currently to our knowledge, discussing our terms with Dom Pedro II about his potential involvement with the Grand Alliance. He is further meeting with dignitaries from Spain, who are there to listen to the Hapsburg claim. From there you will advance on the Spanish Port of Cadiz, ideally capturing her from her Spanish masters in order to establish a Mediterranean port for her Majesty, the Queen Anne.

You are to use any force you deem necessary but wherever possible, you are to defer to the suggestions and requests of Prince George of Hesse, as this is his diplomatic mission. You are in command entirely of the fleet, and the actions of such are at your discretion. Lord Ormonde will be in charge of the forces once they land at the port of Cadiz. You are to assist him in the landing of any troops he requires and further support him with any covering cannon fire you think would be appropriate without endangering the fleet. Once there you are to hold Cadiz for as long as you think is possible, ideally long enough to establish a permanent base there. Should this prove impossible, the value of the fleet is larger than that of the potential of a Port in the region, and you should return to Portsmouth prior to the Winter storms coming in.
I know you will do your duty in line of that which has become expected of you. I expect acknowledgement of these orders in writing returning to me, and to hear news of your departure equally quickly.
Yours

Thomas Herbert, 8ᵗʰ Earl of Pembroke.
P.S. Congratulations on the birth of your son.

So, it was official. The ships and men he had at his disposal were to sail as soon as the tide turned. Around fourteen thousand troops, along with horses, supplies and God knows what else was to leave Portsmouth immediately. The usual feeling of dread mixed with excitement filled him. It would not be the fastest convoy, on the
contrary, the convoy would probably be limited to four or five

knots in order to keep cohesion.

He set about to write his reply. A simple "Read and understood," would have probably sufficed, but he had known Thomas for years as they had both served in Parliament since the mid 1680's. He had been kind enough to congratulate him on the birth of his son, another nice touch of their Kinship.

Thomas Herbert, 8th Earl of Pembroke
Your orders are read and understood. The health of the fleet is the main consideration of this mission. I will therefore report back to you upon the engagement in Cadiz with my opinion on the operation as it stands.
Secondly, I thank you for your kind words over the birth of my son, a joyous occasion all round.
Your friend, Sir George Rooke.

It was a polite enough letter, to an old friend whilst remaining professional in nature. He probably should write also to his wife, they had only been married a short time, and now she was alone, with their son. Due to the orders, although now in July, he would not, unless a complete failure of the mission, see her or his child until at least the winter. He may be home for Christmas, how lovely.

"Richards!" he roared, expecting the young Lieutenant to be about.

He was surprised to find he was not, and it took around twenty minutes to find the young man, and a further ten for him to arrive at the Admirals cabin.

"Sir?" he said, his usual politeness not escaping him despite his clearly flustered face. His rosy-red cheeks, and his shortness of breath indicated he had been running, probably along the length of this Hundred-and-eight gunner.

"Send up the signals," he said simply, allowing the young man to catch his breath. "We sail for Brest and Cadiz today, all army and stores need to be on by this evening, have I made myself clear?"

"Crystal clear Sir," replied Richards. "I'll get a Midshipman on the signals at once."

Butler was frustrated. His sea chest had got wet during the embarkation of his effects. This boat seemed to sway fretfully, and his stomach was not feeling fantastic. His cloak had got caught on a loose nail, and he had raised the issue with Rooke, resulting in Rooke looking at him as if he were a mad man. The cloak was extraordinarily expensive, he would be meeting up with a Prince after all and must be dressed well. Rooke seemed to think it was all trivial, but it most certainly was not.

"Where is the books on speaking German?" he asked his footman abruptly.

"Somewhere in the boxes my Duke," came the man's terrified response. "I have not had chance to unpack them yet. I was trying to get the china out for dinner."

"The cheek of it also," replied Butler. He was still frustrated at being told by Rooke that he would have to provide his own food unless he wanted the same as the common sailor. Not even fresh meat, but some brined beef, sat in the salty mixture for weeks on end. No thank you.

A knock at the door saw a young Midshipman shaking but stood perfectly to attention.

"Yes?" asked Butler, trying not to be impolite to the young man.

"Excuse me Sir," Butler looked furiously at the young man, "I mean Duke. Sir George Rooke would like to invite you to dine with him and the officers tonight," said the young man, looking more frightened now he was waiting for the reply from the Commander of the army. Butler looked at him for a moment, and then finally smiled.

"Yes, that sounds lovely, tell the Admiral I will be there promptly at seven o clock,"

"Excuse me Sir. But dinner is at six." Again, the young Midshipman looked awkwardly around waiting for his superior's response.

Butler forced a smile at the young man, "Very well, I shall see them promptly at *six* o clock. That's what aboard this ship?"

"Four bells, Sir, of the Dogwatch," said the young Midshipman, growing in confidence from this little exchange. He saluted both

Butler, and his footman, looked unsure of himself and left the cabin.

"Poor little lad," muttered the footman to himself, "probably never met a Duke before." This was possible, but his commanding officer was a member of Parliament also. Midshipmen were also often young men starting off in the service with patronages above them pushing them in the right direction. No doubt his father was a Knight or else a Lord of some description.

"Dinner sounds promising however!" said Butler, seeming more pleased that he had been invited to dinner with the Admiral of the fleet, and get chance to rub shoulders with some real seamen. His previous luncheon with the Admiral had been a private affair, just the two of them, and although the food had been only passable, he had enjoyed himself. No doubt that would happen again tonight.

"Yes, I suspect it will Sir," said the footman, rather unimpressed. It would make no difference to him who his Duke ate with, it would still be his fault should the food not be up to the standard he expected, and he had a rather sneaking suspicion that nothing aboard this ship would be to his master's expectations. "Would you like to have your nap now Sir, or a walk on deck?". Butler stood at this suggestion.

"I shall take a walk on deck, there are officers of my army I wish to talk to about the outcomes of these engagements." Butler was not a foreigner to war. In his younger days he had fought against the Duke of Monmouth in his short-lived rebellion, and alongside his

late Highness William III at the Battle of the Boyne. He had in fact disembarked with him at Carrickfergus during the war.

But details were never his strong point. He was part of what some at court called the "Tally Ho!" brigade, throwing themselves into the fight rather than thinking anything through previously. It was probably the reason that Rooke had been given overall command of the expedition rather than him.

The wind was gentle in the summer air as they pulled out of Portsmouth on the fifteenth of July, pulling them down the channel. It would be clear to anyone in France that something was going on, as approximately fifty ships of varying sizes and styles, and an additional twenty some ships from the Dutch were sailing with them. But unless the Atlantic fleet was ready and fully supplied in Brest, it was now too late to do anything. It was around a two-hundred-and-fifty-mile ride from Cherbourg, where they would first be seen, to Brest. This would, even on horses at full speed, and swapping horses and riders at every post office and turnpike, still take over a day to reach Brest. To fully fill ships, even if they merely intended to just sail out, fight and return to port, would take at least a week if they were empty. It all came down to simple preparedness. Were the French ready for a war, ready to sail out and fight, or would they let England's Navy sail straight past her.

As the sun began to set on the first day, Rooke and his officers, along with the officers of the Army, were in his cabin, eating the delight of dishes supplied by Rooke for this occasion. He had wanted to show the best of himself, and what his crew could offer should the opportunity arise, and the smoked pork, roast lamb and a rib of beef was better than most of the young officers would receive in their lives. The table was long and thin, made up of several smaller tables pushed together, and Rooke and Butler took each end, as the two highest ranking officers.

Rooke smiled to himself. He had put on a fine meal for around twelve officers within the service, he could not be called cheap on this dinner that was for certain. The rib of beef alone had been more than some men spend on dinners in a week. He had, for the first time in a while, had chance to speak to his officers, talk about personal matters, such as his young family or the ongoing war at large, rather than being specifically being forced to think about his mission. The usual toasts were done,

"To the health of the Queen!", "To the *Royal Sovereign!*", "To the health of the Army!", "Death to the Spanish!" and other such toasts which were done by naval officers in these times.

"The convoy is making good time Sir," stated Captain Dilkes towards the end of the meal.

"Yes," said Rooke calmly, "We should be round Brest in the next two or three days.

"We can relieve that little fishing boat then," smiled Dilkes.

"All ships have equal value in my service," said Rooke, quietly but firmly. Richards smiled. Without the "little boats" that many post Captains regarded as futile, the messages, the lookouts, the fetching and carrying would have to be done by these larger ships. Slower. Less agile. More work. It was funny how quickly Post Captains seemed to forget the value of the sloops, brigs and ketches they may have once served on.

"How is Smythe doing?" asked Richards.

"As far as I know he's fine. I know he will have taken a more scenic route, hopefully he had the sense to stay on the English side of the channel. Otherwise, I expect we shall see him in around three days."

"Thought you said we would make it in two?" asked Dilkes.

"We could," admitted Rooke, "But arriving in the dark might spook a *little boat*," he said sarcastically, and Dilkes smiled. It was not a formal scalding, but enough for him to remember his place in this command.

At the other end of the table, Butler was also cheerful about the action ahead. "It's as I said to Billy, King William should I say, before his death, we need something in the Med to hold the Diego's off." Whether he was close enough to the previous king to call him "Billy" remained to be seen, but the officers around him were hanging on his words.

"Was he a good man?" asked one of his subordinates.

"Yes, he was in his own way," replied Butler. He was clearly enjoying holding court with his officers, even if he was certain some of them were barely listening.

"What do you think of the mission?" asked another.

"Oh, I expect the Diego's to run as soon as we land a man. They never stand up to anyone do they? God only knows how they took so much land in the Americas, must be the Indians are even worse." The evening was wearing on, and Rooke stood to speak.

"Gentlemen, it is my pleasure to welcome you aboard the *Royal Sovereign*." The usual murmur of assent was given from the naval officers, whereas the army nodded appreciatively. "This ship, no, this fleet, will be remembered I am sure! But not without sacrifice." The mood shifted slightly. Rooke's face was ruddy with the drink he had consumed already, and some of the men looked onward, wondering if their Admiral was having a moment of spiritual awakening to his profession. Children would do that to you. "We dine tonight knowing that we may not all dine together in the future. We will be in Cadiz around mid-August all being well. Some of you may not see Christmas," it was a very sombre speech, Richards thought. What on earth was Rooke planning? "That being said, we are here now. So. Another DRINK!" he yelled. There was a loud cheer from all assembled as more wine and rum flowed as the officers cheered. "It would be a successful voyage" thought Butler, as he looked at his counterpart in the Navy. "Bloody miserable
speech though," he also thought.

Heads were heavy aboard the *Royal Sovereign* the next morning amongst the officers and the crew knew it. Rooke was sure the crew were intentionally dropping more objects on the wooden decks to make that *thud* which hungover was painful every time. It was a crew's way of repaying, what must have been an inevitably late and drunken night for the officers. Unlike the route Rooke hoped the *Lannwedhenek* took, the *Royal Sovereign* sailed proudly down the middle of the channel. This was to ensure he was approximately in the middle of the fleet, allowing him to see as many of his ships as possible.

"Who heads up the fleet?" asked Rooke to no one in particular.

The midshipman around all pulled out their glasses to look, trying to win the favour of the respected Admiral.

"*HMS Mary*, Sir!" replied a particularly squeaky young midshipman. "Captained by, hang on, Edward Hobson Sir,"

Hobson was relatively new to the service, not even serving during the War of the Two Kings. He had been a Lieutenant on his uncle's ship, and his uncle was a man in good standing, and was one of the highest ranked officers in the fleet currently under Rooke's command, all be it aboard another ship.

"Signal to the *Mary!*" said Rooke with energy, "*Compliments of Admiral Rooke. Keep in the lead, and signal once sight of the Lannwedhenek has been made. Signal to make contact with the Lannwedhenek in name of the fleet.*" It was a simple enough instruction. Two of the midshipmen were rummaging through the signal books to make sure they had the correct flags. Rooke debated shouting at the young men. They had been sat in Spithead for months, why in God's name had they not learned the bloody signals? But he breathed out and relaxed. They were young, they would learn, as all midshipmen did, it was easier to put the time in to remember them than to have to look them up. Besides time at sea would increase their effectiveness, real experience was invaluable compared to book learning anyway.

"Response Sir!" replied the same midshipman, "Give me a moment," he asked a little too casually, and remembering himself quickly added, "Sir! Erm, *Read and understood, will remain in lead of fleet. Hobson.*" At least he had a Captain who was diligent in his responses. This expedition might actually be a success after all.

"Oh, I say look, pretty flags, how quaint!" remarked Ormonde from behind Rooke. Perhaps not so successful.

CHAPTER ELEVEN

The *Lannwedhenek* was sitting just outside the port of Brest on the eighteenth of July. They had been sat there for several days now, and tensions were starting to run high. Smythe was frustrated by this. They had not been doing firing drills, the usual practice to keep the crews busy, for fear of being thought as too aggressive. They had been doing sail races with the crews, and races up the rigging and other such competitions, but after four days, the excitement was starting to wear off. His suggestion of sailing in the figure of eight would have kept the men busy for at least a couple of days, but alas, his subordinates, although not able to overrule him, had clearly stated that they disapproved of the idea.

"Dam this infernal fog!" roared Smythe out of frustration. The fog they had found themselves in was as thick as custard, and it would prove difficult to see anything twenty feet away in this, let alone the fleet they were meant to be looking out for, or the fleet they were meant to be meeting up with. Most concerningly of all however, was the fact that they may be simply bumped into by a random French ship of any size.

They had, in the last couple of days spotted the odd French fisherman or merchant ship going to and from the channel and following the trade winds. It was not uncommon, especially in times of war, to simply try to avoid one another, honour being that if close enough to engage, you should, but by active avoidance,

smaller vessels could carry on with their business uninterrupted. But in this fog, the chances of being accidentally engaged were much higher.

"Mister Jones, you've served a while," said Smythe, trying to engage his Coxswain in discussion about their predicament, "What do you suggest we do about this fog?"

"Well Sir, to announce ourselves we could do that gun practice you've been after." That was not a bad idea. No balls in the practice obviously, but firing a few blank charges would, at least give notice to their presence. Most ships would then simply avoid their position.

"What about any French ships who notice a small sloop doing firing practise off Brest?" They probably would not see the *Lannwedhenek* firing her guns, but they would hear her. Nine guns firing in order, it would not take long for the Brest fleet or garrison to work out what was happening.

"We fire in groups of four Sir. Make it look like we are a merchant ship," said Jones proudly, pleased with himself for coming up with such an imaginative idea.

"Won't work," chimed up Jenkins from behind him, idling away at the tiller.

"Excuse me?" said Smythe, rather frustrated that Jenkins had been listening at all to their conversation.

"It won't work," said Jenkins, as calm as ever. "Merchant ships might run out the guns, but they never do firing practice. They only carry enough shot to do exactly what they feel they need to. No merchant ship is going to laden itself down with additional gunpowder when it can carry more cotton or sugar. You're thinking too much like a Navy man Jones," then adding as an afterthought "Sir."

"And you're still a bloody smuggler at heart!" replied Jones in frustration, but Smythe knew Jenkins was right. It would be more suspicious that a merchant vessel was using her guns either way, whether in practice or not. That may cause a ship to come investigate, which would mean a firefight between the *Lannwedhenek* and whatever Brest sent out to meet her. No, it was best to stay put, but how on earth to remain undetectable.

"I have an idea Sir," chimed up Jenkins, who clearly had been leading the conversation to this point.

"Well?" snapped Jones, clearly frustrated with his younger

subordinate. Jenkins had of course been talking to Smythe, but he replied nevertheless when addressed by Jones.

"Yellow fever," he said simply, and continued to mess around with the stationary tiller, despite the fact the ship was anchored.

"What?" said Smythe, evidently confused, but now it was Jones turn to smile in understanding.

"Signal for quarantine," said Jones.

There was nothing worse on a ship, than sickness. The close quarters in which men lived caused disease to rip through a crew

faster than a cannonball. No ship's Captain would allow his crew to actively encounter a ship which had illness on it. It did not matter what the illness was. Just that there was illness would be enough.

"Midshipman Abraham!" shouted Smythe, finally catching on to the suggestion which Jenkins had provided.

"Sir?"

"Run up the signal for smallpox," Even though each nation had its own set of signal flags, every country knew the sickness signals of the other nations. Even if a French first rate came sailing past, they would not risk engagement. A boarding party from the sloop, even a suicidal one, might cause the smallpox aboard their vessel. They would not risk it for such a small prize as a sloop.

"Sir," came the voice of Treen from across the ship.

"Yes?" replied Smythe.

"There's a ship coming from the portside."

Great. Just fantastic. They had been here for around four days without incidence, and now, today, when the fog had come from nowhere to be thicker than he had seen in years, and to top it off, a ship was coming. He would have to explain why there were so many men above deck, why they were sitting stationary in the water just outside one of the largest French ports.

"How big?" asked Smythe, feeling like a small child in the simplicity of his question.

"Not sure Sir,"

"From?"

"Not sure Sir,"

Well, that was lots of useful information. Smythe was becoming irritable, and he knew it. He was a man of action. That was why he never made a good fisherman. But to be told there was a ship approaching to portside and have no information about it was rather annoying for anyone.

French voices could be heard however, coming across from the ship as it approached. Smythe had an idea.

"Monsieur!" he yelled, to the confusion of his crew, both due to drawing attention to himself and the fact he was speaking in French.

"Oui?" came back the reply from the French vessel. Judging by how low down the reply had been it was a small trading brig they were dealing with.

"Parles-tu Anglais?" he said in his best French.

"Yes," a clear distain in his voice, "What do 'ou want?"

"Send a doctor!" Smythe yelled in a panicked voice, "We need a doctor, we have pox aboard this ship!" The panic in his voice seemed almost real. Jones had to commend his Commander for his idea, Treen however looked horrified, not knowing that they were completing a ruse.

"POX!" he exclaimed, causing a murmur of confusion amongst the

crew, Smythe wished he could silence his first Lieutenant.

"Yes, Mister Treen, Pox," said Smythe, trying to regain control of the crew, "Please Monsieur send help!"

"Oui, Oui!" he shouted back, as their ships continued to pass each other by. Smythe was sure that the Brig had turned a couple of points away from the *Lannwedhenek* after finding out the news. Treen came running up to Smythe, red faced and panicked. "Pox!" he yelled again.

"Calm yourself Mister Treen," said Smythe calmly, which had no effect whatsoever.

"We have pox aboard, oh, my God, the signal flags, it's true," the colour drained from Treen face as the realisation set in.

"Calm yourself Mister Treen," repeated Smythe calmly. He was trying to covey there was nothing to worry about whilst not specifically saying it, the brig might still be in earshot.

"We have pox aboard, I bet it's one of the new crew, can't be one of the old crew they didn't have any shore time. Oh my, is it Yin? Is it an officer?" Treen was looking more and more panicked by the moment.

"Mister Treen, calm yourself or I will be forced to sedate you." said Smythe sternly, "We do not have pox aboard this ship, relax."

"But you just said…"

"And by this afternoon, all of Brest will know that the ship which has been stationed outside of the port for the last couple of days
has the pox. No ship will come near for the next two weeks."

"But. Oh!" finally the reason of the rouse came to him. "But isn't that?"

"Questionable? Yes, and it may backfire, no doubt. But the other option was to have a ship sail as close as that with no explanation for our presence. At least now it just seems like we are waiting out some of our quarantine period."

"I was actually thinking illegal Sir, but yes, questionable will do." The four men, Smythe, Treen, Jones and Jenkins all smiled. Midshipman Abraham was trying not to laugh from behind them, having run the signals up himself.

The *Mary* rounded the tip of France in the fog on the morning of the eighteenth of July. Edward Hobson was standing on his quarterdeck staring into the grey mists. "Damn this infernal fog," he muttered to himself. He could not see the rest of the fleet behind him, and he sure as hell could not see the *Lannwedhenek* in front of him. It was a little sloop, less than a third of the size of his Third-rate, and it would be damned near impossible to locate in this weather.

"Let's hope the sun burns through it," he muttered, his mood not improving as the day continued. The fog was starting to look thinner. He ate his breakfast upon the quarterdeck, choosing to stay up on the deck to allow for better vision of the conditions. He had

made the young man's error of not keeping his personal stocks high on ship, feeling there would always have been time to refill them so long as he was in port. He then, almost predictably, had not found time to restock his stores, and was now running out of jam. It was not the end of the world. Just rather frustrating when he knew other Captains would be enjoying that for weeks to come.

"Pull in the sails a touch," he said, "Lets slow down if we are heading into unknown waters." He had not received all clear still from the *Lannwedhenek,* nor could he see the fleet behind him. Slowing down would at least bring him back in touch with the main fleet, and he could signal for further instructions.

"Ship spotted off the starboard bow!"

At least they were spotting something. Hobson jumped to his feet, searching for the ship which had been called. His crew, or at least the lookouts knew they were looking for a ship off the bow.

"They have signals up Sir!" shouted down the lookout. "It's pox Sir!" There was a genuine fear in the voice of the lookout. Everyone aboard ship knew what that meant. Regardless of nation, no crew wanted to lose out to an invisible foe.

"Keep your distance at the tiller if you please!" shouted Hobson. That was not something he wanted to face if at all possible. "Send up the signal, asking for clarification of the illness please!" It was not uncommon for ships to use the signal for pox as a catch all for all illnesses. It may not be as serious as feared. The midshipmen

aboard sent up the signal as quickly as they could. Every second counted.

Aboard the *Lannwedhenek*, Smythe was pacing his deck, as he often did during times of inactivity. It had been an interesting morning, with the encounter with French brig, and now, there was nothing to do but continue to wait for the fleet to arrive.

"Should we take down the quarantine flag Sir?" asked Treen, seeing no reason for it to remain in place. Clearly, he was still unsure of the legality of this action.

"Leave it for now," said Smythe, "I don't want to arouse suspicion from and Frenchmen watching." It was a valid point. If another merchant vessel sailed past them this afternoon, how would it look if their quarantine was magically over after less than a day.

"Sails off the portside stern Sir!" shouted a lookout aloft.

"That must be the fleet," said Smythe calmly. "Have they spotted us?" he shouted up.

"I think so Sir." He said, "They seem to be turning away from us,"

That did not make much sense. They were turning towards Brest, which just seemed foolish for any British ship.

"Any idea who it is?" he asked.

"Can't make out Sir, I can see the ensign is one of ours though!" Well, that was reassuring that at least it most likely was the fleet. From his lower vantage point, Smythe could see the sails and the

masts of the ship, clearly giving the *Lannwedhenek* a wide berth.

"There's movement on the signalling flags Sir!"

"What are they saying?"

"*Confirm ailment?*" said the man aloft, somewhat confused. Not everyone on the crew knew what Smythe had done, he must have been one of the men down below at that point. Smythe thought about how to respond. It would not be an easy thing to explain, but he knew the longer he delayed, the more danger that ship was in travelling toward Brest.

"Ask who they are," said Smythe to Abraham.

The signals went up from the *Lannwedhenek*, and shortly the reply was being relayed down to Smythe.

"*Mary* Sir, 60 gunner, Captained by Captain Hobson," said Abraham. They had got close enough now, and the fog had continued to reduce, allowing for visibility on the deck rather than aloft.

"Send my compliments to Captain Hobson and inform him that there is nothing to fear in terms of sickness on this ship."

There was a pause, whilst the rather complicated signals were sent up. Some parts of the message had to be spelt out, causing more delay. Smythe could feel the eyes of the Captain of the *Mary* burning into the signals he was sending up.

"Response Sir. *Confirm, no illness aboard.*"

"Reply in the affirmative" came Smythe's simple reply. He knew that this would cause some confusion about his previous signal.

"*Report required. Is fleet clear to pass?*"

"Again, reply in the affirmative," came Smythe. He felt like this could be done quicker. The *Mary,* upon reading this response began to sail back towards the *Lannwedhenek*, and more importantly away from the port of Brest. The *Mary* was signalling now, presumably to fleet currently out of sight to the *Lannwedhenek*, and Smythe could start to see the individual men aboard this vessel. They were more clinical in their movements than the crew of the *Lannwedhenek*, more efficient. One day, his crew would be as effective, he was sure.

The *Mary* came about on the Portside of the *Lannwedhenek*. The sixty-gun Third-rate ship of the line towered over the little sloop, seemingly protecting them, like a big brother looking over his younger sibling.

"Commander Smythe, I presume?" shouted Hobson from the deck of the *Mary*. "What was with the Pox signal Sir?"

"Deterrent for the French Sir," said Smythe, he was unsure how Hobson would take this, "Are we to wait here Sir?"

"Yes, until the Admiral is here, we are to wait," came the response, "Good thinking on the Pox, no French ship will come near here until it's too late to stop us. Well done."

Smythe smiled to himself. Although he did not crave the accolades of other men, being told by the Captain of a much larger ship he had done well did make him feel like he was finally becoming

accepted by the others.

Slowly through the day, more and more ships arrived around Brest. By mid-afternoon, the signals were given by the *Royal Sovereign* to move on. They were to sail in a loose formation across the Bay of Biscay, following the trade winds as they did. It would be another week at least before they reached their next stop off point, Oporto.

Portugal was nominally neutral so far in this otherwise Pan-European war. Even in the Great Northern War, the two sides were being aligned, through trade and politics, with the wider war too. Both sides, the Bourbons and the Hapsburgs, were sending dignitaries to the court of Pedro II, trying to sway him one way or the other. He had however, continued to allow ships of all nations to restock in the ports of Portugal, seemingly wishing to profit from the war, rather than enter into it directly. It was thought a show of force was the most likely thing to change his mind, although currently Prince George of Hesse, the man they were going to collect on route to Cadiz, was trying his best for the Grand Alliance.

The sailing down to Oporto was uneventful, the ships' crew being kept busy as ever when she was sailing, with continued maintenance and improvements to the running of the ship being made regularly. The *Lannwedhenek* whilst in Oporto, was used, alongside other smaller vessels in the fleet, as a ship which was tasked with fetching and carrying, as it could go closer into the harbour.

The harbour at Oporto was a deep one, which could easily house the third, second and first raters in Rooke's fleet. However, it would appear that Pedro, despite wishing to profit from the Anglo-Dutch fleet, also did not wish to allow several large warships into one of his main ports. Therefore, the major ships of the fleet were forced to sit outside the port, whilst the sloops, and smaller vessels were tasked with bringing the requested supplies.

Hobson was able, and was elated about it, to get some lime marmalade from one of the vendors in Oporto. Smythe restocked his larder too, getting some hens for eggs that they could keep on board. Rooke was having meetings with his Captains whenever he could and had let slip that they could be in for the long haul after this.

They stayed outside Oporto for a couple of weeks, as per the instructions from Prince George who was still in the court in Lisbon. This was music to the ears of the common sailors, even those who did not go ashore. Fresh food was supplied, contraband like wine and booze, extra tobacco and even livestock could be found on the shores of northern Portugal. The merchants of the town were becoming richer and richer by the day. And for those who could go ashore, there were other pleasures to be purchased. To any upstanding English officer, they would not be caught in the brothels and houses of disrepute, but in reality, many of the men who went ashore would aim to be in them as discretely

as possible. As ever when a force was ashore, problems arose, and Rooke had to intervene to prevent several duels from occurring.

But whenever the rank and file were happy, that meant large bills for the Admiralty. The longer they were sat in port, the more money would be burned through. England, with her Caribbean Empire, made her one of the richer partners in the alliance and they were already helping to fund the war in Europe. Now, they were having to give promissory notes to their Portuguese suppliers.

Discipline in general began to break down. Men who normally would not move without orders were beginning to grumble and moan, orders were being completed slowly or else with complaint. Even the officers of the army were becoming restless, being stuck as they were on the ships, when dry land was ever so close.

"When will we get those bloody orders to sail?" asked the crews every day. And every day Rooke would be given orders stating that until Prince George was ready, the fleet would wait.

CHAPTER TWELVE

On the tenth of August, the orders finally came. The fleet would sail south and meet off Cape Saint Vincent with the *Adventure*, around the twentieth of August, and then sail onto Cadiz. It was a simple enough plan, and after a day of ensuring every store was as full as it could be, they set sail around midday on the thirteen.

Rooke was apprehensive still about the plan. They were now late into August and had been in Oporto for a good couple of weeks. Despite *officially* no Englishman or Dutchman was meant to discuss their orders with anyone, he was not stupid. He knew someone would have talked at some point. Whether it was with merchants in idle discussion, in pillow talk with the prostitutes or as an offer for a *discount* on something, the news would have got out. Even if they assumed it did not get out until a week in, it was less than a week's ride to Cadiz, which meant the news of the fleet was already there.

Like he often did, he paced his cabin, with the charts spread across the desk. The most prominent chart changed, depending on the stage of the expedition. Today's chart was the coastline of Cape Saint Vincent. He had not sailed these waters for a long time, normally choosing to stay further away from the coastline and with the trade winds, this was a newer experience.

He would meet with the Prince, it would add another ship to his fleet at any rate, and then the short sail down to Cadiz and then what? His chart of Cadiz showed a fortified port, with a clear bay.

There were places to land certainly, but far away from the main base, and that would cause different issues. No, he was not sure about Cadiz at all. But he had his orders and that was that.

He went onto his deck to get some air, having been cooped up in his cabin all morning. They were only around a day away from Cape Saint Vincent, and he was leading the fleet, so as to ensure the first ship the *Adventure* saw was his flagship.

"Nice morning isn't it, Sir?" said Richards, more of a statement than a question, and Rooke merely nodded.

"Mister Richards, if you'd be so kind as to actually do some work, it would be appreciated!" barked Dilkes. Richards smiled to himself and moved as was his orders. He went below to drill the gun crews. There were just running them out, rather than live fire drills. He was on time keeping. Which essentially meant he had to stand at the side, shout "Start!", time and wait for the gunnery officers to shout "done!".

All this for a land invasion. But it was the relentless drilling which had proved the difference in the wars which England had fought in. The professionalism and pride the sailors and gunners of the English Navy were a sight to behold. They would be the difference; Richards was sure of it.

Aboard the *Lannwedhenek*, Smythe was also pacing, much like his Admiral, not that he knew it, his deck. He often paced the deck on a morning, but more so in the current situation of sharing his

personal space.

"Remind me Treen," he said as they passed each other for the eighth time that morning.

"Sir?"

"The next time someone asks me to give up my cabin."

"Yes Sir?"

"Remind me of this moment, so I don't make that mistake again," both men smiled. It was not that either man disliked the others company, on the contrary, they both liked and learned off each other on a regular basis. But when you have been used to having your own space, as both these men did, being constantly on top of each other, and with a couple of soldiers added into the mix, made for some discomfort aboard.

Mix in the non-commissioned officers from the army with the petty officers of the *Lannwedhenek*, making what was usually a lovely and spacious ship feel incredibly cramped.

Lord Hempleman was not helping matters around the ship either. Despite being the only man with a private berth, he was constantly moaning to anyone who would listen that he did not have the space he needed to practice his sword work, or that the food aboard was passable at best, despite the fact he had separate rations compared to the crew, which was inevitably worse.

The morning watch was ending, which always meant lots of movement aboard ship. It was incredible to Smythe, who had been aboard a naval vessel for around two years now, that the soldiers

lazing around on deck were confused when there was a flurry of activity every four hours.

"You'd of thought they have learned by now," said Smythe to Jones.

"Lobsters never learn," said Jones with a smile, "its why they always end up in hot water." Treen was close enough to hear the conversation to laugh, but catching the sight of Lieutenant Potter, he stifled it quickly.

"The Major would like a word Commander if you would be so kind," said Potter. He did not look in a good mood.

"What on earth's all that about?" asked Treen, a look of confusion on his face. "I know Jones made a joke about Lobsters but that's not exactly a new one, you'd have thought he'd heard it by now."

"Dammed if I know," replied Smythe. The quick, quiet sail along the Portuguese coastline just became slightly more challenging. "However, you're right, I doubt it was the joke. Ships yours Treen whilst I deal with this."

"Aye aye Sir," said Treen, the confusion still evident in his voice. Smythe went below, trying to find Connolly as requested. It did not take him long.

"How fucking long till we are at Cadiz?" he said, not minding to watch his language in the slightest.

"Not sure," replied Smythe, still rather confused at the whole outburst, "it's more to do with the fleet than me personally. Why, what's wrong?"

"That prick from Hesse, or wherever the fuck it is!"

"Ah the Lord,"

"No, not the Lord, I expect him to be a privileged little wart, it's what they do, no I'm talking about that weasel he lives with,"

"His steward? What has he done,"

"Going through my stuff that's what!"

"What?"

"Yeah, going through my chest."

"Well, where is he now?"

"I put him in irons obviously. But now the actual German we are escorting is demanding we release him."

"Did he actually steal anything?"

"What the fuck does that matter, if we caught one of our lads doing that it would be lashes and you know it!"

In all honesty, this was true, if he were lucky. Going through an officer's possessions by a common solider was most certainly not tolerated. If he were unlucky, the officer in question might just trump up some more charges and end it all for the young man.

"Cos he's a gentleman. And a gentleman is different, and you know it."

"Then I will demand satisfaction."

"That would have to wait until we land," Smythe was trying to be as diplomatic as possible, but he was not sure he was managing it.

"Why can't I just do it out on the deck? It would be quick I assure

you!" the anger of Connolly was evident, the Irish might not have been in him long, but it was definitely up.

"Look," said Smythe, clearly fed up with playing the nice guy role. "I let you have a duel on my ship, then what happens? Either he dies, and Lord Hempleman has us both up in front of

Rooke on a charge of murder. Or else the German gets bloody lucky, and I have to explain to your commanding officer why he is down a major!"

Smythe rarely let his anger get the better of him, but on this occasion, he saw no other option. He would not allow his ship to fall into anarchy. Not for Connolly's pride at any rate.

"If you wish to complete this foolish act, then be dammed, but you do it in Cadiz, on land where frankly its nothing to do with me." The use of the blaspheme was a clear indication of Smythe's frustration and it took Connolly aback.

"Then I shall arrange it for Cadiz!" and he stormed out of their shared berth.

"It never rains, but it pours," said Smythe to himself.

"The Lord does not give us more than we can handle Henry, don't forget that," quipped Will from behind him.

CHAPTER THIRTEEN

The *Adventure* met with the fleet on the twenty first of August. Aboard was His Royal Highness, Prince George of Hesse. He had been in Lisbon now for months on a diplomatic detail. Spending time in the Court of Pedro II had been extremely comfortable, and now he was pinned into a small, damp cabin. Not exactly the expectations of a Prince but needs must.

The *Adventure* came up to the portside of the *Royal Sovereign,* causing the fleet to slow. This, in the *Adventure*'s defence had been the plan all along. The Prince was to meet in person with Rooke to discuss the strategy which would be in place during the siege and hopeful capture of Cadiz.

"May I introduce," said Richards, again using his most regal voice, "His Royal Highness, Prince George of Hesse. Prinz George, darf ich vorstellen, seine Gnade, Sir George Rooke, Admiral der Mittelmeerflotte." The Prince bowed in deference to Richards use of German. He gave a kindly smile, showing nothing but warmth to the Admiral.

"Ah, Ormonde!" he said, finally seeing the Duke in the corner of the cabin. "Good to see you, what it has been…"

"Ninety-one," said Ormonde, answering Prince George's question.

"Yes, yes," the Prince nodded, "and you Sir," he now turned back to Rooke, "George, what a very excellent and regal name!" Everyone smiled at the Prince's joke. Although he was full of pomp and

pomposity, he was clearly a kindly young man, in his early thirties. "This is what happens when you are the third son," he said, looking at everyone's smiles, "You learn a sense of humour."

"Your English is impeccable," said Rooke, trying not to smile at Richards, who, although useful in other ways, was clearly no longer needed as a translator.

"Well, I spent lots of time with the late king, as you may know. But that is ancient history now, there is a new King, sorry Queen on the throne."

"And two new kings on the Spanish one," quipped Ormonde, trying to match the prince in jokes. It was not well received.

"May I introduce, your diplomat to the Court of Pedro II, Paul Metheun, who is escorting me on this journey to see that the diplomatic objectives are not forgotten in this military campaign."

"Pleasure to meet you," said Rooke, shaking the hand of Paul. He had clearly been in warmer climates than Rooke had recently for a prolonged period of time, the tan, and in places burn on his skin was clear.

"It's my job to make sure you cutthroats don't just butcher everyone," he said with a smile which Rooke thought was meant to put the men at ease. The effect was quite the opposite, Rooke and Ormonde both thought it sounded more like a veiled threat. "Kidding," he added, judging by the military faces around him. "No, I know there will be blood, we are attacking an enemy port for

goodness' sake. No, I am here to try and ensure that our mission does not conflict with your mission."

Rooke was once again reminded of the conflicting mandates the Commanders of this mission had been given. He was told to take the port, hold it if possible, but not risk everything on that. Ormonde's task was to lead the ground forces in this, using all means at his disposal. And the diplomat's jobs were to get the dignitaries from Spain to work with them to install Charles instead of Philip. It would not be a quick mission.

"It's lovely to make your acquaintance Mister Metheun. How did you find Lisbon?"

"Warm," he replied, again clearly trying to make jokes. It was not something that came naturally to him.

162

"I understand that we are only a couple of days away from Cadiz," said Prince George, "We should discuss our strategy as the three Commanders."

"I intend to hold a war council when we arrive at Cadiz so we can assess the situation on the ground," said Rooke, "I think that would be better than making a plan and merely sticking to it."

"Of course, of course," said the Prince, clearly not a hundred percent convinced by this logic, "My intelligence suggests that Cadiz is highly undervalued by the Spanish authorities, and as such, the garrisons of the area are limited to say the least."

"Your intelligence?" asked Ormonde, interested in who the Prince
was using as his help.

"You forget," said the Prince, "I have fought these Bourbon dogs before, whilst in Catalonia. I was the Viceroy of Catalonia for his Most Catholic Majesty, the late Carlos II. The men I speak to are old friends and comrades. They assure me that Philip has not seen its value."

Rooke would not be so convince that the new King of Spain had simply abandoned one of the major ports of the country.

"Are you sure of this?" asked Rooke, trying to keep the scepticism out of his voice.

"Quite sure, I trust these men, Philip doesn't understand its value. I am also meeting some more men aiming at improving the chances of success when we eventually land the great army."

The Austrian plan seemed to be that Spain would recognise that a Hapsburg was the true monarch of them and rally to their cause once they landed an army. Then they would march on Madrid, have young Charles proclaimed Emperor of Spain, and once again rule both halves of Europe. Rooke, and Ormonde for that matter, were not so sure of this.

"Then we shall reassess the situation as we arrive but thank you for this information," said Rooke, politely, but clearly ending the conversation.

"Wait!" interjected Ormonde, "If you'd be so kind, I would like to come aboard the *Adventure* with you gentlemen, if that is permitted Rooke?"

"What?" said Rooke, still processing what Ormonde had said, "Oh erm," it would be a burden on the Captain of the *Adventure* to have yet another dignitary aboard, but it would be a lot less haste to him. No, he must consider that of his fellow Captains' wellbeing, and sanity, despite how much he would like to get rid of him. "No, I am afraid this is not possible, the *Adventure* would not have room for you my Duke, and it would mean sleeping in surroundings far beneath your status." He thought that flattery would be the best way to avoid an uncomfortable situation. It seemed to have worked though.

"Yes, I suppose you're correct," conceded the Duke, "Well, I shall at least see you into your Jolly Boat gentlemen, Admiral, Lieutenant." He made his leave with the Prince and the diplomat. After giving a suitable and sensible amount of time to ensure they were out of earshot, Richards turned to his Admiral.

"We could have been shot of him," he said, somewhere between annoyance and amusement. "honestly Sir,"

"And make another Captain in the fleet more annoyed with me, no, better to suffer oneself than cause another to suffer."

It was the middle of the afternoon on the twenty second of August, when the fleet were approximately around fifty miles from Cadiz. News must have gotten out to the locals not to leave any port, as
the fleet had not seen another ship for a couple of days.

"Why are they staying away?" asked Richards, "Surely they still need to go about their business."

"Not willing to get captured," said Dilkes. "We get a boat near enough we are pulling them aboard to question them. You'd lose money if you weren't working. So do they."

"We'd buy their fish," said Richards. "Besides they are losing more surely by not sailing out and fishing or shipping."

"It isn't about us buying anything. Besides how would the authorities of the bay react when they came home without any catch and a bag full of guineas?"

This was a good point. The local authorities would not appreciate, even if the fisherman had told the enemy a load of lies, that he returned with a purse full of gold. Other men might not be as scrupulous.

"Fishing vessel off the portside bow!" yelled a man aloft. The swiftness of the officer on deck, grabbing their glasses to look through, trying to spot this little boat was evident to two key points. Firstly, the desire to have any information from a local source on the defences and garrison of the port of Cadiz. And secondly, the evident boredom of being at sea, seeing nothing different for days on end, to have something, anything else to focus on.

"Are they in range?" shouted Rooke, who had come on deck to see what the fuss was about.

"Probably for the Long nines?" replied the gunnery sergeant, looking through a glass, "Doubt we'd hit 'em though."

"Don't want to hit them, want to show we could hit them," said Rooke, "Stick one in the water, give 'em a scare!"

The gunnery sergeant lined up the gun on the deck, taking care to ensure he missed the boat. It would be a difficult shot, with a combination of trying to fire into the water as close to the boat as possible, but making sure that he did not hit the boat.

"What's he playing at?" asked Richards quietly to Dilkes, "Either blow it out of the water or don't bloody bother."

"Just wait," said Dilkes, smiling to himself. The gunnery sergeant shot the long nine, putting the ball around ten feet away from the boat. It was enough to cause a panic on the boat, they began rushing to pull their nets in as quickly as they could.

"Let's get them aboard, Coxswain, hunt them down!" roared Rooke.

The *Royal Sovereign* turned and sped towards the fishing boat.

"Gunner!" shouted Rooke, "could you hit the side of them again?"

"I'd be less confident Sir," said the gunner in reply. "I might 'it 'em with the uneven surges." That would completely defeat the objective that Rooke was trying to accomplish. This would mean he would have to put the shot further way from the boat to ensure it did not blow it out of the water. A sot wider might embolden the fishing boat, causing them to do something rather foolish, like trying to run, or shoot towards them.

"Leave it then, Coxswain? How long till we are upon 'em?"

"'Bout fifteen mins, they aren't exactly rushing, are they?"

"Still getting their nets in." commented Dilkes to Richards, as they approached the little fishing boat.

They continued to approach the fishing boat, clearing the open ocean between the two vessels. "How about now gunner?" shouted Rooke.

"Aye Sir, should be able to stick it within six to ten feet of them reliably."

"Then do it, I want to scare the shit out of them!"

The long nine was once again primed and aimed, the boat easily within range of the gun. He could be more precise now in his aim, ensuring he hit the water to the side. It was not about hitting them, quite the contrary, Rooke wanted to talk to the men aboard the boat, but it was enough for them to know that they could hit them. The splash around five foot off the starboard side of the fishing boat showed the excellent effort of the gunner. There were smiles amongst the gun crew for their excellent work.

"Again!" bellowed Rooke, "I want them to see the fear in their eyes!"

The *Royal Sovereign* was gaining with every moment which passed. Another shot threw up the spray, again the gunnery crew showing their worth, by this time putting it closer still onto the port side. They were intentionally swapping sides, using this as a perfect

excuse to practice with live ammunition, something they rarely got to do with a hundred guns aboard.

"They're moving Sir!" shouted a midshipman from the stern. The fishing boat seemed to have finally retrieved their nets, and now they were trying to outrun the large ship chasing them down.

"What are you doing Rooke?" asked Ormonde from along the deck, watching, but not understanding the circumstances of the cannon fire. "You're wasting shot! It's just a fishing boat man!"

"Another round!" Rooke shouted, completely ignoring the landsman's input on his pursuit of this boat. From the sound of Ormonde's voice, it seemed that he was under the impression that Rooke had not realised that he was chasing a fishing boat. Despite the skill of the gun crew, Richards was not sure it was having the desired effect. The idea of course was to show the fishing boat that they could hit them if they wished, but were intentionally putting to the sides of them, ensuring they were not hurt, but trying to intimidate them. But Richards thought, that the fishermen, who probably were not naval men themselves, probably thought this was poor aim, rather than an excellent one.

"How long Coxswain?"

"Only another five minutes Sir." They were nearly in range to fire their muskets.

"Shoot one in the water!" shouted Rooke, the fishing boat would not misconstrue that. They would be in range soon for all of them

to have their muskets pointing at the fishing boat. A splash less than a foot from side of the boat made the Captain of the fishing vessel turn and face the ship he had been trying to avoid.

"Richards!" shouted Rooke, looking over the deck for the young Lieutenant.

"Sir!" came the stock response to his Admiral from Richards.

"Tell him we mean him no harm, and I wish to invite them aboard."

Richards was struggling to think how to phrase to someone you had spent the last twenty minutes firing cannon balls at, that they meant him no harm. But he formulated the tone he wanted to use in his voice, as the *Royal Sovereign* slowed to a stop blocking the small, fishing boats path.

"¡Buen día señor! No temas, no deseamos lastimarte. Mi capitán desea que suba a bordo con cualquier pescado que haya capturado, si es tan amable." He stood there, quite still, hoping that the Captain of the fishing boat would agree with him to come aboard. He could see the Captain speaking to the men aboard his vessel, clearing trying to work out whether he could refuse this "invitation" he had been issued. Finally, after much discussion, the Captain shouted back, "Si Senor." and threw a rope from his vessel toward the *Sovereign.* This was, as expected, completely pointless, as the little fishing boat barely came up to the upper gun deck of the first-rate, but it showed the willingness that the crew threw ropes back over to the fishing boat in order to secure her.

There were only four men aboard the small boat, a boy, barely old enough to be useful at sea, a couple of younger men, clearly the main labour for the boat, and the Captain, an old seadog if there ever was one, grizzled and hardened by many years at sea. It seemed likely that despite the insistence from the Spanish authorities to not engage in any fishing or leave port, these men had indeed chosen to go out into the waters of the Atlantic, in hope of catching a Kings ransom worth of fish, when all other fishing boats were moored up in port.

"Be so kind as to invite him to my cabin, if you would Mister Richards," said Rooke, in a softer, gentler tone than was customary. He wanted to put the Captain of the fishing boat at ease on this ship, which was another world away from his tiny boat. The cabin alone would probably be as big, if not bigger than the entire fishing boat.

Rooke stood at the window of his stern, facing out towards his fleet. They had detoured for around an hour, moving offline, and no doubt his Captains had heard or seen the firing of his guns. Hopefully, they will have also seen the target, and understand that this was not a call to action, but an intelligence mission only. None of his ships seemed to have increased their pace, and therefore it must be that with only one gun firing off at random intervals, the fleet assumed that the Admiral's flagship was clearly not in danger. Ormonde was in the room too, having been invited for this

interrogation of the fisherman.

The knock on the door, as was required when entering the cabin of a senior officer, came and Rooke's customary gruff "Enter!" was given. Richards brought in the old man, who looked a mixture of defiant and frightened at his predicament.

"Richards, I assume you would be good enough to translate?" asked Rooke, although despite the friendly nature of the suggestion, refusal was out of the question.

"Of course, Sir," said Richards, "Would you like a direct translation or one where I explain what you mean rather than the specific words?". This was Richards polite way of asking Rooke if he wanted to be as candid as possible as he, Richards, would still ask it in as kind and gentle possible way.

"Whichever you think would be better Lieutenant, so long as we get the information I desire. Now, what does he know of the forces in Cadiz?"

Richards paused, to formulate his Spanish, as he was waiting, Ormonde spoke.

"Señor, ¿qué sabe de las fuerzas en Cádiz?" It was brief and to the point, a literal translation of the Admirals words.

"Nada," replied the Spaniard, almost defiant in his response.

Richards inwardly smiled. Ormonde may well be versed in Spanish, but he was not able to covey a simple message without clear distain from the man he was questioning. A different tact was needed

here.

"Señor, no quiero nada más que, que se vaya a casa con su familia esta noche. Sin embargo, mi almirante quiere saber cuántos hombres hay defendiendo Gibraltar."

"Gibraltar, what are you talking about you, stupid boy, we want to know about," Ormonde began, but a sharp look from Rooke silenced him.

Almost with a laugh, the fisherman spoke. "No hay hombres en

Gibraltar. Todos se preparan para la defensa del Cádiz." And he continued to explain how the cannons were being primed and readied for an invasion of the bay, how more troops were being added to the garrisons at the forts along the sides of the city. He spoke for almost five minutes on the subject, before going deadly quiet. He looked horrified at Richards, who simply smiled at the old fisherman, as he had relayed all the information he could to Rooke, whilst still listening to the fisherman.

"Sí señor, ¿sigue?" said Richards, trying his best to not smile too much at the unfortunate man for revealing too much information. The fisherman, possibly in disgust with himself as much as Richards spat at his feet. Richards could no longer hold in his smile, and turned to Rooke. "I think this is all we will be getting out of him Sir," he said, knowing he had done what was needed of him. "To summarise, increased garrison, both at the main fortifications in Cadiz at Fort Saint Sebastian, and at the secondary forts up and

down the coastline. As for ships, he said rowing boats? I don't know if he means galleys, but if that's all there is then that shouldn't be a problem for us. It's the hotshot which will prove tricky from the guns from Saint Sebastian which will most likely cause us the most trouble."

Rooke stood there for a moment, lost in thought. He wanted to thank the fisherman for his information, but worried that would be too rude. Instead, he opted for the polite, but simpler response of "Thank him for his time Richards, and ask that if he has any fish aboard his vessel I would like to purchase it."

Perhaps in some final defiance of the Admiral, the fisherman shook his head in anger at the idea of selling his product to the Englishman. He said some choice words that even Rooke knew, some even relating to Rooke's parentage, as Richards escorted the old man from the cabin.

"Well, what a load of codswallop," said Ormonde finally as the fisherman was clearly above on the deck.

"How so?" asked Rooke. "I thought the fisherman was quite clear in his explanations."

"Exactly, made up a load of stuff. Now, Prince George's intelligence came from reliable sources in the resistance against the pretender Philip."

"Which is more likely? A fisherman who left Cadiz a day or two ago, or Prince George's contacts who left Cadiz over a month ago. I am

not saying that Prince George's men are lying, nor am I saying that he is wrong. I am saying that the up-to-date information is more reliable."

"I put my faith in Princes, rather than paupers," replied Ormonde simply. "I will not base my plans on the words of an old fishermen who lied to me." His snobbery and expectations of the upper classes were clearly biasing his opinion. Furthermore, Rooke knew that if the intelligence from Prince George was correct, it would make for a much easier Ormonde on the ground, which wishful thinking being what it is, was inevitably playing into the mind of the Army's Commander.

"And I will base my plans on the latest intelligence," replied Rooke firmly. Both men glared at each other until Ormonde finally said, "I think, I shall take some air. Sir George." He gave a small salute to indicate the discussion had come to an end.

"I'd have been better letting him bugger off to the *Adventure*," thought Rooke.

The fleet hove to outside of Cadiz on the twenty third of August. Rooke stood on his quarterdeck, looking over his fleet. It mattered not now whether the Spanish knew they were coming. They were here. And the battlements were clearly in front of them.

The city of Cadiz is based on an inlet bay with a large fortification guarding the main entrance on an outcrop. It is heavily defended by

shore batteries, and unreachable through a direct assault. The bay of Cadiz is much larger, with a sheltered area dug out for ships. There has been a settlement on the footprint of Cadiz since around 1000's BC and is considered to be one of the oldest still occupied cities in Western Europe. It was run by the Moors until the Reconquista and was finally captured by the Spanish King Alphonso X in 1262. It has its own diocese, being granted it by Pope Clement IV shortly after its capture by the Spanish and houses religious buildings such as the Cathedral of Santa Cruz and San Francisco Church and convent. Known for its tight streets throughout the city, it has everything from barracks to house the troops, to Plaza's and market squares, to a Roman open-air amphitheatre.

Rooke had no idea how many ships were stationed in the harbour. But he knew that they would not come out. It was not a large enough bay to house so many ships-of-the-line. The main harbour was protected on each side by forts, on the eastern side, Fort Saint Mantagorda and the western side, Fort Saint Lawrence. Why the Spanish insisted on naming their forts after Saints was beyond him.

There were other fortified settlements too, in Port Royal, Port Saint Mary, and another minor Fort, another saint, Saint Catherine. There was a clear garrison, firing off shots from cannons high above them every few hours, more out of a defiance than anything. The ships of the fleet were clearly out of range.

"Signal to the fleet," he said, "I want a council of war convening in

the next few hours if you please." The request to have all ships Captains and officers from the army would take time to both convey, be relayed to the ships further away from the *Royal Sovereign* which could not see the signal given. Then there would be the time it would take for the Captains and Commanders of the ships to get into their gigs, or whatever other small crafts would be available to them. With some of the ships literally miles away due to the sheer size of the fleet, that would add to the time taken by the fleet also. There would be the salutes and greetings. And there would be over fifty people crammed into the cabins aboard.

The signals went up, and this time Ormonde had the sense not to make a joke about pretty flags. Since their disagreement yesterday, neither Rooke nor Ormonde had spoken to each other. "Perhaps that was for the best," thought Rooke, "let tempers calm down." They would however be in the cabin together today during the council of war. That would also be the case for Prince George, although he had not heard the testimony from the fisherman.

Over the next hour or so Captains and Commanders from around the fleet came aboard the *Royal Sovereign,* often with their army equivalent in tow. They were greeted with a glass of port, purchased of course from Oporto whilst in dock, made and sourced from the vineyards along the Douro River. There was a lull for a little while now, as both the message had to be conveyed to the ships further away, and they then had further to row to arrive also.

Rooke went into his cabin to talk to his Captains which had already arrived. Hobson was there, as was Jennings and Hardy. These were men who had seen at least some action and their opinions could be counted upon. Moreover, they had been in social situations with Rooke before, and could be counted on to be during a fight.

Smythe received the orders relayed from a Dutch ship ahead and closer to the bay itself. He knew that should an amphibious landing on the beaches be required, his ship would be used and placed under fire. "Mister Connolly, if you would be so kind as to join myself in the gig, your presence would also be appreciated too Sir." Which was true. All senior officers had been summoned to the *Royal Sovereign* for this council on the attack on Cadiz. Although the responsibility for the attack lay squarely on the shoulders of Rooke, he wanted the opinion of the officers under his command. Although a formality, it would issue him with some legal cover, should the plan go awry, as Rooke would have on record the several plans available and the reasons they went with the plan they finally reached.

It took them around thirty minutes to arrive at the *Sovereign,* and around another ten to wait until there was a space for them to be brought aboard. The gig had to hold water far enough away from the ship to ensure that they did not encounter any of the wash the bobbing ship was causing. In the choppy Atlantic waters, Connolly looked greener than ever on this small boat. He turned, threw up his guts into the water, and wiped his mouth.

"Better?" asked Smythe with a small cheeky smile.

"Better," replied Connolly, equally smiling at the Commander of the naval ships' amusement.

"Whilst we are here, I was wondering if you had thought on the duelling issue?"

"Already dealt with," replied Connolly, not showing much emotion either way.

"Oh," said Smythe, concerned more for the reputation of his ship than for the safety and wellbeing of the German, "how so?"

"Once we are on land after the invasion, pistols," said Connolly. "I agreed with you, anything on her Majesty's ship could create legal issues. I'm surprised Lord Hempleman didn't tell you to be honest. He seemed to think it was a wonderful idea. Clear his man with honour, I think were his words."

It was a common joke in and around the continent that the only German men without duelling scars were cowards and the clergy, and even they were not always exempt. Even royalty, in their

younger days, may be brought into the martial fold. To a German, the idea of defending one's honour above all else was essential, and they took duelling requests seriously.

"Who'll be his second?" asked Smythe, more out of curiosity than worry.

"We have forgone seconds." Connolly replied, in a calm and relaxed manner. "Although Potter did offer, I saw no point in the matter. Once it's done, it's done." There was an odd calmness about Connolly, perhaps it was the fact he was most likely about to be storming a Spanish fort under cannon fire, that a small pistol bullet did not faze him. It would, however, be equally deadly should it come to that.

Once they were finally aboard the *Royal Sovereign*, the two gentlemen were escorted by a midshipman, who looked as if this had been his job the majority of the day, and as such the usual energy and deference that would have been shown to a Commander and a Major of the army were not present. Smythe realised why the second he entered the cabin. It was packed, with chattering Captains and Majors, Generals, and Admirals. With all these officers present, it was more like a meeting of Parliament in the Atlantic than a military council. The uniforms of every officer had been pressed and shined for the occasion, Smythe wondered if some of the Army men had literally kept it in their sea chests until this moment. There were English voices, Dutch voices, accents of

Yorkshire, Cumbria, Ireland, Wales and some Scottish, as the integration of the forces had already begun. Both men were offered a glass of port, which they took cheerfully, and went about to talk to their fellow officers, Connolly going to the army side, Smythe, to his naval colleagues. It was like the parting of the Red Sea, with the charts on the table in the middle, Naval officers to one side, Army officers to the other. The disunity, even at this stage, was clear.

"Smythe, isn't it?" asked Hardy, offering his hand to the Commander. "We had dinner at Christmas together. How are you finding the fleet?"

"Very well thank you Sir, you know it's my first time in a fleet?"

"Yes, Richards mentioned it during one of our meetings," he said kindly, "Some men think the massive first-raters are all we need, but like Rooke, I feel that every ship has its own part to play, no matter how small it may seem. Ah, but now, the Admiral speaks."

It was mid-afternoon by the time the number of officers which Rooke felt were enough had been assembled in the cabin of the *Sovereign*. The room was stifling, even with all the windows at the back open. The sun, thankfully, was on the southern side, whereas the stern windows were pointing North west. But with all the bodies in the room, and the midday heat near the mouth of the Mediterranean, it was almost unbearable. The charts of the bay were out on the table, with Rooke, Jennings and Vice-Admiral Hobson on one side, and Ormonde, the 1st Earl Stanhope, one of his Colonels, and his second in command Sir Henry Belasys at the other. It was Prince George however, who spoke first, stood at the end of a table, with Methuen at his side.

"My suggestion would be a quick frontal assault. According to my intelligence, there will be little in the way of opposition. The forts are garrisoned as a mere formality and we would easily overpower them."

"I'm afraid your intelligence is out of date, Your Highness," said Rooke.

"Oh, really, not this rubbish again!" voiced Ormonde, clearly frustrated that Rooke still believed the fisherman.

"We captured a fishing boat yesterday, your highness," said Rooke, ignoring the interruption from Ormonde, "and he confirmed that the fortresses have all been reinforced. Some with horses and increased shot." There was a murmur throughout the assembled officers. They all seemed to think that a direct frontal assault was no longer an option.

"With respect Admiral," said Ormonde, showing little respect with his tone, "This was merely the words of a fisherman, I think we can rely on the intelligence of His Highness more than that of a mere Diego fisherman." There was nodding, especially from his subordinates, in particular a man with a rather prominent nose, who's audible "here here!" gave away his fellow Irish roots.

"My information is a few weeks old," conceded Prince George. "If the Admiral has up to date information, I am more than happy to defer to him. If the barricades are indeed well manned then the plan I have suggested would not be suitable." Ormonde was furious. He had just backed his highness, and what was his repayment? To be ignored and have Rooke deferred to. He felt slighted.

"Besides," continued Prince George, "my understanding is that Francisco Fajardo has become the Commander of the Pretender's forces in the region. If that is the case, the troops will be well arranged and prepared to fight. He's steady under fire."

"Then we bomb the city!" said Ormonde enthusiastically. "We clearly have the firepower, so let's just get to it."

"The Romans make a desert, and call it peace," thought Rooke. "That wouldn't work." he said simply. "We wouldn't be able to get our ships close enough to do the damage you desire, my Duke." There was deference in the words that Rooke spoke, but not in the tone. Rooke would not sail his ships into a bay flanked by forts with hotshot. It would turn his fleet into matchsticks within moments.

"Besides," added Prince George, "my remit is to convince the people of this region to declare their allegiance to the true King of Spain, Charles. Bombing the city within an inch of its life would not achieve that I fear." His eyes were saying very clearly that he would not endorse any kind of bombardment of the city of Cadiz.

"Too many cooks spoil the broth," thought Smythe. "May I suggest
something?" said Smythe, unsure of the etiquette of these situations.

"Commander Smythe, of the ship *Lannwedhenek*," said Rooke, which Smythe took as his introduction to speak.

"Well, we can't storm the main bases with men. Nor can we directly attack the harbour. But when you're fishing, you don't just go for the shoal, you encircle it with seals and other boats."

"What are you getting at man!" demanded Ormonde, "If I'd have wanted fishing lessons, I'd have told Rooke to keep that Diego on board." As much as Ormonde was frustrating Rooke, he too was now regretting letting Smythe speak.

"There are forts along the coastline," said Smythe, coming forward to point at the chart. "But they stop here. If we could make a beachhead, then we could attack the forts, one by one, go around not through them." It was an option. Rooke smiled. The new Commander may have a plan they could work with. Prince George seemed to be unconvinced, but he was not as against the idea as the bombardment that Ormonde had suggested. Ormonde spoke first.

"It would take too long." He said, softly. "We could not do all we need to achieve in that time."

"And yet, no other plan allows us to complete the mission either," said Rooke.

"It would not work," said Ormonde, frustrated by what he saw as

his fellow Commanders' unwillingness to engage the enemy. His fellow Army officers began to shout angrily too, which in turn caused the Navy officers to respond in kind.

"Enough!" roared Rooke, his years at sea being used in the gruffness and projection of his voice. "Enough," he said quieter. "It's getting late, and we are getting nowhere. May I suggest we turn in for the night and discuss it again in the morning. I will send for those Captain's input I wish to hear from, but for now gentlemen, goodnight." It was a quick dismissal, before the meeting got completely out of hand. Rooke was angry with himself, he should never have asked for so many officers to come in the first place. Too many personalities, too many opinions. No, tomorrow he would ask back Hobson, Jennings and Hardy, let Ormonde bring the same, and hash out this plan once and for all.

CHAPTER FOURTEEN

Don Francisco Castillo Fajardo, Segundo Marqués de Villadarias, was on the battlement of Fort Saint Catherine. He was a short man, with a pronounced nose, and long silvery hair. He had a wispy short beard which came up and around his mouth into a moustache. He had olive skin, which permanently darker than when he was a younger man; he put down to being on the African coast for so long. He was back on Spanish soil, not home, that was Malaga, but Spain at least would do for now.

It would have been much safer, without question, for him to reside back in Cadiz itself, but the Commander wanted to have an eye on the ground. Since the news of their arrival, around a month ago whilst the fleet were still docked safely in Porto, he had sent out word for a militia to be called, and the cities of Cordoba and Seville had responded magnificently. Perhaps it was self-interest, the cities were supplied by the port at Cadiz, or perhaps some level of patriotic duty caused the upsurge, but in any case, the turnout was awe inspiring.

A sergeant was drilling the troops on musket loading. Many of the men had never even held a musket, let alone shot one. And of those who had, it had been for hunting rather than for war. It was not the best rag tag of soldiers, but it would do.

"Take your cartridge," said the Sergeant, showing the men as he went along. "Bite off the top. Pour some of the gunpowder into the

pan, that's this bit here," he said pointing at the part of the gun he meant. The men were intently listening, as all were volunteers of one persuasion or another. Some men had come for the glory of Spain, some had come because they were unemployed.

"Pour the bullet down the muzzle. Ram it down, and don't forget to remove it because Saint Teresa knows I will tell you to go get it back." There was a chuckle amongst the men, they all seemed to appreciate the old Sergeant's humour. "Finally, add the rest of the powder, put it onto your shoulder, and squeeze." And as he spoke he completed the action, firing a bullet high into the air over everyone's heads, "Only difference is lads, you aim at the enemy, not the air, and we will be fine."

The stone battlements improved after the Reconquista would prove formidable in the defence of this area. Francisco walked along them, inspecting the regular troops as he went.

"Where do you think they will attack Sir?" asked one of his subordinates who was following him. Francisco had thought hard on this. Initially, he was convinced that they would launch an attack on the city itself. But then he stopped and thought a little more. It would be an all-out bloodbath underneath the hotshot of the two forts.

"I think they will land on the beach," he said simply. He was a man of few words, and at already sixty years old, he had been looking forward to a quiet retirement. Alas, Europe decided to plunge itself

into war, and as he done before at Oran, he would defend his Majesty's territory with his life if necessary.

He could see the little English boats approaching the ship which bore the Ensign of an Admiral. Having been in northern Africa for the better part of a decade, he was no longer familiar with the different Ensigns or names of the Commanders of English fleets, but he could see by the size of it its intent. It was not a mere smash and grab raid. It was an invasion force. Not a large one. But still enough to potentially create a beachhead.

"They will attack the beaches," he said again, "and we will be ready." The beach between Fort Saint Catherine and Rota, or the sandy part where landing troops would be possible, was around two and a half miles. Francisco knew he would not be able to defend the entire beach, that would be impossible even if it were fortified. No, he would have to pick his place to place the troops, to ensure that they were as effective as possible.

The cavalry master walked beside him. He was a tall man, taller than the old general at any rate, with a thin moustache and short cropped hair. "Your horse is ready Sir," he said simply. He knew Francisco by reputation and knew he would not apricate unnecessary conversation.

"Thank you, Juan," he replied, as he walked towards the fort's gates. The fort, with its north westerly facing battlements, had twelve sixteen-pound cannons pointing into the bay, oceanside.

Even if the English captured the fort, there were no cannons on the south western fortifications that could fire all the way into the bay proper, ensuring that the combined Spanish and French fleets would remain unscaled.

He rode his horse the ten or so miles north to the unfortified village of Rota, looking out on the beaches all the way for any movement from the Anglo-Dutch fleet. None was forthcoming. It was the hot mid-afternoon sun and the couple of hours ride was pleasant enough.

"Where is the mayor of the town?" asked Francisco on arrival. The town, having seen the fleet had begun to empty. There were donkeys and mules being loaded with the possessions of the locals, along with all weaponry and food. They were busy, and Francisco, rather frustratedly had to repeat himself, this time a little louder.

"Sir!" responded a man from the opposite side of the street. "I have the honour of being the governor of this town, to what do I owe the pleasure…" he paused trying to work out the role of the man who had ridden in on a horse.

"Don Francisco Castillo Fajardo, Segundo Marqués de Villadarias, Captain-General of Andalucía. I have come to look at your defences Sir."

"Defences?" said the governor. "We are leaving Sir!" It was not a request of the Captain-General, it was a statement.

"The English are coming!" roared Francisco indignantly.

"Precisely Sir!" replied the Governor. "We are not soldiers, Sir.

We are farmers and fishermen." Francisco glazed at him. He knew that the governor was probably right. But he had a duty to this area.

"Once you leave," he said "Anything which is usable that is left will be taken and either burned or used by his most Catholic Majesty, Philip. Do you understand?"

The governor sighed, "Yes Sir," he replied simply. There was no possible way that the peasantry of the town could carry everything of use. They would just have to accept that their possessions would be forfeited to the crown.

"Another thing," added Francisco, as he was remounting his horse, "They will try and recruit men from this village and any other in the surrounding regions. Any man who helps the enemy will be tried and executed for treason. Have I made myself clear?"

"Yes Sir. I will return here to surrender the town, to try and secure survival of the buildings."

"Do as you wish governor. But help the enemy. And you will swing." It was not a threat, it was a promise. Francisco rode back along the coast, stopping at positions he felt the English may land their troops.

"How do you know they won't directly attack the forts Sir?" asked one of his aides.

"Because they would have already done it," replied Francisco simply. The fleet had been here around a day now, but apart from
the small boats ferrying what he assumed were officers to and from the flagship, there had not been much movement.

"I want a couple of smaller guns here," he indicated on the wasteland after the beach. "And some of our militia men. Let's not make it a comfortable landing."

"What about the town, Sir?" asked another aide.

"What about it?" asked Francisco, "If they are not willing to fight for it, I don't see why I should. First rule of war gentlemen, never reinforce failure." It was indefensible compared to the forts at any rate. Fort Catharine probably would fall, but the further back forts of Saint Lawrence and Saint Matagorda would be the key points. Holding both of these would ensure that the English could not cut off Cadiz itself, or the Fort of Saint Sebastian, which looked over the isthmus of the bay.

Rota was not that strategically important at any rate. It would serve as a place for the fleet to establish its administration and would give the English an early morale boost. But other than that, it would not be worth much. Once a beachhead had been established, it would be difficult to dislodge the enemy with the men he had at his disposal, with or without the capture of Rota. No, if he were to stop the English, prior to the Fort of Matagorda, it would be here on the beach.

The short ride back to the fort was made just as night was coming in. The fleet had been outside the bay now for around a day and a

half. The cannons would be moved in the morning. And he would send a troop of cavalry to Rota to clean up any messes which were left.

The morning sun rose on the twenty-fifth of August. There was still little movement still from the fleet, which Francisco was thankful for. "Get the militia's set up on the marshland," he said, whilst breakfasting overlooking the bay. "And set the cavalry on their orders if you please." The weather was once again perfect, the sun was shining, and the visibility was crystal clear.

Rooke was still arguing with Ormonde over the landing of troops.

"You should sail up to the forts and storm them Sir!" demanded Ormonde, "A direct assault on their defences and they would not stand a chance man!"

"We directly attack now, after they have had a further two days of preparation would be suicide Sir!" Rooke retorted.

"And who's fault is that Sir?" demanded Ormonde, "If we had attacked, as I suggested, as soon as we arrived, then we would not be in this mess."

"The odds were just as poor then as they are now!" barked back Rooke.

The subordinate officers had left the cabin, being invited by the officers of the *Royal Sovereign* to "drinks on the deck". This was the polite way of getting them out of there, so the higher ups could

argue without interruption.

"Ormonde is wrong," said Hardy to O'Hara, one of the army Commanders.

"I know," said O'Hara simply. "he may have been right initially, but without your support we'd all get mown down like corn in a field."

The officers were milling around waiting for the three Commanders, Rooke, Ormonde and Prince George, to finally come to a decision. The longer they waited, the more preparation the Spanish garrisons would make. In O'Hara's opinion they had delayed long enough.

"Look James," said Rooke, "I didn't think that it was a good plan when we arrived, I sure as hell don't think it's a good idea now after two days of preparations."

"So," grumbled Ormonde, "What do you suggest?"

"Same thing that I have suggested for the past two days," replied Rooke. "here," he pointed at the charts in front of them. "between Saint Catherine and Rota. Land the troops. Hold a beachhead. Flood it with troops. Go from there."

Rooke had made it sound simple. But even Prince George, who was in favour of the plan, felt it had flaws in it. The tidal charts were not perfect, that was for certain. There was always uncertainty with the weather on the Western Iberian coastline too.

"That will waste even more time!" complained Ormonde. "You moan about giving them time to prepare and then you insist on a plan of attack which will give the enemy even more."

Ormonde's frustration was evident. He knew his troops would secure the forts and hold the city for England through the winter. From there, who knows what would happen.

"Rooke," said Prince gently. "Is what the Duke wishes to happen possible?"

"Not without an unnecessary risk to my fleet. Which I cannot allow. We need a potential retreat option, and I am under strict orders from the Admiralty to not allow anything to happen to the fleet unless absolutely unavoidable."

"Then, James, unless you wish to turn around and go home, it seems your only option is to go with the Admiral's plan."

"I am the Commander of the Army, I will say where they go!" retorted Ormonde angrily.

"And you are stood on a ship of Her Majesty's Navy," replied Rooke, "Which *I* will say, where they sail."

If looks could kill Ormonde would have put Rooke straight to Davy Jones. "I will land my troops. But I want it on the record that I disagree and that we should have attacked the forts."

"Understood," nodded Rooke. Basically, unless this is a complete success, I am personally blaming you. Not the best pace to be in.

"I shall come ashore after your men have achieved their beachhead," said Prince George cheerfully. "A toast, gentlemen! To the success of the mission, and to the rightful king of Spain, Charles!"

"To King Charles." The two men said and took a drink of the wine offered to the by Prince George's Steward. Where on earth he had so quickly got three glasses of wine from was anyone's guess. "I shall invite your officers back down to discuss the plan with you gentlemen, if you so wish?"

"That would be good of you, thank you, Your Highness," said Rooke quickly. He did not trust Ormonde not to cut across him, so answered for both.

The officers filed into the cabin, saluting each one of them as they came in. It was not the free for all it had been at the first council of war, but still rather cramped.

"Gentlemen, we have come up with our plan," said Rooke, "Will land the troops, tomorrow morning. Here." he pointed at the chart. "Now we need someone to command the landing party."

"I'll do that," voiced Colonel James Stanhope, one of the Commanders of the troops, and Ormonde gave him the nod of approval.

"Now, as for ferrying the men in, we need smaller ships than what most of us possess. The waters will be shallow, so the smaller bottom, the better."

"Might I suggest the *Lannwedhenek* Sir?" asked Hardy, "Smythe did suggest this plan after all."

He did. And he had some army forces aboard his ship. And he was a gutsy man. "Agreed. Colonel Stanhope you will report to the

Lannwedhenek tomorrow morning with any troops you see fit to land. Expect some resistance, but nothing I am sure you can't handle." Stanhope nodded. "Richards?" shouted Rooke.

"Sir?"

"Go get Commander Smythe. He needs his orders."

CHAPTER FIFTEEN

The *Lannwedhenek* hove to at the low tide as close to the shoreline as it could safely do so. There was a wind in the air this morning, and the soldiers were loading themselves into the gigs. It was overcast, and stormy, most unlike summer they had been having recently. There were around two hundred men in the gigs bound for the shoreline from the *Lannwedhenenk* alone. It was six bells of the morning watch, and the gigs were beginning to row ashore. Major Connolly was sitting uneasily in the boat. Commander Smythe stood on his deck looking over at the landing ground.

Before they had left, the Bosun and his mates had lined up a crew to sing them off;

Come cheer up my lads, tis to glory we steer,
To add something more to this wonderful year,
To honour you all, now as freemen not slaves,
For whom are as free as the sons of the waves?
Hearts of Oak are our ships,
Hearts of Oak are our men,
We're ready, Steady boy, Steady.

"Could we cover them if needed?" Smythe asked Jones whilst continuing to look through his glass at the target.

"I expect so Sir. Not sure how accurate we would be."

"Let's hope Mister Jenkins's drill has been successful," commented Smythe. "If not, we could be accidentally killing lots of Lobsters today."

"Fishermen are we," commented one of the crew sarcastically whilst passing and Smythe smiled. Less than a third of the crew now were from the original men who signed up to protect the coats from the Barbary states. Now they were about to lay siege to a Spanish port. Slightly different from their original mandate.

"What's the bottom?" asked Smythe.

"Not sure Sir."

"Find out. Closer we get, more we can support them."

"But what if they fire at us from the shore Sir?"

"Let them." Smythe said simply. The fear of hot shot, cannon balls heated up in a furnace, was the fear of all navies attacking land. However, from the shoreline they were attacking, there were no furnaces. Even if they had cannons ashore, and Smythe could not see any large batteries through his glass, the best they could have is small guns with small poundage's. So, any hotshot they had would be heated over a fire and at most a six- or twelve-pound ball. That would not do any major damage to his ship and he knew it. By the time it had flown through the air, it would be barely warmer than a shot from an enemy broadside, and depending on the ship, only half the size.

"By the line – nine, Sir."

They had plenty of room then should the decide to go in closer. "Keep the leadsman up there Treen, let's take her in a bit closer."

The *Lannwedhenek* followed the gigs towards the bay. "Heavy weight – eight!" shouted the leadsman. The ship was not in danger until the numbers dropped below five. Until then, it was more an academic exercise. After a shout of five however, the Captain of a ship had to consider slowing and stopping to ensure he did not run aground on the sand.

As the *Lannwedhenek* began pulling into shore, the gigs were fighting against the tide and waves. Connolly and his company could see the boats struggling to keep afloat. "Watch yourself oarsmen!" roared the coxswain to the men around him. The waves were coming up and into the gigs. "Start bailing man!" he roared at the soldiers, who instinctively grabbed a bucket. The waves were getting rougher, the landing crafts were starting to rock even heavier.

"Sir!" shouted one of the soldiers, "Look!" Connolly looked a couple of boats to the north and saw it was taking more and more water on board. Another large wave caused it to capsize, throwing fifteen or so men into the black waters below.

"We need to get them!" shouted Connolly.

"Can't Sir!" replied the Coxswain of the landing craft, "We couldn' take the weight! We'd be next into the water!" This was probably true, and sadly, Connolly knew it. The crew were bailing as quickly

as they could, and still he was unsure they would make it the couple of hundred yards to the beach.

"Cannon fire!" shouted the next boat, and Connolly could see the spray where the balls were hitting the water. They might not be any danger to a ship, but to these little boats, they would be crippled in moments. The oarsmen increased their pace, knowing that the longer they were in the water, the more danger they were in.

On the *Lannwedhenek* Smythe was looking through his glass at the smoke rising from the beach.

"Make a hard to starboard!" he shouted to the tiller. "Mister Treen be so kind as to set the guns off. Let's give 'em some cover fire!"

The *Lannwedhenek* turned, knowing she had more than enough water under her to ensure she did not run aground.

"Hurry man!" yelled Smythe. The longer they took, the longer the boats would be under fire. It was unlikely at this range that they would hit the guns. In fact, Smythe had only seen four puffs of smoke, which lead him to surmise that was how many cannons they had.

"What do you think they've got Sir?" asked Jones, also whilst looking through a glass.

"They're small whatever they are."

"How can you tell Sir?" it was young midshipman Gabriel who asked this question.

"There are a few reasons," said Smythe, always willing to give knowledge to his younger officers. "Firstly, the amount of smoke. The larger the gun, the larger the smoke."

"Makes sense."

"Secondly, the size of the splashes in the water. A larger ball would make a larger splash. Third, they are aiming at the smaller boats. There is no point using twelve or sixteen pounders against the small landing craft when a six or nine pounder would probably do the damage." It was interesting, that even as the *Lannwedhenek* was taking the time to turn on the enemy, that Smythe and Gabriel were having a conversation like it was just another academic problem, something which could be solved or fixed. "What other reasons might there be Gabriel?" Smythe was asking like a teacher asks a pupil. It was of course part of their relationship, but still under the circumstances, when orders were being shouted by Treen and the petty officers, it was an odd time.

"The time they had?" replied Gabriel, unsure of himself.

"Yes, very good. I doubt that it is a permanent battery, and therefore the guns had to be moved. If we assume they didn't move them until we had been here a whole day, and we assume that they didn't know when we were coming, smaller guns would be preferable as they would be easier to move."

"There's a landsman's answer too," said Jones, trying to assist in the young man's education also. Although Treen was the main teacher

of the two young midshipmen, it was obvious even now they were taking different paths. Abraham often worked with Yin, and to all intents and purposes was the Surgeons mate. Gabriel on the other hand was taking his enthusiasm into arithmetic and sailing skills. This was what both Smythe and Jones specialised in, and so, when the young men were apart, often Gabriel would gravitate to Jones, or if he got the chance Smythe, to learn under their experience.

"The forts!" cried Gabriel, after a pause.

"Precisely the forts. They have left all their bigger guns behind nice big walls. More importantly, it means we don't steal 'em. We are going to pound their walls with cannon balls and make a breach. That or rush at the bugger and hope for the best. Leaving us some nice big cannons to fire at them with isn't the smartest move. They will struggle to stop us on the beach, but they might kill a few of us."

"Sir!" came a voice from aloft. "Sir do we have any gigs left?"

"Yes, a couple why?"

"A couple of the craft have flipped Sir!"

Smythe took less than a second to process this. In full gear a soldier was weighed down by about forty extra pounds. Add in the fact that the red coats were woollen and would absorb the water more, and that these men were not sailors, and they may not last long in the water.

"Send out a boat, no wait, I'll go! I want a volunteer crew. Mister Jones, the ship is yours until Mister Treen has finished firing his guns at the beaches."

"But Sir, shouldn't I go?"

"I am not willing to risk the lives of others and not my own. No, Mister Jones, I will go, but thank you for your offer."

The gig was launched with all haste just as they came about and hove to. "Give me a minute to get away from the wash Mister Treen and then fire as you bear, please!" shouted Smythe. Jenkins was at the tiller, and the rowers were ready to heave away. Many of the men in the boat were the fishermen of Cornwall, men who knew how important it was to get out of the cold waters of the Atlantic. Yes, the water would not be as cold as around Lundy Island in January, but being pulled down, into the darkness, would be some men's worst nightmare.

"Heave boys! Heave! Mister Jenkins, hold her steady!"

"Aye aye Sir!"

Yin had been warned that men may be coming aboard with symptoms of hypothermia and other such issues. He had blankets and tea at the ready, but he knew he may be of little use. If they were in the water for longer than a few minutes, they would either be fine with a cup of tea or be in real trouble. His medical skill would be most likely redundant.

Connolly's boat was approaching the beach. He had been lucky, several boats had capsized, and he knew that not every man had come back up. As the boats flipped, it would not take much to hit one's head, and it would not be long till that put you in real trouble.

As the boats pulled up on the shore, Connolly shouted at his men, "Form up lads! Let's show 'em what proper soldiers can do!" Cannons from the *Lannwedhenek* fired overhead at the beach, causing sand to fly up in the air on the dunes. There were musket shots now firing out from the dunes too, behind the scrubland. The skirmish formation which these militia men were showing was impressive, but Connolly felt it would be more likely it was more about taking cover, rather than tactics. They also knew that until a beachhead had been achieved, it was unlikely they would have to receive cavalry, where skirmish formation is most vulnerable. The enemy cannon were still firing, off to the north of his position, they were still firing at the boats. They hit one in shallows, causing the wood and crew to be dispersed. Those who had not been directly hit however, stood up and walked, now soaked, to the beach.

"Go back and pick any men up you can!" he said frantically to the boat crew. "We will be fine, just help them out of the water!"

The men were lining up on the beach, but as the troops were arriving boat by boat, it was becoming ill disciplined and sloppy. Even Connolly's unit, which usually was excellently drilled as far as he was concerned, were struggling without both their officers and the none commissioned officers roaring at them. The man next to

Connolly fell, grasping his shoulder, blood flying from his arm. "Hold steady lads!" shouted Connolly, "Have a pop while we wait, skirmish formation." The infantry he commanded were not light infantry or skirmishers by any stretch of the imagination, but they could spread themselves out. This made them more vulnerable to cavalry, but at the moment, that was not a problem.

Stanhope's boat was just pulling up to the beach. He had known that there would be contest, he was not foolish enough to expect they would simply walk onto the beach, but he had expected some resistance, but this was beyond his expectations. He had been lucky, his boat had been mainly unscathed, the decision to have him in the middle of the fleet of little boats had proved wise. The cannons the enemy had placed were off to the south slightly, as the enemy probably had found the first place they could securely and accurately lay their guns to bear and simply placed them there.

"In line!" his Sergeant barked behind him, and the men fell in as quickly as they could. Another boat pulled up just to the side of him, and the men aboard there fell in too. "By the left, quick march." ordered the sergeant. They had their beachhead. Bullets were flying intermittently from the scrubland as they approached. "Preee-sent!" the Sergeant was continuing to bellow the orders out. A thick line of muskets, bayonets glistening in the sun, aimed indiscriminately towards the scrublands. "FIRE!". As the order

came, there was a set of bright flashes in the air, the roar of guns as the gunpowder ignited, the acrid stench of gunpowder smoke filling the lungs and the thud of muzzles into the shoulders of the Privates in the line.

There was the expected scream from the bushes, any men who had been unlucky enough to not be fully covered by their hiding places had been hit, along with any men hit by the ricochet of bullets off scrub and bushes. The return, sporadic volley, if such a thing was possible, was distinctly less violent than when they had landed, with less men firing than previously. Stanhope could hear the men in the scrub starting to move backwards giving ground to the attackers.

There were more troops coming off the boats now, following their Commanders lead and firing into the bush. The landing

was turning the way of the attackers and Stanhope knew it.
"FIRE!" shouted his Sergeant again, and more noise, more screams followed.

Francisco was atop his horse on the southern side of the beach watching the landing. He had ordered his cannons to spike their guns if the enemy got too close. They were not the most professional of soldiers, but he had them prepare the spiking cartridges prior to the battle. Once started with the slow match it could not be stopped by the enemy without the risk of extreme danger to themselves.

"Sir, they have taken the beach," said one of his aides.

"Taken?" said Francisco calmly. "The battle is still raging. And they are disorganised. Cavalry!"

"Sir,"

"Now, we advance." The cavalry advanced slowly, not wanting to draw attention to themselves. A cloud of dust would be a giveaway to any half decent Commander, a warning to the infantry that cavalry was approaching. But the dampness of the day had stuck some of the dust and dirt to the road. The usually dusty trail which lead from the fort to the beach was damp and holding all the dirt on it. The slow, methodical approach of the cavalry would only be noticed by an eagle-eyed Commander. And they were all currently fighting in the scrublands with militia.

The slow progression of the cavalry was methodical and precise. Francisco, although not the Commander of the cavalry, was assuming the role, and his subordinate was more than willing to defer to his leader.

"We charge at them," said Francisco calmy. "Swords drawn and we run through them. Cut and run. Do you understand Captain?"

"Yes Sir," he said, sabres and swords were being drawn by the men on horse, as were pistols and carbines. They only had about forty cavalrymen in this unit, it was the best that could be summoned on short notice. But now, during the landing

would be the most effective time to use them. When they were in the close quarters of
a fort, the horse's advantages on a battlefield of being able to cover large amounts of ground at once, and also to be used as basically a battering ram into men.

"When you are ready Captain."

"Ready Sir."

"In that case, may Santiago bless your actions!"

Connolly had finally met up with Potter on the beach. The majority of their troops had been assembled and the line was moving forward into the scrub. Connolly could see the Queen's colours aloft with Stanhope north of his position. The cannons however were still firing away, now aiming at the lines of men assembling on the beach to advance into the scrub.

"Take your men and advance on the dunes Potter!" shouted Connolly over the din. Rather than try and be heard over the din, Potter merely saluted his officer, and beckoned his men into the scrub. That would be the hand-to-hand combat, but Connolly was hoping to flush them out. His troops were still in skirmish formation, waiting for the movement within the scrub to pick off the enemy. Once the scrub was clear they could move within it, clearing the Spanish troops as they went. Potter drew his sword his father had bought him as he enlisted. Well, he rebought it from the pawn shop and went into the unknown. The first man ran at him, a simple musket which he had
already fired, in which he evidently intended to use as a club. The Spaniard swung it wildly, and even with the strong parry from Potter, it knocked him off balance. The Spaniard swung it again, and again Potter barely held on. This time the Spaniard used the butt end and shoved it into Potter's stomach. It winded him and he bent over. "This is it," he thought, "One quick blow and I'm gone." But it did not come. A Private who was near saw the action, and whilst the Spaniard had raised his gun to come down on the head of the officer, thrust his bay-

onet into the Spaniard's stomach. Coming out of his momentary daze, Potter swung his sword into the man's shoulder and
neck, causing blood to fly from his arteries, covering both him
and the Private in it.

"Thank you," he stammered, still trying to regain his breath.
The Private nodded, moving on to the next man as he did. Potter got himself up and kept moving. That was the way to survive. He swung his sword at the next man, coming into contact
with his upper arm. He howled in an and swung his gun wildly
at Potter. He was ready for it though, avoided the contact from
it and kicked the man for good measure in the face. He knew
he would not die from it, but he would be incapacitated for a
while.

There was movement ahead and a volley from behind Potter
reminded him of his duty. He was to flush out as many of the
militia as possible. The enemy, not in any uniform, dropping,
as the bullets hit them in the back, causing them to drop, either
dead, or else
incapacitated.

"Company, advance!" Potter shouted, trying to push the enemy
further into the brush, and ideally completely through it.

Francisco's cavalry were getting closer to the edge of the
troops, sabres drawn. "Charge!" he yelled finally, offering the
men permission to cut through the redcoat lines. Many of the
men were in skirmish formation, trying to counter the attacks
coming from the militia scrublands behind. Francisco swung
his sabre into the upper shoulder and neck area of a redcoat.
His blade was sharp enough that there was not much resistance even as it made contact with him, a gurgled scream from
the young redcoat being all that was released. His horse sprint-
ing on, he swung his blade again, this time into a sergeant who
was trying to rally the troops. It hit the enemy in the chest, lift-
ing him off his feet, and all that was heard was the thud of the
body as it hit the ground lifeless.

"Push on lads!" he called, knowing that the confusion his

troops were causing may slow, if not stop, the English invasion plans. He looked around, and except for one or two riderless horses, his fifty or so men had ripped through the English skirmish lines without too much issue. It was now the militia which were causing him issues. In the excitement, the ill-disciplined troops had fired their guns, trying to add to the English confusion, but causing more injury to the horses and men of the Spanish advance.

"SIR!" he bellowed at the man in charge of the militia at this point of the beach, "Take your men and get back to the fort!" he was furious that his cavalry charge, which had been so devastating, was now slowing because of the foot troops. The young officer nodded, calling his troops in his accented Spanish to withdraw, and the cavalry marched on.

Francisco looked around and saw the beach strewn with Redcoats injured or dying. "Leave them!" he shouted. If they were down, they were not affecting the fight, and speed was the most important factor, then dealing with any men would only slow the approach.

"But Sir, the rules of..."

"Militia Captain!" he shouted, "Deal with the Redcoats."

How they were to deal with the Redcoats he did not specify. He officially of course meant, carry them back to the fort as were the rules of war. But whatever happened, his orders had been clear enough. The cavalry would continue into the next line of English troops, continuing to confuse and damage their enemy throughout.

Connolly had ordered his men into line. His troops, under Lieutenant Potter, were clearing the scrublands ahead, allowing them to create a base to work from. Potter was clearly doing a decent job; the militia were moving out from their sheltered positions and into the open. With that, the regimented and skilled shots of the English muskets could pick off the enemy, one by one. The initial shock volley had served to thin their ranks originally, but now the skirmish lines were what were needed.

"Cavalry!" shouted a soldier to Connolly's right. He turned and saw a platoon of cavalry charging towards his troops, all stood neatly in line, ready to be cut down.

"Turn and face!" he shouted, but it was too late, the cavalry hitting the side of their line. The cavalry were throwing men left and right. Connolly raised his pistol and fired it, sending a horseman to fall backwards off his horse. He drew his sword and parried an attack from another horseman too, but as he looked around he could see he was one of the lucky ones.

"Into the scrub!" he yelled. He knew the scrub was not completely cleared and they would have to fight, outnumbered by the irregulars in there, but it was better to fight the irregulars' hand to hand, than to try and stand up against the cavalry ripping through his lines. A horseman rode towards Connolly, and this time he was not as fortunate. The sabre struck his shoulder, causing him to scream in agony. Blood flowed freely as he now stumbled into the brush.

Stanhope was looking over the beach. His troops may be fairing fine, but they were probably the only ones which were. The men on the southern side of the beach had been attacked by a perfectly
timed and disguised cavalry charge. The middle were still being beaten back by the four cannons, repeatedly firing away with a methodical regularity. The north side of the beach however was all but secure.

A cannonball from the ship just off the coast hit into the area where the cannons were. "Thank god for the covering fire," he thought, slowing the cannon fire on his own troops. "Company! Right face! Quick march!" ordered the sergeant.

The ordered discipline of the Redcoats was clear here, as they slowly but surely began to clear a path of the enemy troops. Skirmish formation had been replaced by the doctrine of fire and advance, as rank by rank the troops won the beach. More troops were adding to the line, meaning every time they fired, more and more of the Spanish troops were being downed. As they walked over the injured or dying, any man who showed an ounce of resistance were clubbed in the head with the butt of a musket, or else a quick poke with the bayonet to finish them off.

"Cannons from the ships Sir!" called a Lieutenant from the waterside, and Stanhope saw the smoke coming from the sloop out in the bay. Their cover fire had held the cannons in check, and hopefully would do the same for the cavalry too.

Smythe was pulling for all he was worth, rushing to where the upturned landing crafts were. The spray next to him showed that

despite his gunnery crews' best efforts, the battery ashore still had some fire power in them.

"Sir, man in the water!" shouted an oarsman.

"Only if he's alive!" replied Smythe. It may seem cold, but there was limited space in the gig, and no room for dead men yet. They could wait.

"His arms are up Sir!"

"Then let's get him out of there!"

Time was of the essence. The longer these men were in the cold waters of the Atlantic, drenched and weighed down by their woollen jackets, it would not be long before treading water was not an option, especially in these choppy waters.

"Pull him out damn it!" shouted Smythe. Every moment wasted could be another man's life. There was yet another spray in the water, evidently the battery had decided that the single gig was a better and more realistic target than individual troops around them.

"Hold water!" shouted Smythe, and the oarsmen worked against the currents and tide to hold their position in the water. Smythe lent over the gig, into the water, grabbing the man by his belt and pulling him headfirst into the boat. This was the third person they had pulled out of the water, and they only now had space for two more.

"Ttthhhhannk you." said a shivering young private.

"Anyone see any more?" shouted Smythe over the confusion. There

was no response from either his men, or the two men they had already pulled out of the water, who were now sat up and looking around trying to assist where they could. "In that case, return to the *Lannwedhenek* boys."

Francisco's horse slowed to a gentle trot. The soldiers had fled into the scrub, where his horses would be much less effective. Now, they had pulled away toward the waters edge, putting them nominally out of range of the musket fire.

"Sir, what are your orders?"

Francisco thought hard about this. He surveyed the landscape of the battlefield. Despite their best efforts it was clear to him that it was a lost cause. The English had created their beachhead on the northern side. With the small cannon and inexperienced troops they had, dislodging them would be both impractical and most likely cost more in blood than he could afford.

"Captain! Pick your fastest rider. They are to go to the cannon and order them to be spiked. They are only small, but I want it gone. Understand?"

"Yes Sir."

"The rest of you, start mopping them up whilst returning to the fort. Any Englishman who offers resistance, you know what to do." Francisco would not reinforce the failure, he knew the cost would be most likely too great. He would not personally take part in the

sport he had ordered for his horsemen. If one of those men were to be unfortunate and get themselves caught out, it was not the end of the world, one regular soldier would not change the outcome. But the Commander in chief, that was a different matter. Of course, if he came across a soldier who needed dealing with, he would, but he would not go out of his way to engage, nor did he have to worry about the looting which some of his less affluent horsemen may engage with.

His horse reduced itself to a steady trot, as he observed the battlefield. Although he did not know exact numbers, he knew his troops had fared better overall. That being said, the English had achieved their objective. They had their beachhead. In terms of men, he had won. In terms of strategy, he had most certainly lost.

The explosion from behind him confirmed his notion of glorious defeat. The cannons were blown. That was the understood signal for retreat for all the troops. The English would shortly have all the beach at their disposal, slowly unloading all the equipment the fleet could have carried. It was an unpleasant feeling.

Connolly felt cold. The white of his clothes were stained all over with what he assumed was mostly his own blood. As the Spanish had withdrawn, his troops had brought him back out onto the beach, in the hope that, the more visible they were, the more likely they were to receive any help.

Potter was stood next to his major, trying to organise the wounded and dead of his company. The surgeon's bill would be long and expensive today, he feared. "Any ideas?" he asked the closest sergeant he could see.

"Not sure Sir,"

"Potter," said Connolly rather weakly.

"Sir?" he replied quietly. Even in his short time as a soldier, he knew that voice. It was one of death.

"The duel," he said weakly still.

"Sir?"

"The duel against that German," he said, coughing as he spoke. "The bloody thief man!"

"Yes Sir," said Potter, trying not to get his Major too excited.

"Leave it alone," he said, "Her Majesty and the men are about to lose one officer, best not risk another."

"You're going to be fine Sir," said Potter, although not truly believing his own words.

"You and I know that isn't bloody true."

Smythe was back aboard the *Lannwedhenek*, with several of the men who had ended up in the water. There would be no doubt that some men did not make it, the water had taken them into the deep. "Mister Yin," Smythe said quietly, "how go the patients?"

"Nothing Midshipman Abraham cannot handle Sir," he replied. "Then come aboard a gig with me, I am sure your presence ashore would be most welcome." The wind had mercifully died down now, and the sea was much calmer than in the morning. Several gigs and longboats were making their way from the boats in the fleet, with Commanders of troops who had stayed aboard ships now making their way to the beach to take command.

Smythe's longboat pulled up where he had calculated that Connolly's men would have landed. He had seen through his glass the cavalry which had decimated the southern column within the English lines. Any surgeon would be welcome here that was for certain. It was a blood bath.

"Any men who would recover to be taken back to the *Lannwedhenek*," said Smythe to the crew. "Press any soldiers you think would be suitable to row with you gentlemen. Now, Mister Yin, any men you can save, you better bloody well do it."

CHAPTER SIXTEEN

Stanhope looked across the beach. O'Hara had come ashore, as had His Royal Highness Prince George. There were Redcoats all around, and men who bore no known uniform, the irregulars of the Spanish forces.

"A report, Sir, if you please," said Prince George, standing to attention. He had witnessed the storming of the beach from the *Adventure* and wanted to hear first-hand what had happened. He was not unhappy with the outcome, once he had heard that Francisco was defending the territory, he knew there would be a fight.

"Your highness," said Stanhope, "We landed at the beach at several places. The irregular forces of his Most Catholic Majesty slowed our progress."

"Yes, I can see that," said Prince George, not too unkindly, "continue, if you please."

"We took the northern end of the beach with little casualties; the southern side however was met with a small battery of cannons and a unit of cavalry. I wish to commend the bravery and skill of all of our troops here today Sir. The fortitude of the southern troops, even against the odds was highly commendable."

"Agreed," said Prince George calmly. "the men fought bravely. I saw from the ship they had blown their guns. Smart not to let them fall into our hands. What of the cavalry?"

"I think they knew that it was no use Sir," said Stanhope simply. "It would have taken a gargantuan effort to dislodge us. Men better used on the defence of the forts."

This was true. The fleet may now have its foothold but that is all it was. There was still the small matter of the several forts which separated them from Cadiz.

"I intend to secure the town to the North, Rota it is called." said the Prince regally. "This is after all as much about diplomacy as it is about military matters."

"A civilian government Sir," said Stanhope, understanding what Prince George wished to establish.

"Exactly," he replied, "If we are the official civilian authority here, we may actually remain." It would also give the soldiers a place to billet, giving the Navy more room. Tensions would be eased. That would help both Ormonde and Rooke, both of whom were still clearly frustrated with the other over the truncated plans that had been set.

"Will you ride with me Colonel?" asked the Prince, a request which Stanhope had no chance of refusing.

"I shall assemble a small force to ensure your safety your highness." It would not be too difficult, the main issue was that many of the horsemen, along with their horses, were still aboard ships. It had been a long journey for the horses, they would undoubtably be skittish upon disembarkation, and a disorderly ride would not do for
such an occasion.

"Might I suggest your Highness," said Stanhope, trying to explain delicately to a Prince, "That we ride into town tomorrow, after the horses have had a chance to stretch their legs."

The Prince looked at Stanhope for a moment and smiled. "Then let us walk in, Colonel. I understand your suggestion, but I must insist that we enter the town as soon as possible."

"Yes Sir, the light company shall advance ahead of us then Sir." The orders were issued, the light company advanced slowly into the town. They moved quickly individually, but slowly as a group, the man behind advancing whilst the man ahead stood, musket at the ready to fire should the men be attacked.

They need not have bothered. Rota was deserted. "They have even burned the floorboards," joked one of the soldiers. The town was completely stripped of all wealth and value to an army. But to an individual, there were some trinkets to be had in gold and silver coins.

The Castillo de Luna was the ceremonial town hall, the house of the Governor of the Rota. There had been a building on this site, ceremonial or defensive, since the eleventh century, previously being home to a Muslim minaret under the rule of Guzman the Good. The majority of the current structure had been there since the mid-thirteen century, rebuilt during the time of the Reconquista. The yellow sandstone walls, and towers continued to

look like a formidable fortress, but an engineer would look upon these with an amused eye. They were outdated, and more decorative than defensive, as modern cannons would make light work of what once catapults would have had a prolonged struggle with.

Prince George entered in what he felt was a somewhat anti-climax. However, the army had managed to bring ashore a desk for him to work from. "Where are all the townsfolk?" he asked, assuming that the soldiers had done something untoward.

"Gone, Your Highness," replied the soldier, "they chose to run. Or rather they were ordered to, I fear," said Stanhope coming in behind. "Still, there are roofs over buildings. I shall order the provosts to select billets. How many rooms are there here Sir?"

"A fair few of decent size," replied Prince George simply.

"Then if you would be so kind, I shall also billet the senior officers here until a more suitable arrangement can be made?"

"I would be glad of it."

The larger rooms would be given to the Prince and his entourage, the next rooms down to the Duke of Ormonde. Finally, any spare rooms would be given to the likes of Stanhope, the young Earl next or O'Hara, another man of the Emerald Isle.

The Duke of Ormonde arrived in the early evening, with very little fanfare. This was not to his liking. "You could have at least called out the guard Stanhope!" he shouted in frustration at his

subordinate. Stanhope was used to such frustrations from his Commander.

"Of course, Sir," he answered. It was going to be a long evening.

Smythe and Yin walked slowly to Lieutenant Potter. He looked tired.

"Hell of a morning Potter," said Smythe kindly, "where is the Major?"

"The Major is, indisposed, Sir," said Potter, in a quiet voice.

"How so?" said Smythe.

"He is," he paused.

"YIN!" shouted Smythe, the realisation coming over him. "YIN!"

"Already on it, Sir!" shouted back the surgeon. The men had dined together, had berthed together. It was unthinkable that one of the four of them would have fallen so quickly within reaching their destination.

Yin went over to where Potter indicated his Major was laid. "Lie still," said Yin calmly, his composed nature not changing even in this gravest of moments.

"Will he live?" asked Smythe, almost childlike in his approach of Yin.

"I am not sure," said Yin, still considering his patient, "He has clearly lost a lot of blood. May I ask how long the Major has been "indisposed" Lieutenant?"

"Around half an hour. We tried to stop the bleeding and make him as comfortable as possible," said Potter, unsure if what he had done
was the correct thing.

"Sand," said Yin simply. "You should have used the salted sand to block the wound."

"They tried bless them," mouthed Connolly, clearly trying to exonerate his fellow soldiers.

"Can he be moved?" asked Smythe, knowing that this was not the place for a man to be bleeding out.

"Until I have stabilised the wound it would be highly unrecommended Sir."

"Then stabilise him!" roared Smythe, losing his temper with

his surgeon. He almost immediately regretted his anger however, "Sorry, Yin, that was uncalled for."

"It was, you are quite correct Sir," said Yin, his usual tone when he was politely mocking people in use. "But it cannot be helped. Now," he said, as he often did once he had formulated a plan in his head about how to carry on, "We stuff it with saltwater and sand. The salt will kill most if not all the infection, whilst the sand will act as a physical barrier to stop the bleeding. It is my understanding, from what Hempleman said about Rota that they intend to use that as a base of operations? Then let us take the officer there, he will be surely welcomed."

It was a difficult task, even with Yin's suggestions about packing the wound. Moving him without inducting too much pain would be a struggle. "It may have to come off," said Yin patiently to Connolly.

"As you know, I am no trained surgeon, but I fear you may have to lose it Sir,"

The men bearing his stretcher carried the Major the three miles towards Rota, moaning and groaning the whole way. The wound, packed with sand, saltwater and wadding, was holding up nicely, less and less blood was coming away each second.

"How long?" asked Smythe to the stretcher bearer at the front.

"About another half mile Sir, then we need to find the surgeon."

The roads were sandy, causing many miss steps and jarring of the stretcher. Each movement caused the wadding and bandages that Yin had placed in the wound to move, causing more bleeding to occur. It was about another four hundred yards on when Connolly told them to stop. "Here seems nice." He said simply, and the men stopped. "Let me stand."

"Sir, if you stand, you will knock your bandages, we might be able to-"

"Able to what? Save me?" he laughed and coughed, and a small amount of blood came up with the cough. "My friends, I am dying either way, better do it on one's feet, don't you all think?"

The eloquence of his Grammar school education came through as he was determined to die without showing fear or pain. "As a good and proper Englishman-"

"Irish." said one of the men with a thick Ulster accent who had helped carry him.

"Yes, alright Irish then," he smiled, "Well, better an Irishman than anything else right now." He gently got to his feet, "Did we at least win?". There was almost a pleading in his eyes.

"We took the beach, if that what you mean," said Smythe. Obviously, the overall target was the port of Cadiz. But the landing of the troops to create a beachhead had indeed been a success. The cavalry had been forced to withdraw, and with no other pitched battles, the sting was out of them. The loss of the enemy's guns, albeit small ones, had also been an added bonus to the cause.

"Then it wasn't all in vain," he said as he stood up. The bandages dropped away, but there was not much bleeding from the wound. He staggered on the spot, holding his feet as steady as he could. He took a deep breath, exhaled, and took a second. "Such a shame, to die here, so far from home." He closed his eyes and fell backwards into Smythe and Yin who were standing with their fellow officer. Yin, who although small had considerable strength, caught him, as Connolly exhaled his final breath and his head and body went limp.

"Though I walk through the valley of the shadow of death, I shall fear no evil," said Smythe finally. The men stood around their Commander, the man who had led them off the boats, onto the beach, organised them to stop them from being picked off one by one by the enemy skirmishers, and stood his ground against a cavalry charge. And he had paid for it with his life.

"Commander Smythe," said Potter quietly after a few more moments. "What do we do now?"

Smythe had no idea. At sea, the ceremony was simple and expected. But soldiers on foreign soil, Smythe was honestly unsure of the procedure.

"May I suggest," said Yin quietly, "That you report to Colonel Stanhope as your superior. You currently are in command, but as I understand it, are too junior in rank to have this position?" This was true. It was a minimum of a Major which could command the number of troops under the command of Major Connolly. That number was of course now reduced, but still Potter would be unable to take further command.

"Yes," said Potter, still trying to think through what Yin had said, "Yes, that is the correct course of action. Thank you, gentlemen. Stretcher bearers if you would be so kind as to continue with your task?"

"Yes, Sir." It meant they would not be able to continue with the looting of the dead like many of their compatriots were engaged in, but the sign of respect they could give Connolly was worth it.

"Myself and Yin will return to our ship, should you need a report of this Lieutenant," said Smythe kindly.

"Thank you, Sir. Best of luck on your return to the ship."

Ormonde was sitting at the desk which he had brought for the occasion. He was sat in the Castillo de Luna, having just had his dinner, was waiting for Stanhope to report to him about the day's actions. The butchers bill from the different platoons were being collated, and although it would not have a major effect on the battles ahead, some units may need to be merged in order to keep a cohesive military force.

"Sir," said Stanhope, standing to attention in front of him.

"Ah, Stanhope," said Ormonde, "go one then, how much?" he was asking like he was literally paying a bill in a tavern or shop rather than that of the number of dead an injured in his army.

"Numbers still coming in Sir," replied Stanhope, "but we believe the sea took a few before the guns even started Sir."

"How many?"

"Around twenty, Sir," replied Stanhope.

"Well, that's Rooke's bloody fault," replied Ormonde, "stupid bloody waterboy, demanding I do things in a certain way. See what happened?"

"O'Hara did agree it was probably the right decision also Sir," commented Stanhope.

"O'Hara said it was the right thing after we had been sat outside the port for three days Sir," replied Ormonde, in a rather irritable tone, "we should, as I suggested, have attacked the second we arrived. The damn Diego's wouldn't have stood, you mark my words!"

It had not missed Stanhope's attention that the men that "wouldn't stand" had indeed done just that, holding onto the beach for nearly

an hour before finally withdrawing in the midmorning. But now was not the time for being clever with his superior officer. "Any gentlemen fall?" What Ormonde of course meant was, had any officers died.

"At the moment there are still a couple missing Sir," said Stanhope, "But I can report that Connolly, of your Irish company, had died of wounds sustained in battle. His body is in the butchers if you wish to-"

"I shall look upon him later," said Ormonde, although whether he would or not remained to be seen, "Plantation man, isn't he? New Irish?"

"Yes Sir," replied Stanhope.

"Hmm," came the noise from Ormonde. "Is there anything else I should be aware of or is that everything for the evening?"

"There is a council of war tomorrow to discuss the next steps on the plan Sir, but other than that, no, nothing I can think of."

"Then I bid you a pleasant evening Sir, goodnight." The interview was brief and to the point, and Stanhope was almost certain he knew why. Although the town had been deserted upon arrival, some local ladies had come to ply their trade. Some, as honourable washerwomen or cooks to the officers, as many had not been able to bring their valets due to the confines of the ships. Other women, however, were not so concerned with their honour, or said lack of. Whores of all levels, from the classier ladies who serviced the

officers, to the cheap gutter whores who serviced the common soldiery, returned to ply their trade, relieving some of the troops of their recently gained booty.

"What time is she arriving?" Stanhope asked the guard stationed outside Ormonde's door.

"Don't know what you're talking about Sir," he said, with a cheeky wink at Stanhope. It confirmed his suspicions at any rate.

"Should I wait till later to wake the Duke or-?" he paused waiting for the response from the guardsman.

"No, his Duke doesn't like to share his bed on the evening, says it makes him feel guilty about his wife. The morning will be fine."

"How very noble of him," thought Stanhope, "Very well, I shall return tomorrow," he said to the guardsman and bade him goodnight.

In the morning, but not too early, a council of war had been convened. Ormonde, without too much difficulty, had been convinced to allow today to be a rest day, rather than pushing forward immediately. Some saw this as a tactical blunder, in that they should continue whilst they had the Dons on the run. Cooler heads however prevailed. It was not a lack of skill or organisation which had caused the Spanish defeat on the beaches, but the size of the territory to defend and a sheer lack of men. The forts however, being more compact and in a much smaller area, could be defended much easier, and with less men required. Add into that the mounted guns attached to the barricades and the simple action of having to storm any breaches, the allied forces would inevitably come under serious scrutiny.

Rooke had come ashore to offer his experience and support where possible, although he now understood with the successful taking of a beachhead, that his part in this endeavour was mainly coming to an end.

As was becoming the etiquette for this expedition, the Generals and Admirals however, let Prince George open the meeting.

"I have set up a civilian administration for this region, in the name of his most Catholic majesty, Charles III." It was a very grandiose claim. By set up a civilian government, what he meant was he had issued proclamations in the name of the region of Andalusia, for Charles III, with some other German officials in tow. Hempleman for example had been granted the title, minister for agriculture, without knowing the first thing about farming, agriculture, or what even the hell they grew down here.

"Congratulations your Highness," said Rooke politely, "Have the dignitaries which you discussed previously come to bear witness to this?" That had after all been the whole point of this mission as far as Prince George had been concerned.

"Not yet, but I am sure all-in good time. The people of Rota are returning as we saw last night, they know we pose them no harm.

The good people of Andalusia will of course be the first to swear loyalty to his Highness King Charles, and soon, I am sure, all of Spain will follow!" It was a bold claim which the Prince made, and nobody, not even the Prince, Rooke was sure, actually believed that this little landing party and invasion would cause an entire country to magically change sides in this war to the death.

"To the next steps gentlemen," said Ormonde cheerfully. He may still be frustrated with Rooke, but he would not let this affect his plans going forward. "Fort Saint Catherine is our next target," he said, setting up for the revelation of his plans, "Which, as my Naval colleague pointed out, is heavily defended if attacked from sea. It is however, rather less well defended if attacked from the north east, the land side." A basic recognisance and military understanding told him this. But it was true, nevertheless. They would now be able to advance on the fort from a much stronger position than previously, leaving then only the combined port entrance forts of Saint Matagorda and Saint Lawrence.

"I intend to hit the fort hard and fast, passing through her and establishing a southern base of operations. From there we will pass through the town of Saint Mary, and around the inlet and attack the eastern fort." Ormonde made it sound so simple. And to be fair it was. Whether it went as smoothly as suggested was another matter.

"The Navy will be able to offer limited support," said Rooke calmly. "Once you have engaged, we may offer some covering fire aimed at distracting the enemy."

"Would you be willing to send a ship in before we engage to try to drag some of the troops away from our assembling troops in the east?"

"It would have to be a small ship, one of the sloops, a single broadside from them, intent on simply being a diversion."

Ormonde sighed. Of course, he would not send in one of his precious ships of the line. A small Sloop or brig would be all that was offered to him. The army was doing all the work and the Navy was just sitting, with over a thousand guns no less, idly by.

"Very well," he finally said, nodding his appreciation to Rooke. Better to seem pleased and be pissed off than show it. It would not do him any good at any rate. "Then we shall start to move our guns tomorrow afternoon gentlemen."

"We can help you there, Duke," said Rooke. "You may have as many of my guns as you so wish." Rooke was trying to mend the bridges that Ormonde and he had broken so recently. The surrounding officers smiled, the gesture was appreciated by them.

"Well thank you, Sir Rooke. But of course, I can, it's not like you are using them. Besides, we will have to see whether the artillery need them from you." Ormonde was desperate to not accept any help from Rooke unless he specifically needed it.

"Well, the offer stands," said Rooke.

"I will ride out this afternoon, my Duke and survey the area," said O'Hara, "that should give us some indication as to the need for the guns." He looked directly at Rooke and nodded. Rooke had the sneaking suspicion that the guns would most certainly be needed.

"Excellent suggestion, Charles," said Ormonde. He smiled at the older man, but subordinate officer.

The council was wrapped up with this. No further plans would be made until O'Hara had done his assessment, at which time, no doubt Ormonde would make further plans without discussing it with Rooke.

O'Hara walked with purpose into the stables. Tall, thin, and muscular, O'Hara usually intimidated most people with his physique. His face, worn from years of work, with a small stubble he had allowed to grow since they had arrived in the bay of Cadiz only added to his daunting demeanour.

It was only a few miles ride, nothing compared to his younger days. His friends said he had spent his youth riding horses through the wilds of Ireland. His detractors said he had spent his youth riding horses and robbing people through the wilds of Ireland. The truth, as with many things in O'Hara's life, was somewhere in the middle.

"You and the Duke seem to be of one mind," said a voice behind him. It was the young Lieutenant that Rooke kept close to him.

"Roberts, right?" said O'Hara. He was not sure of the name, but was almost certain it began with an R.

"Richards," said the young Lieutenant as he continued to smile at O'Hara, "Lieutenant of Her Majesty's ship *Royal Sovereign*." He stood, having clearly meant the original statement as a question to be answered.

"Myself and the Duke have been friends for a long time now. I had the pleasure of tutoring the Duke throughout his younger years."

"That is a generous term for riding master." Richards stopped walking, as did O'Hara, who simply looked at him with distrust and frustration.

"I am sorry, do you have something you wish to say to me Richards?"

"Merely stating what I understand to be true."

"Then leave it as your understanding," said O'Hara testily. "I have known the Duke through many times, and my role has changed over the years. Yes, I was once merely his riding master, but I have had the pleasure in later years of tutoring and working with the Duke through all these matters and education. So yes," he added at the end of his speech, one which clearly he had used before to other people who questioned his motives, "it is not surprising that the young Duke follows my suggestions, as he has done now for many years."

Richards kindly, and attentively listened to this speech from O'Hara.

He had been around long enough to know not to annoy or offend the friend of a Duke, it tended not to advance one's career prospects. "Then I bid you a fair and safe ride to view the fort. I'm sure you will come to a sensible and practical conclusion upon viewing."

O'Hara rode south to look at the fortifications of Fort Saint Catherine. It took not all of his inconsiderable experience to see it was an old fort, one which had not been kept well. It was not dilapidated, the walls were not crumbling, but it had been built a long time ago, and was not up to the modern standards of fortifications.

"It wunt tek much cannon fire Sir," said one of the Engineers who had been brought along for the assessment. "I'd sey we'd be in a day or two."

"That quickly?" asked O'Hara rather sceptically. A day seemed very quick, even for the old fort.

"Aye Sir," replied the engineer. "Aim low 'n' it'll tumble like an 'ouse o' cards."

"Size of guns?"

"Size shunt mek much difference. Just aim enough of the buggers at it and we'll stick an 'ole in it big enough that you'd think Moses himself did it."

"If only Moses himself were here to lead the promised people, the Irish, through without harm," thought O'Hara, "Very good, get digging and laying."

"We could use some more guns, if you 'av' 'em"

"I'll get them off a ship or two," said O'Hara.

It was mid-afternoon when the townsfolk began to slowly return to Rota. Evidently the ladies from the previous night had gone away and told the people of their "generosity", and some, but not all, of the inhabitants began to return to their homes. This caused unforeseen problems, where had the people stayed, it was unlikely that the billeting of troops would have happened in such a free and haphazard way. The soldiers had originally been told to simply sleep wherever they so wished, as there had been no opposition to this, with the town being deserted. Quarrels broke out, and one more than one occasion the Provosts had to be called to deal with the ill-discipline of the troops.

The Governor of Rota also returned this afternoon for an "audience with his Royal Highness, Jorge de Darmstadt". Clearly the arrival of the previous Viceroy of Catalonia had been announced through Andalusia. As a war hero of the old, Hapsburg Spain, Prince George, or "Jorge" as the Spanish called him, clearly still commanded respect in this region, even though it was as far away from his exploits as possible.

"Senor, can you assist me please," asked the Governor after the introductions had been made.

"Si fuera más fácil para usted, señor, ¿podemos hablar en español?"

"Eso sería preferible señor, gracias."

Much to the annoyance of both his German counterparts and his English allies, the two gentlemen had their conversation in Spanish. George, however, was no fool. He knew that by putting the Governor at ease, he would get more out of him.

"You were not here when the army arrived, can you explain why?"

"Ordered to Sir," he replied. "The pretender Philip's representative here ordered the town to empty. With armed men. Under pain of death were we to leave anything that your army may find useful."

"Well, I commend your bravery for returning Senor. What can you tell me of the enemy positions?"

"I have no knowledge of such things Senor," said the Governor with a shrug of his shoulders. "The Marquis of Villadarias rode only with his cavalry to inspect the town. I am not sure if he knew of the Castillo de Luna, or its nature as a civil administrational house, rather than a fort, or else just wanted to ensure we left you nothing to use."

"What can you do for me?"

"I can offer you my support as the Governor of Rota," he said as regally as he could. It was a humble and hollow gesture. But it might get men from the surrounding area on side. This mission was as much about gaining the populaces love and care as much as military might. A unit, even a partial unit of local troops would give a large

amount of legitimacy to the whole expedition.

"Well, your support is most welcome!" replied an over enthusiastic Prince George. "Yes, I, as his most Catholic Majesty, King Charles III's representative here, declare you shall continue as the Governor of Rota." The Governor bowed to Prince George, as he left the room. It was an empty gesture and everyone, including the Governor knew it. So long as Prince George was in the town, he would run the affairs of the town with or without the input of the Governor. No, this was his way of ensuring his towns longevity, pride or position be dammed.

A small militia of men from Rota were assembled for inspection by Prince George. "These are excellent soldiers!" he exclaimed, going up to each man and thanking him personally. Stanhope and O'Hara looked on, somewhat in disbelief, somewhat in amusement, as the Prince began declaring that these men were "The true Army of Spain!" and "Defenders of the faith!" and any other honorific he could think of.

"Toy soldiers," whispered O'Hara to Stanhope, "wouldn't stand to a single shot if you ask me."

"I didn't," said Stanhope with a smile, "No, I know what you mean, but the Prince's role isn't a military one is it? It's a public opinion one. And that helps."

"Thirty men who have around fourteen thousand around them asking if they want to join?" said O'Hara with a smirk, "I'm sure

we'd all be more likely to sign up. Anyway, won't make much difference. Not like they are gonna be used in the battles is it? Oh, and the rest of the guns are being placed today. We'll be attacking the fort soon."

"Who's ship they are coming off?"

"*Lannwedhenek*," said O'Hara, "One of the sloops in the bay. Getting the gun crews as well to line and fire the buggers."

CHAPTER SEVENTEEN

Jenkins was staring down the barrel of the cannon. It was aiming at the eastern wall of Fort Saint Catherine. "Sir?" he shouted to the army officer who was inspecting the guns which had come ashore.

"Yes?" he shouted back, clearly more interested in the guns than what a naval petty officer had to say.

"Permission to fire a ranging shot, Sir." He had some idea of how far his twelve-pounder would fire, but without the rocking ship beneath him, or the returning of an enemy broadside, this was new territory for him.

"Granted," said the officer in charge, and with the slow match ready, Jenkins poked the hole. The flame from the cannon seemed less bright in the open air, as did the roar it gave off without the echoing of the ship around it, but the smoke blowing back into Jenkins's face was a new experience he did not appreciate. He coughed and spluttered, as did the rest of his gun crew.

The shot fell short by about forty yards, a poor shot. If they had been at sea, he would be cursing his crew, but in these unfamiliar surroundings he was willing to let it go down to inexperience. "Let's raise the gun up boys." A few degrees of elevation could make all the difference when firing the guns. "Sir?"

"However they bear Mister Jenkins," replied the officer, who was getting frustrated that these seamen could not just think for themselves. The shot this time was much better, but still short.

"Another degree Mister Jenkins," came a voice the crew recognised.

"Mister Treen," said Jenkins, with a small salute, "what brings

219

you to our little battery?"

"Making sure you don't destroy the Commander's guns, Mister Jenkins," he said with a smile, but both men knew he was only joking. "No, in all seriousness I was asked to come ashore as the officer in charge of you lot. You're my section anyway, so it made sense I came along." The informality in which he spoke matched that of his management style. The army officer overseeing looked on frustratedly at this exchange, but thankfully, he had not said anything. This may have been out of professional courtesy for a fellow officer, or perhaps he simply thought it would be simpler not to do anything, after all they were not the men under his command, and it would not make a difference.

The gun crew reloaded, realigned, this time with Treen's "help" and fired. What help the young Lieutenant gave remained to be seen, but it hit the wall of the fort clean enough and judging by the amount of rock which was dislodged it would not take long to make a simple breech. From there, the army would rush in, and overrun the small garrison.

"Why don't they fire back?" asked Treen, still green in the ways of warfare.

"They can't resupply," said Jenkins, who had thankfully never been
on the receiving end of a siege, so only knew this in practice. "If they fire their guns now, when we come to attack, they have nothing to use against us. We fire ours and that mule over there just brings another ball from the supplies." The supply lines of the British were not infinite, but as always when there was profit to be made in war, people did. The Portuguese again, after cleaning up in Oporto, now were cleaning up on supplying the officers of the Army and Navy with better food and spirits than basic rations could provide, and enough gun powder and shot to blast a rather large hole in the side of the forts throughout their Atlantic coastline. Not only would they profit in the literal sense, gold, spices and improvements to the trade agreements being the usual fees for such activities, but a

weaker Spain to the East, meant more opportunity to expand for the fledgling Portuguese Empire.

"Keep firing at 'em like that gunnery crew!" shouted the Engineer overseeing the project, and Treen smiled with pride. His crew smiled too, the boys of the Navy outshining those of the Army or Engineers was a source of pride many of them felt. It would not be a quick job, it would undoubtably take them most of the day, with the assistance of all the other guns firing away at the fort. But unless the Spanish insisted on fighting a pitched battle, something with their significantly smaller size would be ill advised, the fort would eventually fall to the allied forces.

Francisco had withdrawn to the more defendable fort of Saint Lawrence, but he had heard the guns begin to fire on the fort to the north. He knew that meant that fort was as good as lost, the garrison was not large enough to hold off the allied force in any way.

"What's the plan Sir?"

"Plan Captain?" Francisco had been stood overlooking the bay, quite absent from the local considerations, but his Captain's question had brought him back to the present.

"Yes Sir, there is around three hundred men in that fort, how do you intend to get them out of there?"

"In wooden boxes," said Francisco, rather coldly. "Don't you dare look at me like that!" he snarled at his Captains look of horror. "We cannot dislodge those cannons, and it would be very foolish to try. The men in the garrison will not surrender, even if I told them to, they have too much pride, and they know that as long as they kill more of those Godames than are garrisoned there, then it is a small victory, and their sacrifice will be remembered. More importantly, there are not three hundred men inside that fort. More like sixty."

Francisco was again, as he put it, refusing to reinforce failure. He continued to look over the bay, at the fort across the port entrance, Saint Matagorda. That was the real lynchpin of the

whole operation. So long as Spain held that, they would hold both Cadiz, and the several ships in the bay. They may only be galleys, the
smallest of warships, if they could even be called warships, but they would fetch around four hundred pounds apiece. The English of course did not use them, but the Northern war was raging, or if they could slip them through into the Mediterranean possibly gift them to the Austrians, furthering their war in Italy.

"Sir, women from Rota have arrived." All the best spies in the world could work hard, infiltrating the enemy administrations, passing messages through secret channels, building a rapport, all the while hoping they were not found out and hung. It was much easier to hire some whores and tell them to go get information from the enemy. There was one thing which was common across all men, they thought with their cocks.

"Senorita," he said kindly, "What news do you bring of the English?"

"What, no rose for a lady? Sir, you are slipping," she smiled, and Francisco smiled, which was something the Captain thought was as rare as hens' teeth.

"I am sorry, I should have made sure you had something of use. A wine perhaps?" he offered the lady a wine, "Now, what can you tell me."

"Other than the Commander of the English cheats on his wife?" she said with a smile, "They have brought a civilian administrator as you thought they would. Its Jorge de Darmstadt."

"The Hapsburg who used to run Catalonia?"

"Yes Sir,"

That was interesting. Clearly the Hapsburgs' felt that by sending a man who had previously had administrational duties in Spain was a move which could inspire hope and energy into their cause.

"There is more," she added, "Your fears were correct. He swore loyalty to the invading army."

Francisco did not look shocked. He did not even need an explanation as to who "he" was. The governor of Rota had basically told him he intended to do that, if it meant his town would be spared any horrific consequences of an invading army. But it was treason, and he would pay the price for such actions.

"They have raised a militia as well," she said, "Farm boys and the like. Compared to our troops, or the militia's you have raised, they would not stand. It's a propaganda only."

"They still have a musket; they can still pull a trigger." Francisco said, "What of the bakers and butchers."

"Forced requisitions," she said, "No doubt they would sell them to the army, but currently, they are not given a choice."

"Quietly tell them to get receipts," said Francisco, "Once we win, there will be punishments. Any man who can prove he did not have a choice will not be executed."

"Executed?"

"It is treason. Let the word get around with your ladies if you please. Any man, or woman, found working with these invaders will be considered traitors to Spain. And will be punished accordingly."

Francisco's face showed he was not joking. His furrowed his eyebrows and took a sip of the wine. "Does this displease you, my dear?"

"For the glory of Spain," she replied, raising her glass in a toast to the Marquis.

"For the glory of Spain," he repeated and smiled.

The guns were now firing with clockwork regularity at the walls of fort Saint Catherine. The garrison inside knew their duty. They were to hold for as long as possible. Major Juan Diaz stood on the ramparts looking over toward his enemy. They intended to pound them into submission, break holes in his fort and make it worthless in defence. He had around fifty men in the garrison with him, and he was under no illusions that not all fifty would make it out alive. In fact, he seriously doubted how many would. At the rate the cannons were firing at his walls, the invasionary force would have their breech within the next couple of hours.

"Why does he not send help?" asked one of the younger militia men who had been stationed at the fort.

"You will remember your place, Private!" roared the Major, "Just because the Commander of the entire region of Andalusia doesn't share his plans with you doesn't mean he doesn't fucking have any! Now, clean that gun! I will not have some poxy Englishman laughing at us for our equipment not being right."

Juan's opinion was set. Shouting at the Private, even if it was slightly unjustified, would keep discipline in men who were yet to understand the realities of this battle. There was no relief coming. They were on their own. And the longer they held out, and the more English they killed, the better. He would eventually surrender the fort, once it was completely lost, but he would ensure that they put up at least a decent show prior to doing so.

The horses had all been moved the afternoon after the English had landed. The number of stores had also been reduced, leaving the garrison with around only a week of food. As the garrison was thankfully nearly all militia, the amount of food required to feed fifty men looked like a lot to the untrained eye, and as such morale had not yet taken a dip. That would of course change as the food stocks decreased over the next few days, and it became apparent that they did not have enough food. The troops, who right now were ready to fight to the death, might not feel so inclined should they have not had any decent food.

Another cannon ball hit the wall, causing rock to fly up into the air. It would not be long now. He need not have worried about the lack of supplies. The wall was showing serious cracks in multiple places. "Get the men away from those breach points!" ordered Juan. He needed every man he could get, losing men needlessly as the walls fell was not part of this plan.

Another ball hit, and the stone crumbled away faster still. The enemy nearly had their breach. "It won't be long now," Juan mumbled to himself. "Troops!" he yelled, "Get some food in you lads!". Every bit of food which could be deprived of the enemy would be advantageous. The hole was most certainly getting larger in the wall, and the troops, knowing that the enemy were coming, were beginning to get restless. "And another brandy for each man!" he shouted. Anything to keep the spirits up.

Jenkins fired yet another cannon ball into the wall of the fortress. The wall was becoming more and more damaged now, it was clear that it would not hold up for much longer. "Keep pounding away boys! Keep pounding away!". The longer they hit the wall with cannon balls, the more breaches the army would have to flood when the time came. And the smaller Spanish army inside would have to cover more areas.

"What happens when we have made enough breaches?" asked one of the gunners.

"We make more bloody holes!" said Treen, excitedly. "No, we wait for the signal from the engineers to fire one last salvo low and then we wait."

"Wait for what?" asked the same gunner.

"Not sure if I am honest," said Treen, "Just got told we'd know it when we saw it. Once we've seen it, we are raising the guns, trying to hit the top of the fort, kill, maim and blind the defenders I think
is the idea."

It was a simple enough plan. Send a few hundred troops at the enemy, who were undermanned, under gunned and defensively in a very weak position.

"It's a last stand by those boys inside," said Jenkins mournfully. "Bugger should just surrender as soon as we breach. Its over for him then anyway, but at least we then can't use it ourselves."

"If I remember rightly there was a smuggling vessel which, despite overwhelming odds fought a Sloop-of-War for the better part of twenty minutes before surrendering," said Treen with a wry smile.

"Yes, and it needlessly cost men their lives," said Jenkins, looking rather disheartened by the whole situation.

"True, but it saved more. Do you think Smythe would have reacted the same way if you had just given up? No, he'd have tried you all as smugglers if he could prove it. If not, a continued life of crime for you all, only to be blown out of the water by some larger ship on your next voyage. Or worse, captured by the Spaniards or the French. Instead, it meant that many of your lads became honest men, fighting men. Better life for the likes of Abraham and Gabriel. Think of that the next time you put yourself down for not surrendering sooner."

It was comforting that the officers in charge of Jenkins did not hold it against him, and more importantly that he had indeed impressed them. The knowledge his actions had directly improved the lives of

his men, his friends and his young wards, made him feel better about the whole situation.

Another cannon ball hit the wall, and a large crash could be heard for miles around. The first part of the wall had collapsed, causing more damage and destruction to be caused. There was a large cheer from the sappers and engineers in the army's ranks, easily visible from their dark blue uniforms. The cheer was infectious however, as the boys carrying the powder, to the rank and file, realising what the large noise had been also shouted in admiration.

"SILENCE!" shouted O'Hara, who had just arrived at the location to survey the progress. "Major, control your men. Now, how long before we have a couple more of those holes?"

"Not too long Sir, you can see the cracks already beginning to appear Sir," came the reply. Looking through the glass this was indeed true. "Then you have another two hours Major, make as many breaches as you can. Do you understand me?"

"Yes Sir."

"Why only two hours?" asked Jenkins quietly after O'Hara had left.

"No idea," replied Treen, "I can only assume they intend to take the fort tonight, before they have chance to make any repairs, and two hours is the longest they can spare." The cannons continued to fly from their relatively safe positions. One militia man, whether by his own design as a hero, or else whilst trying to desert, grazed an engineer in the arm before being promptly shot down by the

skirmishers spaced out to give nominal protection to the gunners, but other than that, the enemy seemed to be happy to let the English come to them.

"Space the holes out, if you please gun crews!" roared the Major in charge. "Least forty yards apart if you would." The wider the scattering of breaches, the thinner the Spanish troops would have to be, the less resistance any one set of men would encounter on their entrance to the fort. The regularity which the cannons were now firing, the thud of the balls against the walls of the fort, the crumbling rock. Where all the gunners had been firing upon their own spots on the walls, now the gunners were targeting the next major faults within them, causing more and more damage with each shot. The next hour went by without any major change in the state of affairs, the cannons kept pounding, the fort kept becoming more and more broken.

"How are they still there?" asked one of the gunners, feeling that this much barrage was enough to make anyone think twice. But the Spanish flag continued to fly over the ramparts.

"Enough!" shouted O'Hara, and the guns came to a slow finish as the message was passed down the ranks. "Major, send up the signal please. Gunners, realign for the tops of the ramparts."

CHAPTER EIGHTEEN

The flares from the troops on land was the signal to the *Pembroke* to engage the enemy. Having previously intending to merely send a sloop or brig to act as covering fire, Rooke, seeing that the Spanish were not firing on the landcrews, decided to put a larger ship to the task. They had crept up onto the lee shore throughout the day, turned to a portside broadside on the fort, and were waiting for the signal to be given.

"When do we fire?" asked a Lieutenant of Captain Hardy earlier in the day.

"When the signal goes up," said Hardy simply. He stood, eagerly on his quarterdeck, awaiting the signal from land which would enable him to act.

"If they are firing from the shore," asked the same Lieutenant, as everyone could hear the battery as it echoed around the bay, "then what's the point of us firing on the fort later?"

"I think we are the diversion. They are inexperienced troops and being fired on from two different directions may cause them to panic. Despite the fact we would not be able to do anything useful from here."

"What about when our lads get into the fort Sir?" the concern in his voice for fearing the friendly fire which would ensue.

"They intend to send up a second flare, once our "lads" are in range," said Hardy, simply. "Then we will stop firing upon them." It

was late afternoon when the flares went up over the eastern sky. "That's the signal, Gunner, in your own time, fire at that fort!"

The broadside of thirty guns, all of varying sizes, from the *Pembrooke* hit, with varying degrees of accuracy, Fort Saint

Catherine. Bits of rock flew in all directions, and predictably, the inexperienced troops rang the oceanside warning bell.

Almost as if the gunners on land had been waiting, once the bell had been rung on the wall, the guns exploded from the batteries ashore. This caused the bell to ring on the land wall too, and Hardy, looking through his glass, could tell that the men inside were unsure of where to go. This confusion would not last forever, but for now, it would be useful.

"Keep that barrage up gunner! Another ration of rum if the pace is as high at the end compared to drill!"

Keeping a bombardment of the fort until the last second would allow the infantry as much time as possible to infiltrate the fort. He could see through his eyepiece cannon balls landing, now in the fort itself from the land batteries. An explosion within suggested they hit a powder cache, and a fire had broken out. The battle would not be long now.

Major Diaz was trying to retain order. The militia he had been left with were either not prepared for this onslaught from the English artillery, or else were happy to run, and live another day. They were
not career soldiers; they were groomsmen and farm boys, poachers and gamekeepers. "Forget the seawall, it's from the land they are coming!" he shouted, but to no avail. A fire had started, and the men were more concerned with putting the fire out than anything else. Others were rushing back to their bunks to gather their things, rather than risk leaving it to the English. He saw two men rushing towards one of the breaches, clearly trying to make their escape. He pulled out his pistol and shot at the one furthest away. He fell, whether dead or dying was irrelevant at this point, and the one behind turned, gun still pointing at the floor. Diaz pulled out his second pistol, cocked it, and shouted "Don't even fucking think about it. Now get your arse back in line!"

The cannon balls were coming from both sides still, causing more panic and confusion. They were almost simultaneous, hitting both walls and barricades at the same time. Diaz had ordered barricades to be erected in the breaches, but they were no use. A few cannon balls from the land battery had seen to that. No, his men would have to stand in and around those breaches. And what then? After a single volley from his now depleted troops would wound and injure the first wave of men, but what of the second, or the third?

Another cannon ball came through the gap and smashed a cart not two feet from him. He was going to die here, he knew that, but how many of his men would stand and fight, that number would be few.

"Form three ranks!" he shouted, and a few men followed his orders. "Form three damn ranks!" he shouted again, and this time more men, evidently impressed with the coolness the Major was showing followed the order this time. "They will come through those breaches," he said, continuing to remain calm whilst the cannon balls were landing around them, "And we will fire on them. We fire, and we reload. Then we charge."

It was a simple plan. He did not intend to over complicate it. Had he had more time, he would have relayed one of his cannons. But he knew that was not an option now. The increased barrage, the guns from the oceanside as well as land meant only one thing. They were coming.

O'Hara had lined up his troops. The batteries from land and sea were undoubtably doing their work, causing havoc inside the Spanish fort. "All troops ready?"

"Ready Sir" replied Lieutenant Potter.

"Then take the damn thing, let's get it over with."

"Very good Sir! Company, forward quick MARCH!"

The company of troops set off; they were in range of the guns from the battlements. But no fire came. Either the enemy had no shot to fire, in order to ensure they deprived the enemy increasing their stores, or else they had no men who were able or capable enough to fire them with any accuracy that the men needed would be more effective simply holding a musket until

the enemy came through
the gap.

The smoke was growing thicker as they approached the fort. There were flames clearly visible from within, whether by design to distract and hinder the advancing enemy, or out of control and just happened to be an advantage, Potter was not sure. They were less than a hundred yards away now; the green flare had been sent up from behind him. That was the signal for the cannons to stop, but he knew that the offshore batteries would fire their last balls from now.

The last cannon balls from the land batteries were going overhead too, causing more rubble to tumble from the fort. There were men on the ramparts, their muskets began to fire. But at that range, it was more pot luck than skill, and as of yet, no bullets had hit. He heard the officer inside the garrison shouting at his men, either to get them into some form of order, or else chastising them for firing whilst the enemy were too far away. One of the breaches was just ahead of the unit Potter was with. Another breach had another unit pass through it, as a flash came from the other side, followed by the unmistakeable crack of a volley of muskets. Men fell all around, grasping arms and shoulders, a Sergeant putting pressure on his leg where the blood was squirting out between his fingers. But still the Redcoats moved on, standing atop the breach, firing their own volley down into the fort. The flash, this time brighter, most likely due to the superior number of
guns, and then the charge.

Potter's unit reached the breach and were met with a similar fate to that of the unit to his left. Whether there had been less men originally at this breach compared to the other, or originally there had been the same but as the breach to the west fell troops had moved over to plug the gap, or simply that the troops here had not been as lucky with their volley, Potter did not know. What he did know however, was that the effect had not been as devastating. One Corporal grabbed his shoulder, but on quick inspection it was only a graze, and a Private had dropped, clearly dead or dying a few men to the right of Potter, but otherwise, they remained unscathed.

"Present!" shouted Potter over the din which was ensuing. He could see Redcoats on his left starting to overpower their opponents throughout the fort. The final couple of cannon balls were being hit into the ocean wall, causing the inexperienced Spanish troops to look around and become distracted. "FIRE!" he roared, and the crack of muskets all around him rung through his ears. The smoke with its usual acrid taste, the blinding flash, all these things he would never be used to. "Charge!" he shouted. Men ran past him, bayonets glistening in the firelight coming from inside the fort. Potter pulled out his pistol, took aim and shot an enemy trying to reload his musket in the chest. He stowed it away, and drawing his second pistol and his sword, entered the fray.

Major Diaz's plan could not have gone worse. The organisation his men had shown prior to the Redcoats arriving ended as soon as they arrived. The troops which had been around him fired off their volley at the first sight of Redcoats at the breach but had forgotten to reload as soon as the Redcoat volley followed, despite having time. Many tried to assist their dying or dead comrades, wasting precious time. The charge from the English caused many of the troops to panic, adding confusion to the already disorganised defence.

He looked to his left, and saw another breach being captured by the English too, and a Sergeant, who had tried to establish order in the same way that Diaz himself had, was shot from the returning volley from the Redcoats had caused complete disarray. The men had simply run in all directions, unsure how to respond, even to such a simple action. The bayonets glistening from the muskets of the English as they poured like a river bursting its banks over the breaches now.

Diaz drew his sword, and prepared for the onslaught of troops. Several of his men ran forward to meet the English head on. The clunk of bayonet against the muskets of the militia, the sparks as metal made contact with metal. The groans of men as either a steel bayonet or musket muzzle made contact with their bodies, men dropping as they were struggling to keep their feet under the pressure. Another volley of musket fire came from on high, causing

both sides to fall in front of him. There were only a small number of his men left fighting now, and an uneasy hush seemed to have fallen over the siege.

A unit of Redcoats had flanked him, all now pointing their loaded muskets at the ten or fifteen men which surrounded Diaz, their own muskets pointing outwards.

"Senor!" shouted an English voice from the side of one of the lines. "Suelta tus armas!". It was broken Spanish, but the meaning was clear. Essentially, surrender. Diaz looked around at his broken, young militia. Yes, they may take a few Englishmen with them, but to what end? The men around him were scared and even with the poor quality of the officer's Spanish, they understood. They looked at their commanding officer, with almost pleading in their eyes.

"Drop your guns boys," said Diaz to his troops. "No point us all dying today." Most dropped them almost immediately, but one man, incensed with the idea of surrender, ran at the English line. Whether it was honour which caused him to do so, or his blood was up in the heat of the moment, Diaz did not know. The English officer took pity on him, aiming his pistol at the man's leg. He went down, dropping his musket and grabbing his leg. He joined the screaming of the other men, of which there were many. Diaz looked around. He had started the day with fifty-seven men holding the fort. He was now surrounded by the last few, twelve by his count. Forty-three men dead or injured. And the fort was lost.

CHAPTER NINETEEN

O'Hara looked on from the cannon batteries at the fort. He watched on as his troops had piled over the walls of the fort, and after a brief amount of shooting, there had been silence. One final pistol shot rung out across the bay, then silence. When the flag of Spain began to be pulled down, O'Hara smiled. It had not been a long battle for the fort, but it had been decisive. Fort Saint Catherine was in the hands of the Grand Alliance.

"A good win all round Sir," said one of the gunners and O'Hara smiled. It was a good win. Now, there was nothing in the rear which could affect the continuation of the attack. They could have continued to press on without capturing the fort, but military theory clearly stated not leaving an enemy in the rear. "Get the butchers bill and secure the fort." said O'Hara calmly. He knew his report would be smaller than that of Stanhope's from the previous couple of days. In fact, his list might be smaller than that of Stanhope's today, as men continued to die from their wounds they received from the landing.

But it was not a fair comparison and he knew it. One was a breached fort, when he knew there was a maximum number of men, the other, an amphibious landing with an unknown number of hostile troops. That is not how the papers would report it. "Bring me a horse please."

He climbed upon the horse which was brought to him, a brown thoroughbred with white socks, and rode gently towards the fort. There would be a surrender to formally accept, prisoners to organise, stores to be placed within the fort for safe keeping. There would have to be a Commander of the fort assigned, a quartermaster too. But it would alleviate the pressure on Rota, the town which had for the most part, been the central command and civilian administration of the invasion. With many of the troops rehoused here in the fort, Prince George would be able to get on more effectively with the running of state affairs. He rode through the open gates, with two Redcoats stood on sentry and saluted. At least whoever had taken the fort had had the sense to post men on the outside. He came to a stop in the middle of the fort and assessed the situation. There were dead men, both in Redcoats and in brown overalls of men in militia. A quick count showed O'Hara that there were more men in brown. Not only had the fort been taken, but by all accounts, had been taken with relative ease.

"Major-General," came the voice of a Sergeant, who saluted his officer. "Lieutenant Potter said would you be so kind as to meet him in the Commander's office, Sir!"

The office was small, large enough for the fort's paperwork, but not much else. There was, Potter had already found out, an officer's mess, which would have sufficed for any larger meetings. The paperwork was all over the place. Clearly the Spanish had not been

too careful in the last days of their garrison of the fort. That, or there had been a wilful destruction of the information regarding the fort, knowing it was inevitably due to fall.

"Sir," Potter stood to attention as O'Hara entered the room.

"At ease Lieutenant." O'Hara looked around the office, "Anything of use?"

"Not really Sir. Seems they anticipated our arrival and took everything that could help us and burned it or relocated to one of the other forts. My Spanish isn't that good either Sir, so I might not be the best person to judge." O'Hara nodded in frustration. He had expected that from the moment he walked into the office and saw it such a mess.

"Did the officer have much to say?"

"Not a word Sir. I think he's just upset he had to surrender Sir," surrender or die had been his options, but to some men, the decision to surrender came with disappointment and regret, feeling that perhaps it would have been better to have died, and done it honourably.

O'Hara nodded again in agreement with his young officer. He felt for the Spanish officer who had been in charge of this impossible defence, but he still had to be talked to. "Where is he?" O'Hara asked.

"Downstairs, in his quarters. There is a couple of Privates with him watching his movements and a couple more on the door. Thankfully, we have plenty of troops to keep an eye on all the prisoners."

"May I recommend you use the prisoners to assist in clearing the bodies?"

"Yes, Sir, thank you, Sir."

"How many bunks are there here Lieutenant?"

"Haven't done a full count yet Sir, but around a hundred. There's not much food been left behind; seems the enemy knew what they were doing in terms of that. About three days left for the garrison which was here."

That was frustrating. O'Hara could have gone on with the plan regardless, fifty men and less than a weeks' food. They would have been surrendering themselves in a few days. He was not sure how many men he had lost, but more importantly than that, he had had to use the bloody Navy and their cannons to ensure victory. This meant that dispatches would have to reflect this. Instead of a smart Commander waiting out the patient victory against the enemy, he had lost men, and would have to share the glory of the victory with seamen. Rooke would be enjoying this, as inevitably would Stanhope as he realised the outcome.

"Then I leave the fort in your command Lieutenant." The fort was secured. The few extra billets they had earned would indeed relieve the pressure on Rota, but there was not any rooms which were of a high enough standard to move the Duke from Rota. He would go

speak to the Spanish Commander of the fort, knowing that he probably would get nothing, but hopefully gaining some otherwise unknown gem of information which could assist them in this battle.

"Senor," he spoke in Spanish to put the Commander at ease, and with a slight nod to show his deference to the man. "My name is Captain-General O'Hara, and who do I have the pleasure of addressing."

The Spanish gentlemen looked with angry eyes at the Englishman. He knew he was being polite, but it did not make it any easier. "Major Diaz, of his most Catholic Majesty, King Philip V." as he said the final part of his name, he gave a small bow of deference. "May I assume you are taking command of this fort?"

"I am leaving the Lieutenant in command, unfortunately Major, I have other business to attend to." And he offered his hand to the Major who took it. He knew that he would have no trouble from this man. The militia he had commanded had all but wasted away, some no doubt would even join Prince George's local Spanish militia, to ensure they continued being paid for their trouble. O'Hara felt that he had done his duty in respect to the fort. He climbed upon the horse he had ridden into the fort and rode out back towards the batteries.

"Duke of Ormonde?" he said upon returning to the batteries to see his commanding officer present, "What is it that I can do for you, Sir?"

The Duke had ridden the five miles or so from Rota to join O'Hara at the fort. His hair was slightly unkempt, probably due to the breeze blowing in from the bay. He had dismounted and was trying his best to mingle with the common soldiers without seeming too much out of place. "Oh, I saw the signal flares go up and I thought I would come and have a look for myself as to the progress of the siege. Nice to see it has played out as we expected. No jolly Spaniards in our rear causing mischief and all that." He was his usual mock jovial self, almost as if a caricature of an aristocrat had been made.

"No, Sir," replied O'Hara, unsure how else to respond.

"No, we shall remain here for the night, but the town of Port Saint Mary awaits us tomorrow!"

"For the discipline of the men Sir, we should pass straight through it." Any army of size would inevitably try to sack, loot and plunder a hostile town. They had managed to maintain order so far, but that would not last forever. An easy target, such as an undefended port town, was almost too good to be true for the poor privates of the English army.

"Yes, yes, whatever," said Ormonde absentmindedly, "Just ensure we have the control we need alright O'Hara? There's a good chap."

"We should re-billet some troops in the fort Sir," O'Hara added as Ormonde was climbing up onto his horse.

"Yes, well, make sure these gunners are all taken care of. Then send a man back with some numbers and we will see what we can do.

Goodnight to you Captain-General."

Aboard the *Pembroke*, there was celebration. From the green flares being sent in the air, signalling to them to cease their fire, until the Spanish flag had been pulled down, the crew had been on tender hooks, seeing if their exploits had assisted the troops in gaining the fort. Once the flag had come down however, the celebration had begun. The rum was flowing freely, as Hardy looked on over his ship. The enemy, whether due to confusion or the lack of numbers, had not fired a single shot back at the *Pembroke*.

"Good win all round Sir," came the voice of the familiar Lieutenant, and Hardy smiled. It had indeed been a successful encounter, which Rooke, always pushing for naval supremacy over the army would inevitably push for recognition of the hard work of the *Pembroke*. From the *Pembroke's* point of view, it could not have been better. They had shot a few broadsides at the fort, received no return fire, and therefore no casualties, but would share in the glory of the dispatches sent back to England. It was a successful day.

Major Diaz sat in the officer's mess of Fort Saint Catherine. Less than forty-eight hours ago he had been sitting here toasting the health of the King Philip V. Now, he would be spending the next however many years in an English Prison. Even if they chose to leave the militia men behind, no point taking home untrained

troops, the major would not be so fortunate. As a commissioned officer, he was, if nothing else, wealthy, not overly, but enough that the English would not let him remain here in Spain and continue his career.

The Lieutenant who had taken his surrender walked in, and Diaz could not help but feel resentment towards the man. He looked kindly enough and did not walk with the arrogance that his senior officer had, but still. It had been the officer that had cost him his honour, his freedom, and for this he could not help but be angry.

"Senor Diaz, I presume?" asked the Officer, as kindly as he could. It had clearly been a long day for him too, the bags under his eyes gave away his fatigue.

"Yes," replied Diaz, trying not to let the anger in his voice come through too much. The officer had merely been doing his duty, exactly the same as him, and he had been the man who had held his troops in check from a massacre. More than that, he had been controlled enough to shoot the man who had broken the line and charged at his troops in the leg, rather than letting his troops riddle him with bullets, and likely, shoot some men behind who had already dropped their weapons.

"My name is Lieutenant Potter. I was wondering if you would be so kind as to join me in a brandy?" A Lieutenant. He had been beaten by a Lieutenant. Not a Major, not even a Captain. But a mere Lieutenant.

"Have you been soldiering long Lieutenant?" asked Diaz, not wishing to give his answer to the Lieutenant too quickly.

"No, not too long. This is my first major action Major. But I was on the landing at the beaches a few days ago as well. My Major fell there. I have been acting command of this unit ever since." Well, that was something at least. Green he may be, but willing to lead men in a crisis of leadership and he did not seek revenge for the death of his commanding officer. Such men were rare in this world.

"Then a toast, Senor." said Diaz, "To the fallen dead, whether they be Spaniards or Englishmen, the valiant dead."

"The valiant dead," replied Potter. They both raised a glass.

"Do you not have duties to see to Lieutenant?"

"Mainly done thankfully," said Potter, "Your troops are assisting with moving the bodies, being generally useful thankfully. Once that has been completed, they will be disarmed and set free."

"Set free?"

"Yeah, we know they aren't soldiers, it was clear from our skirmish. So, let them go home. A simple promise not to raise arms again against Charles. They won't be any trouble." Lots of the men were from neighbouring towns anyway and would probably rush at the opportunity to go home. It was a blow to the numbers, but also a blow to the cause of Philip V. Charles the Pretender was clearly trying to win the hearts and minds of the people, not just smash a
hole in the side of Spain.

"And me?" asked Diaz, he was almost certain he knew the answer to this.

"You Sir, will remain in the custody of her Majesty's army.," said Potter, not unkindly, "If you offer me your parole, then you remain free to roam around the fort."

"And should you fail to hold this position Senor?" There was an air of arrogance, almost certainty to the Spaniards' voice.

"Should we fail to hold on to this position Senor," said Potter with a smile, "Then you will have the pleasure of returning to England with me Sir." Diaz nodded. He had expected such an outcome, but now, with it being confirmed, it seemed more real.

"Then I hope to enjoy my time in an English home." Both men smiled to each other, took another drink of brandy, and settled back into their chairs. It had been a long day. But it was finally over.

Francisco stood on the battlements of Fort Saint Lawrence overlooking the brief battle which had occurred at Fort Saint Catherine. He had listened to the batteries pound away at the walls, the falling of the rocks as they crumbled away from the ramparts. Fort Saint Catherine was an old fort. Built mainly to withstand the weaponry of a bygone age, it had not taken long for the guns of the Allies to pound hole in it. The forts closer to Cadiz proper had had their defences improved over the last few decades, meaning they

would not fall so easily.

He felt for the young officer he had left in charge of the Fort. If he were still alive, his career would now forever be tarnished by the defeat and surrender of the fort, regardless of how valiantly he fought. For his honour, it would almost be better if he had died, at least then he would be amongst the valiant dead. Francisco's focus could not dwell on his poor Major, however. He had to focus on the next steps of the defence of Cadiz. Unlike Rota, which he had expected to fall regardless of the size of the allied force, prior to the battle he had not known if they would have the firepower or manpower to capture Fort Saint Catherine, and as a direct consequence, Port Saint Mary. Therefore, unlike his prudence with removing everything of value from the town of Rota, and sparing it a viscous sacking by the English, the same care and attention had not been taken in respect to Port Saint Mary, and it was too late to change that now.

"Sir?" came the voice of one of his subordinates, "They have taken the fort."

"Yes, I assumed as much when they removed our flag," he replied, slightly sarcastically. This was slightly unfair, as it was his subordinate's duty to ensure that he was up to date with information on the battle, but Francisco was not in a mood to be given obvious statements.

"We wondered Sir," continued his subordinate officer, "When you intended to counterattack?". Counterattack. That was what his troops expected? Truly to Francisco at least, this was unexpected. If they had expected a counterattack, then surely, they would have expected a more vigorous defence of the fort initially.

"I don't." he said simply. And his subordinate had the good sense not to question him further on the subject.

"Very good Sir," he said, looking uncomfortable about the whole situation. "What orders do you have now Sir?"

"Send more stores to Fort Saint Matagorda. We will hold that Fort."

"Yes Sir!" There was a definite energy in this response, as if his troops had been worried that Francisco had given up prior to this, allowing Fort Saint Catherine to fall so easily. By ordering a reinforcement of Saint Matagorda, this showed them this was not the case.

CHAPTER TWENTY

The morning mist in the bay of Cadiz reminded Smythe of the mists of the coast of his native Cornwall. Less than half the crew of the *Lannwedhenek* now were from his home county, some of course leaving immediately after their victory over the *Niazmehr*, others had left in the following months following their time in Spithead. Some had transferred to other, and larger ships, taking the opportunity to sail under the command of more distinguished Captain.

He watched, as he had done from the deck of the *Lannwedhenek* for the previous few days, after the funeral of Major Connolly. His Lieutenant Treen had of course gone ashore, as had a few gun crews with half of his cannons, and they had spent the morning organising with the Admiral's and General's staff, respectively. As of yet, he still did not have his cannons back.

"Gig approaching!" shouted a man aloft, "Looks like Richards Sir!" Richards. This almost certainly meant he was not getting his cannons back anytime soon. In fact, it almost certainly meant that the *Lannwedhenek* would have some undesirable task which nobody else really wanted, but as one of the smallest ships in the fleet, commanded by a man who did not have any patronage at court, meant Rooke, although not unkind to Smythe, did not have to worry about any fall out from the higher ups, should anything befall them.

"Let's give him the proper welcome lads," said Smythe rather frustratedly.

Richards came aboard, his usual boyish smile beaming as he came over the side. The whistles blew and salutes were given.

"Commander Smythe," nodded Richards. It was an almost automated response from Richards, having spent a large amount of time in Spithead on the *Lannwedhenek*. "Your presence is required…"

"On the *Royal Sovereign?*" asked Smythe, cutting off Richards, and turning to smile at Jones.

"On shore, Sir" came the unexpected response from Richards, who had clearly expected the sarcastic response from his superior officer and was waiting for Smythe to make the remark, and then having the pleasure of cutting him down. "The Admiral is once again stuck in a council of war, seems to be spending half his time in them now, and after your, erm, suggestions previously, he would appreciate your input, Sir."

Smythe looked uncomfortable about his previous outburst and assumption, "Mister Richards," he began, but was unsure how to phrase his apology for his rudeness.

"Oh, think nothing of it Smythe," said Richards, the friendly familiarity had returned to his conversational tone, "Most people treat me like a large inconvenience, always bearing bad news or orders, at least you have the humour to hide your frustrations, *Sir*."

He added the *Sir* at the end, emphasizing the nature of the word. It was an oddity of the Navy that Commanders, like Smythe, were in an inopportune place, beyond the point of Lieutenants, but before that of full Post-Captains, leaving them in a limbo where Lieutenants did not see them as their own, or respect them, and Captains did not respect them as they were clearly beneath them.

"Still, my rudeness," commented Smythe, struggling to apologise in a way which was fitting of the differences in rank.

"A rum, Sir," said Richards with a smile, "Whilst I wait for you to get ready? Or slightly longer, Will, you do excel yourself in this role my friend, don't you?"

Will had heard the call of Richards arrival and gone to get Smythe's greatcoat, hat and sword, knowing this would be expected upon arrival with the Admiral. The response of the crew of the *Lannwedhenek*, such was the regularity of Richards' presence on board, was nothing out of the expected, with the majority of the crew acting almost as if the Lieutenant had not even boarded, or a mere nod or quick salute at the best.

The quartermaster brought Richards a rum in a pewter tankard, which Richards graciously accepted. "Mind if I take it with me?" asked Richards jovially, as Smythe was ready to board his gig, and the quartermaster waved him on, knowing full well that one pewter tankard was neither here nor there, and to deny a superior officer, even Richards, something was not worth the hassle it created.

The two men were rowed ashore, landing around the same area in which the troops had made their amphibious landing previously. The row across the waters had been pleasant enough, another sign that the amphibious landing had indeed occurred on the worst possible day for it. "Such were the plans of great men," thought Smythe, "Wind and weather simply make fools of them."

"To the town?" asked Smythe, having been to Rota only briefly to escort Major Connolly's body with Lieutenant Potter.

"No, the fort, we have moved military operations to there. It seemed more appropriate to plan military plans from a fort, rather than a town. The Prince is trying to establish a civilian government and having lots of troops skulking around was not exactly what he had in mind." It was a short ride from the beach to the fort, but Smythe was not looking forward to it.

"Can you ride?" asked Richards. He himself was not an overly confident rider, preferring ships to horses, but he at least had had to ride sometimes during grammar school.

"Erm," Smythe hesitated long enough to make Richards ask what was probably a kinder question.

"Would you prefer to walk, Sir?"

"Yes, Lieutenant, I think that would be for the best." It was not that Smythe could not ride. He had ridden a few times in his life, but living in the coastal areas of Cornwall, you did not ride, you rowed, or you sailed, to your destinations.

It was a three-mile hike to the fort, more than long enough for the two friends to catch up on their voyages so far.

"Nearly had a bloody duel aboard the *Lannwedhenek*," said Smythe concernedly, "The German's butler was found rooting through Major Connolly's possessions."

"You're fucking kidding?" Richards looked at Smythe with a look of pure frustration, "Oh God Henry, I am so sorry, I arranged for Lord Hempleman to be aboard with you, I knew he was a pain in the arse, but I didn't think for a second it would cause such issues!"

"Well, I managed to get Connolly to agree to call him out once we had landed thankfully. Although I needn't had bothered, Hempleman was more than happy for his butler to fight for his honour, should have let them do it on the deck."

"Ah yes, but if it had been a crew member, and not the German's butler, it would have been a gauntlet at best for the thief. Probably not the best idea to suggest that someone has to simply request a duel to defend themselves. You would end up with no crew left." The final part was said with a smile, but the point was well received.

"That's true. But still. What with that, and Hempleman seasick, and four of us being forced to share what is normally just Treen's berth, our wardroom isn't exactly large now is it?"

"Church mice have more room," smiled Richards, "Seriously, the wardroom on the *Sovereign* is larger than your cabin, you should think about going back to just being a Lieutenant, you'd have more

room." The two men continued on their hike, now with Richards discussing the tension aboard the *Sovereign*.

"Well, Ormonde is a tool," said Richards, which made Smythe raise his eyebrows with shock. It was rare to hear Richards speak ill of his superior officers.

"How so?" Smythe lowered his voice to barely a whisper, in fear of being heard, but Richards just laughed him off.

"Oh don't worry about these lads, they feel the same." All the men around them around them were seamen, all from the *Sovereign*, nodding along with Richards, "Aye Sir," came the response from the sailors.

"He's just an arrogant aristocrat," said Richards, "Yes, I get the irony," he said quickly before either Smythe or his men could interject, "but honestly. Looks down his nose at everyone, if you don't agree with him, he has a temper tantrum. Only person he listens to is the Prince. Thankfully, the Prince seems to have some idea of how to run an operation, because if they were as bad as each other we'd be done for. He is so rude to everyone, including Rooke. He's a fucking Lord for God's sake, and he still has zero respect for him." It was clear from the tone of his voice; it was the last part was what he found so offensive. It was one thing to be rude to him, he was a young Lieutenant, who's family had some money, but little influence at court, but Rooke, who was a Lord, in Parliament, and a member of the Admiralty, could be spoken to

with such disregard was unthinkable.

"Well, everything is separate now, surely." Smythe was trying to see the lighter side of the situation, but Richards shook his head.

"Any troops on the ground, whether sailors or soldiers now come under the command of that wart," said Richards, clear disgust at officially, even if nominally, ordered around by Ormonde. They reached the fort in the mid-afternoon, with troops moving around in all directions.

"What the hell is going on here!" shouted Richards, the commotion being offensive to the ordered Naval officer.

"What's it to you!" shouted a Private, then seeing the naval officer's uniforms quickly changed his tone, "Oh, sorry, Sirs. We are moving onto Port Saint Mary, and the General wants us ready to move in the hour."

"Where is your commanding officer?" demanded Richards, still frustrated with the lack of order, "And why the hell are there no sentries on duty, and what," the latest thing to have caught his eye seemed to cause the most offence to him, "in the name of all that is holy is that damn Diego doing walking around?" He had seen the Spanish officer walking around without even a guard escorting him. Clearly the Spaniard had heard the commotion, and came over, evidently trying to ease the tension.

"Major Diaz, of His most Catholic Majesty Philip V at your service. To whom do I have the pleasure of introducing myself to?" The rules of the military dictated that even a captured enemy of higher rank must be treated with respect equal to that rank. "I am Lieutenant Richards, First Lieutenant on Her Majesty's Ship, *Royal Sovereign*."

"And I am Commander Smythe, of Her Majesty's Sloop, *Lann-wedhenek*,"

"Is it customary for Lieutenants to give orders in your military whilst Commanders stay silent?" asked Major Diaz, the sneer in his voice clear as day, enjoying goading the Englishman. "In his Most Catholic Majesty's Army, the senior officer is normally the ones giving them, no?"

"Do your Sergeants not give orders, Senor?" asked Richards with a smile, "Perhaps that is why we managed to relieve you of this fort, without too much trouble." It was Richards turn to enjoy the moment, and Diaz's turn to try not to look out of place.

"Now, where is the commanding officer for this Fort?" asked Smythe, trying to get the conversation back onto topic.

"He is in the officers mess Senor," replied Diaz. The tone was politer to Smythe than he had been to Richards. Richards and Smythe were unsure whether the tone was due to the fact that Smythe was yet to insult him, or that Diaz was simply more inclined to speak to the officer of equal rank to him, "As far as I am aware, he is discussing logistics with your Admiral Rooke and General O'Hara. Now if that is all."

"No, it isn't bloody all!" shouted Richards, "What the hell are you doing simply walking around?"

"I offered my parole as a gentleman," said Diaz calmly, "And so O'Hara and the young Lieutenant, I forget his name, it's a job, like baker or butcher,"

"Potter?" asked Smythe, having sailed the young man all the way from Portsmouth.

"Yes, that's the man!" said Diaz, cheerful that Smythe had assisted him in remembering the name. "Well, gentlemen, they accepted it. And unless you have the authority to overrule a General." He gave a short bow to both of them, walking away from them with a smile on his face. He knew that neither of them had anywhere near the power to countermand General O'Hara's orders.

Smythe and Richards walked into the officer's mess. There was a large map laid out across it, weighed down by rocks at each corner. It was a detailed map of this half of the bay, with Fort Saint Matagorda the clear target for the military minds.

"If we take that fort," said Richards, "We can slide a rated ship into the bay, should we wish. But more importantly, we can fire on those galleys from an elevated point, or better yet capture them."

"Not worth that much, are they?" asked Smythe, but moments later he wished he had not.

"I'd have thought you of all men would have understood the value of a Galley, Mister Smythe." Rooke had entered the room, a broad

smile on his face. "Welcome Smythe, and you too Richards, I believe you all know Captain-General O'Hara," the gentlemen nodded to the General, who out of professional courtesy nodded back, "And I know that you Mister Smythe know young Lieutenant Potter here." Potter smiled at Smythe, but Richards, clearly simmering from Major Diaz's relative freedom simply glared at him.

"So, the army is marching on, as you can see," said Rooke, "The Duke of Ormonde wishes naval support, mainly cannon fire, for the capturing of Fort Saint Matagorda. This may involve some groundwork." The last statement made the naval officers around the table look uncomfortably at each other.

"We are sailors Sir, not sappers." said Richards, as politely as he could. The dismay however could not completely be kept out of his voice.

"You will serve Her Majesty however the Duke sees fit," said

O'Hara, and he seemed to think that settled the matter.

"We *sail* where Her Majesty decides. We are not ponies for the army to do with as it wishes, Sir," said Richards, again as politely as he could manage.

"Gentlemen, gentlemen," Rooke looked frustrated as Richards was, but clearly trying to keep the peace as best as possible, "Before we do anything, I believe Mister O'Hara you have to move your troops?"

"Yes," said O'Hara, also happy to return to the task at hand, "We intend to move the army beyond the town. It will not be the easiest of actions, on account of-"

"The army being full of ill-disciplined, drunken louts?" said Richards, enjoying any opportunity to poke fun at the army's expense. He was not wrong, however. Many of the men had been "invited" to join by the courts, a way of escaping jail, or else had been too drunk to escape the pressgangs.

"Well, quite," said O'Hara, not wishing to create conflict on a point which was already lost. "The longer we spend in and around the town, the higher the chance of the discipline breaking down. We wish the Navy, and more importantly, your officers to assist us in this."

"We are to act as your provosts." Richards scepticism was growing by the minute.

"Exactly," said O'Hara. "Well, I have lots to attend to, gentlemen." He left the mess, leaving the naval officers alone in the mess.

"I am calling the rest of the Captains here to discuss it with them, but needless to say, I am not overly confident or pleased with the plan," said Rooke, "For starters, there are around five thousand troops and around twenty Captains that we can spare. I can't assign all the Captains because A, some of them are Dutch and honestly, I don't trust the soldiers to respond to the Dutch officers the same, which would in turn cause issues, and B, I need to leave some Captains aboard."

"Even if we used a Lieutenant or Captain from every ship. It still puts us to around fifty. A hundred soldiers per officer. Lord above knows what O'Hara wants us to do with it." Richards frustrations, as poorly as they had been held in check during the conversation with O'Hara, were now on full show.

"I know, I know," replied Rooke, "I'm not entirely sure it's all O'Hara's doing, but yes I get your point. Now, to you Smythe. I am sorry, but you aren't getting those cannons back any time soon. Or the men. Ormonde in his infinite wisdom has insisted any men who are on land who aren't officers are under his command. Treen is obviously an exception, but I think it would be better to leave him with the troops in command, give us at least a semblance of control over the situation."

"Whatever you think is best, Sir" said Smythe. He knew there was no point arguing, it would not do any good. It was not Rooke's fault anyway, he knew that Ormonde had clearly demanded those cannons and men without Rooke having much of a leg to stand on. At least leaving Treen with the men, and the men with the cannons should help keep them all in one piece, and in working order.

"I think the idea is for us, as officers, to line the streets of Port Saint Mary on horseback, along with some provosts that the army has supplied. The Army isn't staying in the port, thankfully, they are going through it, our job is simple. Keep them from misbehaving whilst travelling through."

"Just that simple Sir?" asked Richards, slightly sarcastically. It was a testament to the friendship which had clearly grown on board the *Sovereign* that Richards, a mere Lieutenant, could get away with such blatant rudeness to a superior officer. Rooke merely glared at him.

The troops filed out of Rota and Fort Saint Catherine in the late afternoon. O'Hara and Sir Henry Belasys rode at the front of the column, with all the flags and ceremony which accompanied such an event. The band was playing away, drums rattling to the tune and the soldiers marching, in somewhat orderly fashion, through the town of Port Saint Mary. The people of the town, both out of fear and awe had come out to watch the precession, as Redcoats, blue coats and even some golden coats of the Spanish irregulars recruited from Rota by Prince George. The naval officers, again in full regalia, were sitting on horseback, lining the streets and facing the Allied soldiers, saluting. To an onlooker, it may have seemed like a powerplay, a show of strength having these officers face away from the crowds and towards the troops, but in all honesty, it was anything but. O'Hara believed if his men got a sniff of freedom, then the warehouses and taverns of Port Saint Mary would be ravaged by nightfall.

The passing through the town was completely uneventful, save a little bit of shouting from the population. Many of the merchants

there, although on the paperwork they were all Spaniards, clearly once conversations between the officers and merchants themselves began, it became evident that they were actually Englishmen, Dutchmen, Frenchmen, and any other nationality. So long as the Portmaster's pockets were lined enough, the taxes, or prohibitions in the case of any merchants from the Grand Alliance, would happily be forgotten. It was close enough to Cadiz to be able to use its surrounding economic power, but far enough away so that it did not fall foul of the main Spanish Authorities which were housed there.

"All quiet so far," said Rooke, riding along the lines of Provosts and Naval officers alike. Although born to the sea, at the dismay of his father, he had of course grown up on their country estate. Therefore, he was not as awkward as many of the other naval officers in the saddle, especially the younger Lieutenants, who had joined the sea as soon as they could. Smythe, who had only ridden a few times in his life, hated sitting atop this horse, which of course was not his own, in the blistering summer heat.

"Indeed Sir!" shouted back Lieutenant Potter, who's troops were now passing the Admiral, and although not knowing him personally, had seen him in the fort with O'Hara earlier on. The troops continued on their march through the town, as the night was closing in.

"Well, troops are through," said Rooke, a smile on his face at a job
well done. He turned to his fellow Naval officers, everything between Vice-Admiral Hobson, all the way down to the lowly Lieutenant of the sixth-rate *HMS Myude*. "Had a look around, and besides a basic garrison, Fort Saint Catherine is basically deserted. I had my steward set up a supper there for us gentlemen, if you wish to retire there. We can sleep there too if you don't mind roughing it, before returning to our ships in the morning." There was a general murmur of consent. No one wanted to row into the bay at night, even if it were a clear night.

"Excellent, then you boy!" he shouted at the young Lieutenant, "Ride ahead and tell him we are on the way, the wine needs time to breathe."

"We make camp here!" shouted O'Hara, the place where the engineers had identified a couple of days previously. Tents were set up, fires lit, mess tents sorted. The camp seemed to be sorted, O'Hara turned in for the night. He had taken the fort, he had moved the troops on. His job was done.

"Sir, there isn't enough food for everyone!" shouted one of the cooks to the quartermaster.

"How short are we?" he asked. He knew that he probably would not have enough food to give full ration until the supply waggons caught up, but he might be able to give a part portion tonight, and double in the morning. The men would moan this evening, be
unhappy until the morning, and completely forget about it tomorrow morning when then got more breakfast, and grumble tomorrow dinner when they did not get as much food as they got for breakfast.

"It's like trying to feed the five-thousand, but without the Son of God assisting," he shouted back. So not enough even for that.

"Where are those God damn waggons?" asked the Quartermaster, more to himself than anyone in particular. "If we can't feed the buggers."

"They'll have to get their own," said one of his cooks. It did not do well when soldiers had to get their own food. They tended not to pay for it.

"Send for Sir Henry," said the Quartermaster. He needed to send some men back through the town to move the waggons faster. Any men into the town had to be approved by the Commanders of the army. O'Hara had turned in early, having had a couple of days of rather hard work taking Fort Saint Catherine. The only other person who could authorise soldiers entering the town was Sir Henry Belasys, the official second in command of the entire expedition.

"What's the problem Quartermaster?" Sir Henry was clearly tired and not in the mood to be disturbed. He was only half dressed, and there was lipstick on his neck. He was clearly enjoying the company of a friendly local lady, and as the second in command of the army, he would have his pick.

"Running out of food, Sir," he said simply. "Waggons too far back." It was a logistical nightmare, and one unlikely to be solved that evening.

"Let the men into the town. There's taverns there isn't there."

"But Sir," said the Quartermaster trying to think how to diplomatically put this.

"Let them go!" shouted Sir Henry, "Now, if that's all, I have business to attend to."

CHAPTER TWENTY-ONE

It was not until the morning when O'Hara realised something had gone horribly wrong. He woke around nine in the morning, a lie in, which in its own was surprising. He stood up, walked over to the water bowl in his tent and washed his face. It was quiet. Too quiet. It was nine in the morning, he was in a camp of several thousand English and Dutch troops and it was quiet.

He dressed quickly, shouting out to his guard patrol as he placed his jacket on. He rushed out half dressed, looking around. The camp was half full at best.

"Where are the men!" asked O'Hara to his guard unit, "And why did no one wake me?"

"In the town, Sir," replied one of his guardsmen.

"What?" O'Hara could not believe his ears. "Which idiot allowed the men back into the town?" The whole point of the convoy, of the provosts being lined up with the naval officers, all that planning had been to keep the troops out of Port Saint Mary.

"Sir Henry Belasys, Sir." O'Hara looked back at him. There were two people in the army he did not have the authority to overrule. The Duke of Ormonde, and Sir Henry. And one of them had allowed the troops into the town.

"Damn him!" said O'Hara, more to himself than anyone else. This would only end in tears.

Around fourteen hours ago, the first English troops had entered the town of Port Saint Mary. It had started innocent enough. One unit of troops trying to hurry the supply waggons along. But as time went by, more and more troops were entering the town.

"Wine!" shouted one soldier, forcing open a warehouse door on the waterfront.

"The hell do you think you're doing?" asked one of the merchants inside. His English accent was evident through his voice.

"Shove off you stupid Spaniard," shouted the soldiers pushing past him, shoving him with their muskets.

"I'm from Dover you git!" he retorted and shoved back. The soldier, already a little drunk, dropped back into another soldier. He did not see the funny side of it, pointing his musket at the merchant, who looked aghast.

"Fucking leave, you Spanish prick!" he shouted. He aimed it, and held it pointing at the young man's face. The merchant, although furious, was not foolish enough to risk his life over it. He had insurance with Lloyds, he could claim it back. Fuck the army and fuck this man.

"Be dammed to you Sir!" he shouted as he left.

"Ah, balls to him!" shouted one of the soldiers.

"Brandy!" shouted another, and the rest of the Soldiers cheered.

Occurrences like this went on all along the waterfront at Port Saint Mary. The Provosts had tried initially to stem the tide of soldiers,

but as news spread back to the camp, the flood became too much.

Lieutenant Potter was in a tavern enjoying the evening on the Spanish coast. He has been joined by First Lieutenant Treen, as both men knew each other intimately from their journey south on the *Lannwedhenek*. Potter had not had a night off since he had landed at the beaches, and even more pressure had been added to him now that Major Connolly was dead. Treen was just glad to be out and about having been onboard for around two years almost constantly. Three Redcoats rushing through the door was not what they had in mind.

"GENTLEMEN!" Potter bellowed, as loud as he could muster. It at least caused the soldiers to pause. Realising they were in the presence of an officer, and not yet too far under the influence of alcohol allowed them to regain their order, standing to attention to address him.

"Sir," they all said, standing stock still. It had been clear to both Potter and Treen that these men had intended to drink large quantities of alcohol, the better question had been did they intend to pay for it?

"What are you doing here Private?" asked Treen, his naval uniform contrasting with the uniforms of the army.

"Having a drink," he replied, then remembering that despite not an army officer, he was still an officer he added, "Sir."

"Excellent," said Potter, this time at more of a stage whisper, still

loud enough for all to hear, but no longer a booming shout. "They require payment upfront for the first drinks gentlemen. So as soon as you give them the tin, we can all sit and drink." His eyes burrowed into the soldiers, all three of whom were now looking at each other.

"Problem?" asked Treen, both officers still standing and looking at the troops.

"We, erm, well,"

"We don't, umm"

"Have any money?" asked Treen. "Then how on earth were you going to pay for it?"

"Erm,"

"On credit, Sir," said one of the men quickly. "We wos hoping to get it on credit, Sir."

Treen smiled. On credit was the quickest way out of the situation. None of the five men present believed it, but it was a good enough story that they could all accept believing it. Looting, if caught, was a hanging offence, and with officers' present at the crime, it would be an open and shut case. But pretending that they had intended to purchase them on credit and pay him back later, they had saved themselves from the rope.

"Well, sorry chaps," said Treen with a finality in his tone which made it clear it was time for the soldiers to leave, "but they do not run a line of credit even to officers, so I am afraid you will have to
leave."

The soldiers stood, unsure if they had been dismissed, clearly frustrated they had walked into one of the few places that they could not get free alcohol like the rest of their comrades. They eventually about turned and left the tavern, causing the other patrons to relax slightly and the tavern owner to visibly calm down.

"Two more drinks over here, if you please Senor!" said Treen. His face, which had been firm and focused during the exchange with the troops, but now they had left, it eased into that more cheerful, relaxed nature which he had grown into these two years at sea.

"Well done Sir," said Potter, pleased that the officer had deescalated the situation brewing around him. Despite the word being the same, Potter was subordinate to Treen, as a Naval Lieutenant was equal to that of a Captain in the army.

"Think nothing of it," smiled Treen, as the tavern keeper placed two wines on the table.

"La Casa!" he said, pointing to himself, with a smile. It was clear he appreciated the officers making the soldiers leave, rather than leaving his tavern at their mercy.

"De nada," replied Treen, having been in Spain long enough to pick up this basic term. "What's home like Potter?"

"Home isn't much Sir, not like yours I'm sure."

"Potter," Treen began, "I'm the third Grandson of a Cornish Trader. The only reason I am Lieutenant is because my Grandfather gave
the Navy the *Lannwedhenek* on the understanding I would be a commissioned officer within it. I went to Greenwich and passed the Lieutenancy exams. So, they promoted me straight

to it. Let me tell you, if I were in a better position with inheritance, I would not be a Naval Lieutenant." Potter smiled. He had assumed that Treen would be a richer man, but it sounded like the fortyish pounds he had earned from the *Niazmehr* was probably the extent of his wealth.

"Then maybe similar," smiled Potter, "My dad's a farmer from County Antrim. Been there a couple of generations. We've somehow managed to keep ourselves out of Cromwell's wars or the Jacobeans attempts, but I decided to join up. I have an older brother who'll inherit the farm, thought I'd best make some money for myself. So, here I am. A farmboy, who bought his commission, and hasn't a sodding clue what he's doing."

"Makes two of us then," smiled Treen. The noise from outside the tavern was growing, it was clear to the two officers that raiding, and looting was clearing happening.

"We are protecting this tavern, right?" asked Potter, hoping that Treen would agree with him.

"Potter my friend, as far as I see it, we are the only protection it has." Treen replied, and he smiled, and the tavern keeper brought them yet more wine.

O'Hara was livid. A whole day of planning. Promises issued to Prince
George. Owing favours to the Navy. All that wasted because Sir Henry wanted to get his cock wet.

"How many men are currently in the town?" he asked the head of the Provosts, after he had received the report from him. As a Provost, he was subordinate to no one, not even the Duke of Ormonde, acting completely separate from the rest of the Army. The Army could ask or request the placement of the Provosts, but even a direct order from Ormonde could not change their decision.

"By the last count, couple of thousand. Some have already been in and come back, drunk as monks mind you." It was bad for discipline. It was bad for motivation. And it was horrendous for O'Hara's career. "And Prince George wants a word, Sir."

Of course, the Prince wanted a word. O'Hara had planned out the troop movements with him, given personal promises that the troops would behave like civilised men, not like a bunch of gutter rats that the world had come to expect from the Redcoat. And what had the Redcoats done? They had acted like the scum of the earth, stealing and breaking stuff, no doubt getting into fights with both each other and the locals and undoubtably there would be an increased number of babies born in nine months, hopefully for a fair price, but O'Hara was not holding his breath.

"I need to speak to Sir Henry first," he instructed the Provost, and began to move, but before he took more than a step the Provost cut him off.

"Sir Henry is already there, Sir," he said simply. "Now, I must insist that you accompany me Sir." It went from a polite request to essentially a summons. "Now, Sir," he added. The statement ended all debate. Either O'Hara could go there "freely", or else the Provosts would escort him all the way.

"Then lead on," O'Hara said, deciding that the illusion of free will was better than the loss of prestige by being forced was the lesser of two evils, picked up his jacket and went along with the Provosts. "Where are we heading?" he asked, as he mounted his horse.

"Back to Fort Saint Catherine Sir," said the Provost, "The Prince would like you to see the damage caused by the soldiers under your command." Clearly, this would not be a pretty sight. There was no other reason that he would force him through the town. The destruction was evident from outside the town. There had been small fires lit at different points, there was still some smoke rising from parts of town closest to the waterfront. There were empty bottles strewn around the ground, as the horses slowly trotted through the streets. It was clear from the noise that the town was yet to be cleared of English troops. What was more, as the Provosts had indicated, was now thousands of men were working their way through the town, giving themselves up to its pleasures.

The destruction and chaos caused by the troops was evident throughout the town. As they continued to ride through, it was clear the troops had made it with an almost systematic precision

their mission to work through the warehouses of the town. It was not a large town, but the damage was done.

They rode into Fort Saint Catherine around lunchtime, still with a paper-thin garrison. A couple of sergeants came to tend to the horses, and O'Hara was led into the officer's mess. The Prince was stood at the far end, with Rooke stood by his side. Ormonde was stood to one side, as was Sir Henry, who looked like he had been suitably chastised already.

"Charles," said Prince George, his eyes now boring into him like barnacles onto a ship. "Thank you for joining us. We would like to discuss the actions of the troops over the last twelve hours or so. Care for a drink?" he took a bottle of clearly stolen wine from the table next to him.

"No, your highness, I am fine without thank you." The Prince was clearly furious, his anger barely being concealed by his face. O'Hara was furious too, his honour and promised now seemed to mean nothing. "You wished to discuss the happenings of last night. What do you wish to discuss?"

"I want to God damn know how, despite your fucking assurances and promises, you lost control of your troops and they ran a fucking muck through Port Saint Mary?" The Prince's voice although starting calm, raised throughout the sentence as his anger grew and got the better of him.

"The Navy were involved too!" stated Ormonde, clearly not wishing

for the Army to take all the blame for this fiasco.

"The amount of damage the few sailors which are ashore have done compared to the Army is like comparing a plague of locusts to missing a meal. I have no doubt," he added, before Rooke could interject, "that given the opportunity that they would, and may still, wreak an equal amount of havoc upon the town, but as for now, my Duke, do not trivialise it. After what the army had left, it was like crows to carcass after the fox has had it." The Prince, who up to this point had always kept his frustrations at the soldier's disrespect for the political outcome in check to smooth over the overall success of the missions. Now however, the troops had overstepped the mark, and he would not be made a fool of.

"There were two clear missions to achieve," said the Prince, his voice still quaking with the rage the actions of the Army had caused. "To capture the Port of Cadiz, should that be possible, and to lay the political groundwork for the eventual coronation of His Royal Highness, the rightful King of Spain, Charles III." His voice was still quaking with rage, as he now turned to the Duke of Ormonde. "Tell me, my Duke, how do you intend to change the public perception?" There was a prolonged silence from the assembled men. O'Hara was seething from the chastising he was clearly receiving from the Prince. The Prince himself was not to know that he had turned in and not personally given the order. But that was not important now.

"I have spoken to your commanding officer," continued Prince George, "But unfortunately, he does not seem to think it warrants any further action." His face turned to Ormonde, who smiled.

"War is war, Your Highness. It is simply part of what is expected."

"War is order!" Prince George shouted back in retort. "War is soldiers fighting soldiers, not reckless abandon of one's honour! Warehouses is one thing, but Churches?" O'Hara closed his eyes in frustration. He had not known about the churches ransacked.

"Churches," continued the Prince, "And Convents? The Nuns sure as hell are not combatants my Duke, or are you suggesting that they keep pistols in their habits?" Prince George took a deep breath to steady himself. O'Hara, coming from the rougher parts of Ireland suspected that some Nuns there did keep pistols up their habits, but he was smart enough not to mention this to the Prince. He did not want to come across as flippant at such a time.

Prince George continued, "As your commanding officer has decided not to take action, it has left me no choice. I cannot hold him to account for your actions, he was in Rota, and clearly not involved in the decision making." By the way Prince George spoke, he clearly did feel that Ormonde should carry the burden of responsibility. "However, I have written to Parliament to relay your actions and have demanded an inquiry. You will answer gentlemen! And by God, there will be answers!" His face, normally jovial and energetic was puce and flush, his eyes were bulging with frustration. "Now,"

he said, a tone of finality to it, "I intend to try and fix some of the mess you have created, with any luck, I can smooth some of this over, and stop the flow of rumour and information out of here. If it gets to Lisbon and Madrid, by God there will be hell to pay." He stormed off, to the apparent amusement of Sir Henry.

"Eyes front!" roared Rooke, clearly not in the mood for the immature Army Officer. "If you'd done your bloody job right, we wouldn't be in this shitstorm!" Rooke, although not as visibly angry as the Prince, seemed to understand that damage had been irreparably done.

"You're just angry your men didn't get their fill!" shouted Ormonde. It was one thing to be chastised by a Prince, but he would not allow a sailor to do such a thing.

"The job isn't finished yet!" retorted Rooke. "We still have at least two forts left to capture. Not to mention overpower a militia and take command of one of the largest ports in Western Spain." It had been clear to Rooke from the beginning that Ormonde had never fully grasped the extreme difficulty which may occur in this endeavour.

"We took this fort in day!" exclaimed Ormonde, seeming to think that put an end to the argument. It did not.

"We took this place, because the Spanish let us. Fifty men, and a major, with no repelling cannon fire? They are saving themselves Ormonde and you're gonna walk right into their trap if you aren't careful. Not to mention the soldier's motivation."

"The soldiers follow orders Sir!" said Ormonde with an air of his aristocratic upbringing.

"Soldiers follow their pockets and their cocks Ormonde," retorted Rooke, without any intention of hiding his meanings, "And now thanks to sleepy and horny," he indicated to O'Hara and Sir Henry in turn. "They've had their fill." It was clear from his tone who he placed the majority of the blame at, and thankfully, O'Hara thought, it did not lay with him in Rooke's eyes at least. That would help come the inquiry which would inevitably come now that the Prince had demanded it.

"We need to take command of the situation," said O'Hara finally speaking after his clear telling off from the Prince and Rooke. "I don't think simply ordering it will cover it Sir. We need to be methodical and flush the troops out of the rat runs, one by one." Like ferreting at home, if you threw all the ferrets in all the holes, most of the rabbits got away. They would have to go, warren to warren to continue the analogy, and flush the rabbits out one by one.

"It will take time," said Rooke gruffly, but shaking his head he looked at O'Hara. "But you're right, we go door to door and pull the men out of the buildings if we have to."

"Punishment?" asked Stanhope who had been so far silent on the whole issue. After being side-lined during the capturing of the fort,

despite his relative success on landing the troops, he was one of the few men left untarnished by the action.

"We can't," said Ormonde, horrified by the idea of punishing his soldiers for what he saw as spoils of war.

"He's right," said O'Hara quickly interjecting before Rooke or Stanhope could argue. "We'd need thousands of Provosts and as many men not looting to give out the lashes. We simply don't have the manpower. Any man who leaves when we turn up and goes back to camp, will simply have to be left to it."

Rooke looked furious at the clear lack of discipline being discussed by the officers of the Army, but Stanhope simply sighed. O'Hara was right, and reasoned. Yes, Ormonde did not want punishments anyway, which would cause problems down the line, if the commanding officer started cancelling punishments, but moreover they simply could not carry out the number of punishments needed for the crimes committed. The soldiers had robbed, raped and raided the town of Port Saint Mary. And they were going to get away with it.

Francisco looked out from the fort in the morning to see the slowly rising smoke from Port Saint Mary. The anger and frustration he felt towards the men who had perpetrated this egregious act of violence against his province quickly began to soften. He smiled, as the realisation of the opportunity dawned on him. The Grand
Alliance had landed troops under the auspices of a diplomatic mission. And what had they done? They had committed the sins that all invading armies did. And he would use the propaganda to its fullest effect.

"She is here, Sir," said one of his aides, and he smiled. What better way to get the news out than with the same way he gathered information?

"My lady," he said softly, as he kissed her hand. She mock blushed, and smiled at Francisco, who though much older, gave off the feeling of energy in all he did. "A wine perhaps? I know it is early, but I would hate for you to think me a poor host. So, what news can you give me from Port Saint Mary?"

"The best," she said, with a smile, "or the worst, depending on how you wish to look at it. The oldest sins committed by savages. Or at least that is the news which will spread round Spain."

"How true is it?" asked Francisco.

"Oh, very true. They spared nothing and no-one. Nuns, monks, even their own merchants on the black market were not spared the plundering. It's like they wanted all of Spain to be enraged at their actions."

"How quickly can you get the news out?"

"It'll be in Seville in a couple of days. From there, round Spain as quickly as it can. By Christmas everyone will know what happens to towns that peacefully surrender to the Grand Alliance." That was

the difference. It was expected that towns which had been besieged and frustrated an enemy would be plundered, that was just the rules of war. But a town which was peaceful, that had not shown any signs of resistance. It was like the Spanish propagandists had written the story for them.

"Don't exaggerate," said Francisco, eager to put the point across. "I know there isn't a need to, but don't. I don't want the English to have anything fight back with. No lies, no made-up stories. Keep to the facts."

"When do I ever do such a thing as exaggerate?" she asked, fluttering her eyelids at Francisco. He smiled with his old, warm grin.

"I imagine, in your line of work, exaggerating the size of things for men is part and parcel of the job, is it not?"

"Something I am sure that you have never experienced," she winked at him, with her cheeky smile.

"Thankfully, no," smiled the old man. "Now, we both have business to attend to, so if you would be so kind,"

"Always work, never play," she said, but with jest in her voice. She bowed kindly to him, and made her leave, as Francisco's guard watched her leave with interest.

"She is both out of your league and price-range," said Francisco, not even bothering to look up at his guard. His guard stood quickly to attention, trying to pretend he had not been doing anything.

As much as the destruction of Port Saint Mary was a political boon to the cause of Philip, especially in the long term, in the short term it would have repercussions, both good and bad. On the positive side, the local populace, both Spanish and merchant, had no respect or love for the invading forces. The negative however, was now that the cat was out of the bag, there was no telling what the Allied invasionary forces would do. That would put the men in the forts of Matagorda and Law-rence on edge without question. They were better provisioned than Saint Catherine had been, and Francisco had not been willing to reinforce such an undefendable position, but still morale might become shaky amongst the militia.

Francisco looked over Cadiz from his vantage point on Fort Saint Sebastian. If the English got this far, he was in real trouble and he knew it. This would be the place of their last stand, should it come to that. But Francisco did not think it would come to it unless the Allies intended to besiege him through the winter.

Smythe was in Fort Saint Catherine and had overheard the anger coming from the Officer's mess. The Prince had stormed out, almost mid flow, jumping straight on his horse and into the town of Port Saint Mary. Smythe hated riding. He found horses too wild, too unpredictable. The bob and sway of a ship, even in a storm, could be predicted. Men may joke about the sea being a living entity, but it had nothing on the freewill of horses. He was sitting, drinking the

tea he had managed to beg off of Richards, waiting for his inevitable orders. He had been invited to dine last night with Rooke, and the evening had been going pleasantly, with food and drinks being provided by the Admiral being a nice distrac-tion and change from ships biscuits and salt beef.

But that had all changed. Treen had returned to the Fort some-where around eleven, to report the debauchery going on in the town, but he was not the first man to do so. What had been considered a celebratory dinner for capturing the fort and suc-cessfully moving the army on, now seemed like a cruel joke by comparison.

Rooke came out, face like thunder. O'Hara, who previously been standoffish with the Admiral, seemed to simply quake in his shadow now, knowing that he at least held some of the blame for this fiasco. Ormonde however, seemed unfazed by the meeting, or the smouldering town which his troops had left.

"Saddle up Smythe," said Rooke, not unkindly to him, but with an urgency which left no time for pleasantries. "We are rooting out this evil once and for all!"

"Aye aye, Sir!" he said, drinking down his mug of lukewarm tea in one. He saddled a horse which the army had kindly lent him and rode into the town. The officers were going door to door, but this was causing nearly as much harm as good, as the abruptness of officers looking for their own troops was now becoming almost as

large of an inconvenience and disruption of their forced entrance into homes and businesses was causing issues. It was also a never-ending task, and men would leave one dwelling, merely to have to be dismissed from another around an hour later. There were that many rat-runs and alleyways, that the men could hide and circumvent the officers looking for them. In addition to this, now that the troops had plundered and pillaged, as well as drunk their way through most of the town, the taverns were becoming a hotbed for the troops to somewhat legally unload their ill-gotten gains for yet more alcohol, food and whores.

It was a thankless task. The troops hated them for stopping what they thought, like Ormonde had suggested, was their right to plunder an enemy town. Some of the local's were angry that they had not intervened faster, or at least protected the churches and convents of the town, feeling that religious buildings being sacked was equivalent to that of the Berber Muslims centuries before. And finally, there were the currently profiting locals, who were now becoming increasingly annoyed that they were stopping the soldiers at least putting the money back into the town that they had stolen it from, rather than taking it all back to Portsmouth with them.

"Move your arse; and get back to camp!" shouted one of the Provosts, the third time he had moved this particular soldier on. The Army officers, at a unit level, had been ordered back to camp, and were to drill their troops in order to sober them up

should they
be drunk, or else tire them out, so not to have a repeat of the
fiasco. Trouble was, more and more sailors, at the behest of
Ormonde feeling he needed more troops on the ground, were
now entering the town also, and seeing the utter destruction
in front of them, decided to take it upon themselves to continue in this vein and cause yet more chaos.

"Ormonde better have a damn good plan for all these men
coming ashore," grumbled Rooke to Richards, as they now
were dealing with drunken sailors as much as Redcoats. As far
as Richards could tell however, Ormonde did not seem to have
a plan at all.

CHAPTER TWENTY-TWO

Prince George was sitting in Rota, wondering how on earth he was to fix the problem which the English had created. Firstly, there was the immediate need to try and stop information from getting out in the short term. That would be difficult to say the least. But what would be immeasurably harder, would be having to try and stop the flow of information should the attack on Cadiz fail. Once the troops had all packed up and left, there would be no one left to stop the information from spreading, and Francisco would ensure that this information would spread as far and as wide as possible. It would not surprise him if the news were already speeding away now to Seville or Cordoba, even now as he was still trying to find a way to stop it.

He sat in the Castillo de Luna, papers and lists strewn all over his desk. It had been a stressful couple of nights. He was still awaiting confirmation from the nobles who had been unable to visit him in Lisbon, during his time in the court of Peter II. And now would they come at all. The loss of honour, prestige and a sense of fair play which the sacking of Port Saint Mary had created meant he no longer knew if the dignitaries would come at all.

"Long day?" said Hempleman, "Well, me too. Trying to stabilise the agriculture in these times. The price of grain will be going through the roof through the harvest."

"How so?" said Prince George, taking any excuse to think about something else for a moment or two.

"Brewery's demanding more due to your problem. Same with the wine also, but that will most likely be felt across the continent the rate the troops seem to be going through it." Despite everything which had happened through the recent days, the Prince had to smile.

"Well then, better make sure the harvest comes in, my Lord Hempleman," he said with a smile, the first real smile he had had in a day or two now.

"And you got some mail Your Highness."

"Mail?"

"Yes, that thing people write on when they want to convey a message over distances."

"I know what mail is, thank you." replied the Prince, again catching himself smiling in spite of himself. "I meant, who is it from?"

"Some of the local nobles, I think, it's in Spanish anyway. My Spanish isn't that great I am afraid."

"Then why did you offer to come on this trip if your Spanish isn't great?"

"See the world." Hempleman simply shrugged as if to show this was merely his Grand Tour.

Prince George shook his head and took the letters from him. As he opened the first letter, he was full of apprehension. If they were writing rather than attending him in person, it was not a good sign.

To; His Royal Highness, Prince George of Hesse-Darmstadt

*My dearest Jorge, it is a pleasure to be writing to you on such an occasion as your visit to Andalusia. It is my understanding that you wish to meet with me to discuss the eligibility of His Royal Highness, the Archduke Charles. This will be rather difficult, my Lord, his Highness Philip has specifically banned any discussion of the Archduke's claim to the throne **on Spanish soil**. Might I suggest a meeting which does not take place on Spanish soil as this would satisfy both yourself and my King Philip?*

Yours
Juan Tomás Enríquez de Cabrera y Ponce de Leon, VII Duque de
Medina de Río-Seco.

There were other letters which offered similar condolences and confidences, of promises and requests. Meeting, not on Spanish soil, but in the water, was a way around such a predicament as discussing treason on dryland.

"What do you suggest?" the Prince asked Lord Hempleman.

"Meet them on a ship?" he said, rather flippantly. However, this was not a terrible idea.

"We could meet them on a ship," said the Prince, more to himself

than to Hempleman. In the bay of Cadiz, a small gig would not be noticed amongst the fleet. It would allow enough deniability to the nobles, and they would be able to argue Philip's orders of not on Spanish soil had not been broken.

"We are moving away from Rota anyway," said Prince George, almost as an afterthought. Hempleman was not upset. Rota, with its empty houses and taverns was not the most hospitable place to be staying. Add into the mix that the militia which had been raised had been moved to the town of Port Saint Mary, to act as a paramilitary police force, stopping the looting which the Grand Alliance's troops had been engaged in. It was causing friction between all parties, but more than that, it had left the town of Rota without any real garrison. Finally, the governor of Rota had pledged his loyalty to Charles's cause, meaning that without the presence of people that the locals probably considered foreigners, the town may return to something resembling normal.

"To Port Saint Mary?"

"No, to the fort. a defensible position should things go poorly. Besides, after the army's actions, I doubt we would be overly welcome in Port Saint Mary anyway. At least closer to supplies from a populated town."

Fresher food, wine which had not been found under a floorboard somewhere. It would be better to be nearer at town.
"What of the army?" asked Hempleman.
"The Navy are going to use the fort as a base of operations. But that will leave only a skeleton staff. We, the civilians, will be close in number to them. The army are going to be based on the far side of Port Saint Mary, where this time, I have been assured, they will stay."

Treen was walking through the Army camp in the late morning. He was not used to being in such places, and as yet, was unsure if he preferred it or not to that of his small, Lieutenant's berth, in which at least people seemed to knock before entering. The food was better on land also, fresh, not baked several weeks prior and kept in barrels.
"Sir," came the voice of a sergeant walking towards him, ensuring his attention was gained. "Your presence is requested his Duke's tent." It was only a short walk, but his naval uniform made him stand out to the extent that the troops would still look up and stare. He could do without the staring.
"Sir," Treen said, seeing O'Hara stood also waiting outside the tent. O'Hara looked up at Treen, then realising it was the naval officer who had assisted with the guns at the fort, smiled and bade him well as they waited for the Duke. They were not alone, as there were engineers, and men in Dutch uniforms also, as the Duke clearly had a further plan of attack. They did not have to wait long. Sir Henry stood at the tent opening, looking at the assembled
officers.
The table which had been in Rooke's private rooms was now in the middle of the tent. It had maps and sketches of the next fort on the way to capturing Cadiz, Fort Saint Matagorda. There were colours on the maps, and although meant nothing to Treen, were evidently drawn on by the engineers to assist Ormonde in his attempts to take the fort.
"Thank you for all joining me gentlemen. As you can see the

engineers have made sketches, and suggestions as to the progress we can make. Admiral Rooke, in his infinite wisdom," the bitterness in his voice was such, you'd have thought he was sucking on lemons, "has point blank refused to move his ships into a more useful position, here in the bay. Something about winds and leeshores and autumnal gales, honestly, it didn't make much sense to me, but he refused at any rate. Which means that we need to move the men and materials across this marshy country. Which won't be easy. Lieutenant," he finally turned and spoke directly to Treen, "You will be the liaison between the army and Navy. I have been assured by Captain-General O'Hara that you are a man who can be trusted to do tasks well. Your men will be reassigned to an engineer's unit, as they will be used there anyway. I have a letter for Rooke, if you would be so kind as to take it now?" Although framed as a question, it was clearly an order.

"Of course, sssiir," said Treen, his stammer seemed to be coming

back in the presence of a Duke.

"Excellent!" said Ormonde excitedly. "There should be a horse ready for you, if not ask for one, don't think about walking, it'll take too long. And I would like a response please, sooner rather than later."

Treen left the tent, rather frustrated he had lost his sailors to the Engineers, but otherwise not too flustered. Depending on where he was at times of the day, he might even get better food, or, a rarity, double meals. The horse was indeed ready for him, as was an escort of Provosts. "You are riding through the town, and it has become slightly more hostile," said the Provost nearest him. "We have been advised that no persons are to go into, or through, the town alone, Sir."

The streets were deserted through the main street of the town. There was some hustle and bustle on the side streets, deliveries being made to shops and taverns, but nothing compared to the energy and fanfare the army had entered to only days previously. As they entered the fort, the feeling that summer was at an end was clear. The early days of autumn were starting to fall in on the Western coast of Spain, with the winds beginning to increase.

"Sir," Treen stood to attention in front of Rooke, letter held out in his hand. "And the Duke requests an immediate response, Sir." Treen could not have looked more uncomfortable if he tried. Rooke for his part tried to keep his clear anger under control. It was not

this Lieutenant's, a Lieutenant who had been taken from his rightful place as a Naval Lieutenant, to be a messenger boy.

"Best read the bloody letter then, hadn't I?"

Rooke still had not calmed down three hours later. It was early evening, and Rooke was so angry he still had not started his dinner. Despite keeping his reply as short as he could, and in the affirmative, the lines from Ormonde's letter were being re-read in his head over and over. Terms such as *I am disappointed at the lack of support you have shown me* and *It has been noted that your ships have been less than helpful during these times, and I hold you personally responsible for their inaction.* It was however the presumptive nature of other lines within the letter which were ringing through his ears. *It is requested that all sailors be put at the use of the Army* and *ditches need to be dug and your men are the best options available.* And now, he would have to bear the bad news to his officers.

Ormonde's plan, with the assistance of the Engineers, was to build a causeway across the marshlands separating Port Saint Mary from Port Royal. Port Royal was the last settlement prior to the fort of Saint Matagorda. The engineers planned to make a dry and secure point on the sandy isthmus, which the Spanish called, the *Puntales*. From there, a battery and breach could be sought. But first digging. And relaying of rock. And land. It would not be easy.

"My sailors are expected to do what?" asked Hardy, furious at such a suggestion. "They are sailors Sir, not labourers!"

"Don't take that tone with me Thomas!" roared Rooke, himself angry at Ormonde's demands, but rather little he could do about it. One plan alienated the men. The other risked their lives and the health of the fleet. "I know its bullshit. I know. But by God, I will not give the Duke more reason to blame us for any mistakes made. His army is in complete disarray, do you not think he will be looking for any scapegoats. I can justify not putting the fleet into a leeshore under cannons from a fort. Any politician can understand that. But not allowing the Army to use able men. That may be seen as us putting the dampers on an otherwise credible plan."

"Better to let him fail on his own?" Jennings commented, as he took a look over the numbers being suggested by Rooke. His ship, the *Kent* was not too badly affected. Most of the sailors looked like they were coming from smaller ships, such as the *Lannwedhenek*.

Jenkins was tired. He was tired of mud. He was tired of sand. He was tired of digging in general. He was frustrated too. Having spent years at sea, he unsurprisingly he thought, new a fair bit about wood. He knew when it would float. He knew when it would sink. He knew how much weight it would hold in a given situation. So why, he and his gun crew were digging through the mud and sand, was completely beyond him. They were being overseen by a

Provost too, as Treen had been taken by the army. So now, not only were they digging, but they were being watched by the Provosts. It was like a prison labour camp.

"Keep digging lads," shouted one of the sergeants. Jenkins noticed he was not digging. So the Army's NCO's were not digging, but the Navies were. How interesting. "I said dig! Or I'll av you on a charge!"

"Fuck you!" shouted Jenkins back, "I'm a mate, same rank as you, you prick."

The sergeant's face flushed with anger at been spoken to in such a manner, but he held his tongue. As much as he did not like it, there was nothing he could do. Jenkins was correct, he could not put him on a charge.

"He can't, but I will sailor!" shouted the Provost, trying to maintain order and discipline. "Come on lads, lets dig faster than that team over there!" The encouragement which may work for the labourers of the Army, or the Engineers, did not have any effect on the sailors. They raced at things like running the guns, or unfurling and tacking the sails. Being challenged to dig a hole faster than the next group of people, was not their idea of fun, nor a motivational tool.

The trenches were however, being dug at a reasonable pace. They would eventually be used to lay the foundations of the basic road that the engineers needed to transport the cannons. The weather, though not what it had been a month ago, was still sticky, and much

higher than what the sailors would experience at home during this time. The Dutchmen were digging too, as were conscripted labourers from Port Saint Mary, men who, despite the injuries the troops had inflicted upon their town, were still taking the silver of England.

The digging went on all day. And the next day. They were at least, Jenkins' thought, making progress. But it was slow work. The Spanish troops from Matagorda, amongst other places, had begun to come and harass the diggers, to further slow their progress. Jenkins diggers alone had lost one man, with a bullet in his leg, before the Allied skirmishers, and light cavalry came to drive the enemy away. It was a guerrilla war which the Spanish were fighting now, with men coming and going from the column and disappearing, face coverings and banditry. These men may be digging for England one day and shooting at them the next. What was more, the trenches and ditches being dug needed to be guarded all hours of the day. Jenkins group had found this out the hard way, as overnight, the Spanish Guerrillas had taken to filling in the holes with whatever rubble, sand, and other slightly smellier things, making digging them out all the more unpleasant.

The longer they dug for, the more unpleasant, and frustrated they became. What made things worse often, was the soldiers not digging. Ormonde's reasoning to Rooke had been that they would be needed for storming the breaches, which was true, and

therefore needed as much strength as they could get, whereas the sailors would be able to rest. On the face of it, this sounded plausible, until of course you remembered that the Engineers still had to blast a hole or two in the side of Fort Matagorda. By Ormonde's, and the Engineers own estimates, this would take a day or two at least, plenty of time, in Rooke's opinion, for the army to rest up.

It came to a head on the seventh of September. Men from the crew of the *Adventure,* the ship which Prince George had been sailing on, were charged with insubordination by the provosts, for not digging quickly enough. Rooke did not bother with a letter this time. He went to the camp.

"This is a bloody outrage!" he roared, his face turning that rare shade of purple only shown when his anger was beyond control.

"They did not dig fast enough for the Provosts approval." Said Ormonde simply, attempting to avoid being pulled into the conversation.

"You know damn well that they aren't trained for it Ormonde!" Rooke was now almost beyond himself with rage. "Moreover, you've charged the buggers who are on Prince George's ship!"

"Shit." The word slipped out before he could stop himself. Ormonde had not been told that by the provosts. He knew some common sailors had been charged, but the ones which had personally aided

the Prince throughout his voyage would not sit well politically.

"I am telling you now formally," said Rooke, a finality in his tone which Ormonde knew there would be no negotiation from this point, "You can use my guns, if needed. You can use the gun crews from the ships, if needed. But they don't dig anymore. Such slavish labour is not for seamen."

Ormonde opened his mouth to retort, but without even saying goodbye, Rooke left the tent.

"Fucking Sailors. Think they rule the God dam world." Ormonde chunnered to himself. A difficult task had just become that much harder.

CHAPTER TWENTY-THREE

Prince George was aboard the *Lannwedhenek.* All the crew, barring a skeleton one left on for basic maintenance had been removed. All the officers had been removed, except one midshipman, a young black boy named Abraham. These were the terms which had been negotiated for the delegation arriving from Faro. They had refused his larger ship of the *Adventure,* despite it being more comfortable, as it was seen as a ship of war. The small sloop was much more acceptable for such talks. The delegation was made up of Spanish nobles who had missed him, despite his own prolonged stay, in Lisbon, and now, were travelling by cutter to listen to what the Prince had to say.

It had been agreed that only Sir Paul Methuen, who had accompanied him from Portugal and who was officially still one of England's Special Envoys to the country, could remain here. All other military officers, save the one Midshipman, had to leave the *Lannwedhenek.* It was not, by any means a popular decision. Firstly, the crew and officers of the *Adventure* had felt snubbed, after keeping the Prince for all these months, only to be disregarded at such a crucial time. And the crew of the *Lannwedhenek* were not much happier. Although they would now receive the honour of hosting the meeting, none but a few crew members would be aboard. But Rooke, who knew how important this meeting could be to the future of both the invasion and subsequent capture of Cadiz, and the larger war as a whole, smoothed the egos over as much as he could. All that was left was for the dinner to occur.

A dinner had been made by Prince George's Valet and assisted by the Commander of the ship's Steward, William. The courses, which had been prepared in a ships galley, would not be of the standard Prince George knew his Valet could achieve, but never the less would be as good as could be expected at sea. Furthermore, with an assistant, something he did not normally have at sea, it may even be better. Often, he made some form of meat pie, the herbed and peppered pastry being able to hide the toughness of the salt beef that would inevitably be within.

Around a dozen men, all in their military regalia, had come onto the deck. Depending on the previous relationship, both between them and Sir Paul, depended on the familiarity of the greeting, with some men shaking both their hands, some merely the Prince's, and some merely nodding in acknowledgement to both. One man actually hugged the Prince, confusing everyone in attendance, and continued to be extremely familiar with him, to the point another man had a polite word in his ear, that this was not the way to address royalty. The feast was set out on the deck of the *Lannwedhenek*, the Commanders berth being considered far too small to host such a prestigious affair.

"Gentlemen! Gentlemen!" said Prince George in Spanish, after the first course of Chorizo with minted peas. George had chosen this as

a sign of his Spanish loyalty. It was not Spain he was at war with, it was Philip V. "Welcome, and thank you for meeting me here. It is a pleasure to see you all here. I know that coming aboard this English ship is something that some of you are not happy with, so again thank you." He was unsure how to continue. What he wanted, and what the men aboard were willing to give him would be two very considerably different things. "A toast," he said finally, "to the late Charles II, may God bless his soul now!" It was a safe toast to make, as all men aboard had either directly served, or in the single exception of Sir Paul, had nothing against Charles II.

The second course was indeed a rosemary crust beef pie, which, with a gravy and mashed potato was delightful. The chatter continued as the wine flowed.

"Now, Prince Jorge," said one of the dignitaries, "You simply are asking too much of us."

"How so?" asked Prince George, unsure how they could lessen what he asked of them. It was either adherence and loyalty to Charles or it was not.

"You ask us to start a rebellion for the man considered by many as the rightful King of Spain. But you ask us to do so, without any support whatsoever."

This was a valid point. The men at this table would surely be exiled at least should knowledge of their presence be known by certain authorities. Depending on the severity of the charge, it could of

course be death, perhaps by execution, perhaps by suicide to ensure the family honour.

"What would be required for such an action to be taken, Sir?" asked Sir Paul, who for the most part had stayed quiet through the conversations, his Spanish not being as good as his Portuguese and not wishing to embarrass himself or Prince George too much. However, an opportunity to gain support was too good to miss, and if the question were considered too crass, he had asked it and not the Prince.

"What we would need is some sort of protection. Legally and militarily," said another nobleman, who had been listening to the conversation. "We are isolated in our support currently; we need more aid from the Grand Alliance. I might add, that your Army's recent exploits have not helped your cause, either with us, or with the locals of Spain. The Clergy are furious I might add. Talking about invading forces and desecration of Spanish maidens. I am personally questioning the purity of said maidens they think were in the taverns of Port Saint Mary, but by God Sir, they are riling up the populace like something we haven't seen since the Reconquista."

"Ormonde has a lot to answer for," thought Prince George, "My friends, surely you do not believe the rumours of a broken and beaten army, trying to apologise for its own defeat by spreading lies,"

"Jorge," said an older man closer to him, "how many years have I

known you?"

"A fair few," said George, uncomfortably. He had a vague idea where this was going.

"Then don't lie to me, Jorge," said the old man simply. "We know that the Englishmen ravaged through Port Saint Mary. We also know that the Governor of Rota has swore allegiance to you. I tell you now," he said, eyes boring into Prince George, "not for the safety of the Governor, he will either be punished by the Spanish or become a national hero depending on the winner of this war, or maybe even just the winner of this battle, but it means you have someone in your camp giving information to Francisco."

"Of course we have people in our camp giving information to Francisco," said Prince George, completely unphased by the accusation and assumption the old man had made. "With the number of people coming and going within our camp, the butchers and bakers who are locals. Not to mention the whores who probably were servicing both camps. It isn't a question of does Francisco know what the Army is planning, it's a question of can he stop it." Prince George seemed thoroughly unconcerned about the accusations that spies were in his camp. In fact, he was almost certain there were. Despite his best efforts to curb information leaving the camp, he knew that Francisco had planned everything so far, the easy capture of Fort Saint Catherine, to the spread of information from the town of Port Saint Mary. And the militaries

latest plan, even if kept in the height of secrecy, was not difficult to decipher with half the free rock in the country being used as foundational deposits. They were building a road across the marshland to enable them to besiege the Fort of

Saint Matagorda. There was no need for spies to work that out. "What we need Jorge, is assurances." Finally, after a couple of hours they were getting down to terms. "A continuity of the Hapsburg's would be preferable to many nobles here in Spain. It was not that long ago we were at war with our new allies, Bourbon Frogs." It was clear from the faces around the deck that many of the men present agreed with this assessment. They had all spent their lives, including Prince George, protecting the frontiers from France. Indeed, the most supportive area of a Hapsburg ruler of Spain, was Catalonia, where the French, and Prince George personally, had seen off a French invasion only five years previously. It was difficult for people whose homes had been burnt and possessions stolen to now just accept them as allies.

"So, what can we assure you?" asked Sir Paul. Although not a military man, he, as a diplomat could asked such uncomfortable questions.

"We need protecting," said one of the nobles from the far side of the table.

"A one-off attack on a city in the south of Spain will not make Madrid listen. It needs to be sustainable. I know you wish to take

and hold Cadiz, giving the Grand Alliance a landing point to funnel all their troops through. But without the long-term support of the Spanish nobles, and the Pope, you will fail before you start. Jorge, you need us," said another. It was clear from the way the nobles were speaking that this single action would not be enough. Moreover, from how it sounded, if this action failed, it would be considered too risky for the nobles to join the cause at all. What Prince George wanted to create was, essentially, a civil war inside of Spain. Currently, most if not all the nobles had fallen into line and followed Philip, possession being nine tenths of the law. George needed to create such energy behind a victory, that the Spanish nobles thought twice about that decision.

"We are not fools," said the old nobleman sitting to his left, "We know it is too late in the campaigning season to march all the way to Madrid and force Philip to abdicate. Moreover, we know it isn't simple should you get a foothold here for the armies of Spain to dislodge you, should you set up a supply line from England."

"So if we take this place…" said Prince George.

"And hold it, and support us through the winter, we will swear loyalty to Charles in his quest to become King of Spain. If you cannot do this Jorge, then tell us, and we will be on our way. We will not actively hinder your cause, but nor shall we support you in it either."

The terms of the agreement were simple. Take Cadiz. Hold it through the winter, with support. And some nobles of Spain would indeed throw their support behind Charles.

"I must speak to my English Allies before I can make any assurances," said Prince George, allowing him to buy for time. He knew the campaign on land was not going perfectly. And he knew in politics and diplomacy, it was better to promise low and deliver high, than the other way around. This was the safest way of ensuring these things.

"We can wait," said the nobleman, now smiling. He had Jorge's interest and he knew it.

Rooke and Ormonde were still barely on speaking terms. The refusal by Rooke to allow his sailors to dig the trenches and buttresses needed for the task at hand was infuriating to Ormonde. Rooke, for his part, was more worried about a munity amongst his men being forced to dig, whilst soldiers, tired as they may be, were sat idly by. His men had done all the work getting them here. They should not have to do all the work once they arrived.

Prince George, as he had promised, had brought the two Commanders together to discuss the terms set out by the Spanish noblemen. He had a shrewd idea he knew what both men would say. Ormonde, energetic as he was and an optimist to the last, would tell him that it was a splendid idea, and easily achievable. Rooke, ever the pessimist on this expedition, would indicate that

they would have to refuse. Prince George, although hoping he was wrong, was more inclined to go with Rooke on this. It was already the ninth of September, and Rooke had orders, rather vaguely written, not to risk his fleet. Should the Atlantic gales come, his fleet would indeed be at risk. He needed to sail home, sooner rather than later. They were meeting back in Fort Saint Catherine, as this was the middle point between the fleet and the army camp.

"The Spanish want assurances," said Prince George, after relaying the conversations he had had aboard the *Lannwedhenek*. "They want men and money to carry on this war whilst we cannot through the winter. Without the supplies and manpower, they will not assist us at this time. The easiest and only way that is possible, is with the successful capture of Cadiz. What I need to know gentlemen is, is that possible?"

Ormonde, predictably, jumped straight in. "Of course, it is, your Highness. We are, without any help I would like to add, building the road that will allow us to move our cannons into range of Fort Saint Matagorda as we speak." His subtle dig at Rooke has not been missed by Prince George, but thankfully for expediency, Rooke had either missed it, or more likely, was simply choosing to ignore it.

"We need to sail away soon. We cannot be stuck an open bay in Spain through the winter with no chance of being resupplied. Our supplies are healthy now, but they would not last through the winter."

"We will be in the city by then!" exclaimed Ormonde excitedly, "And you can harbour your precious ships within the confines of the harbour itself."

"We cannot risk the fleet," said Rooke, simply. He was not willing to risk the destruction of the fleet on a promise from Ormonde, regardless of how delusional he seemed.

"What is the latest you are willing to sail for home Sir George?" asked the Prince, trying to find a middle ground which both men could be satisfied. Or at least humour Ormonde long enough to get him to agree to some form of plan.

"Late this month," said Rooke simply. "It'll take us around two to three weeks to get home, depending on the winds. It'll take a whole day at least also to get the ships into Portsmouth. And I don't think our relations with the Dutch would do well if we lost their twenty or so ships. I already have Philips van Almonde breathing down my neck, trying to find out when we intend to go home." Philips van Almonde was the Lieutenant-Admiral of the Dutch fleet, and although Rooke was in over-all command of the Naval expedition, it would not do well to anger his allies unnecessarily.

"Then, Ormonde, you have three weeks to capture Cadiz."

"Three weeks to capture the Forts of Matagorda and Law-rence," said Rooke, softening slightly. "The final fort is incon-sequential at that point. We can simply starve them out if needs be or offer terms. But unless you capture both those forts, I can't get my ships

into shore. If I can't do that, I have orders from the Admiralty to ensure the fleet returns to safe ports by the autumnal gales."

"Three weeks." Ormonde seemed to be talking to himself more than anyone else. Three weeks to blast through two forts as yet untouched. Matagorda would be the more difficult of the two. The swampy land outside would prove difficult to lay his guns, even if he managed to pull them through the mud to get them in range. "Three weeks gentlemen!" he repeated with his previ-ous vigour. "We will be toasting to the downfall of that French puppet which sits atop the Honourable Throne of Espana!"

His enthusiasm was not infectious, however. Ormonde, hav-ing to travel back to the camp to issue his orders, left Prince George and Rooke in the room.

"Chances of him managing it?" asked Prince George, knowing that Rooke would at least give him an honest assessment.

"Low," replied Rooke, in an almost bored tone. "But best let him try. God knows he thinks I'm sabotaging him at every point anyway, might as well let him have a crack so at least we can say "We told you so.""

The short ride back to where the army were encamped was uneventful, and Ormonde summoned his officers to inform them of the meeting. He knew that some would be excited about the prospect of a time limit on their exploits, whether that was due to

wanting to be back in England, or the excitement from the pressure of having to have the job done in a specific amount of time.

O'Hara and Belasys were in attendance, as was Stanhope, along with the Dutch officers. "Gentlemen. We have three weeks."

"Can't be done," said Stanhope, immediately, shaking his head. O'Hara secretly agreed, but seeing the dejection on Ormonde's face, decided not to share his opinion.

"It is plenty of time!" roared one of the Dutch officers. Stanhope looked over, a look of shock hardly hidden on his face. The Baron Sparr, Commander of the Dutch forces had spoken. And he had clearly meant it too.

"We will be laying the guns in less than a week Sir!" said the Baron excitedly. That was probably a fair time frame, even with the digging. The fort, although better made than the previous one, probably would not last more than a day or two under heavy fire. What would be more important, was how many Spanish troops the fort housed. The previous one had been a rabble of militia, of around fifty men and provisions to last only a couple of days. Fort Matagorda would, in all likelihood, be better defended than Saint Catherine was.

"Give me the command then Sir!" shouted the Baron, "If your Generals are unwilling, then I will smash a hole in that Diego fort and I will win this battle for you!" His comrades did not share his confidence, but Ormonde smiled so enthusiastically at him that

they all stared at each other in disbelief, knowing what the next words would be out of his mouth.

"Then the command you have Sir!" he said with all the delight he could muster. "You may have the guns Sir! And the men! Do the United Provinces proud my man!"

CHAPTER TWENTY-FOUR

The digging of the road took the week which Ormonde had anticipated. The army moved onto the town of Port Royal, however, probably due to the lack of time, there was thankfully, no repeat of the actions from the troops in terms of looting or plundering. The ditches were dug, and the approach to the Fort of Matagorda was open to the army.

Baron Sparr led the army, with Ormonde by his side. He was not quite as energetic as he had been a week ago when the decision had been made. The morale, and drive of the troops had dwindled slightly in the past week. It was most likely the digging, but also the weather was still in the high twenties. Unless it were an Indian summer, back home the temperature would be lower, and the men seemed drained of energy because of it. Match that with the full pockets of gold and silver they had taken from Port Saint Mary, and the fact they will not have seen England for over four months upon their return home. For some of the troops, the Irish ones in particular, it would have been nearly a year once they were home, since they last set foot on their own soil.

"Dig them guns in!" shouted Sparr, knowing that the Spanish would most certainly fire back this time. He had been an observer at the attack on Fort Catherine. He knew that he would not have it as easy as O'Hara, not that he begrudged him of that. The dispatches home, especially in Amsterdam, would be showering him in praise, should
he take the fort, the odds stacked against him as they were.

"How long till we get the guns laid!" he shouted, first in English, then in Dutch. The problem with the mixed army meant most orders had to be given twice. Despite being Dutch, the majority of Sparr's men were English, so it made sense to give the order in English first.

"Not long Sir!" shouted a man back. It would take some digging out, but once they were set, the barrage would begin. The Engineers, who had made a road in less than a week, were more than capable of laying the guns to fire at Matagorda. What was a better question, was did they have the energy. Having done a large amount of work moving the guns through the swampy territory, to continue to dig the guns into a defendable position would take time and energy.

Rooke, along with some of the other senior officers of the Navy had come forward too, mainly to see how the Army were getting on. Sparr was as energetic as ever, but there was a noticeable lull in enthusiasm from the remainder of the army. "Troops seem unenthused Baron?" asked Hobson, unhappy with the lethargic nature of the troops.

"There are just saving their energy, my friend!" replied Sparr. Hobson was not sure who Sparr had been trying to convince, Hobson or himself. There were Spanish skirmishers taking shots at the engineers, but with little effect, as either they had no inclination, or had specific orders to keep their distance from the

enemy. The English sent some men forward too, giving the Engineers plenty of support to continue the dig.

It took the remainder of the day to lay the guns, with a few firing and ranging shots to ensure the distance was correct. A couple of shards of brick and mortar flew off from the walls of Fort Matagorda, but it was too late in the day to begin the bombardment of the fort.

"Make sure there is a suitable guard sergeant," ordered Sparr, concerned for the batteries, "We've done all this fucking digging, let's not make it for nothing."

Jenkins stood deep in the soil. Its grainy texture, as sand made up a large amount of the mud here, made the digging easier here than it had been for the road. Despite Rooke's sweeping declaration about Naval servicemen not digging, Ormonde had dug his heals in about any men who had been present during the storming of Fort Catherine. In order to keep the peace, and as a small offering of the olive branch, Rooke had relented, allowing any men who had been present there to remain under the command of the Army.

Everyone in the fleet, and service, knew of the argument between Rooke and Ormonde. Despite the senior officer's best efforts, the word of their meeting, and subsequent orders which came of it, were proof enough. Three was a marked increase in the workload of the troops pushing forward towards Port Royal and Fort

Matagorda.

The conditions for the crew of the *Lannwedhenek* ashore had, however, markedly improved. The length of time they had spent digging was reduced, giving them more leisure time. The uniforms of the Navy were not as despised in Port Saint Mary as the army, and they could still be served in the taverns and brothels without fearing for their lives or causing too much offence. The locals still needed some form of income.

As the army had moved forward, it became Port Royal where the men went to spend their gains. Most of the loot that Jenkins and his men had acquired was from the dead men in Fort Catherine, but he knew that some of the bounty had come from Port Saint Mary. He had won the equivalency of two guineas in a game of cards against a couple of sergeants three nights ago and was under no illusions where the coins had come from. It was not his problem however, and he was more than happy to spend others money, regardless of where they got it from.

The ranging shots they had taken had hit the walls, to great fanfare amongst the other Engineers. Having played a large part in the breaches at Catherine, it felt right that they also assist with the breach at Matagorda. There were a few other naval gun crews, but now, most had re-joined their ships. Jenkins, as much as he was enjoying his time on dry land, he could not remember the last time he had had such a prolonged period on dry land, he would be glad

to return to the relative safety, comfort and familiarity of the *Lannwedhenek*.

They saw Treen from time to time, he was still acting as liaison between the fleet, Rooke, and the Army, Ormonde. Ormonde was now of course being heavily assisted by the Baron Sparr, and for all intents and purposes, he was the de facto Commander of the Army. Treen, and Jenkins for that matter, was not sure if this were preferable to Rooke or not. On the one hand, it was no longer Ormonde, a state of affairs that nearly everyone in the service could agree was an improvement, not because Ormonde was a poor general, but because the relationship between Ormonde and Rooke was so badly damaged that it was having a detrimental effect on morale and cohesion. On the other hand, Sparr was Dutch. Not that there was anything inherently wrong with being Dutch, but working with Allies rather than with your own troops always posed problems. What if Sparr decided to use exclusively English troops in his assaults, risking their lives over those of his own countrymen? What if he did the exact opposite and took all the credit for the Netherlands? This provided problems, which had Ormonde still been in command, simply did not exist.

It was for men more important than Jenkins to worry about. He looked over at the Fort he would be spending the next two- or three-days intent on breaking a hole large enough in her side that an army could pour through her. The roads around the bay were

kept by the Spanish in excellent condition, the supply routes being needed by the ports. That hopefully would give them enough time to smash a hole in the side of Fort Lawrence too. There were a lot of hopefully's and maybe's in the Allied plan.

Francisco was stood on the walls of Fort Lawrence across the small straight from Matagorda. Through his glass he could see the cannons set, ready for the bombardment to begin in the morning. He could, at a push, see the camp of the army, set now just outside Port Royal. Judging by the size of the camp, the English must have left only a skeleton force in Port Saint Mary, Fort Catherine and Rota.

"Your Excellency?" said one of his subordinates, bringing Francisco back to Lawrence, "Your Lady is waiting for you." So, she was his lady now, was she? Francisco smiled to himself. If that is how the men saw it, let them. It mattered not to him how the men saw him, so long as they fought hard for Spain.

"Your Excellency," she curtsied for him, smiling at the assembled soldiers, knowing that they were all watching her. "so lovely to be invited here." Where some thought that she and Francisco were having an affair, others, more in the know, knew her real purpose was much more vital. She was in effect, his spymaster in the enemy camp.

"My lady." Francisco said, with a smile on his face knowing that he

had fanned the flames of rumour for his men in regards to her role. "Leave us," he said to the assembled troops, which they did quickly, not knowing what their Commander had planned. After they had all left, and were out of earshot, Francisco's demeanour changed to the more business-like one he reserved for affairs of state, "What news do you bring?"

"Your troops have stopped harassing the troops now they are in position," she said, a look of frustration in her eyes. She seemed to think it was cowardice which had caused the troops to stop harassing the English, but Francisco shook his head.

"I need every man I can have defending those walls, what about their Navy?"

"Impotent," she said, a wry smile, "Not the only English thing which is, I can assure you." they both smiled at her little joke.

"That is information for once this battle is won." said Francisco, "How many did we kill?"

"Hard to say," she replied, "I can tell you that we have put around fifty or so out of action but,"

"Out of action will do." Francisco said, more to himself than his guest, "Where are the troops."

"Mainly around Port Royal," she replied. "There is a small force in the town of Port Saint Mary and at the fortress Saint Catherine."

"Nothing in Rota?" asked Francisco, a slight surprise and delight in his voice which could not be hidden.

"Not that I know of," she replied, "Small militia maybe, but my ladies are not plying much trade there."

The plan was formulating in Francisco's mind as the conversation progressed throughout its stages. He knew that it was a potentially risky, but it would deal an almost killer blow to the Allied cause.

Rota had a sporadic militia. The majority of the people had returned to the town, but most of the residents were simply staying inside their own homes. Nothing good would come of supporting this new regime. Not until it was secure in its position at any rate. The Governor may have signed up to this new Archduke's demands of fidelity, but the populace of the town was not so quick to jump ship.

The Governor had set up his administration in the Castillo de Luna as was to be expected of a Governor of Rota. Prince Jorge had left the town in his hands, and this was only a sign of things to come. When the Archduke Charles officially became Charles III, he would surely appoint Prince Jorge, who was his mother's cousin, as a high official, thanks to his stellar work throughout his accession. Men who showed loyalty to the regime early, would surely also be rewarded with such powers. He may find himself as a Viceroy in the Americas, or perhaps in Prince Jorge's old Viceroyship of Catalonia. Wealth, power and prestige would be his before the end of this war.

A crack of a musket brought him back to earth. The first one made

him stop daydreaming. The second shot fully brought him back to his office. He threw on his ceremonial General's jacket and ran through the door, pistol in one hand, sword in the other.

Looking down the main street, his militia were in a fire fight with troops marching down towards them. They had two flags flying, one of Spain, the other of Philip V. The cracks of musketry, both of his own troops and that of the enemy were flying in all directions.

"Take cover men!" shouted the Governor, "Where is the army?"

"What army?" shouted back a sergeant. "This is all we have Sir!"

More smoke and gunfire came from the enemy troops. The troops were merging from the northeast and northwest, as clearly a group of King Philip's troops had worked further round. The flanking manoeuvre which his enemy had undertaken, had inevitably been successful. The roar of a volley from the troops, and although not in perfect unison as fully trained troops would have conducted themselves, the effect was similar. Militia men falling down left right and centre, as the Governor took the best cover he could. Another crack from the enemy closing in on them, and the militia ran.

"Let them run!" shouted a voice which the Governor recognised. Francisco. The Governor could feel the men running around him, with individual men choosing to run than fight. Francisco letting them go showed that he had only one target in mind. Guns were aimed at the troops.

"Throw down your arms, if you aren't an officer, you can go home!" shouted Francisco, and most of the men threw down their weapons immediately. They were not willing to die for a king who had never set foot on their soil. They threw down their weapons and ran.

Such a choice was not open to the Governor and he knew it. The military of Francisco was not in a forgiving mood for him. A line of infantry walked slowly towards the Governor, guns pointing directly at him. He stood up, looking defiantly at the enemy. He raised his pistol, dragged at the trigger, but due to his shaking hand, he fired the gun over the head of his enemy. Francisco walked in front of the line, guns pointing over his shoulders. "Senor," he began, "I warned you. I warned you what would happen if you were to disobey your King. You have been found guilty, by your actions, of treason to the Crown of Spain. Do you have anything to say before sentencing?"

"I protected my town."

Francisco looked around at the dead and dying men around them, the blood and chips of brick from where the bullets had hit them. "You seem to have done a good job," he said sarcastically, "Would you like a blindfold?"

"No need," he stood, defiantly watching the line.

"Take aim," said Francisco, his eyes fixed on governor, "Fire!"

The guns cracked at as Francisco shouted fire, all the men ready to execute this traitor of the nation. The bullets hit the governor's

chest, blood coming out slowly, dropping to his knees, blood now coming out of his mouth. He smiled, knowing his life was coming to an end.

"Death is freedom," he said, as his body softened, and he flopped to the ground.

"Time for us to go," said Francisco.

Prince George was furious. Not only had Ormonde failed miserably in capturing the forts so far. Not only had they ransacked the town of Port Saint Mary. But they had failed to protect the allies they had gained. It was a complete failure. The delegation had left the *Lannwedhenek* now. It was unlikely to join without a complete victory here in Cadiz.

"How likely are we to capture the town?" he asked Ormonde, his patience at breaking point. It had been nine days since Ormonde was given a three-week ultimatum and although the army had progressed, they were still not through the walls even at Matagorda, let alone fort Lawrence across the straight of water. Without both, Rooke could not dock his ships in a haven for the winter, and would have to return to Portsmouth. "Sparr is in command of the breach of the fort, Your Highness, perhaps we could-"

"I asked you damn it Ormonde!" shouted the Prince, once again losing patience with the Duke. "Give me a simple answer, how likely

are you to capture Cadiz?"

There was an uncomfortable silence, as Ormonde stared at the Prince. Eventually, Ormonde, with reluctance answered. "Not high, your Highness."

"Thank you," the Prince, though frustrated, was glad to finally be getting a straight answer out of him. "What are the plans for a withdrawal, should that be needed." It did not take a genius to see, looking at Ormonde's face, that this had not crossed his mind. "May I suggest asking Rooke to dock some ships closer to the shore and ferry the cavalry back at least?" Ormonde nodded. The cavalry, with the lack of a pitched battle, were in-effective at the tasks at hand. He had more than enough foot soldiers to make the numbers up, without them.

"Yes, your highness. And now, if you would join me, I was intending to inspect the lines with the Baron Sparr at any rate this morning."

It was a short ride between the camp and the front lines of the batteries, but as was the tenseness between the two men, it was completed in perfect silence. Only the neighing of the horse as they trotted broke the otherwise graveyard like quiet. Sparr was thoroughly enjoying himself by the looks of things. He had been effectively side-lined during the two previous en-gagements within this battle, and now he seemed thirsty to prove his worth.

"Your Highness!" he exclaimed with delight, eager to show the Prince what progress they had made. "Take a look through the glass

Sir! You will see the cracks appearing already!" It was true that you could see the cracks beginning to appear on the walls of

Matagorda.

"No returning fire?" asked Ormonde, who, after the capitulation of Catherine, was starting to become suspicious of the Spanish inactivity.

"Oh, yeah they've been firing all day," replied Sparr, unconcerned. "They have yet to hit anything of importance, a couple of engineers dead. But no doubt we have put worse on them."

As he spoke, the unmistakeable thud of a cannon ball struck the ground to their right. It caused the horses to jolt, forcing all riders to fight to control their animals. Another couple of cannon balls hit around them, making Sparr's comments seem a laughable joke.

"What the fuck?" he shouted, furious at this sudden attack, which was now more accurate than it had been all day.

"Its coming from the galleys Sir!" shouted an Engineer taking cover in the ditch for the gun. Sure enough, as Prince George looked over to the shoreline, he could see the wafting of white smoke blowing gently away from the ships.

"Well fucking fire back damn it!" shouted Sparr, incensed that his batteries were under attack, and from the sea no less.'

"With what Sir?" asked the Engineer. "All the guns are set on the fort." And it was true. Every large gun that the army had was pointed squarely at Fort Matagorda.

"Well, realign them!" he roared, clearly the obvious answers were not to the engineers this morning.

"Pointless Sir," replied the man. "It'll take us a good couple of hours to redig the trench, reinforce the floor and relay the guns. They can move out of range within ten mins max, they'll just row away, wait for us to reset, then fire again."

"So, what do we do?"

"Hide?" suggested the Engineer, trying not to laugh out loud to his commanding officer. "Ain't much we can do 'part from fire a few smaller balls at 'em. Won't stop 'em mind, might just annoy 'em enough to bugger up."

"So, Baron," said Prince George, trying not to be too annoyed at the additional errors made here, "We will be under constant fire ourselves on the south side of the siege. Meaning we will have to breach in the north, is that fair?"

The Baron coughed, sat up straight in the saddle, and looked defiantly at the Fort. "Yes, your Highness, that seems to be a rather fair summation. Engineer! Start to pack these guns up. Relay them pointing toward the bay, let's make sure the buggers don't try and surprise us on the flank."

"Aye Sir!" replied the Engineer, before turning to his men and bellowing orders. Sparr looked over at Fort Matagorda. It was his nut to crack. Unfortunately, the nut was proving rather difficult.

CHAPTER
TWENTY-FIVE

Sparr's orders were followed to the letter. The guns were moved, with only a mild amount of damage being felt. The manpower lost was negligible, a few gunners and sighters were hit, as were some Spanish local labourers. No doubt they would insist that they had been forced if the English were displaced from their positions. It made little difference to the galley's guncrews, they had shot in any case. It probably helped that most of the ships in the harbour were French, and therefore, were certainly not firing cannons at any of their own citizens.

The larger casualty were the guns. They lost several guns to a combination of the galley's fire and mishandling during the movement. Whether by design of the French Navy or through opportunism, the galleys had fired repeated salvos over the course of a few hours at the English batteries, with barely a scratch on them.

Despite the small six and even some smaller four pounders from on shore being fired to try to distract the French fleet, it was to no avail. Most of the shots, due to being fired over such a large distance and at a relatively small weight, became affected by the wind. Out of hundred of cannon balls shot towards the French ships, only a small few hit their targets, with most of those merely making a nuisance, rather than any serious damage. A couple hit masts, cracking and splintering them, but nothing major that the
carpenters aboard could not fix. It mattered not what the Brit-

ish cannons did to be fair. If the harbour remained secure, the French fleet would remain, for the most part, unscathed, with the English having much more pressing issues. Should the harbour be breached, the French fleet would, most likely, scuttle their vessels, rather than have them taken as prizes of war by the invading fleet.

The loss of the cannons meant one simple thing for Sparr. Delay. Although not all, a number of his guns were now, unable to fire. The Engineer had of course been correct. Once he had moved his guns to be able to hit the fleet, the fleet had simply moved out of range of the guns. It meant Sparr did not have the fire power on the fort he had accounted for in his estimations for creating breaches, creating an outcome of either a; less breaches, or b; longer time needed to create the breaches.

"Gun Crews, hit your targets!" Sparr was ready for the fight. The breaches were coming, but it was slow work. The cracks were coming, but the same crews which had blasted holes in the side of Saint Catherine in a day were taking a few to even put one hole in.

"When are we returning to the *Lannwedhenek*?" asked one of Jenkins gunners, clearly ready to return to the relative comforts of the ship. "Damn this warm weather!" It was still in the mid-twenties and the heat emanating from the guns did not help matters. Aboard ship, and away from mosquitos, the men in this weather would most likely be topless, but here, out in the open sun and with the
biting devils, being covered up was the better option.

"I don't remember you complaining in Nassau?" said Jenkins, with a wry smile.

"In Nassau there were naked women and ample rum," he replied.

"We have wine." smiled Jenkins. "Let's have a song for the Lieutenant boys!" Signalling to Potter, who's men would again be pushing into the breach in a couple of days.

For we, sailed on the Sloop John B,

My Grandpappy and me,
Round Nassau we did roam,
Drinking all night,
Got into a fight!
Well I feel so broke up, (Oh yeah!)
I want to go home!

It was sung in a round amongst the gun crew with such gusto, that men from the *Kent* who were also firing at the fort, joined in too. Sparr, who had evidently had a different approach to that of O'Hara, was on his horse, pretending to conduct the gun crews in their music. Prince George was inspecting the lines as well as Rooke, who, seeing his naval crews in such high spirits, smiled. Still the cannon balls roared towards their targets, as light skirmishes were happening ahead. The Spanish made periodic raids to disrupt

the gun crews. But in the open ground, they were not as effective as they had been harassing the road builders earlier in the week. Eventually, they stopped all together. By the sergeants count, the Spanish had lost as many men as they had, and being besieged, they could not afford to lose any men more than the enemy.

On the twentieth of September, Sparr and Rooke stood atop one of the batteries.

"It needs to happen soon, Baron," said Rooke, not wanting to sound rude, but equally the urgency of the situation becoming apparent.

"I am aware of your deadline Admiral." said Sparr kindly. "Admiral Almonde has made his position equally felt, and he, like you, would prefer to winter in the channel should it prove impossible to capture Cadiz."

The breaches were still incomplete as far as Sparr was concerned. "I will need every man I can have going up and over those walls."

"Speak to Ormonde about as many soldiers as you wish," said

Rooke, a stern look on his face, "But under no circumstances are you to use my gun crews Sir." It was an order that Sparr would not be foolish enough to ignore. An order of such clarity given by Admiral Almonde would carry equal weight, and ignoring it would have dire consequences. The alliance between The Dutch Republic and England was now, by no fault of either party, weaker than it had been prior to the death of the Prince of Orange, William. Whilst

a protestant Dutchman sat upon the throne of England, the alliance was strong. But after the death of William, the friendship had, understandably, become cooler. Should a direct order be ignored, in order to maintain the alliance, the punishment would be severe and quick.

"Your using Lieutenant Potter and his boys again," said O'Hara joining the pair overlooking the fort.

"They served you well in their breach," said Sparr simply. "I hope the Lieutenant is as fortunate in the storming of Matagorda."

The mood of the army was one of optimism. As of yet, despite the setback of Spain recapturing Rota, they were yet to receive a setback aside from time. Now however, their sternest test stood before them. The attack on Matagorda was imminent, there was an atmosphere in the air which showed it.

The breaches were as broken as they would be. Another full day had been given to the Engineers to make the holes as large as they could. The ladders had been prepared; wood taken from the rafters of the houses of Port Saint Mary. "They already despise us," commented Ormonde. Even he had to admit that the actions of his troops had led to detrimental effects. Most clearly on the rank and files discipline.

It was dark. The night had fallen in on Fort Matagorda, with braziers and torches on the walls being the only source of light. The
Spaniards who manned this position knew what was coming. It was the longest the guns had been silent since they had been

laid a few days previously. Sparr looked over the battlements with his glass, sitting atop his trusty horse.

The briefing of the officers had been positive that afternoon. With around a thousand Englishmen and five hundred or so Dutch soldiers forcing the breaches it would come down to simple numbers. Could the Spanish hold that many men back, or would they fold?

"You three," he pointed at three English officers, "will attack here, on the northern side. You will need ladders. The Engineers have estimated that the breach is around twenty feet wide, but the wider you can make it with the ladders. Unless one of you wishes to volunteer, you will draw straws for the Forlorn Hope. I will not be the one to send a man to potential death, but it must be done."

The Forlorn Hope was the name given to the first set of troops going towards a breach. Unless the enemy were especially lax, it meant that these men were almost certainly meet with the most resistance, with every gun loaded, sometimes mines and cannon fire depending on the time the defenders had to prepare. The troops at Matagorda had known of the enemy troops now for around a month. Cannons with grape and shot would be filled on the walls, waiting for their red and orange coated victims to fall in her range.

The men remained silent at the suggestion one of them volunteering. This surprised Sparr somewhat. Despite the obvious risks to ones health, the rather high chance of death, there was one rather attractive thing which the Forlorn gave back to the officer in charge of it. Whilst death was not a certainty, a successful Forlorn was almost certain promotion without purchase. It was clear however from the faces of the officers assembled that they did not think that promotion would be achieved during this Forlorn, whether due to the time which the Spaniards had had to prepare their defences or just a general lack of faith in victory, Sparr was not sure.

"I will lead the Forlorn" said a Lieutenant eventually, and Sparr beamed with pride.

"That's the spirit Mister Potter!" he shouted, making many of the surrounding men shift uncomfortably with the shame of being outshone by a young Lieutenant.

"Now, men of Netherlands!" Sparr continued, this time in Dutch. Whether because he was speaking in Dutch, a language he was clearly more comfortable with, or because he simply expected more of his own countrymen, there was a clear elevation in his voice. "We will attack the southern breach," again he pointed to the map. "It will not be easy," he said, "But I expect every Dutchman to excel himself in his duties."

"Does everyone understand the plan?" asked Sparr after another

twenty minutes or so of discussion. Potter thought it would be harder not to understand. At nine o clock this evening, he, the Forlorn Hope, along with his southern Dutch counterpart, were to advance on the Fort. From there, it would simply be a fight to the death, and the fort itself.

"What if we are unsuccessful?" asked one of the English officers, "Will we regroup and go again?"

"Alas no," replied Sparr, causing some stir within the men assembled, "The Admirals, and I include both Rooke and Almonde in this, feel the need to sail home prior to the Winter Gales affecting the Atlantic. As I am not a Naval man, I cannot comment on such issues, and therefore must defer to them in such matters. Should we fail, we are to withdraw to Port Saint Mary, where we will reembark onto the fleet."

This furthered the looks of frustration and defeat which the officers were displaying. The fighting morale of the men was at rock bottom. Or rather the fighting desire of the men, was at rock bottom. They had money in their pockets, and more waiting for them once they had returned home. Unless the Spanish had a complete capitulation, which under the command of Don Francisco was looking increasingly unlikely, even taking Fort Matagorda would unlikely end in the capturing of Cadiz.

"Well gentlemen, you have your orders. To the Joy of the day."

Jenkins stood besides his guns. He knew even as he was receiving the order to stop firing, that the breaches were not as big as they had been at Catherine. And yet somehow more men were expected to force their way over those small breaks in the otherwise solid rock wall. And unlike Catherine, in which, the enemy were few in number, and lacked spirit, the troops in Matagorda knew the importance of their fighting and sacrificing. It would be the major skirmish so far in the siege, with the winner of this going a long way to winning the battle overall.

The wind was blowing in slightly from the sea, bringing a thin mist through the air. Jenkins looked over his gun crew. They were tired sure. But energised too, running off the adrenaline that had been coursing through them since the bombardment started.

The Redcoats were starting to assemble readying themselves for the attack on the fort. Potter had drawn his sword, ready for the assault.

"Mister Potter, Sir," said Jenkins, causing Potter to turn and face him. Whether it was the mist, the bad light, or simply that Potter was so focused on the task at hand, but he appeared to not recognise him. "Lieutenant?" asked Jenkins again, trying to ensure that Potter was ok. He had watched Potter go through a breach point already, and it had an effect on a man that was not always positive.

"Mister Jenkins," replied Potter eventually focusing on Jenkins stood in front of him. "how good to see you in this place." There was a nervousness to his voice, as clearly his mind was on the task at hand.

"You been lumped with taking another fort Sir?" Jenkins thought that this was beyond a cruel joke. They had been on the beaches at the landing, losing their Major in that offensive. Then they had been part of the storming of Fort Catherine, which admittedly had not been that taxing, in terms of energy or men, only three men were casualties in Potter's unit, but there was all the work afterwards securing the fort. And now the same men were being asked to get themselves over yet another wall and fight once again.

"Foolishly I offered," said Potter, "no other bugger would so I thought, "If it has got to be someone might as well be me.".". Daresay I will live to regret that decision." Hopefully, he would live to regret the decision, but that was a slim chance. There were only so many times a man could go into battle and walk away.

"Well, you are a braver man than me," laughed Jenkins, "I'm happy with the guns I think."

"Sure I can't tempt you?" said Potter, with a smile on his face. No one in their right mind would join after someone else had already offered. But the offer just hung there. Jenkins stared at Potter for a moment.

"Could I join you?" asked Jenkins quietly. Potter checked himself to

make sure he had heard Jenkins correctly.

"You want to join us?" said Potter, barely believing his ears.

"We have seen you this far," said Jenkins, looking at his gun crew around him. "Might as well see you all the way."

Potter smiled to Jenkins. "Well, then you'd better do it." The men shook hands. Despite having only met three months ago, a friendship had been made between the men of the *Lannwedhenek* and the troops they had transported.

"Bring the colours!" shouted the Sergeant towards the back of the line.

"Fall in where you can Coxswain's mate. And you're a Cornishman, aren't you?"

"Aye Sir."

"Well then, Saint Piran's blessings on you Jenkins."

"Thank you, Sir,"

The mist was clearing now, leaving a crystal-clear sky. It was eight thirty according to Potter's watch. Only half an hour more before they were due to march on the enemy positions. The tension in the air from the troops was so evident it could be sliced with a bayonet.

"Mister Jenkins!" shouted Potter, eager to lift the spirits of the troops in his command.

"Sir," came a voice back, the Navy uniforms sticking out in the middle of the Redcoats.

"A Cornish song if you please, lets lighten the mood aye?"

"A Cornish song Sir?" came the reply.

"Aye, a Cornish song lad! Let's show 'em what the west country is about!" the energy which Potter was showing was evident, he was clearly trying to rub some off on his men.

"A Cornish song," said Jenkins, "A Cornish song." He paused for a moment. He then turned to his gun crew, around half of which were from the Tin County. "Let's show 'em what Cornish lads can do," he said and the gun crew smiled. They knew exactly which song Jenkins had in mind.

"In Kernewek or English Sir?"

"Leave it in English," said Jenkins, "Not sure I know it all in Cornish anyway."

A good sword and a trusty hand!
A merry heart and true!
King James's men shall understand
What Cornish lads can do!
And have they fixed the where and when?
And shall Trelawny die?
Here's twenty thousand Cornish men
Will know the reason why!

And shall Trelawny live?
Or shall Trelawny die?
Here's twenty thousand Cornish men
Will know the reason why!

It continued for two more verses, and during the chorus, even the non-Cornish members of the gun crew joined in, such was the knowledge of the song aboard the *Lannwedhenek*. By the end of the final chorus, even members of the Redcoats were joining. O'Hara, who was back in the camp could hear the singing and smiled. He personally did not like that style of leadership, feeling that he as a General should be further away form the men. But for Lieutenants to push such cheerfulness was their prerogative, and the spirits of the men about to go over a wall was so high, that they were willing to sing about it. It was remarkable.

On the southern side, Sparr could hear it too. "That's the ticket Potter!" he shouted out loud. "Keep the troops happy!" Sparr hoped that the troops would be equally happy in a few hours' time.

CHAPTER TWENTY-SIX

The troops were ready. The flags were unfurled. And the clock was ticking down to nine. Potter was ready. His sword was in his hand, which he was still barely able to keep steady. Be dammed if he knew how men fought duels. he could not keep himself calm when no one was firing at him personally. Be sure as hell he would not be able to keep his hand steady when they were aiming a pistol at him and him alone.

Jenkins, who had the rank equal to that of a Sergeant had crept towards the front. "It's approaching time Sir," he said softly, the troops having been ordered to be quiet until their presence so close to the breach had been spotted by the enemy. They had crept forward under the darkness of the night. There was cloud cover tonight, meaning little light would give away their position. With any luck, they would be able to get almost to the breach before the Spanish knew what was happening.

"Let's get closer lads!" whispered Potter, creeping forward in the mud. Despite the heat, the humidity and the digging had found the ground water. Although sandy in texture, the mud was wet, sticky and slow moving.

The dark sky above continued to darken as they made their approach. Spots of rain could be felt on the men's faces as they etched ever closer to the ramparts readying themselves for the off.

"We waiting for a signal Sir?" asked Jenkins, remembering the flares

which had been sent up during the capturing of Fort Catherine.

JOSHUA BARRACLOUGH

"No, going in quick and hard, Sparr thinks that's the best chance we have," replied Potter. The nerves were upon him now. He had not felt this since the beach when in the scrub he thought he was about to die. Curiously, he had not felt it at Fort Catherine, perhaps that was due to the expectation of victory. Matagorda was a completely different feel. It seemed like a last-ditch hope, rather than that of a triumphal march.

Within a hundred yards of the fort, Potter signalled for the men to stop. "Catch your breath lads," he said, "Worst yet to come." It was five-to-nine. They were to attack at nine sharp, hopefully hitting the breach at the same moment as the Dutch troops in the south. It was unlikely that they would hit the breach at exactly the same time, but hopefully close enough to-gether that the Spanish were unable to get anymore reinforce-ments to the breaches.

Potter took out his glass, looking at the breach. There were a few men atop it, couple of men sorting out the swivel guns, it seemed that the enemy had an idea that they would be attack-ing, if not tonight, then sooner rather than later. It was getting late in the campaigning season, and winter, all be it milder in Spain than in Northern Europe, or even the Poe Valley in Italy, would still prove most likely too stubborn an opponent on its own, let alone the Spanish troops awaiting them.

"Now?" asked Jenkins.

"NOW!" said Potter, and he lifted his sword and charged. His troops followed, some stopping to take shots at the Spanish, who were now sounding the alarm. Jenkins was at Potter's side, pistol in one hand and cutlass in the other. One of the swivel guns erupted in flames, the flash catching both their eyes, as it blasted out a one-pound ball flew towards them. It skidded off the dirt in front of them, causing sand and mud to fly into the air, filling their mouths with a wet, salty grit.

The trumpeters and signals were going off all around them now, in the fort ahead of them, in the rear with their fellow comrades to come join in the fight. They could hear the Dutch advance, as near as dam it the same time as they were. "Come on boys!" shouted Potter, "Onto glory!".

He looked and saw that remarkably few of his men had been stopped, as yet more gunfire cracked from the fort. Jenkins was still stood beside him, urging the men on. They were a mere twenty yards or so from the start of the incline to the breach point, they would be there in moments.

More gunfire, now from both sides, English muskets behind him cracking, making everything an inaudible mess. It was becoming impossible to give orders by his voice, the cacophony of noise from all sides making his head spin. They were at the incline now, only a short climb to the enemy, and, for the third time in around a month, Potter would be engaging the Spanish enemy.

A shot skimmed the rock in front of Potter, causing him to lose his footing for a moment. He looked up and saw a Spaniard reloading his musket as quickly as he could. Jenkins, around a yard behind the Lieutenant had seen the bullet ricochet as well, took aim with his pistol and fired. He did not miss. The Spaniard fell backward, as the bullet lodged itself in him. Whether he was dead or merely injured, neither Potter nor Jenkins knew, but it was one less man firing at them, so both men took that as a positive.

Jenkins, having fired his first pistol threw it to one side. It was a standard issue pistol, which having been fired, was now a six-pound club with a wooden butt. He would not have time to reload it any time soon, so discarding it and drawing the second one he had had stowed away on his belt was the sensible move. They were reaching the top now, with men all around them short of breath. Then Potter heard it. The click of muskets from a troop of soldiers readying themselves to fire. He turned and looked at his men, unknowing of what was about to befall them.

"Down Sir!" shouted Jenkins, tackling Potter to the ground. The muskets fired seconds later, as a mix of the acrid taste of gunpowder and iron from the exposed blood of the Redcoats behind him.

"¡Recargar!" shouted the Spanish officer and the clanking of the ramrods on the muzzles of the muskets.

Potter, having had his face in the rubble of during the volley looked

behind him at the carnage. Redcoats down behind him, and Jenkins had a scrape on his shoulder. He had covered the officer during the volley and had paid a small price for it.

"Don't falter lads!" shouted Potter, helping Jenkins up to his feet. Jenkins, rather angry at being shot, even if it was just a scrape, pulled out his second pistol. He did not bother this time to aim too carefully, there were enough Spaniards on top of the ridge to ensure that his bullet would surely hit someone, anyone. It made contact with a leg of one of the line, causing him to howl in pain, his hand trying to apply pressure to the blood coming out of his leg.

"Onward Sir!" said Jenkins, "Be like a shark, if you stop, you'll drown." In their own blood most likely. There were Englishmen behind them, the gargling of their blood coming out of their mouths now becoming one of the defining features. Another volley, this time to their right, aiming further down the breach. The Spanish were evidently not willing to waste bullets on individual men, but at the larger columns coming toward them. The swivel gun, this time filled with canister shot exploded, causing a ladder crew to fall to the right of Jenkins. The next men ran up and took it, next man forward mentality kicking in for these troops.

Potter reached the top of the breach, sword glistening in the flaming torchlights. He swung his sword at the nearest man he could, and sparks flew from the bayonet of the gun. Another thrust of his sword, this time making contact with something softer, told

Potter he had done damage. A shoulder barge from Jenkins sent the man, bleeding, flying backwards. The breach was theirs now, so long as they could hold it.

"Get the colours up here!" shouted Potter, taking on the next man. The task was far from complete. The ratatat of the drummers from inside the walls of the fort, the reorganisation of the Spanish troops. Another volley from the right this time, felling the Redcoats like oaks for the timber yards, the screams of the injured and dying penetrating the air. Potter stormed on, the swivel gun on his left being his first target.

A sergeant this time stood in his way, bayonet point for him. Potter paused. Sergeant had aimed his gun at him. He had been lucky already once in this war, it would run out here. He could hear the click of the trigger being pulled. And. Nothing. The gun misfired, causing a tiny amount of smoke but nothing which would cause damage. The sergeant, focusing on his gun, and his frustration was distracted, and Potter lunged at him with such vigour and anger that only a man who thought death was upon him could muster. He buried his sword into the sergeant's chest and regretted it immediately. It was very difficult to pull it out, and there was no time to lose.

The swivel gun fired again, and again more Englishmen went down in agony. The Spanish were holding their own this time, any fanciful ideas that it would be as easy as Catherine had gone completely out

of the window. Jenkins picking up the musket of a dead man fired it at a Spanish officer, who dropped down, causing momentary confusion amongst his men. The Redcoats were piling up on the breach now, but just as many were climbing over their fallen comrades, pushing on for the glory of England.

Another shot from the right swivel gun caused more carnage on the breach. The troops seemed to have forgotten about the ladders now, intent on simply clambering over their friends, who lay dying with shot running through them. More volleys from the disciplined troops, organised and ready saw more Redcoats fall.

Yet still they came, flags unfurled and raring to go. A private shoved his bayonet into the operator of the swivel gun and with the butt of his musket hit its stand till it broke. He paid for his attack on the gun by a shot from a skirmisher further back. He fell too and his fellow troops, now cautious of the snipers in the rear hesitated at pushing forward.

This of course was a mistake as the skirmishers would not fire in close quarters with their fellow Spaniards, but were happy to pick off the individual troops as they came over the wall.

"Forward boys!" shouted Potter, his mouth was dry from the salt and powder in the air, and hoarse from all the shouting he had already had to do. "Forward, don't just fucking stand there, move!". And more volleys came from the guardhouse now, only fifty feet away. Potter and Jenkins had taken cover, along with other troops

as they continued to secure the breach.

The fighting had been furious, the blood shed by both sides excessive. And yet both sides kept throwing men at the breach like a battering ram against a door. Jenkins fired yet another musket at the guard house and saw a flash as a gun flew up in the air.

The constant stream of Redcoats was thinning now, less and less men were coming forward. The columns of Redcoats which so far had seemed unstoppable were slowing, even coming to a standstill. The fighting was still fierce but it was now the Spanish who were clearly gaining the upper hand. The guard house opened, and the ranks of Spanish troops marched out, slowly and controlled. The skirmishers behind continued to take shots at the individual English troops.

"Form line, form a God damn line!" shouted Potter, and those troops still aware did form a line. "Present!" he shouted and the rattle of muskets dropping down was a testament to the drill which the troops underwent. "FIRE!" he roared, and the roar which answered him was one of defiance. England may be struggling in this fight, but by God they were not out of it yet. Jenkins finally having time had reloaded his pistol, steadied himself and took aim at the Spanish officer. He hit his mark, causing the officer to fall, but the Spanish troops, who previously had been outfoxed by such an action, this time carried on, the ratatat of the drums beating out a solemn tone for the line to advance on. More

Redcoats now joined the fray, and the line was bolstered by this.

"Arrodillarse de primera fila" shouted the sergeant in charge, and the front row of men dropped to one knee. The Englishmen were still reloading their guns as the sergeant gave the order to fire. More blood now, clear through the white breaches of the Redcoats was coming, and a swivel gun on the ramparts further down finished off the line that had once stood there.

Some men began to turn and run now, after seeing so much blood, Potter could hardly blame them. But he had a job to do. "Reform!" he yelled. "Reform!". But it was no use. Those who did reform were being picked off one by one. The men turning and running had caused a pause in the men joining the fight, wondering if the outcome was already decided. The number of Redcoats pushing through the breach had stopped, and now atop the wall on Fort Matagorda, Potter knew the outcome. They had been defeated.

"Company," he shouted, taking a pause to ensure that his voice did not crack too much under the strain of the order. "Company, withdraw." It was done. The Forlorn Hope had failed, and with it, any chance of a victory on the North breach. He knew not what would happen on the Southern Breach. Had they failed too? Or would they have succeeded if the Northern breach had taken the brunt of the Spanish defence.

Jenkins was walking backwards now, pistol cocked and ready, as the Redcoats withdrew back down the breach point. The Spaniards,

whether under orders, or whether due to control, were not firing. Then a volley. The last volley which the Redcoats would face. The men, who had been controlled in their withdrawal now turned and fled. Only Potter and Jenkins now held a controlled retreat rather than an all-out free for all.

The officer in charge of the Spanish lowered his pistol. He took aim at the English officer who had nearly successfully captured his defensive position. He was intent on making sure he never did that again. Potter was looking over his shoulder,

making sure he did not lose his footing. He had not seen the officer in question lower his pistol. He had not seen him take steady aim. Jenkins however had. Without time to aim, he shot wildly at the officer, hoping against everything that he could kill him and save Potter. The bullet grazed the officer's shoulder, jolting him as he fired his own pistol. Rather than shotting Potter in the chest as he had been aiming, it diverted down, hitting Potter in the thigh. Potter howled in agony and dropped down to the ground. Blood was coming out, but not in the spurts and surges of an artery being hit, but evenly and constant. Jenkins began to rush over to him but Potter seeing his friend shouted, "RUN JENKINS, just fucking run and get out of here!" Jenkins paused, but a bullet hitting the floor next to him from an unaimed musket fire caused him to think twice. Another misaimed shot hit the ground around him, and with one final glance at Potter, he ran, retreating as ordered to. The Northern breach had been
attacked. And it had failed.

The next morning the carnage was clear. The southern breach had not gone any better than the northern one, and many of the injured had become prisoners of the Spanish. The dead simply lay there in the positions where they had died, except for on the ramparts where, depending on which officer had taken control of it, depended on whether they were moved with dignity or simply slung over the side like fish at sea. Francisco had been sent a letter from The Duke of Ormonde, whoever that was, asking him if they would be permitted to remove their dead from the siege. Francisco agreed, so long as they did not come within a designated area. He marked it out with flaming torches, and told Ormonde clearly in his reply, that if any man were to come inside that area, his men would not hesitate to fire.
He need not have bothered. The English were a beaten army, slow and lethargic. There was no fight left in them. Francisco had been Commander of Andalusia throughout this crisis

point in the history of Spain. And he had held triumphantly. "Write to Madrid," he said softly to one of his secretaries. "Tell them that by the time they read this letter, it is likely the English will be gone. They have no fight left in them."

Ormonde, Rooke, Sparr and Prince George were in the command tent. Some of the other officers were present too, as was the Spanish Major Diaz.

"Tell them to reform!" said Ormonde with his usual optimism now matched with his indignation at being defeated. "Tell them to reform and go again."

"No," said Sparr softly. "The morale is too low. At the sound of the first guns, they would run like chickens from a fox. Uncontrollably and without order. No, my Duke, I will not order them to."

Ormonde looked around in anger at his fellow officers, all of whom seemed to accept the fate of the army. They were beaten. "We should have bombarded the harbour, from the ships as I suggested!" he shouted at Rooke, not bothering to hide his anger. "Will you now do this one favour of me Rooke?"

"On our way out, Ormonde, yes I will if I can." He looked and Prince George as he finished speaking and the two men understood each other. There would be no bombarding of the city.

"Lists Sparr?" asked Ormonde defiantly, like a schoolmaster talking to a naughty pupil about their homework.

"Couple of officers accounted for Sir. Only one missing. A Lieutenant Potter, he was the Forlorn Hope on the southern side. He was not amongst the dead and did not return, so I can only assume this means he was taken prisoner."

Diaz could not help but smile at this news. It had been Potter who had forced him to surrender at Fort Catherine and now he too had surrendered at the next major action. Justice was sweet and imminent.

"Well, I will write to Don Francisco and ask to see if he is there.

Otherwise, how many did we lose?"

"Hard to say. Some men hobbled back but won't make it. Couple of hundred dead, wounded or surrendered at least Sir."

"It is done then," said Rooke firmly. "Gentlemen, you have a week. Pack up this mess, and let's return to England. No doubt there will be fallout from this, but at least if we return with men and the ships, we won't all get court martialled."

"No, not *all*," said the Prince, his eyes boring into O'Hara. O'Hara stared back at the Prince, a small smile on his face.

"Sir," he said finally to Ormonde, "Perhaps I could write that letter for you."

"You Sir, but you don't speak or know Spanish."

"I'm sure Major Diaz would only be too happy to help, wouldn't you?"

Diaz glared at O'Hara for a moment, before seeing what O'Hara had seen.

"Of course," he said, "I would only be too happy to assist, Senor."

EPILOGUE

A week had passed since the failed assault on Fort Matagorda. Despite his promise to Ormonde that he would bombard the city as they left, Rooke had decided on the morning of departure that "The weather just was not right for it." And therefore, the fleet had sailed away, leaving the city unscathed. Perhaps in irony and pleasure at their failed attempt to capture the city, or perhaps as a genuine appreciation that they had not bombed them on departure, the Fort at Saint Sebastian gave the English fleet a salute as it vacated the bay.

Smythe and Treen were sitting in Smythe's cabin. Jones was stood at the Stern window, which although small, allowed for a small view of the ships around them. The fleet had just set sail away from Cadiz.

"Well, that was a waste of time," said Treen, "But still, I got to spend lots of time riding. Not all bad." Both men smiled, whilst Jones still stood stock still, staring out of the window. The two officers were sharing a small glass of Port, one of the last bottles they still had from Portugal. Oporto seemed like years ago now, but it was a mere two-and-a-half months since they had sailed from Portsmouth, with all the intent and fury of the English Navy. Now, they were sailing home, tails between their legs, the stunned silence of an English Navy in defeat.

"You sure about this?" asked Treen, "I mean, I agree I do, but he is what you might call a loose cannon. Might backfire on you."

"I'm sure it will work out for the best," said Smythe simply, and Jones nodded in his agreement from the Stern Window.

There was a gentle knock at the door, and Treen, first looking at his Commander for confirmation, shouted, "Enter."

Jenkins, army in a sling still, walked through the door, "Sirs." He stood to attention, awaiting their instructions.

"Do you know why I have requested your presence here Coxswains Mate Jenkins?" asked Smythe, his face had suddenly turned frosty and angered.

"No Sir," said Jenkins, but this was a lie. Despite being back aboard for a couple of days now, he had not spoken to the Commander since he had volunteered the gun crew to join Lieutenant Potter in the Forlorn Hope.

"Articles of War, Jenkins," shouted Smythe, "Twenty-one, say it!"

Jenkins continued to look blankly straight forward. "If any officer, mariner, soldier or other person in the fleet, shall strike any of his superior officers, or draw, or offer to draw, or lift up any weapon against him, being in the execution of his office, on any pretence whatsoever, every such person being convicted of any such offense, by the sentence of a court martial, shall suffer death; and if any officer, mariner, soldier or other person in the fleet, shall presume to quarrel with any of his superior officers, being in the execution of his office, or shall disobey any lawful command of any of his

superior officers; every such person being convicted of any such offence, by the sentence of a court martial, shall suffer death, or such other punishment, as shall, according to the nature and degree of his offence, be inflicted upon him by the sentence of a court martial. Sir."

"Sir indeed!" continued Smythe, "And how do you think this relates to you."

"It does not Sir," said Jenkins, still staring blankly forward.

"It does not?" asked Treen, confused.

"No Sir, I have never, whilst in Her Majesty's Navy disobeyed a direct order Sir."

"Like hell!" continued to shout Smythe.

"Well, not in relation to this action specifically, Sir," said Jenkins.

"Admiral Rooke's orders..." started Treen.

"Beginning your pardon Sir," said Jenkins, cutting off his Lieu-tenant, "But Admiral Rooke's orders were that no sailor could be compelled to storm the breach. We volunteered Sir." For the first time since entering Jenkins looked directly at his officers. Jenkins was trying his best not to smile. As were Treen and Smythe.

"Bloody brave thing you did Jenkins," said Smythe, his face changing from anger to admiration. "I'd be happy with your decision no matter who you had been assisting, but assisting Potter, to see through our orders to ferry safely the army. And helping a friend. Just to let you know, we are all very proud of you aboard the *Lannwedhenek*."

"Sir," Jenkins paused, "Thank you, Sir."

"Now, Mister Jones, you had something you wished to discuss." Jones, who had not turned around since Jenkins had joined them in the cabin, continued to stare out of the window. "Never did get this view enough," he sighed, and turned to Jenkins.

"I'm done," he said, "Finished. I was done before the Admiralty convinced me to join the *Lannwedhenek*, but now, I'm sure as hell done." There was a tiredness in his eyes which suggested that after this voyage he may not be long for this world.

"You're retiring?" asked Jenkins. Most men died at sea who took to it, whether from old age, disease or shot. It was rare for someone to have the chance to walk away.

"I have some money stored at the Admiralty," said Jones, "I never spent much of me prize money. It'll see me through. My sister and her husband have a cottage just outside Abertawe, they have always said if I want to stop, I'm welcome, so long as I pay my way. Well, the prize money should pay it for a while, till I'm just part of the furniture and she wouldn't kick me out." He smiled, his mind seemed at peace and made up.

"Well, it has been a pleasure serving under you Sir," said Jen-kins, and he meant it. They may not have started on the best terms, but Jenkins respected the old sea dog, and, in his own

way, had begun to like the standoffish and grumpy old man who he worked with
daily.

"There's just the position of Coxswain," said Smythe, looking directly at Jenkins. It took Jenkins a moment to realise what Smythe was saying.

"Me Sir?" asked Jenkins, shocked at his Commanders rather off the cuff appointment.

"A brave, brazen sailor who, rumour has it, once took on a ship twice his size, managed to damage her slightly, and keep himself and many of his crew alive. I couldn't think of anyone better."

"Congratulations Francis," said Treen, and Jenkins balked. It was the first time which his Christian name had been used by anyone aboard the *Lannwedhenek*.

"What do you think Jones?" asked Jenkins.

"Which idiot do you think recommended you?" smiled Jones.

"Will, bring that bottle in," shouted Smythe and four glasses were poured. "To promotion," said Smythe, nodding to Jenkins, "To retirement," he nodded to Jones, "And, to friendship." And all four men raised their glasses.

There was another knock at the door. Smythe, who had taken a small sip of his wine looked around to see if any of the group had been expecting anyone. Evidently, they had not. "Well, Mister Jenkins, call them in."

"Enter!" said Jenkins, clearly pleased at being given such an honour.

Dressed in his finest uniform, bandage around his leg where the
bullet had been removed, and crutch to boot, in hobbled Potter, smiling at the evident delight on the faces of the officers assembled.

"You're up!" shouted Jenkins, smiling at the Lieutenant. "And walking!"

"Thanks to you," smiled Potter, "And O'Hara. He negotiated my release apparently. Gave them back that Major Diaz we captured at Saint Catherine. I guess that's fair, an officer for an officer and all that." He hobbled over to the nearest chair, still clearly unable to stand. "Spanish doctor took out the bullet. Took his sweet time too. But it should heal."

"Mister Jenkins has just been promoted to Coxswain upon our return to Portsmouth, Lieutenant. And Mister Jones will be sadly leaving the service," explained Treen, "Though we wish him the very best in his retirement. Would you care to join us in a glass to celebrate?"

"No, but this Captain," he said, pulling papers out of his breast pocket, "would love to!". The cheer on his face was clear. "*For gallant bravery in the face of overwhelming odds, and not withdrawing but continuing despite the clear obstacles ahead, we do confirm your promotion to Captain Potter.* Basically, well done for not dying during the Forlorn, here's some more money and responsibility."

"Well congratulations Captain," said Treen. "You're finally as important as me." The four men looked at Treen with astonishment, as it was not in his character to joke so darkly at a fellow officer's expense. Then they all laughed. The expedition may have been a failure. But aboard the *Lannwedhenek*, there was at least, merriment.

HISTORICAL AND GEOGRAPHICAL NOTES

Direct aftermath

It is difficult, if not impossible, to state the direct aftermath of the Battle of Cadiz, for one major reason, the Battle of Vigo Bay. Had the Battle of Vigo Bay not occurred, the returning expedition would have been unquestionably different in its public opinion. However, there were some issues which would not be resolved. Despite a victory allowing both parties to claim a victory, Rooke and Ormonde never saw eye to eye again. They never reconciled prior to Rooke's death, and never worked together again.

The Parliamentary Inquiry into the sacking of Port Saint Mary may also have gone differently. O'Hara was cleared of wrongdoing, with the blame landing almost squarely at the feet of Sir Henry Belasys. It was felt that Ormonde, who had known O'Hara since his youth, may have influenced the inquires members, but this was, and remains, unproven. Had they have come home under a defeat; would the Parliamentary Inquiry have led to the clearing of anyone? Or a more severe punishment for those involved? Even Sir Henry, although never holding a military role of any note again, was a Parliamentarian for nearly the remainder of his life.

The one concrete effect it did have, was a complete loss of support for Archduke Charles's claim to the Spanish throne in the south of Spain. In areas where Hapsburg support remained high, such as in northern Spain where Bourbon France had invaded less than a

decade previously, it was also knocked. Furthermore, despite a couple of nobles defecting, it had little to no major effect on the Spanish aristocracy overall.

The battle of Cadiz therefore can be considered a failure in nearly all its objectives.

Fictional Characters

The crew of the *Lannwedhenek*, although based on real people, are all fictious, as is the ship itself. Based on a trading sloop from the 1680's, the research for the book used *Sloop-of-War 1650-1763* by Ian McLaughlan. For all the other ships, and also the *Lannwedhenek*, the book *British Warships in the Age of Sail – 1603-1714* by Rif Winfield was used. In times of war, the Royal Navy could, and would, requisition such vessels as the *Lannwedhenek*. Equally, merchants wishing to curry favour with local officials could "donate" their ships to the Navy, as is the case with the *Lannwedhenek*. Often these crews would remain intact, as the Navy did not have the men to spare. The discipline on these vessels was often worse than the rest of the Navy, and it was a practice which, by Nelson's day, was almost all but forgotten.

Smythe, Treen, Jones, Yin and Jenkins are all fictious, although based on real people. In Smythe's case, the Quakers, and other non-conformists' Christian offshoots of the Church of England, had only been allowed to practice in private since the Act of Toleration 1689, although Quakers had not taken the brunt of the hatred, that being

saved mainly for Catholicism throughout the Kingdom. They were Abolitionist (against slavery) from the start, and although modern Quakers are anti-war, this was the largest group of conscientious objectors during the First and Second World War in the UK, in a world where so much warfare was present, it was impossible to completely avoid.

Smuggling and Piracy had had its day too by now, as this is the time when Piracy is on the decline. With the exception of the Pirate Republic of Nassau, in 1708, Piracy, on a large scale, was basically at an end. What was much more common was *Privateering,* where people would be given permission to raid the shipping of a specific nation, for another nation. These were known as *Letters of Marque.* Piracy in all but name, it gave nations the ability to decline any knowledge of the action, whilst continuing to profit. The Pirates for their part, were allowed to trade and sell their ill-gotten gains in actual ports of the country of their employment, regardless of the origin, rather than trying to illegally supply ports, usually gaining the Privateers a better deal.

Lannwedhenek is the Cornish word for Padstow. Padstow is a small fishing village, on the Northern coastline of Cornwall, England. There has been a fishing town and Parish in and around the area since before the Doomsday book, 1086, and possibly dating back as far as the fifth century.

Lieutenant Richards, although based on real experiences felt by the

English sailors and officers at that time, is also fictious, as are Connolly and Potter. The back stories of these men are based on a combination of backstories of actual people.

Historical Characters – in order of appearance

- Mayor John Hawkins – I must apologise to the Mayor John Hawkins, who has no links, as far as I could find, to smuggling in 1700. He happened to be the Mayor of St. Ives during the year of 1700, and also, was mayor only for one year. Giving him a backstory as to why he never became mayor again and allowing me to give a solid introduction to the fictional character – Jenkins – in the story.

- Admiral Ashore Sir John Molesworth and George Courtenay – both members of Parliament, and both Admiral's Ashore, administrative roles during the time period. John Molesworth was a parliamentarian of many years, and by all accounts his Admiral duties came second to this. Not to say he was not good at his job, merely inattentive.
- Sir George Rooke – Sir George was born in 1650 in Canterbury, Kent, making him in his early fifties during the time period we are looking at. A career sailor, he actually was fortunate enough to go back home to Canterbury in Kent, where he died peacefully in 1709.
- Captain Henry Greenhill – Henry Greenhill made his fortune in the Caribbean, working with the merchant service. He was rewarded for his time with desk jobs within the Admiralty and becoming a member of Parliament.
- Captains mentioned during the Christmas dinner – although the Christmas dinner is a fictious action, all the Captains mentioned, and the ships described, were the ships which Rooke took into the Battle of Vigo Bay. For example, within the list there is Thomas Hardy, no, not that Hardy, but the Great Uncle of that Hardy, of Nelson fame.
- Duke of Ormonde – The Duke of Ormonde had voted not to oust Charles II during the Glorious Revolution, but later proved himself a loyal man to King William III by fighting alongside him in the War of the Two Kings (The war which the Battle of the Boyne occurred). He later kept faith with the House of Stuart, despite all remaining candidates being Catholic and upon the accension of the Hanoverians, was exiled due to a failed uprising in Ireland. His lands, and titles, were purchased from the crown by his brother. He later tried to mount an ex-

pedition to restore the Stuarts, in another Jacobite rebellion, from of all places, Spain. Although never official, it was suspected he was a Catholic, and he died in the Papal Enclave of Avignon, though his body was brought back to England to be interred in Westminster Abbey.

- Lord Hempleman – there is no evidence to suggest that the twenty some year-old Lord Hempleman was in attendance during this period. He was, however, a Lord in the Holy Roman Empire, so it is plausible, and he was a supporter of Charles's claim.

- Prince George – Prince George, to the best of my research, is how I described him. The younger son of a German royal household, he knew that he would need to distinguish himself, were he to rise to fame and fortune. He had also fought at the Boyne alongside William and converted to Catholicism upon his return. There were suggestions at the time, and now, that this was a way of improving his relations with his new Emperor, the Holy Roman Emperor Leopold I, who was his cousin by marriage.

- James Stanhope – James Stanhope, although a distinguished officer and later the Commander of the army in Spain, eventually made his name in politics. Along with Robert Walpole, he is considered one of the first men to be "Prime Minister", of course holding the office, as today, of the First Lord of the Treasury. He married into an up-and-coming family, who had made their money in India, Lucy Pitt, making him the uncle, by marriage of William Pitt the Elder.

- Charles O'Hara – Charles O'Hara's early life is a mystery. Charles himself seems to have liked to keep it vague, leading some to suspect him of being a highwayman, or at least on the wrong side of the law in his early years. He was at least involved in the education, at some point, of the Duke of Ormonde, and fared better in the political fallout from the sacking of Port Saint Mary than Sir Henry Belasys. He continued his military career, eventually rising to the Commander-in-chief in Ireland under George I.

- Sir Henry Belasys/Belasyse/Bellasis – Following the battle of Cadiz, became a Parliamentarian for firstly Durham and then Cornwall, eventually becoming the ceremonial military position of Governor of Berwick-Upon-Tweed. All the above spellings of Sir Henry's name are in use, there was no reason for the picked preference used in the book.

- Don Francisco Castillo Fajardo, Segundo Marqués de Villadarias – Having fought for the Spanish Hapsburgs throughout his life, when the decreed successor, by Charles II himself, took to the throne, Francisco immediately became an ardent follower. He had previously fought in what is now modern-day Belgium against the French for Spanish territories there, and over in North Africa in Oman, against the Ottomans. As a war hero, and a well-practiced defender of forts and, in particular ports, he was given command of Andalusia, as it was felt by the Spanish Government (rightly so) that the Grand Alliance would try to strike here. By Stanhope's own accounts of the landing at the beaches, another fifty or so cavalry under his command, and it may have been a different outcome.

Barbary attacks

The Barbary attacks on Western and Southern Europe had, by the most part subsided by 1700's. The pirates were based mainly in out of the ports of Tunis, Tripoli and Algiers, which acted as autonomous regions of the Greater Ottoman Empire. For the better part of three hundred years, the coastlines of the South-Western Counties were peppered with attacks from the pirates of these waters. The cargo that the pirates were taking? People. Much like the transatlantic slave trade, although not in the same scale, the value was in people and slaves.

During its zenith, the situation was considered so dire that a Parliamentary committee was set up in 1640, specifically tasked with the ransom and repatriation of the people taken from Cornwall, Devon and other such counties. In 1645, a delegation went to Algiers to secure the release of captives taken from in this case, Cornwall, where over two-hundred people had been captured in a single raid. A price of thirty pounds (approximately three and a quarter thousand pounds in 2021) per man, and more for women, was secured for the release of these captives.

Eventually, the English, and other European governments decided this could not continue. Despite international outrage, and of

course hypocrisy (the Trans-Atlantic slave trade having been established for over a hundred years at this point, and continued for another couple of hundred afterwards), there was never an effort to work together to solve the problem.

Individual efforts, such as that of Cromwell, were made. It is hard to establish the credibility of the claim that Cromwell ordered any Pirate to be *Drown slowly upon capture,* given the nature of the ruling and the often-slanderous way in which Cromwell is portrayed. The use by, and effective ownership, of the pirates of Lundy Island, an island in the Bristol channel off the Northern coast of Cornwall and Devon, however, is established fact. The attacks mainly finished in the UK following the peace and bombardment of Tripoli and Tunis in the mid-to-late 1670's. Future attacks, by Britain, Spain and France on Algiers put all but an end to organised raiding.

The legacy was such that, even today, the Royal Navy still has a Fisheries Protection unit, ensuring the safety, and rights of British, and overseas, fishing vessels within the internationally accepted boundaries of British waters. They are also responsible for inspections of said fishing vessels, and peacefully sorting any disputes between fishermen at sea.

Battle of Cadiz

The Battle of Cadiz was the first, in many coastal battles throughout the War of Spanish Succession. It was English (then British policy) to try to establish and ensure a friendly port, or multiple friendly ports, in and around the Mediterranean. To some extent this plan did not change throughout the remainder of the Empire, and arguably with the control of Gibraltar even today, has still not fully been forgotten. The plan for Cadiz however, by all accounts, was half thought through at best. With so many different agendas being sought, the Navy wanting a port, but not willing to risk a fleet in the process, Prince George who seems to have passionately believed that this was mainly a diplomatic mission and finally, the Army, who by all accounts and Parliamentary inquires afterwards, with the noted exception of James Stanhope, seemed to be there mainly for personal glory and enrichment. By not establishing a workable supply chain, something the British Navy would successfully do in the future, and not enough troops to begin with in Rooke's opinion, the venture was all but doomed to fail from the start. Add in the sacking of Port Saint Mary, and propaganda effect this had on the Hapsburg claim to the throne of Spain, it was mainly considered by all as a failure. The Battle of Cadiz would only work, by the opinions afterwards, if the Commanders had been willing to risk more, and act quicker. That was not a criticism, as many felt that it had been an ill-advised venture to begin with. The inspired defence from Don Francisco was

also credited, both in Spain and in the UK as a vital factor in the defence of Cadiz. Had the out-of-date intelligence which Ormonde thought should have been acted on was taken, it would, it was believed, have most likely ended in not just failure, but disaster. It also remains to be seen whether Cadiz would have been the great victory the allies thought it would be. The plan had been to use Cadiz as a springboard into Spain, but only a couple of years later, the Rock of Gibraltar would be captured by the English, by Rooke and Prince George, allowing the English to fulfil the plans they had laid down only two years previously, and yet the war continued after this point for another ten years officially.

It did however lead to two directly positive actions for the Grand Alliance, one direct, and one indirect.

The direct positive action of the battle was on the voyage home at the Battle of Vigo bay. It allowed the Tory, the precursor to the modern-day Conservative Party in the UK today, government to claim a victory, which otherwise would not have been possible. With a victory, they stabilised their government, which a defeat may have rocked. Moreover, a victory allowed the factions within the military, Rooke and Ormonde, to claim a victory. Rather than a defeat which would allow for blame to be assessed to one or the other, and a prolonged dispute between the Navy and Army, Rooke and Ormonde were not on speaking terms as they sailed out of Cadiz, it gave the ruling class an opportunity to revel in a victory
together and close ranks.

Furthermore, although blown up in the Press at the time, the value of the treasure ships captured was if not significant, then at least a blow to the Spanish finances. Finally, it brought Peter II, and Portugal, into the war against Spain and France, as Portugal, seeing a weakened Spain, looked to expand its own Empire in the new world, and achieved preferential trade agreements with the members of the Grand Alliance (Britain, The Netherlands and Austria).

A major indirect consequence of the Battle of Cadiz was it brought together, for the first time, the formal partnership of Rooke and Prince George. Although they had both been involved in the War of the Two Kings, on the side of William, they had, prior to this, never formally worked together. It created a working partnership would later capture and hold Gibraltar for England, causing long term consequences which last to this day.

Geographical notes

Where possible, the places described are, as they would have been in 1700 onwards. The bay of Perranporth is a large bay on the Northern Coast of Cornwall, currently very popular with tourists (this author included) due to its long beach (which large parts are dog friendly), stretching for miles, and the currents which give excellent waves for surfing and bodyboarding. There are visible remains of a settlement from around the twelfth century, but there has been Christian footprints there since around the seventh.

Saint Ives, again on the Northern Coast of Cornwall is a tourist hotspot. Its long beaches stretch on both sides of the bay. With a headland cliff coming out slightly in the middle. On the western side of this is the quay and docks, with large amounts of the shops you get at the seaside in the United Kingdom. On the Eastern side of the bay are hotels. There is a pub at the top of the central cliff, which has a roof balcony, giving spectacular views of the bays. If you intend to visit, may I suggest that you park at the Rugby Club, it is reasonably priced and runs a park and ride into the town centre, although the walk is not a long one.

Bristol did indeed become one of the largest ports in the United Kingdom and has a somewhat strained relationship with its history today. During the 2020 Black Lives Matter protests, a statue of a prominent Bristolian, who was a slave owner, was torn down. It caused outrage on both sides of the political spectrum, on the left questions being asked about many other statues we had across the country, and on the right about a defiant desire to "keep our history".

Portsmouth in 1700 was much smaller, but still an important cog in the English naval picture. Now adays it is the beating heart of the British Navy. Home to HMS Victory, it showcases something of our history that few other places do. Still a working Naval base, and a commercial dock, it remains strategically

essential. Spithead still to this day catches out inexperienced sailors and sometimes larger
trading vessels, causing both embarrassment for the Captain of such vessels, and financial implications during such events. West Porthmear was a fishing village in what now is the beating heart of the area known as Charlestown, near Saint Austell. Developed in the late 1700s and early 1800s, the dock today hosts many restaurants and bars. I would advise anyone going to dine at the Longstore, and ask for a balcony table, the views are incredible.

Cadiz itself has not been described much in the book, as the English never got there. Now a popular tourist destination for Brits wishing to have a city break on the coast in Andalusia, it was the first major port Spanish ships coming round from India would see. However, the trade winds (now what we call the gulf stream) makes an easier voyage towards La Coruna. This is where many of the trading vessels went. It was strategically important however, at assisting the Spanish on controlling shipping, being only around eighty miles from the Rock of Gibraltar and the entrance to the Med.

Rota is a quaint little town, where you can still see the landmarks described during the book. The Castillo de Luna is now a museum which gives an insight into the history of Rota and surrounding areas. The churches in the town are, as many are in the south of Spain, an odd mix of Christianity and Moorish inspiration, to ease the transition during the Reconquista.

Printed in Great Britain
by Amazon